SMOOTH SAILING

WILD WEST MC SERIES
BOOK 3

KRISTEN ASHLEY

ROCK CHICK
P R E S S

Smooth SAILING

NEW YORK TIMES BESTSELLING AUTHOR

KRISTEN ASHLEY

Author's Note

If there was a skill I'd love to have, it would be to be able to write an entire story, and instead of using over a hundred thousand words, do it so you feel all the feels in three minutes.

In other words, do it in a song, like any great songwriter is able to do.

If you've read my books before, you know I often use music to set a mood or help tell the story.

There are two very important songs mentioned in this book, so when you get to them, if you don't already know these songs, and even if you do, I encourage you to look up the lyrics and listen to Helen Reddy's "You and Me Against the World" and Bob Seger's "Roll Me Away."

I hope I've written it, when you hear those songs, and allow their lyrics to move through you, those scenes are more profound and deepen this story for you.

My mom used to sing that Reddy song to all three of her kids. The final seconds never fail to send me.

And well, all of our lives we roll away.

We just gotta hope, while we've got the time, we do it right.

Rock On.

AUTHOR'S WARNING

Please note that there are frank discussions of sexual assault in this novel. If this causes you distress, I hope you have love and support around you, and if you need it, you find help. However, if this distress can get to be too much, you may wish not to read this book.

PROLOGUE
BEAT-UP CHAIRS

Big Petey

Denver, Colorado
Not too long ago...
Thursday Night

THE BAR WASN'T the worst Pete had been in, it wasn't the best either.

But it was a bar, a busy one, and shit went down in bars, busy, seedy, or neither.

And shit was going down.

That was why he tensed, and Rush, sitting across from him in a back corner booth, tensed with him.

They'd seen the dipshit on the barstool cop a feel of a woman's ass as she walked by with her friends. They'd seen her negative reaction to that unwanted touch.

And they'd seen how Harlan McCain hadn't missed either.

Now, Harlan, a bouncer at the bar, was on the move.

Pete knew Harlan also hadn't missed the man on the barstool had a crew with him.

And that bar had one bouncer.

Harlan.

That didn't stop the man from walking right up to Barstool and having a few words.

Unsurprisingly, those words didn't go well.

Even if Harlan appeared to be going about things calmly and rationally, the situation deteriorated. Barstool got off his seat, going right into a two-handed shove on Harlan without the man doing a thing to stop him.

His buds all exited their seats and gathered around.

Harlan went back a step at the shove, but that was it.

Except Harlan kept talking.

Barstool got in his face, and it was clear he wasn't sharing the weather.

Harlan stayed cool, and when Barstool finally shut up, he kept calm and kept talking with some easily read head and hand motions that indicated Barstool, and his buds, were invited to walk out the front door.

Barstool, either drunk, stupid, or both, took a step back, cocking an arm to throw a punch.

This caused Pete to prepare to move.

It also caused Harlan to dodge, and while dodging, take Barstool by the back neck of his shirt, the back waistband of his jeans and frog-march him right out the front door.

His crew followed, and their set faces and body language shared what they intended to do when this shit went outside.

Pete and Rush instantly slid out of their booth.

Harlan was a big guy. Tall. Built. And the man's muscle wasn't lean, it was bulky.

If he knew how to use it, it would pack a mean punch.

If he didn't, it could slow him down. Make him vulnerable.

But four on one wasn't good odds for anybody, no matter how they could handle themselves.

This being why Pete and Rush quickly wound their way through the bar to the front door and out of it.

Rush was young, fit, and he knew how to take care of business.

Pete had long since passed his days where he could throw down.

Shit, he had to brace in preparation just to stand up from a chair. His knees were bad. His back ached most days. His neck got stiff easily. Even his hips got to hurting on more than the rare occasion. Cold weather seized him right up. He went through ibuprofen like he owned stock in that shit.

The thought of throwing a punch, or catching one, made his stomach curl into itself.

But this was Harlan.

This was Jackie's boy.

So Pete would get trounced to dirt if it came to it.

Rush pushed out the door first, Pete followed, and they both stopped in their tracks right outside.

Barstool was flat on his back on the pavement, and he looked like he was out cold.

One of his crew was bent double, his hand to his face, blood streaming through his fingers, hollering, "You broke my nose, asshole!"

Another was on his knees, both hands clutching his junk, a look on his face no man needed translated.

The last was backing off from Harlan, his hands up.

"Well...shit," Rush whispered.

That said it.

What, it took them half a minute to get out there?

Impressive.

"Banned," Harlan's low, rough voice came, his gaze centered on Hands Up.

"You just earned a lawsuit," Hands Up threatened.

"Got cameras everywhere, man. They caught that genius"—

Harlan jerked his head toward the prone man on the pavement—
"doing his grab-ass shit in the bar. Caught him refusing to leave when
it was made clear he was no longer welcome in this establishment.
Caught him shoving me and winding up to land a blow. Out here,
caught him doing the same, then that professor"—an additional jerk
of the head to the one bleeding—"jumped on my back." Another jerk
in the other direction. "That one tried to pile on. Now, you tell me,
what judge is gonna see some assclown grab a woman's ass, refuse to
leave when asked, all four of you throwing down against one guy, and
give you that first dime for me protecting myself and the women in
the bar, something I'm employed, in part, to do?"

Before Hands Up could speak, Harlan kept at him.

"None of 'em. Trust me on this, I been doin' it for a while. Now
gather your troops and get gone. Don't come back either. Lifetime ban."

Hands Up was pulling Nuts Busted straight and talking trash.
"Was a shit bar anyway."

"Good you won't miss it," Harlan muttered.

Hands Up, Nosebleed and Nuts Busted dragged Barstool, who
was regaining consciousness, to his feet, at the same time they glared
at Harlan. Pete noticed their attention often bounced to Rush, who
was standing not near, but not far, from Harlan's back.

They ignored Pete. Then again, even he had to admit he wasn't
much of a threat.

Harlan didn't move, nor did Rush or Pete as they watched the
four men make their way to an SUV.

They still didn't move as the vehicle drove out of the parking lot.

Once it exited the lot, Harlan turned to them.

He glanced at Rush, but his focus settled on Big Petey.

"If I wanted in, I'd have hit the Compound, man."

"You ride," Pete replied.

Harlan's wide shoulders went up and down. "Lotta men ride
bikes. That don't mean they got patches."

True.

But this was Jackie's boy.

"It's time," Pete replied.

Harlan shook his head. "I'm not a joiner."

"Joker isn't either, but he's a brother. Snapper, the same," Pete told him. "It isn't about joining, son. It's about family."

Harlan had a mess of blond-brown hair and a full, thick beard that couldn't decide if it wanted to be blond or brown, and there was even some black vying for space.

Pete could still see his lips thin in that mass of whiskers at the mention of family.

Pete was too old for this shit.

And he was tired.

He'd survived two wars with his Club. They'd lost men, to both death and dishonor. They'd put their asses on the line. They'd seen their women in danger.

Personally, he'd watched his only child, his beautiful daughter, waste away from cancer.

But he had to do this. He had to find the energy for it.

This had to happen.

For Harlan.

For Jackie.

Therefore, Pete pulled out the big guns.

"She'd want you with us, Harlan," he said quietly. "You know that. You know it, son. I heard her say it myself."

It was all about direct eye contact, until Pete said that.

When those words came out, Harlan looked away.

And Pete knew he was right.

He also knew Jackie died wanting that for her boy. She wanted that purpose, that solidness, that brotherhood for her only child.

And she died without him having it.

Rush entered the discussion.

"Listen, this decision doesn't need to be made now. We're havin' a get-together Saturday. It starts at one o'clock. Come whenever. It's

FFO. That way, you'll get a feel of us. Be able to make an informed decision."

And we'll get a feel for you, he did not say, but Pete knew that was a part of it.

Rush was too young to know.

Tack knew. Hound. Hop. Dog. Brick. High. Arlo. Boz.

They all knew.

Rush didn't know.

Pete had told him, but he didn't *know*.

Harlan already was one of them.

The tightness in Pete's chest relaxed a hint when Harlan asked, "What's FFO?"

"Friends and family only," Rush answered.

Now it was direct eye contact with Rush. A lot of it. And it lasted awhile.

Finally, Harlan said, "We'll see."

Both he and Rush knew that was as good as they were going to get.

They left it at that and walked to their bikes.

They'd see on Saturday.

And on Pete's part, he'd hope.

And that hope was all for Jackie.

Diana

Tucson, Arizona
Several years earlier from Big Petey and Rush's visit to the bar...

WAS THIS HAPPENING?

Was this crap really, freaking *happening*?

I pushed. I shoved. I bit. I scratched.

And I shouted.

Had everyone gone *deaf*?

It was late, but a woman shouting didn't wake at least one person up?

Not to mention, we were in a college dorm. Half the occupants didn't get to sleep until early morning hours, if they slept at all.

But no one came.

And this was happening.

I could not let it happen.

The problem was, the longer it went on, the more I felt like I was slipping into a haze. The disbelief was retreating, the fear was increasing, he was so obviously stronger than me, the hope was fading that I'd be able to get away, and for some shit reason, my mind was taking this opportunity to shut down.

Suddenly, though, I got my opening and did not hesitate to haul up my knee as hard as I could, and I slammed his balls into his pelvis.

He grunted, moaned, rolled off me, grabbing his crotch, and I immediately rolled the other way, off the narrow twin bed in my dorm room where he'd forced me.

Once I got steady on my feet, I realized how hard I was breathing. I could actually feel my heart pounding in my chest, my skin tingling with the rush of adrenaline and fear.

And, thinking of nothing but being absolutely certain he was incapacitated, I punched him in his dick with all the power I could muster.

It was a cheap shot in a vulnerable area, but for heaven's sake, the guy was trying to rape me.

His groan shared agony as he curled into a fetal ball.

I ran out the door, down the hall and to the RA's door.

I hammered on it as my heart continued to hammer in my chest and my breath came out in explosive bursts.

She opened it and blinked at me.

Of course, most of the dorm was probably awake, but this woman had been sleeping.

"Did you not hear me shouting?" I demanded. "My study date just tried to rape me!"

Her face went pale, and suffice it to say, my adrenaline was still flowing, I was freaking out, pissed, scared, shocked, and still, I saw the myriad of emotions drift through her expression. Surprise. Concern. Anger. But also hassle.

This was going to be a hassle for her.

Seriously?

"Um...now's the time when you call the campus police," I informed her.

"Right," she mumbled. "Come in."

I walked in.

I sat on the side of her bed.

That was when I started shaking.

Bad shakes.

Cataclysmic.

Dang.

I'd never been sexually assaulted.

I hoped I never was again.

It wasn't as bad as it could be, but it was still awful.

Terrifying.

I knew, sitting there, it would change my life forever.

What I did not know was that it definitely would.

But in ways I'd never imagine.

Harlan

Denver, Colorado
Several years later from Diana's attack...
Saturday

HARLAN SAT AWAY from the crowd in a white resin chair in the forecourt behind Ride, the auto supply store, and in front of the other part of Ride, the custom car and bike garage that sat at the back of Chaos Motorcycle Club's property.

He was on Chaos.

Again.

Though, this was the first time in more than a decade.

No.

More than two.

Harlan didn't want to like what that resin chair said.

But he liked it.

It was the kind you bought for twenty bucks (if that) at Walmart.

These men, with their businesses (they had auto supply stores all over Colorado) were raking it in. Their builds from the garage were so phenomenal, they'd had magazine articles written about them.

His mom had collected every magazine, saved special in little plastic sleeves.

So now, he had them.

But that chair was not only cheap, it was bought in bulk (because there were a lot of them scattered around). They were nicked and scraped and obviously had been there awhile.

No one bothered to replace them.

No airs, no graces.

White resin chairs. A man at a huge-ass grill that was far from brand-new (and that grill had seen years of action), frying up burgers, brats and hotdogs. Potluck dishes all over a table. So much food, double the FFOs could show at this shindig and walk away stuffed. Kegs in barrels filled with ice. Massive coolers with bottles of beer, pop and water sticking out. Music playing. It was metal, it was loud, but it wasn't so loud you couldn't talk and listen. Kids running around everywhere.

Lots of kids.

Everywhere.

And women.

It was the women that shook him.

There were some in expensive clothes that even he could clock as pricey (though they were expensive in a casual way), wearing high-wedge sandals on their feet (that were also costly ...and casual). There were others who were born old ladies and wore that proudly with their jeans and Harley tees and silver jewelry.

Christ, one of them had a cute dress on, a mass of honey blonde ringlets and looked like a goddamn cheerleader.

All of them mingled together, laughing with each other, gabbing with heads bent close, a clear sisterhood among the brotherhood.

Harlan was really young the last time he was here, and his mother was desperate. He didn't remember much, except he felt powerless because his mom was in a situation he couldn't help her with.

He also remembered those men treated her differently than practically anybody.

She'd been unsafe.

They'd made her safe.

His gaze drifted to Tack Allen then to Hopper Kincaid, and finally to Hound Ironside.

Yeah.

With Big Petey, they'd made her safe.

He still felt the change from then to now.

This was what Pete said it was. It was what his ma told him Tack was building.

It was family.

He heard a chair scrape and looked to his side to see Rush, Tack Allen's son—and his heir, since Rush was now president of the Club, a position Tack used to hold—was dragging another beat-up white chair to Harlan.

Once he got it where he wanted it, Rush sat in it and slouched, testing that old chair's viability in a way that Harlan, who had to have at least fifty pounds on the guy, would never consider doing. Rush took a drag off his bottle of brew and kept his Oakley sunglasses aimed to the forecourt.

"You gettin' it?" Rush asked.

"Hard not to," Harlan answered.

"No one has to know," Rush assured him.

It was a laid-back day. Sunny. Autumn was coming in, but the weather was still great. He'd had a brat and a burger and some of the best homemade potato salad he'd ever tasted. And these were clearly good people.

He didn't want to get pissed.

"Not ashamed of it," he stated tightly. "Ma wasn't either."

Rush looked to him and repeated, "No one has to know."

He got it then.

If he joined, he'd be in the brotherhood, but that didn't mean they owned him. That didn't mean they got every piece of him. That didn't mean he owed them dick.

He came as he came. He gave what he gave. And both were his choice.

Harlan had to admit he was surprised about that.

Especially coming from Rush.

"So how does that work, considering what I know of this business, you join up, it's all in for life?" he asked.

"You do your time as a prospect," Rush explained. "Warning, it's gonna be shit. It's not about hazing. It's about duty. Loyalty. Commitment. The brothers decide you've done enough time, we patch you in. Through this, and after you earn your patch, you work the store or the shop. You get paid like any brother, a percentage of the monthly take. Except it's less as a recruit. You patch in, you get what we all get."

More surprise.

"Equal?"

"No one is above anyone else in the Club, Harlan."

"No matter the time they got in?"

Rush shook his head. "No matter anything, outside your status as recruit or patched-in brother."

"And that's it?"

A smile curved Rush Allen's lips. "You haven't been a recruit. It sucks bein' at the beck and call of a bunch of assholes who might be in the mood to bust your balls."

That did not sound fun.

"You do it?"

Rush jerked up his chin. "Everyone does it. Even a legacy, like you."

That surprised him too.

It also cut him.

He took his own drag from his beer, looked away and said, "Nah, man. I'm not legacy."

"I think Pete, Dad, Hop, High, Hound, Arlo and Boz would disagree."

"They were good to her," Harlan muttered.

"We're good to a lot of people, man. You decide to let me sponsor you, find out for yourself."

Harlan tipped his head toward the forecourt. "You gotta know, life I've lived, that seems too good to be true."

"What you should know is that Big Petey shared the essentials, nothing else, so I don't know," Rush told him. "That's yours to give or keep to yourself."

Harlan found that interesting.

Rush kept on. "It isn't like we don't have rules, we just don't have many of them. We also have structure. There's a hierarchy. It isn't about lording over anyone. It's about keeping balance and order. This is a democracy. Every man with a patch has a vote that's as equal as everything else. But prospects have a voice, and we all got ears, so they might not have a vote, but they're heard."

Harlan nodded that Rush was also heard, and Rush kept at it.

"Straight up, no drugs. Weed, okay. That's legal. Other shit, that's a problem. You do you, but if you get a woman and you do her dirty, you have kids and you fuck them up, or you mess with the brother-hood, that'll be a problem, and the Club will deal with it. You'll be given the chance to have your say, but you won't have the choice but to abide by the decision of the brothers."

None of this was an issue for Harlan.

Harlan turned back to him. "I like my job."

"I get it. Action."

That wasn't it, but Rush didn't get that.

Not now.

Maybe not ever.

"You join, you learn, we don't just run a store and make kickass cars," Rush informed him.

And again, he was surprised. His ma told him they got out of all that shit.

"Outlaw?" he asked.

Rush's lips curved again.

"Not the bad kind," he said and took another drag from his beer.

Harlan did too.

But this time when he did it, he found he was intrigued.

Beat-up chairs.

Potluck party.

The screeches and giggles of kids mingled with men's and women's laughter and metal.

The "rules" being no drugs and treating your women, kids and brothers right, and that was it.

"Not the bad kind" of outlaw.

Harlan threw back some more beer and settled in.

Because...yeah.

Harlan was intrigued.

Very intrigued.

Diana

Tucson, Arizona
Several years earlier than Harlan and Rush's conversation...
But also a Saturday.

THE COLLEGE ADMINISTRATOR came out of her office, gave me a

look I couldn't decipher, and then said, "Your father wants to have a word with you. You can use my office."

She smiled a tight smile, and I could decipher that.

Nolan Armitage wants to have a word with you, you come in on a weekend to have that word with him. He wants a private word with his daughter, you let him use your office to do it.

As I passed her, I mumbled, "Sorry."

I couldn't stop myself. It was habit. I did it a lot when Dad got involved.

She said nothing and closed the door behind me.

Dad was standing there, and when he had picked me up earlier to bring me here, I knew he wasn't messing around. It was the weekend, and he was in a full three-piece, look-at-me-I'm-*important!*, custom-tailored suit.

"Well, that was costly," he sniped.

I was confused.

"I'm sorry?" I asked.

"Taking care of your situation required a donation that was costly."

My...

Situation?

I shook my head. "Dad, I don't—"

"Fortunately, it's early in the semester. They'll be removing you from the class you share with that young man..."

That young man?

Not, *that absolute cretin who attacked my daughter in her dorm room?*

"...you'll be re-enrolled in it next semester," Dad went on. "And this situation will be expunged and not reflect on your record...or his. It will be as if it didn't happen at all."

My mouth dropped open as my lungs hollowed out, mostly because I couldn't believe what I was hearing.

"Really, Diana," Dad carried on. "What were you thinking, studying late at night with a young man who made it clear he had a crush on you? Of course he'd read that particular situation a certain way."

Uh-oh.

Oh no.

Oh crap.

I was going to start crying.

Angry tears.

Very angry ones.

And maybe yelling.

Loudly.

I couldn't do either. I'd learned that.

Boy, had I learned.

I had to be strong, smart, ambitious, hardworking, busy doing things that mattered, and although tears weren't verboten, they were discouraged and only accepted in certain circumstances.

Those didn't include when I butted heads with my dad.

"He's agreed to steer clear of you," Dad shared. "I suggest you do the same."

"Well, yeah, Dad, I'll do that since he *attacked me*," I snapped.

"Diana—"

"You're telling me you didn't come here to make absolutely certain, at the very least, this predator was expelled from this institution, but also doing what you could to make certain what should happen actually happens, that being he's arrested and charges are filed. Instead, you smoothed things over *for him*, and *I* have to change my schedule to avoid *him*?"

"Listen to me," he said in his well-known and oft-used *I fear you're too dim to understand, but I'm going to try to explain anyway* voice. "You haven't had a great deal of experience with men—"

I cut him off again. "I've dated a lot, Dad, and none of the guys I've dated have wrestled me to a bed and tried to tear my clothes off."

I'll hand it to him, when I said that, he flinched.

But he recovered quickly.

"Those were boys in high school," he retorted. "They were not men."

Like boys in high school might not have the same inclinations.

Was he crazy?

"I'm a sophomore here," I reminded him. "And I didn't do a nun impression my first year."

"Diana—"

"So what you're saying is, now that I'm dealing with 'men,' I can't be safe in my own space and instead have to have a mind to how some loser might feel about whether he wants to have sex with me or not. But *he* doesn't have to have a mind *to me* about whether I want the same, and maybe, you know, use his words to share what he wants and *asks me* instead of attacking me in order to simply take what he wants."

"It's the way of the world," Dad said stonily.

Oh yeah.

I couldn't believe I was hearing this.

I should believe it. This was my dad. Nolan Armitage. The epitome of the heartless, power-mad, money-hungry, workaholic attorney who found his way to getting what he wanted by any means necessary, and what he wanted, obviously, was power and money. All other things—his daughter, his wives (yes, plural, though not at the same time)—didn't factor.

Not to mention, he was the man who ground my mother to dust.

But still, I couldn't believe it.

I thought I'd learned how to deal. I thought I'd built appropriate walls that would keep the pain at bay. I didn't think he had the capacity to hurt me anymore.

Every day you learned new things, though, and today, this was my lesson.

And it hurt like hell.

"Do you have any clue how terrified I was?" I whispered.

He softened, slightly.

But not enough. Not near enough.

He proved that with what he said next.

"You need to have a mind to keeping yourself safe."

"I *was* safe. In my dorm room. With people right next door on both sides and across the hall. On a study date with some guy I barely know, so obviously, I don't want him ripping my clothes off."

"You barely know him, and you let him into your room?"

"I'm not on trial here, *Dad*," I bit out. "Save the courtroom machinations for re-traumatizing assault victims your rich clients pay you to get off."

Dad's face got hard. "That was unnecessarily nasty."

I stared at him.

He scowled at me.

He honestly didn't see what was happening here, what had happened to me, *his daughter*, and what he was doing to me, *his daughter*.

He didn't freaking *see it*.

But I did.

Oh, yeah, I so totally did.

Crystal freaking clear.

I shouldn't have wasted time building walls.

I should have used that time to form an escape plan.

"I'm done," I stated.

Dad nodded. "Yes, it's done. We'll have an early dinner and then I'll head back to Phoenix."

"No, I mean, I'm *done*."

His brows drew down. "With what?"

"You." I swung an arm out in front of me. "This. All of it."

He released a heavy sigh. "Please make sense, Diana. It was kind Ms. Bainbridge allowed us to use her office, but we can't stay in it all day."

"I'm dropping out of college."

An angry flush started up his neck.

"You are not," he stated flatly.

"You're paying for it, and I want nothing more from you, so until

I can pay for it, I'm out. I'm out at home too. I'll move in with Gram and Gramps."

His lip curled with distaste. "Now is not the time to throw a tantrum, Diana."

At his words, a sudden calm stole over me.

No, not a calm, a chill. But I welcomed it completely.

"I'm not five, I'm nineteen," I reminded him. "I'm officially an adult. I can vote. I can serve my country. So please don't mistake me. I'm not throwing a tantrum. I'm making a decision and carrying it through."

"This is ridiculous. You've had something unpleasant happen to you and you're being overly emotional."

"I can assure you with one hundred percent accuracy, until you've experienced your own sexual assault, you cannot make that first judgement about the level of emotion of a person who's experienced one. I can also share what happened to me wasn't *unpleasant*. It was terrifying. It was shocking. It was *unconscionable*. And it was *felonious*. You are a student of the law, but more, you're *my father*, and you making it easy for that asshole to get away with what he did to me, which might mean he'll do it to someone else, is utterly unthinkable."

"A lady doesn't curse."

Oh my God!

That was what he focused on in all I said?

"Yeah?" I asked.

"It's *yes*...and *yes*, you know that, as I've told you repeatedly I do not accept that kind of language from my daughter."

"Well, hear this, Dad. I'm not a lady. I'm a woman, and I can talk however the fuck I want. So fuck you, Dad." I leaned toward his stunned straight body and bit, "*Fuck you*."

With that, I walked out of Ms. Bainbridge's office.

She was standing outside it. Her eyes came immediately to me and the softness and concern in them almost blew it for me.

"Thanks," I muttered and got the heck out of there.

I'd fall apart somewhere else.

Not here.

Not now.

Not with him close.

Later.

I'd give myself that, but not much of it, because I'd need to put myself back together, build myself up and stay strong so he didn't grind me to dust too.

This was right.

This was good.

I needed an education. I needed to think about my future.

What I did not need was to owe that man anything.

Some might think it crazy, or even stupid, but they'd be wrong.

This was the smartest thing I'd ever done in my life.

Harlan

Denver, Colorado
Present day...

Rush had been wrong.

Being a prospect for the Chaos MC wasn't that tough of a gig.

Hugger and his ma had some rough times, more lean ones, some scary ones, so he'd been cooking and cleaning and helping his ma at the laundromat since he was in single digits. He got his first job, getting paid under the table, when he was eleven.

In his life, he'd lugged more kegs than he cared to count, cleaned up puke and blood, took punches, meted them out, got talked down to, taken for granted, screwed over.

Pulling a beer from a tap for a brother at his demand and driving home drunk biker bunnies was not a hardship.

Sure, there was tougher shit than that to do, a lot tougher, but it was shit that had to get done.

Hugger had learned in his life, if something had to get done, just do it. Don't waste your time trying to figure out how to con someone else into doing it or assessing the easiest way to get it done. Just get stuck in and do the job right.

Then move on.

He worked out his time as prospect, got paid for it (which, seriously, made it just like a kind of shitty job), then got patched in, and now he got paid a helluva lot more, which was not shitty at all.

And the brotherhood was good.

They were all like those beat-up chairs he'd had to stack more than once when he was a recruit.

They were all a lot like him.

Nicked. Scraped. Worn. But still standing and doing their jobs.

Those jobs were, as he'd noted over the years he'd spent with them, being good husbands, good fathers, good brothers and keeping the businesses strong and thriving, mostly so they could keep their families the same.

That was it.

There was other stuff they got into, but it was up to you if you wanted to get involved.

Hugger had signed on to that right away.

He suspected they all knew who he was, of a sort. Definitely the older brothers did.

But no one got up in his shit. No one pressed for more than he wanted to give. No one did anything but let him be who he was.

Though, they might give him crap about it, like making his Club name Hugger because he wasn't a big fan of being touched, unless he was having sex with a woman. But after, he was not a cuddle guy. If she stayed the night, she had her side of the bed, and he had his, and if she tried to encroach, he put her back where she should be. If she kept at it, he was out the door, or she was.

He didn't give a lot of headspace to trying to understand that. It was obvious.

He and his ma were a team of two.

The end.

His ma died, he was one, and he was down with that, not on the lookout to let anyone in.

Until he got Chaos.

But the way they were, no pressure, hands off, he was down with that too.

He headed through the tatty, lived-in bar area of the Compound, a place where he felt at home the minute he'd first re-entered it, and that had nothing to do with the fact he'd been there before, to the brother's meeting room.

He'd been called in.

He walked through the door to the meet room and was surprised, though also not, when Rush and Big Petey were the only ones sitting at the big table with the Chaos flag enshrined under a Plexiglas top.

Rush, because Rush was the president, and he was involved in everything the Club did.

Pete, because Pete had been trying to fashion himself as some kind of dad-like dude to Hugger since Hugger signed on to recruit.

Hugger didn't have a problem with this. Pete was a good man.

But he didn't encourage it.

This wasn't about Club family dynamics.

This was something else.

Not many of the brothers weren't in to do what needed to get done when the Resurrection MC, another Denver club (also known as the Angels of Vengeance, a name they earned in a number of ways, they were further known as the Angels of Death, and the same applied), came calling for assistance with their vigilante missions.

There was a lot of history there, it was tied up with Chaos, he'd learned it all as prospect, and he was in two minds about Resurrection.

What they did that forced them on the never-ending path to seek redemption was something he could never forgive. It didn't happen to him, and it was well before his time.

Still, he could, and would, never forgive them doing something that entirely fucked up.

But there was no doubt every one of those men was on that never-ending path, and not a one of them would ever stray from it.

So there was that.

He did a chin lift to Rush and Pete, got them in return, and took his seat at the table.

He reckoned he knew what this was about.

When Rush spoke, he found he wasn't wrong.

"That situation down in Phoenix needs some attention. I talked with Beck. He's sending down Muzzle and Eightball. They didn't ask for our assistance, but I'm not feeling the digging that's getting done by that particular player in the Valley of the Sun. Chaos history that needs to stay buried is getting dredged up. I don't know what he's got up his ass about us and Resurrection, but we have links, and he's making them. I want one of ours down there too."

"I'm in," Hugger said straightaway.

Beck was president of Resurrection, also known by his club name, Washington, or Wash. Muzzle and Eight were brothers in that crew.

Rush and Pete shared a glance.

It was Pete who spoke next.

"This guy you'll be looking into is some serious shit."

Hugger nodded. "Imran Babić. Bosnian gangster. Has his finger in every pie he can shove it into, as long as it's unlawful. Also, certifiable. Case in point, he played with the president of the Aces High MC's old lady."

"You prove you listen good, but you've already proved that," Pete replied. "But recently, shit has gone south for this guy."

"No surprise. He lives south, and I don't mean Arizona," Hugger returned.

"He's recently been arrested and made bail, after a brutal rape," Rush said.

Hugger sat perfectly still.

"She's messed up. But she pressed charges," Rush continued. "It's making him vulnerable. The kind of vulnerable he'll pull out all the stops to do something about."

Hugger's voice was ragged when he forced out, "She got protection?"

"That's part of what Muzz, Eight and you will be doing."

Oh yeah.

He was down with this.

"I'm coming with," Big Petey stated.

Hugger kept his mouth shut about Pete being involved, but he didn't like it.

The man was not young, for one.

And he was not well, for another.

Someone gave you no shit, no pressure, let you be who you were and always took your back, you returned that.

So Pete not reaching out about the way he was losing weight, slowing down, and sometimes seemed hazy meant they all had to lock down their concern and let him do it like he wanted to do it.

But Hugger knew he wasn't the only brother who was worried.

So it was Rush and Hugger who exchanged a glance after Pete spoke those words, but other than that, they didn't open their traps.

At least, not about that.

"There's a slight hitch in that plan," Rush went on.

"Yeah?" Hugger prompted.

"She's already got protection. A woman named Diana Armitage."

Oh shit.

"A chick?" Hugger asked.

No shade. Women could get the job done.

But one chick against a Bosnian gangster with a massive crew was not good odds.

Rush nodded his confirmation.

"She security? Ex-military? A cop? What?" Hugger asked.

Rush shook his head. "None of that."

This wasn't *oh shit*.

It was *oh fuck*.

And Rush wasn't done.

"She's also Babić's attorney's daughter."

Nope.

Now it was *oh fuck*.

He had no idea why the daughter would wade into this, but he did not sense good things.

Hugger looked to Big Petey.

"When do we leave?"

Pete grinned. "Pack for hot, son. The heat isn't off the Valley yet. Soon's you're ready, we ride."

Hugger stood.

Then he walked out to jump on his bike, go home, pack his saddle bags, and get his ass down to Phoenix.

1

NOT A FATHER

Diana

"I'M SORRY, Mr. Armitage. She just walked in and wouldn't leave."

"That's all right, Janie. She's my daughter and I asked to see her. I apologize I didn't tell you. It's fine. You can go back to your work."

I sat behind my father's big fancy desk, watching this exchange, marveling at the newfound knowledge the man could apologize.

I then watched him close the door behind Janie, who was rather young to be the personal assistant for a man of my father's stature. That being a named partner in a massive practice, who had a corner office that included a conference area with an eight-seater table and a sitting area that had four armchairs and two couches facing each other.

Oh, and fresh flowers.

Fresh flowers all over the place.

Their weekly flower budget had to equal my monthly mortgage, if not exceed it.

And let us not forget, his art.

I'd finally earned my degree (yep, in art, actually, two of them), which I paid for (thank you very much—it took seven years, but by damn, I earned them). I did restoration, conservation and cleaning, so I knew art, and I hated to admit it, but Dad had a good eye.

But he always did.

He'd picked Mom.

And then he'd picked Nicole.

Enough said right there.

Dad walked to stand in front of his desk, his attention never leaving me, and he said, "I asked to see you, however, you didn't reply to my voicemail."

I was lounged back in his cushy chair, my legs crossed, and I threw up both hands. "Consider this my response."

"This isn't a good time. I have a busy schedule. I'm due in a meeting in ten minutes. Regardless, I'd like to speak to you in private," he said through his teeth.

"It's been a long time, Dad. But with nineteen years' experience starting from birth, I still think I can translate Dad-ish." I sat forward and rested both elbows on his desk, putting my chin on top of my linked fingers. "What you mean is, your vile, cruel, practically inhuman client, who also happens to be rich, and that works for you, in fact, that's all you need, has requested I cut Suzette loose so he can have a clean go at silencing her."

"Again, I'd like to set some time to speak to you in private."

I sat back and feigned excitement. "No, wait...he wants to bribe her?"

I watched my father visibly lose patience. "Diana, I'll repeat, I don't have time at this moment, and I'd rather not do this here. We haven't connected since the situation in Tucson, so it would also be nice if I had the chance to get caught up with my only child."

"Ooo, good one. The guilt card. Well played."

"Diana—"

"You get discovery. Have you received it yet? Did you see pictures of her?"

"Diana—"

"You did, but what's your hourly with a client like Babić? Four hundred? Five?"

Abruptly, he leaned forward, resting his weight into his hands on his desk, the move so sudden, I jumped.

"Can't you see you've put yourself in danger?" he whispered, unease in his gaze.

I ignored the unease, as I'd been ignoring it since Suzette moved in with me a week ago.

Instead, I stood and assumed the same position so we were eye to eye. "Can't you see I'm the only safe place she's got? That man is a psychopath, but he's not going to kill his own attorney's daughter in order to get to the woman he viciously assaulted."

"You don't know what he'll do."

"I'm laying odds."

"This is messy, the accuser of my client living with my daughter."

"I'm afraid I fail to see how that concerns me."

"If you want to punish me, there are other ways to do it. Say, cutting me out of your life for ten years. I can report, that worked quite well."

"Sorry, Dad. This isn't about you. It's about Suzette."

He shook his head. "Don't think I'll fall for that nonsense. You've got your mother in you."

God, sometimes I wished I was a violent person.

In considering that, how bad was it to slap someone? Was that like, level three violent? Or more level five?

I was pretty sure I could do a three. I wasn't so sure I could live with five.

"Diana!" he snapped, straightening from the desk.

"I live in a high rise. We have security. What, are his men going to storm the building?"

"You don't mess with a man like Babić."

"I *have* seen the pictures, so that isn't lost on me."

He took in a deep breath that expanded his wide chest, and I noted he looked good, as always. His dark hair was turning a glinting silver, not gray or white, and it was attractive. He'd always kept fit, getting up early to hit the home gym or the one at the office to put in at least a solid forty-five minutes of cardio and strength training. It was noticeable he hadn't changed that habit.

I wondered, though, if he got Botox, because without the silver in his hair, he looked to be a man in his early forties, tops, not late fifties, which he was.

"I didn't handle that situation well," he announced. "The one on campus. I see that now. I was thinking like a man of my generation. What we'd been taught and what I knew women had been taught in terms of how to look out for themselves. I didn't consider that line of thinking was not only outdated, but wrong."

I didn't know what to say to that.

"And I'd like to have a relationship with my daughter," he finished.

I knew what to say to that.

"Well, if we're entering negotiations, drop Babić as a client, make sure no one in your firm picks him up, and maybe use some of the influence you've spent decades amassing to make it difficult for him to find someone in the legal community that would help him out."

He shook his head. "It doesn't work like that, Diana. Even if I withdrew, it's my duty to protect a client's interests. I'd have to recommend new counsel and advise them on the case."

"So that takes our short negotiations to a close," I muttered.

"I'm proud of you," he announced, apropos of nothing. "You got your degree. You took that further. You did it on your own, which I'm sure was difficult. I have friends who have gone to you for conservation work. They say you're talented."

Oh no.

No way in hell.

He didn't get to do that.

I began to walk around his desk, stating, "We're not doing this."

"Diana, please come to dinner," he requested of my back on my way to his door.

I turned to him.

And I said what I said next despite the sharp pain I felt at hearing the undisguised and genuine entreaty in his tone.

"I'll consider it, but before then, I'll share that it wasn't your outdated...and you're right, wrong line of thinking that was the problem. It was that you thought like a man, not a father. You, my father, after what I went through, put me through a different kind of onslaught by taking the stance of a man, and in so doing, you protected another man, one who had harmed me. *That* was why I walked away and never come back."

I had to hand it to him, once I'd said this, he looked stricken.

Okay, no.

He looked wrecked.

But I couldn't let that affect me, because I wasn't done.

"If you're standing there, telling me you want to be my father, then I'll tell you, it'll never work, and I'm not putting myself through it, if you don't figure out what being a father means. Now, this may seem extreme to you, but representing a man who very obviously brutally attacked a woman physically, sexually, and having a daughter, is not in the slightest bit okay. I don't give that first shit he's entitled to a defense. Let someone else offer it to him. You are not a struggling lawyer who needs to take cases to put food on his family's table. Babić had a retainer with another firm, he did this, they dropped him. You picked him up. *You.* A man with a daughter who's survived a sexual assault. Think on that, Dad. Think why I might have an issue with that. Think what it might mean to me that you're defending this man. Once you do, contact me. And then maybe we'll chat."

"So it *is* about you," he declared, and there was a hint of a smirk on his lips.

I did not forget how very much Nolan Armitage liked to be right.

I just forgot how irksome it was.

"No, it's about you," I retorted. "My entire life, it's never been about me. It's always been about you."

His head jerked like I'd slapped him.

And I didn't even have to commit level five (or three) violence.

This worked for me.

I walked out of his office, closed the door behind me, and looked right to Janie.

She was very attractive.

But she was so freaking young.

Too young to be put through my father's wringer.

Taking her in, I made a decision I didn't like, but in the end, for the sisterhood, I had no choice.

I walked to her and stopped in front of her desk.

"My father fucks all of his PAs," I announced.

Her eyes got big.

But her face got red.

Right.

They were fucking.

I suspected she was younger than me by several years.

Gross, but still...no surprise.

I did not wonder if she called him "Mr. Armitage" when he was doing her, because just skating over the thought gave me the serious skeeves.

Instead, I shared, "He gets a new PA every year, and the old ones don't get moved to another attorney in this firm. Think about that, Janie. Your time is limited, and I can assure you, you will not win him over where the others failed. You will not be presented a ring and then plan a fancy wedding and move into his big Paradise Valley house. You will not carry his children and admire what an energetic mature father he is. He doesn't want children. There were times I wondered if he even wanted me. He doesn't want a partner, he wants a status symbol. There's only one end to this sad tale. You will get nothing you're promised, and nothing you wish for. Instead, when he's done, you will simply be replaced."

I felt terrible because she looked about ready to cry, and I belatedly reconsidered being so blunt about it.

But bottom line, even if she was pretty, and he was attracted to her, she wouldn't have the job if she wasn't good at it.

She needed to find another job where the expectations were a lot more realistic, on both sides.

And with that, my work done, I left my father's practice.

2

WE DOIN' THIS?

Diana

I DROVE HOME from Dad's office pretending I wasn't being tailed.

Mortifying Fact: One could say I'd been *overly emotional* when I decided to wade into the whole Suzette Snyder/Imran Babić situation.

Or, perhaps, highly delusional.

I'd read in the *Arizona Republic* about the woman who'd all but dragged herself into a hospital emergency room after a brutal attack.

At the time, I couldn't say I had much of a reaction to it, except vague distress, considering the appalling fact it wasn't a rare occurrence, and as such, I, along with the rest of society, was inured to that kind of thing.

I'd then heard she'd named her attacker, he'd been arrested, and it was big news, because he was reportedly some Tony Soprano-esque player in Phoenix, and due to that fact, his arrest was a big win for law enforcement.

After that, I'd read my father was taking his case.

I'd successfully avoided my father for a long time.

The only thing that leaked in was when he defended Rogan Kirk after he stole all those people's pensions a few years ago, and that, too, was big news, so Dad was in front of the cameras a lot.

But I could ignore that, because Rogan Kirk was just a greedy jerk who stole from people.

Not a sexual predator who stole even more precious things from people.

So Dad taking this particular case was when things got overly emotional (or delusional, take your pick).

Alas, yes, I knew I was not only regularly tailed, they'd had eyes on my condo since I'd moved Suzette into it (don't ask how that happened, it involved some Google sleuthing that wasn't all that appropriate, some fancy dancing with hospital staff, some girl-to-girl conversations that might, on my part, have been mildly manipulative, and some angry cops who felt it was their responsibility to provide protective custody for Suzette—one in particular, Detective Rayne Scott, was not over it and frequently phoned me in an effort to change this situation).

I didn't lie to Dad about the security in my building.

I had a great job, even if it would never make me a millionaire. Still, it was a niche market that served rich people who paid for the care and conservation of stuff that mattered to them, and they paid a lot for it.

Experiencing a rare wild hair, a few years ago, I'd let some video poker winnings ride on thirteen black on a roulette wheel at Talking Stick Casino, and to my shock, when the little ball dipped down into that particular slot, I won a crazy amount of money.

Immediately after, I cashed out. And as one who had learned not to push her luck (except for when, say, I got another wild hair and decided to stick my nose into the dangerous situation of a woman I'd never met), I walked away from the casino, never to return to it, or any casino, again.

This, along with the nice, but not outlandish, inheritance Gramps left me, gave me a down payment that would make the mortgage (and ridiculous HOA fees) manageable in a really nice condo complex close to Fashion Square Mall in Scottsdale.

There was security in the form of actual security guards patrolling the premises.

Also, you had to have a key fob to get into any complex elevator vestibules, not to mention to get the elevator to take you to your floor (and your fob only worked for your floor) or into a stairwell.

So there was that.

Moreover, the place was lousy with cameras, and I had a security system in my unit.

And after Suzette moved in, I'd had one of those steel bars installed on my door, the kind with two thick plates, and when you hit a button on the center knob, they slid into anchors on either side of the door. It wasn't pretty, but considering my door was heavy-duty anyway, it would make it hard work to get through.

This was no lock-picking situation. You could only open that thing from the inside or with a remote.

This did not make us impenetrable.

What it did was demand a good deal of effort from someone who was trying to break in, and that effort would need to be noisy and violent. This would give Suzette or me a definitive heads-up and the chance to call the cops before they were able to get through.

As such, Suzette hadn't left my condo since she moved in. Not even to sit on one of my two balconies (one off the living room, one off my bedroom), each having views to the massive courtyard.

This was because the lower level of the complex was all businesses open to the public. There was a sandwich shop, a nice restaurant, a brunch café, a coffee bar, a neighborhood pub, a cocktail lounge, a hot-yoga studio, a Pilates place, a cute boutique, a hair salon and a day spa, among other things.

Some of this had outdoor seating.

And yes, I'd noticed from my balcony there were men enjoying lattes lounged in that seating, and they had eyes to my unit. Not all the time, but it wasn't infrequent.

They weren't making a show of it, but they weren't hiding it.

They were watching.

What got into me to get involved in this tense situation, I wasn't quite sure.

It had been a rocky road at first when I'd quit school and gone out on my own.

Gram and Gramps had helped, Mom had provided moral support from afar, but mostly, I was determined to make it under my own steam. It was multiple-jobs, burn-the-midnight-oil, get-so-exhausted-you-felt-you'd-never-be-refreshed-again, have-zero-days-off-from-work-school-or-study-for-an-entire-eighteen-months-at-one-point kind of determination.

I could not deny some of this was about Dad. About showing him, even if I was intent never to see him again. About proving not only myself, but something about Mom that I didn't quite get, but I knew it was there.

He was a terrible father, but a great motivator.

This sitch with Suzette was something else entirely.

It was scary, stupid and dangerous.

But Suzette agreed with me. I was the wall she could hide behind that Babić wouldn't tear down. She'd been clear about what happened, and her many injuries corroborated those facts. There was DNA collected from under her fingernails along with seminal fluid (that had not yet been tested, but it would be incontrovertible when it was).

Because of this, Babić really, *really* needed a very good attorney.

Last, Babić really, really, *really* did not need any more problems with the law, or bad PR, and the death of his accuser, and anything happening to the woman who was offering her protection, would be pretty damned bad PR, and would lead to more pretty danged serious problems with the law.

In other words, Suzette was understandably being a little nuts because she'd been through hell and maybe wasn't thinking straight.

As for me, I didn't know what the hell I was doing.

What I did know, and what troubled me greatly, was that I, too, was not thinking straight.

I parked my little, baby-blue Fiat 500 (satirically, but adorably, I'd named her "Baby Shark") in my underground spot and grabbed my keys, primarily the hand-held Mace on my keychain. I flicked open the snap on the strap that kept the button covered, palmed the tube with my thumb on the button, took a look around through windows and mirrors, and only when I saw nothing, I got out.

I kept alert on the way to the parking level elevator lobby. I fobbed myself in. I called the elevator. I got on the elevator. I fobbed my floor.

And then I let out a sigh of relief as the doors started closing.

Only to have a man slip through.

Then another.

And another.

And a last.

Suddenly occupying the elevator with four large, rough-looking men, I opened my mouth to scream and lifted the Mace to press, but the second guy through, a very tall, brawny man with lots of wild, wavy, thick blond-brown hair and a massive beard, came at me.

Quick as a flash, he caught the wrist of the hand in which I was holding the Mace, and he redirected the aim away from him (or any of them). He then squeezed my wrist firmly, but not painfully, and yanked the canister out of my hand.

Well, that was humiliating.

And alarming.

He then bellied up to me, forcing me to the back of the elevator. He dipped his head down. His dark-brown eyes locked to mine, nothing touching me except his hand still at my wrist.

And he spoke.

"You're safe. We will not harm you. I'm Hugger. With me are Eight, Muzzle and Cruise. We share a Bosnian problem and we think we can help you out."

Oh.

Well then.

The elevator doors closed and we started to ascend.

He let me go and stepped back.

I cast my eyes through the men.

Hugger was tall, but one of the others was taller, as in crazy-tall. The final two were also quite tall, one had a man-bun and a hint of a beer gut, the other one was just good-looking (as were Hugger and the crazy-tall dude).

They did not look like the shiny-golf-shirt-and-slacks-wearing gangsters who drank lattes and kept an insidious presence in the courtyard.

They looked like men who didn't know what golf shirts were, and I would lay money down none of them owned a pair of slacks.

"I'm a brother of the Chaos MC in Denver," Hugger carried on as the elevator went up. "Eight and Muzzle are brothers of Resurrection MC. Also in Denver. Cruise is a local, and he's Aces High."

"MC?" I asked.

"Motorcycle club," he answered.

That explained the no-slacks-owning.

"And what problem do you have with the Babić?" I asked.

The elevator doors opened.

The three other men filed out.

I stood in the elevator with Hugger.

The super tall one kept his hand on the door so it would remain open.

"We doin' this?" Hugger queried.

"What does 'this' refer to?" I returned.

"Talking, explaining, and us offering you and your girl protection because you by no means got that buttoned up," Hugger replied. "They're casing you. They're figuring shit out. They're making plans. And they're gonna put them in play when they think they can get the job done without blowback."

Thus my need to layer concealer under my eyes due to missing sleep because I knew this exact thing was what was happening.

I stared at Hugger.

If he didn't look so serious, he'd be cute.

There was a lot of handsome under all that hair.

So much of it, even all that hair couldn't hide it. Straight, strong nose. Thick, curling, dark eyelashes. Full, ridged lips.

But with all that hair, and his big bulky body, he was the kind of guy you wanted to tease you while you pretended it annoyed you, but you secretly loved it. The kind of guy who would chop onions beside you while you seasoned the meat. The kind of guy who would open his arms in invitation so you could curl up on his lap and he'd make you feel better just by engulfing you in him after you had a bad day.

In other words, cute.

He might not be into excessive grooming (or any grooming at all), but he was fit. He was wearing a Rage Against the Machine black tee, faded blue jeans and black motorcycle boots, but they were all clean.

And he smelled of a hint of clove, a hint of sandalwood and the barest trace of citrus—warm, outdoorsy and fresh, which seemed to define him completely, even if I knew nothing about him.

A quick sweep of the other three said much the same thing (*sans* the scent, they weren't close enough I could smell them).

I made another important decision that day and stepped through the doors.

Hugger came out after me.

I stopped just outside and didn't move.

Neither did they.

"There are cameras everywhere," I told him (or them, but I directed it at Hugger).

"We know," he replied.

"We're having this chat here. I'm not letting you into my place until I understand what's going on," I shared.

"Acceptable," Hugger grunted.

"Okay then," I continued. "What's going on?"

"Babić got a hankering for the president of the Aces High MC's old lady. He kidnapped her to share this info," Hugger stated.

That fucking guy.

"Ugh," I muttered.

"She was unimpressed with his attention, and that was communicated. He then began to fuck with other old ladies of Aces. Leaving notes on the windshields of their cars. Sending them flowers and gifts at their work and homes. Subtle shit that's not illegal, but would mess with their heads," Hugger continued. "And it's messing with their heads."

"Ugh again," I said.

Hugger ignored my utterance.

"Somehow, he got hooked up with a biker bunny who has a beef with Aces," he carried on. "She's cousin to an old lady of a brother of Resurrection." Hugger tilted his head to the super tall guy and the one standing next to him who didn't have a man-bun. "And for some reason, this has translated to him having an interest not only in Aces, but Resurrection and Chaos. We don't know why. We just know no good can come of it. That's why me, Eight and Muzzle are down here. To work with Aces to find out."

"And Suzette factors into this...?" I trailed off in my prompt, and then I stiffened and fought taking a step back when he answered, but his tone had deteriorated significantly.

"Suzette factors into this first, because we are not okay with any motherfucker doing what he did to any woman," Hugger gritted. "But he did, and that shit cannot go unanswered."

Even if I agreed with him, I swallowed nervously, not only at his tone, but the sheer wrath that glittered in his dark eyes that accompanied it.

"Side benie of that, she takes him out, it makes his operation vulnerable," he continued. "We can then neutralize it before they fuck up anyone else's life. So she needs to stay healthy because she just needs to stay healthy. But also so she can testify and get his ass in a cage."

"As you obviously know, we share the same goal," I told him.

"Yeah, we know that," he replied.

"Though, I'm not sure what you can do to help," I said.

He blinked.

Then he stared hard at me.

After that, his brown eyes swept me top to toe. Twice.

I knew what he saw.

I was in cropped, white jeans, muted gold pumps and a light-weight, pink, man-tailored shirt. I was also carrying a sleek, rose-leather tote.

Further, I was five six. I was an ice cream, frozen custard, pie and cookie aficionado, and I wore the evidence of that on my ass (also my tits, and okay, maybe my thighs and belly too).

Assisting that situation, I didn't adhere to taco Tuesdays. Tacos for me were good any day of the week. And my stylist (who happened to have a chair in the salon in the forecourt of that very complex) was a master with the balayage, and as such, my dark hair had golden highlights added by the hand of an artist. But it was my hand that put the perfect, soft, beachy waves in the long tresses.

What could I say?

I could do good hair.

I also was a dab hand with makeup.

Neither were hobbies of mine.

Both were leftovers of being the daughter of a father who drilled into me that appearances meant everything, and furthermore, I reflected on him, and that reflection better be positive, so I got good at doing both.

Now, it was just habit.

What I did not look like was a badass bodyguard or kickass commando.

He didn't look like those either.

He looked exactly like what he was, a biker (though, without the leather jacket or vest I saw club members wear on the streets of

Phoenix, which was a biker haven, considering you could ride all year).

But seeing as he had to be at least six three, and the impressive bulges at his biceps and the sinews and distended veins on his forearms were clearly not just for show, I suspected he was far from a pushover.

Same with the other three dudes (though, man-bun guy appeared a little older, but not by much, and I wasn't fooled by his mini beer belly for a second).

"Not sure why you put yourself in this, Diana," Hugger spoke again, and I returned my attention to him when he did, and not only because he was talking.

Oh no.

It was because he said my name.

And it wasn't because he knew my name, which was a little disconcerting, seeing as I hadn't introduced myself.

It was that in his deep, masculine, attractive voice *he said my name*, and I was a little freaked I had a physical response to him doing it.

A highly pleasant one.

He was not at all my type.

So what was that?

"And the security in this building is tight," he went on. "But I don't think you understand the severity of what you're dealing with."

"When I met her, she was two weeks out of the attack," I said quietly, "and she still looked like she'd been dragged behind a truck for ten miles. I know the severity of what I'm dealing with."

At receiving this knowledge, Hugger's eyes got that scary glint again, but he quickly powered through it.

"You gotta know you don't have the resources to see this through," Hugger rejoined.

"And what resources are you offering?" I asked.

"Safe house," he responded.

I shook my head.

"Not for you to decide," he stated shortly.

"You're right. It's Suzette's," I agreed. "But I can tell you, she feels safe with me, and I can't go with her to a safe house. I have a mortgage to pay."

At this juncture, the very tall dude joined our convo.

"Maybe you can explain why she didn't accept protective custody from the cops," he suggested.

I looked to him. "She thinks Babić has someone, or someones plural, on the inside."

This was true, and it was how I could manipulate her (mildly) into coming to stay with me.

Man-bun guy now spoke. "Your father is Babić's attorney. Wanna explain that?"

Ah, so they pretty much knew everything, which obviously would include my name.

So I wasn't being quick on the draw, sue me. I'd never been cornered by a pack of bikers before. I was learning that threw you off your game.

"Until today, I haven't spoken to my father in ten years," I told them something they clearly didn't know.

They all looked among each other at that.

"It'd be good to know why you're in this at all," the last guy to speak, spoke.

"I'd explain that if I knew myself," I said honestly. "I don't. I heard about what happened. I knew nothing about Babić, though I also heard he'd been arrested. But when I saw my father, who, I'll warn you, is very good at what he does, was going to defend him, I felt compelled to...get involved."

"By putting yourself in the path of a criminally insane lunatic?" Man-bun guy demanded to know.

It was a good question, one with no good answer.

"I will admit, I may not have been thinking clearly," I confessed, not about to share it was more about being *overly emotional*. "But I did it and we are where we are, so the reasons why we're here don't matter."

I felt Hugger's attention, so I turned to him, only to wish I didn't because I suddenly felt naked. Like he could see every inch of me, not just on the outside, but deep down, places I didn't even dwell, and by no means did I explore.

Therefore, I quickly turned my eyes away.

"If she won't do safe house, or protective custody," the tall one said, "then it's about security. A man in your place and patrol outside it."

A man in my place?

"You mean, a man *staying* in my place with Suzette and me?" I asked to clarify. "Or a man to take my place?"

"Although you bein' nowhere near this shit would be optimal, if you won't relocate, then you're getting another roommate," Hugger decreed.

Oh boy.

"Listen—" I started.

"No," Hugger bit out so sharply, it cut like a razor.

I felt that pain, so I shut my mouth.

He then laid it out.

And me while he was doing it.

"You got no idea what you're doin'. You don't even have any idea why you're doin' it. We got muscle. We got guns. We got manpower. We got a stake in this. And we got experience. You either got an axe to grind or something to prove to your pops. You gotta work that out, but not at the expense of a woman who needs someone looking out for her, not whatever she's workin' out for herself. You got her to the point she feels safe with you, whatever. We'll take your back too. Now you're gonna walk us into your crib, introduce us to Suzette and tell her you recruited reinforcements. And we're gonna take it from there."

"Excuse me, but this isn't about me at all," I snapped.

"It isn't?" he bit back.

That hit uncomfortably close to the bone.

"Maybe why I started it, but it isn't where it's at now," I retorted.

"Bullshit," he shot back.

He was a little right and a lot wrong.

The wrong part pissed me off.

"You've known me maybe five minutes," I returned. "You can't make those judgments about me."

"Remember that part I said about experience?" he inquired sarcastically.

"Yes, I do," I replied. "And maybe you'll explain that, since you've shared only you're members of motorcycle clubs, not top-notch security consultants *or* behavioral scientists."

He leaned his strapping torso back, and asked, "You think you got this?"

"No, I do not. But tell me, if you were me and four dudes cornered you in an elevator and offered assistance, out of what apparently is the goodness of their hearts mixed with some vague camaraderie with the victim of a violent crime, and you'd promised a woman you'd do what you could to keep her safe, would you let those four guys waltz in and take over?"

He swung a long arm out to indicate the others and replied, "They looked like us and were offering when you got nothin' to offer, fuck yeah, I'd let them waltz in and take over."

He had a point.

"Again, it's not this woman's choice," man-bun guy said. "It's Suzette's."

It was, damn it.

Don't get me wrong, these men showing out of the blue was a gift from God. Especially if there were more of them.

I wasn't a fan of the "we got guns" assertion, because I wasn't a big fan of guns. Though, I suspected Babić and his boys had them, so at least that evened those odds.

I also was a little confused about the "we got experience" portion of his litany.

But I'd texted Suzette when to expect me home. She was expecting me home. I didn't want to worry her and this was waylaying me from getting to her so she wouldn't worry.

I had another decision to make, and it was a big one.

I wasn't really sure what was going on.

What I was sure of was, if Babić made his play, I did not have the skills to counter it.

These guys might not either, but it was evident they'd be better equipped than me.

Shit.

"Let's go meet Suzette," I muttered.

Hugger glowered at me.

Man-bun grinned.

Tall guy looked to his boots.

Other guy let out an impatient breath.

I turned and led them down the hall to my door.

3

WE EAT IN AN HOUR

Hugger

Hugger was pissed right the fuck off.

There were many reasons for this.

First, Diana Armitage was traipsing around this hot-as-shit, sun-drenched, parched fucking city—a place no one in their right mind would willingly choose to live—and she was doing it in high-heeled gold shoes, driving the smallest, most unsafe car he'd seen in his life, all while being tailed by two gun-toting henchmen of a local mob.

Yet she did it like it was just any other day. She was just going where she needed to go, like two gun-toting henchmen of a local mob weren't on her ass.

Which meant she was either bravely stupid or stupidly brave, but neither was smart.

Second, the bitch was gorgeous.

Lots of tits. Lots of ass. Perfect makeup. Sparkling green eyes. Long, thick hair any man would get a hard-on to have his fingers in and have it spread all over his lap when she was blowing him.

She had sass. She had attitude.

And she was messed right the fuck up, considering she inserted herself into this situation because she had a beef with her pops, and that was so fucking dumb, he wanted to turn her over his knee and spank some sense into her.

Third, she had a tight-as-shit crib.

It didn't take a behavioral scientist to call her favorite color was blue, considering the color of her car, and her pad was mostly white with a lot of blue. It was crisp, stylish, comfortable-looking and feminine.

Even if it wasn't his gig, he liked it. It looked good. It suited her. It was feminine without being girlie, and that was her to a T. And he dug she knew herself well enough she could stamp her space so clearly with her style.

He was on a mission.

He did not need to want to bang this woman.

But he seriously wanted to bang this woman.

Last, Suzette Snyder showed after having a brief conversation with Diana in a room down a hall.

When she showed, her arm was in a sling, she had a limp, and there were still stitches in her lip and across the cheekbone under the end of her left eye. The bruising hadn't all disappeared either, even after three weeks.

But she couldn't be taller than five three. She couldn't weigh much more than a hundred pounds. And she looked about thirteen years old, even if he knew she was twenty-six.

It meant Babić didn't bother picking on someone his own size and he might have some pedo shit going on.

For the first time in his life, Hugger understood what "it made my blood boil" felt like.

Suzette didn't come close to looking any of the men in the eye. She also didn't come fully out into the open. She lingered at Diana's back, just to the side, and she had her fingers wrapped so tightly around Diana's forearm, Hugger could see the white come out around the beds of her nails.

That hold was going to leave bruises, but Diana didn't flinch or give that first indication she even felt it.

Hugger partially understood this, considering his vibe was joining the other men's when they caught sight of her, and these were not happy vibes. He wanted to control it, but the state of Suzette, he was finding that impossible.

The other part he understood was that a man did this to her, so men freaked her.

"This is Hugger and, uh..." Diana started to introduce them.

"Eight," Eightball grunted.

"Muzzle," Muzz said.

"Cruise," Cruise put in tightly.

"Like I told you, they're here to help us keep things steady and cool while the DA builds his case and then..." Diana trailed off.

"Stick until Babić is locked up," Eight bit out.

"So, um...for the long haul," Diana concluded.

Suzette said nothing.

Diana turned to her, pried her hand off her forearm but held it in hers, grabbing the other one too.

"They need to know you're okay with that," she said gently. "So now you've met them, you and I'll go back to your room and talk about it. Okay?"

Suzette nodded, let Diana go and nearly sprinted back down the hall.

Hugger's hands closed into fists.

Diana shot them a look and swiftly followed her.

Hugger concentrated on her ass swaying because he needed that goodness to chase out the bad.

"That motherfucker..." Muzzle gritted.

"Cool it," Cruise murmured.

Hugger needed some air, even if that air was dusty, dry and hot as fuck.

So he walked to the sliding glass door that led to a balcony, which had patio furniture that was mostly blue (the cushions and pillows) but also white (the frames).

He stepped out and homed right in on the two sleazeballs that were sitting outside a coffee place across the courtyard from Diana's unit.

One of them lifted his paper cup Hugger's way.

Hugger considered flipping him the bird but decided against it.

He also considered going down there and knocking their goddamned heads together.

He decided against that too.

Instead, he stepped closer to the railing and cased the courtyard in the middle of the square complex.

Six breezeways to unit entry vestibules. Two in the middle on each side and one at each corner.

Total fucking open-to-all space in the middle, with ample visitor parking on the north side.

Slip in behind a resident at an elevator lobby, like they did earlier with some unsuspecting resident, then slip in behind some health-conscious moron who takes the stairs, you're right at their door.

The only good thing he saw was that steel bar which might take explosives to get through.

But a desperate man did desperate things, and Hugger had no doubt Babić wouldn't blink at setting a few charges to open the way to get to his prey.

He felt company come up at his side, and he looked up at Eight.

"We need to get her in a safe house," he stated.

"Yeah," Eight muttered, gazing through the courtyard. "We need to get her in a safe house."

Hugger then watched Eight jerk up his chin toward the coffee place, like he was saying hello to an acquaintance.

Then he looked at Hugger.

"Your take on Armitage?" Eight asked.

"This is personal to her because of her dad, which is some serious stupid shit."

"It's personal to her all right," Eight mumbled.

"She's got a beef with her pops," Hugger noted.

"She does. She's also got a beef with Babić," Eight replied.

"That's not hard, with what he did."

"It wasn't what he did to Suzette. It's what some other fuck did to Diana."

At these words, it felt like a tidal wave pounded into him, stealing his breath, pulling him under, dragging him out.

It sounded like Eight was ten miles away when he heard, "Hug."

It's what some other fuck did to Diana.

"Hug!" Eight called sharply.

Hugger struggled to the surface.

Eight watched him do it, and then asked, "You didn't clock that?"

"No," Hugger grunted.

"You got a lock on your shit?" Eight asked.

"No."

Eight crossed his arms on his chest and studied him. "You're into her."

"You're not?"

"Oh, I'd do her if she gave me a shot, but that's not where you're at."

It wasn't, considering he wanted to land one in Eight's throat for saying what he just said.

"You're inside," Eight announced.

Hugger stared at him.

Eight was the leader of this mission. And when Resurrection called it, Chaos didn't say dick.

This had to do with the fact that those men picked up assignments like this on the regular, so they had a lot of experience, and they kept their skillset sharp even when they weren't out in the world doing vigilante shit for the downtrodden.

On the other hand, Chaos jumped in occasionally, mostly because it was always for a righteous cause, like this one, but partly for shits, giggles and to keep life interesting.

Regardless their motivation, you didn't question the leader.

But considering Eight had sensed where he was at, Hugger had to question it.

"Don't think that's smart, man," Hugger noted.

"I'll tell you what I've learned, Hug," Eight began. "You got skin in the game, you go balls to the wall to win it. It's not like any of us are gonna slack. But you got incentive to keep her ass healthy so you can tap it, that works in a big way."

"We all need focus."

"You'll be focused all right."

He had zero interest in hashing Diana Armitage out with Eightball.

"You're lead, I'll do what you say. But I'm on record," Hugger finished it.

Before Eight could reply, they heard, "Brothers," come from the door and saw Muzzle standing there.

Looking through the window, Hugger also saw Diana had returned.

She'd kicked off her shoes.

With them on, she was only four inches shorter than him.

With them off, it came clear he could throw her over his shoulder and haul her sweet, round ass to bed.

Fuck.

He and Eight entered the room, Hugger sliding the door shut behind him.

She waited until he did, before she said, "Suzette is okay with you guys helping out."

"She know Hugger's gonna be sleepin' on the couch?" Eight asked.

Hugger watched closely as her eyes got big, some pink came into her cheeks, and neither helped matters, because both were fucking cute, and both told him she was where he was with this shit.

Terrific.

Her voice sounded slightly strangled when she replied, "She knows, yeah."

"We're gonna need fobs, keys, and I need a piece of paper to write some numbers down," Eight told her.

She nodded and headed to the kitchen, which had gleaming white modern cupboards and quartz countertops. But there was a subtle blue in the pattern of the tile that made up the backsplash, and there were cobalt blue glass globes around the three dangling lights over the island.

She pulled out a keychain that had a fob on it as well as a set of keys. She tossed it on the counter.

Eight nabbed it and instantly turned and lobbed it to Hugger, who caught it.

Diana watched this, took a deep breath, then she rooted around in the drawer, saying, "We'll get some keys made and I'll order some extra fobs from the complex office." She came out with a pad of paper and pen, which she slid across the counter to Eight.

He bent to it and started scribbling, offering so much info, he had to take out his phone and copy shit off it.

When he was done, he straightened and pushed the pad back her way.

"You program those into your phone. Get Suzette to do the same. Just precautions, you're gonna be covered," Eight said.

Diana nodded.

"We got another man with us. His name is Big Petey. He's older, softer, less of a visible threat, but he's still got it goin' on. He's gonna hang with Suzette during the day while Hugger stays on you"—her eyes raced to Hugger on that—"and other brothers make sure shit is copacetic here at home base. You with me?"

Her attention swung back to Eight. "I don't need a bodyguard."

"Okay, yeah. Right. You don't quite get what you agreed to. I'll elucidate," Eight said magnanimously. "Suzette and you just turned this over to us. We got this now. You do what we say when we say it.

You don't question it. We got you how we need to get you. And how that is, is never open to discussion. You still with me?"

She opened her mouth.

Hugger nearly smiled when Eight kept going before she could say anything.

"Great. It's not gonna be tough. Unless shit gets fucked, nothing will change. You go to work. You come home. Except, when you do that, you got a man at your back in case Babić gets any ideas. Suzette stays here. She's covered, inside and out. We keep things good, and in the meantime, you and us talk Suzette into vanishing somewhere safe so you're out of this equation, and we are not havin' to deal with providing protection in what amounts to a huge-ass apartment complex on top of a mini fuckin' mall."

She opened her mouth again, and again, Eight got there before her.

"I heard you when you said she wasn't down with leaving you. We'll get her there, and you're gonna help. But you got no business being a middleman in shit this heavy. You need out from under it and she needs to be somewhere we got total control of her environment. We'll have a sit down with Buck to see if there's some local cop he knows is squeaky clean, so we can get word to them that she's vanished, but she hasn't *vanished*, and he can keep the case moving forward."

He took a breath, but even so, she still wasn't fast enough to get in there.

"Sooner rather than later on all this shit. We'll get her used to us so she can trust us. Then we'll extricate you. Sound good?"

"Who's Buck?" she asked quickly in order to get the words out, and Hugger felt his lips quirk.

"President of Aces," Eight answered.

"Um...as for Hugger—" She didn't quite begin.

"Yeah, we dropped our shit at our local crash pad. Muzz is gonna hang with you, Cruise and I will go out and get the lay of the land and provide presence, and Hugger is gonna go get his shit and bring it here. He'll be back in around an hour. It'd be good you talked her out of her room. Hug's a big guy, but he'd end his own life before he'd hurt a woman. She'll learn that, but not if she's in her room."

Diana pushed back on that. "You have to give her space to do what she needs to do."

Eight nodded. "Sure, she can have space, but we don't got a lot of time. You are not a dumb broad. You know what I'm sayin' to you. You're either on this team or we're gonna have to huddle and figure something else out."

Hugger could not only see, but feel Diana getting pissed.

The fuck of it was, he liked it. That grit and the fact she wasn't a fan of letting anyone, even someone like Eightball, steamroll her.

"Figure what else out?" she demanded.

"I don't know, that's why we'd need a huddle," Eight told her easily. "What I do know is, whatever way it goes down, you're out and she's safe. That's our goal line. And we're gonna get the fucking ball over it if it kills all of us."

"You'll have to excuse me for being a mite confused as to why you all are so dedicated to this task," she remarked.

"Maybe we'll share that over a beer one day when Babić is rotting in a cell and his crew is scattered to the winds," Eight replied. "For now, you're just gonna have to trust we'll do what we have to do to get the job done."

"I'm not sure I have any choice," she bitched.

Eight smiled. "Good we're on that same page."

She glared at him.

Eight turned and said to the men, "Right, let's get this shit rollin'."

Hugger started to move to the door, which was through an opening that led to a room that had nothing in it but a long, white dining table (with blue upholstered chairs), a built-in bar and a glassed wall that held a walk-in wine cooler.

She clearly inherited that with the pad, because there wasn't much wine in it.

"Hugger," she called.

He stopped and turned to her.

"I'm starting dinner," she stated. "We eat in an hour."

Was she serious?

"If I'm not here, eat without me," he said.

"And how's Suzette going to get to know you if you're not at dinner?" she asked.

Fucking hell.

"Like Eight said, I'll be about an hour."

"It's rush hour now. That gets hectic in Phoenix."

"Then make something that keeps warm, woman, 'cause I don't have control of traffic."

"Fine," she snapped.

"Great," he said. "Can I go now?"

She shrugged. "Sure."

Christ, he wanted to bang her.

Shit.

He scowled at Eight, who grinned in return.

Then he got the fuck out of there.

4

LIKE THESE GUYS

Diana

"Oh my God, Diana, how could a completely untenable situation get *more* untenable?" Nicole demanded to know in my ear.

Yes, Nicole had once been my father's PA.

Yes, Nicole had been the only one of them who'd achieved the aim of earning a ring and a trip down the aisle to exchange vows with a man who had no intention of keeping them.

Yes, Nicole had been Dad's PA when Dad was still married to Mom.

Yes, in the beginning, this was a big issue for me.

And last, yes, Nicole had won me over along the way, because she was just that awesome.

Part of that awesome was owning her shit, learning life's lessons when they slapped you across the face, sharing that knowledge and being there for me even, I hated to admit it, in the important times my mother wasn't.

Like when I started my period, when I went on my first date, when I needed the perfect prom dress, and when my first boyfriend broke my heart.

FYI: all of that happened after Dad scraped her off.

Including, obviously, when she was there for me after I was sexually assaulted on a study date.

I lost Mom to Dad's betrayal and her spiral afterward that she never pulled herself out of (and I could say that even if she currently lived what she took pains to show was an idyllic life in Idaho, though she was doing this with an alcoholic asshole who had a side coke habit and a Neanderthal's take on the role of a woman in society—but he had money, Mom had three Birkin bags, so for her, it was all good).

But in all that, I gained Nicole.

I never tried to figure out if that balanced the scales.

It was just what it was: my life. So I lived it.

And in the end, Nicole always gave me the steady when I was never sure of my footing with a father who expected things from me I wasn't certain he should expect, but nevertheless, I constantly fell short. Also, when I had a mom who I adored, but who my father broke beyond repair.

Needless to say, Nicole, who I told everything, was not a yay vote on me wading into Suzette's situation.

And she was not a yay vote on all I'd just told her, including me visiting Dad for the first time in a decade by hijacking his office, me laying the unblemished truth on Janie, and me accepting the assistance of a bunch of bikers I didn't know from Adam.

"You need to talk to that Detective Scott again," Nicole advised.

"Suzette doesn't trust him," I reminded her.

"I'm sure the police know just how bad a man this guy is. They want him out of commission, and they'll do everything they can to keep her safe so she can testify."

"I agree. But she doesn't trust them."

"Diana..."

Uh-oh.

She said my name in that *brace, I'm about to impart wisdom* tone.

I was all in for wisdom, but sometimes getting it wasn't a lot of fun.

"...I could verbally flay Nolan for hours for the way he mishandled what happened to you at school."

Yep.

She was about to impart wisdom.

"But that can't be changed," she went on. "Not by him. And also, sweetheart, not by you."

I was in my bedroom. I'd retreated there after the men left so I could call Nicole and get my head straight before I started dinner and tried to coax Suzette into coming out to help, even though Muzzle was still there, and then coax her to staying out when Hugger returned.

The thought of Hugger returning made a little happy wiggle dance in my belly, something I staunchly ignored.

To aid in that endeavor, I moved to the wall of windows that led to the small balcony, rested a shoulder against one, and stared unseeing at the courtyard.

"You're so like your dad. I wish you both saw that so you could both celebrate it," she stated.

My head twitched in shock.

"I'm like him?" I asked.

"Scary smart. Check. Headstrong. Double check. Stubborn. Triple check. Mostly the good kind of stubborn, though. Except in this case. But definitely when you get your teeth into something, you don't let go. You also don't let anyone walk all over you. You stand up for yourself. He came from nothing and built an enviable life. You gave up everything and did the same."

As noted, sometimes, wisdom sucked.

Like now.

One thing in this world I didn't want to be was like my dad.

But she was not wrong in any of that.

I'd just never noticed.

"I don't know what he expected you to be," she carried on. "I fell in love with him and married him, and I'm not even sure what he expected me to be. I just know it's all about expectations with Nolan, and the only one who meets them is him. He just doesn't see that's because he can control what's expected of him, he can decide if it's worthwhile pursuing, then, if it is, meet that challenge. He can't do that to other human beings. You have to make your own goals and reach for them. He can't do it for you."

Oh yeah.

Wisdom sometimes totally sucked.

I mean, I knew all of this, of course. But having it confirmed was another matter, and for some reason, it didn't make me feel validated.

It reminded me of how I used to feel.

Like I'd forever be a disappointment to Dad, no matter how hard I tried not to be.

And this in turn reminded me, just that day, he'd told me he was proud of me in a way I knew he meant it, something I'd wanted from him all my life.

"You should have dinner with him, Di," she said softly.

"Nic." That was all I could get out, because, yeah...

I still heard the entreaty in his tone when he asked me. I could also feel the sharp pang it sent through me.

"And as much as it alarms me four strange men showed in your complex to offer to help, I trust you're a good judge of character. So you need to work with these bikers to get Suzette somewhere so people who can truly help her are helping her," she concluded.

I'd already figured that part out.

"I'm on board with that," I shared. "I don't know what I was thinking. I should have let Detective Scott take care of her."

"Has she explained why she's all on her own yet?"

Suzette hadn't exactly opened up. And when I said that, I meant *at all*.

I just knew there was no boyfriend, apparently no close friends, and her parents were a no-go subject. I didn't even know if she was ditching a job by holing herself up at my place, or where she lived before she came to me.

So yeah again...

Oh yeah.

This was a complete mess, and I'd stepped right into it.

"I haven't thought it wise to push her," I said.

"It probably isn't, but eventually, she's going to have to come back to the land of the living. What's going to be required of her to see this through takes mettle. Everyone needs time to lick their wounds. But you can't keep licking them, or they'll never close."

They'll never close.

Dang, crap, shit.

Shit.

Sensing my epiphany with her kickass ex-stepmom powers, she called, "Di?"

"I did that, didn't I? After what happened in Tucson, not with that guy. With Dad. I didn't let the wounds close."

"No, baby, you didn't," she said gently.

I let my forehead fall forward until it butted against the glass. "I think Dad misses me."

Nicole was silent.

"Nic?"

"We can't make people love us the way we want. We either accept their love as it comes, or we reject it. With that said, Diana, he loves you. He's always loved you. It might not be how you need him to do it, but that doesn't mean it isn't there."

Dang, crap, *shit.*

I was going to cry.

I couldn't cry, not only because I hated crying, but Hugger was going to be back, and I didn't want him to see me all puffy-eyed.

I also didn't want to spend time thinking about *why* I didn't want Hugger to see me like that.

Fortunately (but also unfortunately with the confusing things she said), Nicole spoke again so I didn't have to consider that.

"You're old enough now, I think what he has to say, you're mature enough to hear."

That made my head come up from the glass because, what the hell did that mean?

"What are you talking about?" I asked.

"I'm not sure I know," she said, sounding uncomfortably like she was hedging. "What I do know is that being frozen out by you for a decade undoubtedly gutted him, and that's not a guilt trip, sweetheart. He's been perfectly capable of extending an olive branch over these years, he didn't do it, and it was his place to do. So that isn't on you. But now that seal has been broken. Reconnect with your dad. If it's still damaging to you, step away. But I know you. If you don't try, you'll regret it. And if you let it last too long, and you two can find some footing you both are good with, you'll regret you lost even more years you could have had with your dad."

"You having it together can get really trying," I groused and heard her soft laugh.

"He's a flawed man, but we all have flaws, including me," she declared. "One of them, falling in love with a man who was not right for me. It brought me into your life, so I don't regret what I did, because it earned me you."

"You need to stop being awesome so I can see while I make tacos for a woman with a target on her back and a biker. No one wants tears in their tacos. I suspect, not even bikers."

I heard the humor in her tone when she replied, "Okay, I'll let you go. Larry sends his love."

Nicole met Larry about a year after Dad divorced her. They got married two years later. I was a junior bridesmaid.

He was good-looking, worshiped the ground Nicole walked on, and had two kids from a previous marriage. He didn't want more. Nicole didn't want any of her own, but she was all in to spread her awe-inspiring stepmom goodness around, so she did that with Larry's kids, just like she did with me. They adored her. Larry (and the kids) adored me. I adored all of them.

It was a win-win-win-win.

So...again, Nicole was the only steady I had in my life.

And it meant everything to me.

I sent my love back, disconnected and headed out of my room to the closed door to Suzette's.

I knocked. "Suze? It's me."

"Yeah?" she called.

I opened the door to see her curled up on her bed with her (actually *my*) iPad.

She was a pretty little thing, but so tiny.

Damn.

Lots of blonde hair, big blue eyes, and what had once been perfect peaches and cream skin.

I couldn't imagine anyone laying a finger on her in anger, doing so to harm her in any way.

Just standing there in the door to her room, I wanted to gather her in my arms and will all her hurts away.

I couldn't do that.

So I did the only thing I could do.

"I'm making beer-battered cod tacos with slaw. Wanna help?" I asked.

"Are they gone?"

I shook my head. "No. Muzzle is still here. But he's leaving when Hugger comes back."

"I think maybe I'll stay in here. I'm not real hungry," she replied.

Truth told, she didn't eat much, which was beginning to get concerning. She was a wee thing. She needed to eat.

She'd also endured a massive trauma, was descending deeper by the day into a depression that was likely affecting her appetite, so she needed to be sure to eat even when she wasn't hungry. She could tackle the depression later, but not if she starved to death.

I took a second, then entered the room, which used to be a workshop from which my boss let me do some projects at home, minor ones, but it was a nice option to have.

With the help of Nicole, Larry, Gram and some friends, we stored my stuff and got her a queen-size bed, nice bedclothes, nightstands, lamps, a dresser, and a TV.

It was all secondhand, but it looked good.

Girlie, welcoming, like she mattered.

The blinds were drawn, the curtains pulled over them, the lamps were on, and it being September, thus still light outside, but it was dark as a cave in there (outside the lamps).

"I'm not going to be pushy," I assured. She stiffened because she knew I was winding up to be kind of pushy. "But I am going to encourage you to let the sun in and maybe get out of this room more often."

"I don't understand why all of a sudden four huge guys show up and wanna help me out," she remarked.

I didn't totally understand it either.

"Like I said, they have some history with...you know."

I didn't want to say his name. She winced when it was said, so I tried to avoid it.

"So they're using me to get at him?" she asked.

"No. They're genuinely, and I'd say extremely, from what I could read, pissed about what he did to you."

There it was.

The wince.

Crap.

"And that's why they want to help you out," I finished.

"But they get something out of it."

I pulled my shoulders forward in a shrug. "I don't know, honey. They don't even know why, um...he-who-will-not-be-named turned his attention to them. They're trying to figure that out too, like I explained when we talked about this earlier."

"This seems wonky to me."

I smiled at her, came farther in and sat down on her bed. "I agree. But in case you didn't notice this, I'm not Jason Statham."

Her lips tipped up.

"We're safe here, I truly believe that," I told her. "But I cannot deny we're a lot safer with those guys hanging around."

"Yeah," she said quietly.

"So, you gonna come out and help me with tacos?"

She bit the side of her lip while her right shoulder inched up before she let both go and requested, "Can I try tomorrow night?"

"No pressure. I said I wasn't going to push, and I meant that. But warning, I won't push, but my encouragement might take a harder slant."

She smiled at that, not a big one, but it was a definite smile before she said, "Consider me warned."

"I'll bring you in some tacos," I offered.

She nodded.

If she ate them, along with her smile, that would be a win for the night.

I left her room, returned to mine, changed out of my clothes and into some cutoff jean shorts and a cute black tee with ruffle sleeves and a plunging V neckline (and I was ignoring why I chose a semi-fancy tee with cleavage, when it was unlikely I'd wear it to hang around the house, it was more a going-out-for-coffee or a movie item of apparel), and I headed to the kitchen.

Muzzle was sprawled in all his faded-jeans-and-tee biker badass on my couch, his focus to the TV, where a true crime doc was playing.

"True crime fan?" I asked as I moved toward the kitchen.

His gaze came to me, it dropped to my legs, his eyes got lazy then they came to mine.

So noted: Muzzle was a leg man.

"Misery loves company," he replied.

"What?" I queried.

"It's not good to know there are other sick fucks people have to deal with out there. It's still good to know we're not the only ones who are constantly dealing with sick fucks."

Interesting.

"So that means...?" I prompted.

"People have problems, cops can't sort it, or they don't got the money for lawyers or private dicks, or whatever they need to get the problem gone, they come to us, and we get the problem gone."

Interesting.

"And *that* means?" I pressed.

He looked to the wall beyond, which was the guest bathroom, and beyond that was Suzette's room, then back to me.

But he spoke no words.

I realized his look to the wall was his answer.

Sadly, it also wasn't.

"I'm afraid our short acquaintance has not guided me to under-standing your meaningful glances," I said as I began to move around the kitchen to get dinner started.

I returned my attention to him when he busted out laughing.

He also turned off the TV, rose to his hot-biker-guy height, and moved to the kitchen island.

"Had a lady whose teenage daughter was being sexually black-mailed by some anonymous twat on social media. The girl couldn't deal. She took her own life. The cops were going too slow, and bottom line, this fuck was doing it to other girls. We found the guy and put him out of commission. Gratis. She got justice, other girls got out from under his thumb. And done."

I stared at him. "How did you put him out of commission?"

He shot me a panty-melting, white smile. "Now that, even old ladies don't know. There's brotherhood shit, Diana, where no one gets in. And it isn't about keeping the women out. It's about keeping anyone who isn't a brother out. Learn that early."

I wasn't sure I needed that lesson for the hopefully short time it took us to get Suzette to someplace that was genuinely secure.

But I filed it away anyway.

"What's for dinner?" he asked.

This was a good question, because I needed to know quantities.

"Are you eating?" I asked in return.

"Depends on what's for dinner."

"Beer-battered cod tacos."

"I'm eating."

I smiled at him.

He tipped his head to the side. "This gonna be homemade?"

"The cod, yes. The slaw, yes. The salsa, afraid not."

"You want help?"

"Do you cook?"

"Not if I can help it. But if a woman with a great rack, a sweet ass, killer legs and a pretty smile asks, I can wing it."

I'd never had a man speak about my person right to my face in such direct terms, and still, I felt highly complimented.

Even so, I narrowed my eyes at him. "Are you flirting with me?"

"Yes, but only out of habit," he stated. "If I was serious, you would know. But I can't be serious because Hugger would feed me my balls for breakfast, and I like them where they are."

My heart did a weird squeeze when he said that.

"Why would he do that?"

"Babe," was all he said.

"Is that an answer to my question?"

"Uh...yeah."

"I hate to inform you, it actually wasn't."

He winked at me, then went to the fridge, came out with a head of cabbage, and said, "I'll let you figure it out."

Hmm.

I didn't press because I promised Hugger dinner would be ready when he got back, he'd been gone a good twenty minutes, so we needed to get cracking.

I learned Muzzle was good with shredding cabbage and grating carrots.

I also learned he was what I expected he was: all man.

This happened when I got the fish salted, the batter resting, and he muscled me out of the way when I unearthed the skillet and oil.

Men did the frying.

Good to know.

Through this, surreptitiously, I took Muzzle in.

His strength was lean and defined, whereas Hugger's was hulking and, well...also defined.

Muzzle had dark-brown hair; it was longish, unruly and thick. He was scruffy, with stubble but not a beard. He had hazel eyes that had a mesmerizing tawny center.

Clean him up a bit, put him in a button down and newer jeans, he'd be my type. Long, lean, dark and handsome.

Hugger was none of these things, and yet I found myself cooking beside Muzzle without the barest hint of that uncomfortable excitement you get when you're around an attractive man you want to get to know.

Instead, it was just comfortable and friendly.

No. The tenterhooks I was riding was waiting to hear the front door open, heralding Hugger was back.

This was a problem.

I didn't tend to be shy around guys I liked, so that wasn't it.

No, it was that I was a realist.

Hugger lived in Denver.

I'd been around snow. It was pretty if you were sitting inside, drinking hot cocoa and watching Hallmark movies.

Other than that, I wanted no part of it.

That wasn't the only reason I had no intention of leaving Phoenix. The others were more important, and they were named Nicole, Gram, Larry, and all my friends. Also my job.

Not to mention, I'd never heard that first story where a long-distance relationship worked out. I'd also never heard of it working when one or the other (and it was usually the woman) moved somewhere for her man. That was always a disaster, costly and emotional.

It had to be noted, the biggest part of the problem was, I wasn't even sure he liked me, but instead, he thought I was an idiot.

The slaw was macerating. There were six crisp cod strips sitting on a paper towel, with three more in the oil, and I was seeing about warming up the tortillas when we heard the front door open.

My heart jumped.

Crap.

Hugger walked in carrying odd-shaped, square-ish, beat-up, black leather bags that were closed with straps and buckles, one in each hand.

He stopped, looked at me, looked at Muzzle, looked at the fish frying in the skillet, then looked back at me, first to my cleavage, then to my eyes.

"Dinner isn't ready," he declared.

I started laughing.

Then I said, "Come with me."

I left the kitchen and went down the hall to my room.

I stopped at the door to my walk-in closet and turned back to see Hugger standing a couple of steps inside the room, looking around.

There was no happy wiggle in my belly at that.

Nope.

The happy wiggle I felt at Hugger in my bedroom was somewhere south.

"I don't think you should share a bathroom with Suzette," I stated, and his attention came to me. "She needs her space and to feel totally safe in it. So you can park your crap in my closet and use my bathroom."

"Right," he replied.

"If I'm not in here, feel free to come on back. If I am, and you need something, obviously, just knock."

"Right," he repeated.

"Not to feed into antiquated gender norms, but I'll put some towels out for you. Yours will be blue, mine will be white."

"Got it."

"I have two sinks in there. Go for it in unpacking. You'll see which one isn't used and that's all yours."

He said nothing, just stood there.

"Do you need me to clear you some closet and drawer space?" I offered.

"I'm not movin' in."

My brows drew down. "I thought you were, at least temporarily."

He didn't respond to that.

He asked, "You got a problem with my shit bein' all over your closet floor?"

I gave that a second's thought.

But I only needed half a second.

"Totally."

He shook his head in a this-bitch-is-a-trip way and said, "Yeah. Clear me some space."

"I'll do that after dinner," I told him. "And just so you know, I don't have a pullout couch, but we'll take the back cushions off and the seat is wide. I fall asleep there all the time. It's super comfy."

"You're a hundred pounds lighter than me."

Aw, wasn't he sweet?!

"If it's uncomfortable, maybe we can get an air mattress," I suggested.

"I'm not here on vacation," he reminded me.

"Everybody needs good sleep," I reminded him.

"I've crashed on couches. I've crashed in the back seats of cars. I've crashed on floors, in tents, out of tents on the ground in a sleeping bag. I crashed once on the top of a bar. I don't have a problem getting to sleep just about anywhere that's available. Don't worry about it."

Man, I wanted to know the story behind the "top of the bar" thing.

I didn't ask after that.

"Okeydoke," I replied.

"We done here?"

"Yep."

"Can I drop my shit so we can eat?"

I smiled at him. "Yep."

He didn't move.

I also didn't move because he was staring at my mouth in a way no man had ever stared at my mouth before, and that gave me so many happy wiggles all over my body, I wasn't certain I could move.

He broke the spell, came toward me, I scooted out of the way and he "dropped his shit" in my closet.

He then walked out of my room, and I watched every step, marveling that such a big man could hold that kind of forceful grace.

Hugger's new spell was broken when Muzzle shouted, "Fish is getting cold, and I'm not slavin' over this oil to present soggy-ass fish!"

This made me smile again because, call me crazy, but I was beginning to like these guys.

5

CRAP

Diana

It was the next morning.

I was dressed, ready for the day, and preparing for dinner that night.

When I'd come out earlier to start coffee, I saw Hugger on his back on my couch (which I'd made up with a sheet on the sofa, another for him to pull over him, a blanket and two extra pillows, and I'd also pulled off the back cushions—still, he engulfed the space).

He had an arm thrown over his eyes. And as far as I could tell, outside his boots being on the floor by the couch, he still had his clothes on from the day before.

Last (something I put right out of my mind the second my eyes landed on it), there was a gun lying close to him on the coffee table.

He didn't move as I made coffee.

When I came back out, dressed and ready for breakfast, he was sitting on the couch, staring blankly at the coffee table and sipping from a mug. His hair was messier than normal. Even his beard seemed messier than normal.

Both were fabulous.

More fabulous, he'd stripped the couch and everything was folded and tucked away on the floor on the far side so you couldn't see it.

Bikers tidied.

Who knew?

He gave me a sleepy-eyed look (that was even more fabulous, by, like *a lot*), got up, and without a word, strolled down the hall to my room.

I made some oatmeal, trying not to think of Hugger in my shower when I heard it go on.

I ate it, failing not to think of Hugger, naked and slippery, in my shower.

I was getting out the Crock-pot when Hugger showed.

I ceased moving entirely when I saw him in a black tee stretched tight across his pecs, faded jeans, his hair wet and combed back from his face, making the handsomeness come out in stark relief.

Topping that, his quickly drying hair curled up at the back of his neck, which added a one-two-knockout punch of cuteness to his handsomeness.

"Do you want breakfast?" I forced out.

"Yeah," he said, going direct to the coffeepot, and I sure was glad I made a full pot, because it was clear he imbibed his caffeine like I did.

"I have oatmeal," I told him. "I can make you a smoothie. There's also cereal."

"Cereal," he said, shoving the pot back in.

"Cupboard over by the wall," I replied.

He spooned two sugars into his coffee then wandered over to the cupboard.

He sipped as he opened it.

He then whistled low and added, "Shee-it."

I was not confused by this response.

"I'm a grocery store aficionado," I informed him.

"I can see," he muttered, ignored the Fruity Pebbles, the Cap'n

Crunch, the Lucky Charms, the Cocoa Puffs and the Cinnamon Toast Crunch, and homed right in on the Trix.

I approved of this choice.

"Bowls in the cupboard by the dishwasher," I said as I set up the Crock-pot.

He went there and I watched as he got down a pasta bowl, not a cereal bowl.

I almost said something, just to give him shit, but decided against it and instead just smiled.

He didn't need instruction on where to find the milk.

He'd just poured and put the milk back, when he pulled his phone out of his back pocket, looked at it then looked at me.

"Big Petey's here. Whatchu gotta do to let him up?"

"Buzz him in. It's that console over there." I tipped my head to the wall. "Hit the green button, that'll let him in to the vestibule. Then hit the blue one. It gives him five minutes to call the elevator and will allow him to tag my floor."

He went and hit the buttons. He returned to his cereal.

I went to the refrigerator to get the chicken breasts.

When the doorbell rang, Hugger moved to answer it.

He came back as I was arranging the breasts in the bottom of the Crock-pot.

I froze for a second time that morning when I laid eyes on Big Petey.

He looked like a biker grandpa, with emphasis on the *grandpa*.

The good news about this was, it was unlikely Suzette would have any issue spending time with him. Like all the other guys, he was rough around the edges, but the kindness in his eyes was not hidden.

The bad news was, if trouble came calling, I was pretty certain Big Petey wouldn't be much of an obstacle to it finding its prize.

"Pete, this is Diana. Diana, Big Petey," Hugger said on a series of grunts before he went back to his mug and his bowl.

"Sorry, I have chicken juice on my hands, just a sec," I said, dashing to the sink to wash off the juice.

After I got that done, I approached Big Petey with hand raised. "Nice to meet you."

"You too, doll," he replied, taking my hand, squeezing it firm and friendly, then letting me go.

"Have you had breakfast? Coffee?" I asked.

"Got covered on the way over," he said.

"Suzette hasn't come out yet, but I'll go in and get her so I can introduce you before Hugger and I leave. I just have to get the Crock-pot sorted, and I'll do that."

"Got nowhere else to be but here, Diana," he assured.

I smiled at him, "Make yourself at home, with everything. Food, drink, TV streaming, whatever."

"Thanks, darlin'."

I returned to the kitchen and got a carton of broth.

I was pouring it over the chicken when Hugger asked, "What are you doing?"

"Setting up dinner."

"Now?"

I looked up at him. "It's a slow cooker."

He glanced inside the Crock-pot then back to me. "What's for dinner?"

"Shredded chicken tacos."

His head twitched to the side. "We had tacos last night."

"And we're having them again tonight. And if you have an issue with that, suck it up, because we'll probably have them tomorrow night too."

"Tacos are tacos. You can never say no to a taco," he spoke the gods' honest truth. Then he veered off the righteous path. "Unless you have to eat them every night."

"Don't worry. I've got a whole repertoire of tacos. You've had the beer-battered cod. Tonight, shredded chicken. Then there's shredded beef. And ground beef. And shrimp. And grilled fish. Also grilled chicken. And then there's fajita tacos. And steak. And—"

He put a palm up in front of my face and commanded, "Stop."

Not a fan of that palm (though definitely a fan of his big, long-fingered hand—God, someone kill me), I wrinkled my nose at him.

He stared at my nose a good deal like he'd stared at my mouth last night, and his hand went away.

I ignored how much I liked the expression on his face and retorted, "Don't be dissing my tacos."

"So you're sayin' you're a taco aficionado too."

"I'm an aficionado of a lot, and all of it revolves around food."

His eyes dropped to the vicinity of my hips and he mumbled, "Approved."

My clit pulsed.

Hugger put his bowl to his mouth and drank the milk from it.

And God help me, my clit pulsed at that too.

Big Petey cleared his throat.

I turned to see biker *grandpa* had turned into *Biker Grandpa!* because he was grinning hugely at Hugger and me, his eyes were dancing, and the very air around him sparkled with glee.

"I love tacos," he announced.

"Well, good, because there'll be plenty," I replied.

On that, Big Petey wandered to the couch. I got on with setting up the Crock-pot. And Hugger, to my shock, rinsed his bowl, spoon and coffee mug and put them in the dishwasher.

Proof.

Bikers tidied.

With nothing else available to delay it, something I wanted to do because I wasn't sure she was ready for it, and I knew I wasn't ready to push her on it, but I had no choice (not to mention, I needed to get to work), I told Big Petey, "I'm going to go get Suzette now."

"All right, honey."

I walked down the hall, knocked softly and was taken aback

when the door immediately opened several inches and Suzette appeared.

She was dressed, and this was a thing for her. I'd seen her precisely once wearing pajamas. This when I was in the middle of a TV binge in the living room, it was late, and she'd shuffled to and from the bathroom.

All other times, she was ready to rumble at any given moment, for the most part, even wearing her Chucks.

It hurt my heart, understanding why.

But I understood why (we could just say, after the incident, I'd had no study dates anywhere but in public places, and no man, to this very day, was allowed in my house until after the fifth date, no exceptions (wait, there was one: unrequested biker security services)).

Understanding this, I didn't say anything about it.

"Hey. Big Petey is here. I want you to meet him before me and Hugger have to take off."

"'Kay," she whispered, opened the door and slithered out.

She wasn't wearing shoes.

Perhaps improvement?

We walked down the hall.

Hugger kept his distance, and I loved he knew to do that.

Big Petey rose from the couch.

On sight of her, a fleeting moment of unadulterated fury swept through his face before he controlled it and smiled at Suzette.

"Hey, girl," he greeted.

"Hey," she whispered timidly.

"I'm Big Petey."

"Yeah," she mumbled.

"You have breakfast?" he asked.

"I'm not super hungry," she answered, and since she ate two tacos last night, this time, she might actually not be hungry.

"Maybe not, but we all gotta eat, and breakfast is the most important meal of the day," Pete returned, then looked at me. "You got eggs and bacon?"

"She's a grocery store aficionado," Hugger answered for me.

"Yes," I also answered for me.

Big Petey was aiming a massive grin at Hugger. He stopped doing that as he made his way to the kitchen.

"Come keep me company, darlin', while I make you some breakfast," he invited Suzette.

She tentatively edged her way to the kitchen island even as she said, "I'm really not hungry."

Pete turned to her, and he did not level *Biker Grandpa!* eyes on her.

He leveled *Concerned Dad So You Better Listen to Me!* eyes on her and replied, "You really gotta eat."

Suzette tentatively moved even closer.

I was seeing this might just work on one level, that being Pete being pushier than I was comfortable with and doing it in a way Suzette apparently responded to.

I still had concerns about his age and his ultimate reason for being here.

Suzette's protection.

Though, as she watched him familiarize himself with my kitchen, it was clear Suzette didn't have those same concerns.

"Babe," Hugger called.

Don't ask me how I knew he was referring to me with that word, except for the fact he was likely not calling to Suzette, and definitely not Big Petey, but I turned my attention to him to see he was indeed referring to me.

"We goin' or what?" he asked.

"Right. We're going," I answered. I looked between Big Petey and Suzette. "You guys good?"

"We're golden. Go. See you later for tacos," Pete replied.

Suzette just nodded to me.

I smiled at them both, went to the dining room, grabbed my tote and headed out with Hugger at my heels.

When we were at the elevator, I reached and tugged at his tee at the side of his abs.

Slowly, his head dropped to look at my fingers on his tee.

I let it go.

Equally slowly, he lifted his head and looked at me.

"Um…"

I didn't know how to begin.

I plowed forward anyway.

"I'm not sure about Big Petey."

"What aren't you sure about?"

"Um…" I repeated but said no more.

"Spit it out, Diana," he ordered.

"He's not young."

"Impressed with your powers of perception."

I squinted irritably at him.

Hugger spoke. "Stop worrying. He can take care of business. Ink and Driver are out there with Muzzle keepin' an eye on shit. And we hacked into the complex cameras last night."

I stopped squinting so I could stare.

The elevator doors opened.

Hugger walked in and automatically, I followed.

He hit the button for the lobby level.

"You hacked the complex cameras?" I inquired.

"Resurrection has an ally who can do that kind of shit. This ally's also got facial recognition software and their hands on pictures of all known associations of Imran Babić. Any one of his boys, or just anyone they don't got a good feeling for, strolls anywhere near an elevator lobby, we'll get a call."

I was feeling a whole lot better about the scope of biker security services as the doors opened and we walked out.

"Ink and Driver?" I asked.

"More Aces."

"How many of you are there?"

"A lot."

Definitely feeling a whole lot better.

It was then I realized he was shoving out the door to the main entrance of the complex, and we weren't on my parking level, as of course we wouldn't be, because neither of us used a fob.

I stopped. "My car is down two levels."

He turned to me, half in and half out of the door. "We're taking my bike."

Oh hell to the no, we were not.

"I've never ridden on a motorcycle in my life."

Something heated flared in his eyes, but he just said, "Today's your day."

"It'll mess up my hair."

His gaze went in that direction and his voice had a rough edge to it when he replied, "It absolutely will not."

"Wind does that."

He locked his eyes with mine. "Trust me."

My voice was getting shrill because, really, I wasn't sure about riding on his bike *with* him on the same bike.

And that wasn't all about my hair.

"I'm wearing pumps!"

Yes, nude, patent leather pumps, along with pale pink crop pants and a silky baby-blue crewneck blouse. I was top to toe business casual, not biker babe.

"I'm gettin' it," he declared.

"Getting what?"

"Tyra, Lanie. Millie."

"What?"

"Never got it before, definitely getting it now."

"*What?*"

He came in so he wasn't half out anymore, the door closed behind him, and he didn't do this in order to explain his words.

He said, "One, I don't think I'll fit in your car."

I hadn't thought about this, but now that I was, I saw it was a concern.

"Two, your car is ridiculous and a deathtrap."

I hadn't thought about this either, but now that I was, it pissed me off.

"It is not!" I snapped.

His brows shot up. "You against an SUV or a dually, which is mostly what they got in this town, a town where I've noticed people pretty much go their own way no matter the widely accepted laws of the road, which are actual laws of the fuckin' road, you're toast."

I'd never thought about this either, and I couldn't say he was wrong.

Especially about Phoenix drivers.

I'd long since learned to park any inclinations of road rage, seeing as I'd be harboring murderous tendencies on every inch of asphalt I encountered. And that crap took way too much energy.

Now, I just let everyone go their own way. As long as I got home in one piece without feeling the need to sharpen any knives, I was good.

I felt my lips thin because I hated to be wrong.

Annnnnnnd another thing I shared with my dad.

Crap!

"Three, because of one and two, my ass will never be in that silly piece of metal you call a car," he concluded.

"Maybe you can follow me to work," I bargained.

"Maybe you can shut it and just get on the back of my bike."

"Okay, Hugger, I may be in day three of my blowout, but that doesn't mean I want it destroyed."

"Your what?"

I jabbed a finger at my hair. "Blowout."

"For fuck's sake," he muttered.

He then said no more.

I said no more.

We went into stare down.

I wasn't sure how much time passed, but if I had to guess, it was a full five minutes before he spoke, which meant we were edging toward me being late for work.

Not that my boss would care, she wasn't even going to be there.

It was the principle of the thing (as Dad had taught me).

"You ready to go to work?" he asked.

Gah!

"You're annoying," I complained as I forged his way.

He turned and went out the door before me, humming, "Mm."

That low, rough hum did a number on my nipples, and in an effort to ignore it, I huffed.

Hugger led me to a shiny bike parked in the visitors' section.

Crap.

6

HE GOT COOKIES

Diana

IT WAS LUNCHTIME, and I was introducing Hugger to Sack's sandwiches.

Hugger had ordered the Overture (prime beef, sweet onion, horseradish sauce and fixin's).

I went for the Symphony (turkey, bacon, avocado, sprouts, cream cheese and fixin's).

He paid.

I didn't fight him on it because fighting about paying was one of my pet peeves.

Someone offered or elbowed their way in to do it, why argue?

This, of course, made me hone my skills at elbowing my way in to do it, but this time, Hugger got there before me.

He was able to accomplish that because I had a lot on my mind.

It started with the fact that I'd learned that Hugger's presence at work wasn't going to be him stealthily hanging around outside the workshop, keeping an eye on things.

No, he came right in and sat in my studio with me.

This made me happy my boss had a day of appointments away from work because I wasn't really sure how I was going to explain why I needed a man hanging with me at work.

Fortunately, it was a Friday, and I didn't have to come up with an explanation until Monday.

Further fortunately, my boss was a little ditzy.

Okay, a lot ditzy.

Annie might not even notice he was there.

Also on my mind was, at first, it felt awkward, having Hugger there while I did my thing.

But most of the time, he did stuff on his phone, and for about a half an hour, his head was tipped back, his arms crossed on his chest, and his booted feet were up on the windowsill, and I could swear he was taking a catnap (I just *knew* that couch wouldn't be comfortable for him).

In the end, it didn't seem awkward at all.

The last thing that was on my mind was, riding on the back of Hugger's bike, with Hugger, was the new meaning of my life.

There was something freeing about it. The sun on your skin. The wind in your hair (and I'd been wrong again, and Hugger right, there wasn't too much of that, my hair had needed some taming—both at work and after we hit Sack's—but not as much as I thought, probably because we couldn't go superfast on city streets).

But mostly, it was about giving over to Hugger. Trusting him. Smelling him. Hooking my thumbs in the belt loops at his sides. Feeling the heat come off his body. Sensing his strength. Watching the alert concentration on his sunglassed face as he navigated the roads, keeping us both safe together on the back of his bike.

It was amazing.

And I had to admit, I further got off on the fact he was him, in jeans and a tee, messy hair, big beard; and I was me, balayage, pink crop pants and pumps.

The dichotomy that was us, together on his bike, was a specific kind of turn-on that practically begged me to lean into it, embrace it, wrap my arms around his stomach, press my cheek to his shoulder and be one with him on his bike.

It wasn't lost on me Hugger was a certain kind of trouble and I needed to tread cautiously.

But it was now dawning on me he was definite trouble, and I had to watch myself carefully.

I'd had two long-term relationships.

The first was a heartbreaker. I was deeply in love (I thought). So when I found he was emotionally cheating on me via texts with his high school girlfriend, I'd been gutted.

After I broke up with him, she broke up with her boyfriend, and they got together. They were that way for a while, even got engaged, then in a rather spectacular (and humiliating for him) fashion, she returned to the boyfriend she dumped, and he tried to return to me.

That didn't happen.

The second just petered out. He knew it, I knew it. We went our separate ways and were still friends, in a more friend/acquaintance/used-to-sleep-together kind of way.

I'd never dated a biker. I'd never dated anyone outside my social or cultural stratum.

The thing with Hugger wasn't that.

It was Suzette and needing to focus on her. It was also Suzette, and her needing all kinds of support, and not having to witness right in her face two people circling each other (and what might come of it). It was Denver, and the fact he lived there.

And it was that he gave no indication he wanted my thumbs out of his belt loops and my arms wrapped around him, my cheek to his shoulder.

Oh yeah.

That was the biggie.

"I don't get it," he said, bringing me back to us sitting opposite each other in a bodacious sandwich joint.

"You don't get what?"

"You spit on paintings for a living. How did you get your sweet crib?"

I put aside my unsettling thoughts, laughed at what he said, and told him, "Saliva has enzymes that help gently clean away dirt."

"I suspected. Still, you live in Scottsdale, which is class. And so is your complex and your unit. It's a lot for someone who cleans paintings with spit and a Q-Tip."

"I won at roulette, thirteen black, about three months before my grandfather died of a stroke and left me some money."

"Right," he said, munching into a potato chip.

"Most of my place was like it is, but Larry is a contractor and he put in the kitchen at a massive discount using stuff some rich lady ordered, paid for, decided she didn't want, and just ordered something else even though it was custom and she couldn't get a refund on it. She didn't want it hanging around, so she told Larry he could have it."

"Rich people do crazy shit," he muttered, picking up his sandwich and taking the last big bite.

"They do," I agreed. "Anyway, his guys did some adjustments so it could work in my space. Larry was able to get his hands on some top-notch appliances that had some scratches and dings you can't see. And *voilà*! Fantastic new kitchen."

"Who's Larry?"

"My...I don't know. My ex-stepmom's husband. So I guess he's kind of my sorta-like stepdad, once removed."

Hugger studied me, his deep brown eyes active, but I didn't know exactly what he was mulling over.

"I take it you're still tight with your stepmom," he noted while I took a bite of my own sandwich.

I chewed while nodding.

Then something occurred to me, so I blurted, "I'm not that woman."

He tipped his head to the side. "What woman?"

"The kind who lets daddy pay for everything. I quit school

because he and I had a thing. I was fed up with having those kinds of things with my dad, although, that was the worst thing we'd ever had. Since he was paying my tuition, not to mention for everything else, I walked away. In the end, I did it myself. Sure, Gram and Gramps and Mom gave me very generous checks for my birthday and Christmas to help out. But it was mostly me. It's all mostly me."

"I wasn't takin' a jab at you," he said.

"Just so you know," I mumbled. "It's a point of pride for me."

"It should be. You told your dad to fuck off and built all that, and you're not even thirty. Yeah. It should be."

I suddenly felt warm all over.

"What brought you to the biker life?" I asked.

"My ma wanted it for me."

I smiled at him. "She a biker babe?"

"No. She was a prostitute."

I choked on saliva that would clean a good inch of an oil painting.

"Yeah," he whispered, and now the brown in his eyes that were locked on me was like petrified wood. Dry and impossibly hard.

I pulled myself together and promised, "My reaction was about surprise, nothing else."

"Right," he muttered, throwing his head back with the edge of the chip packet to his lips so he could consume the last bits.

And man, he was just him. In my kitchen. At a sandwich joint.

I liked it.

I totally had to be *very* careful.

Especially now.

"I'm serious. I have no issue with sex workers," I asserted.

"Let's move on," he said on a sigh.

"Let's not," I returned sharply. "I don't know your story, but I can read some of it, considering she wanted the life you're leading, and you're leading it. So I can assume you were close and she mattered to you."

"She mattered to me," he said low, sharing just how much she did.

And it was so much, a shiver slithered up my spine at the intensity of it.

I adjusted my tone and asked, "Since we're talking in past tense—?"

"Dead," he stated flatly. "Breast cancer that metastasized and totally took her over."

"God, Hugger," I whispered, feeling my eyes sting. "I'm so sorry. She had to be young."

"Too young to die."

"God," I pushed out, reaching across the table to wrap my fingers around his wrist. "I'm so, *so* sorry."

"She was a good woman," he stated while gently, but firmly, extricating his wrist from my hold.

I felt that loss, too much, but I buried it and nodded again.

"I bet. Since she made a man like you," I noted.

"What's that mean?"

I fished a chip out of my bag and asked, "What do you mean, 'what's that mean?'"

"You think you know the man I am?"

I stared at him.

Then I said, "Well...yeah."

He sat back, already done with his food, outside the cookie they included with every sandwich (maybe he didn't like cookies, and even though that would shock me to my core, if he didn't, that meant I could eat it), and he asked, "Enlighten me. What kind of man am I?"

"Well, you rode down from an entirely different state to see to the safety and protection of a woman you've never met. Doing so requires you to sleep on a couch, which, for a man your size, I know isn't comfortable, no matter what you say. I've noticed you're you. People take you as you are and that's it. The confidence of that is striking. You've inspired the loyalty of other good men and give it back. I haven't known you long, but there's a lot there. Of course, this could all be about you and that was who you'd grow up to be. But I suspect she didn't play only a small part in that."

His voice sounded strange, coarse, even guttural when he stated, "She didn't. I am what she made me."

I reacted to his tone, thinking this was deep for a sandwich joint and two people who were probably ships passing in the night. And as much as the last part sucked, since it was likely true, I didn't need to put him through it.

I popped my chip in my mouth, chewed, swallowed and said. "Anyway, I'm sorry you lost her."

"I am too."

"Are you gonna eat your cookie?" I asked.

"Yeah."

I frowned.

His beard moved as his lips tipped up.

It was hot.

Crap!

It was a small cookie, and he made a show of putting the entire thing in his mouth and chewing it.

"Very uncool," I noted.

His lips tipped up again.

Then without a word, he got up and walked away.

I suspected he was going to the bathroom. What I knew was, there wasn't a lot left of my lunch hour, and I had a deadline on an oil-painting cleaning. I needed to eat so we could get moving.

I focused on my sandwich and chips (I was going to save my cookie for an afternoon snack), and was trying to decide if I could get myself to a place I didn't care what people thought if I shook the dregs of the chips into my mouth straight from the bag, when I heard my phone vibrate in my tote.

I pulled it out and saw it said FATHER CALLING.

Ugh.

I wanted to let it go to voicemail.

After yesterday and my conversation with Nicole, I couldn't let it go to voicemail.

I took the call and put the phone to my ear. "Hey, Dad."

"Hello, Diana."

"Listen—"

"I've paid Janie a generous severance and recommended her to an attorney I know who's looking for an excellent PA and has been having trouble finding one."

I sat very still and listened very hard.

Dad kept talking.

"And this morning, I filed the papers to withdraw as counsel for Imran Babić."

Oh my God.

Oh my God!

Oh my God, God, *God*!

Dad kept going.

"I've spoken to Detective Scott, and he assures me he has full departmental approval to provide a safe location and protection for Suzette Snyder until she testifies, regardless that will be months from now. He's also speaking with the FBI, who has some interest in this case, and they want to talk to her, and depending on what she has to say, they might be able to offer her witness protection."

Oh my God!

"I know you're old enough to make your own decisions, and advice from your father might not be welcome," he continued. "However, I still strongly advise you to speak to her and urge her to accept this offer from the police."

"You withdrew?"

"Yes."

I put my elbow on the table and dropped my forehead into my hand.

"Diana?" he called.

"I can't—"

I gulped.

I was going to cry.

Shit!

I was so totally going to cry!

"Diana," Dad called again.

"What the fuck is goin' on?" Hugger demanded.

I lifted my head and looked at him.

It appeared he was carrying a bag full of cookies.

God, this guy.

A tear fell from my eye and slid down my face.

Immediately, Hugger reached in and pulled my phone out of my hand.

"Who's this?" he barked into it after he put it to his ear. There was a pause, then, "It don't matter who I am. I asked, who the fuck are you?" Another pause and, "Props, motherfucker, she's crying."

"Hugger," I whispered.

"What?" he bit into the phone. And then, "Fuck no, I'm not handing the phone back to her. Don't contact her again unless she contacts you. Got me?"

With that, he pulled the phone from his ear, dropped the cookies on the table, and jabbed the screen with his finger.

It vibrated in his hand.

He declined what I knew was Dad's call.

I took a deep breath to corral the emotion and shared, "It wasn't what you think it is."

He moved into the space between tables, dragging his chair with him, and he sat in it, so he'd be so close, our knees would brush (and they did).

God, *this guy.*

Once in position to be *right there* for me, he asked, "What was it?

"He's withdrawn as counsel for Babić." I swallowed and finished, "Because I asked him to."

"Fucking hell," he whispered.

"There's more. A lot more. I can't...I don't—"

I was losing it again.

"Not here. At your work. No one is there. Let's go."

And with that, he got up, pushed his chair away, grabbed my hand and pulled me out of my seat.

I had just enough time to nab my cookie and shove it into my mouth (couldn't leave that behind). He snatched up the bag and handed it to me, and then he pulled me out of Sack's.

I stowed the cookies in my tote, swung it on my shoulder, and after he got astride his bike, I jumped on behind him like I'd done it a thousand times and not only two.

There was a lot going through my head. Janie. A plea to have dinner with Dad. Babić. Suzette. The FBI.

It was too much.

So much, I didn't even think as I wrapped my arms around Hugger and rested my cheek to his shoulder as he pulled out of Sack's parking lot.

It hadn't even been a day.

Dad and I had our first conversation in years, and it hadn't been a day when he did what I asked, even things I didn't ask him to do (Janie) and...and...

And he withdrew as representation of a mob boss.

I stiffened and took my cheek from Hugger's shoulder.

"Almost there," he said.

Almost there.

He got cookies.

I rested my forehead against the base of his neck.

Not long later, Hugger pulled into the small and empty parking lot outside the workshop.

I swung off. He swung off. But when he grabbed my hand to pull me inside, I tugged him to a stop.

"Dad withdrew as representation of a mob boss," I said.

"Yeah, you told me. Let's get inside."

"No, Hugger, I mean...this guy." I shook my head. "He's not right. Is this going to piss him off? Is my dad in danger?"

Hugger had put on his sunglasses (mirrored aviators—yes, they looked insanely good on him) and a lot of his face was covered in whiskers.

I still saw the tightness enter it.

Oh my God.

I put a hand to his chest and pushed close. "He had another firm he worked with. Babić. They dropped him after he was arrested for what he did to Suzette. I'm not a rabid news hound, but I haven't heard of a local attorney meeting an untimely death. So maybe he won't call a hit out on my dad, or whatever guys like him do."

"Can we go inside, baby?" he asked.

We could.

We could do anything he asked if he ended it in that sweet "baby."

I tugged his hand again and led him to the door.

He took the keys from me, unlocked it and pulled us inside.

He locked the door behind us and guided me to the room that held my personal work studio, one of only two, since it was only me and Annie who worked there.

He sat me down at my stool in front of the painting I was working on. He then dragged the chair he'd been sitting in over to my stool. He folded into it, bent forward so his elbows were to his knees, the entire time his eyes were on me.

Once in position, he ordered, "Tell me."

"We...like I mentioned, we had a falling out. It was bad. I froze him out. When he learned Suzette was with me, he asked to talk to me. I kinda sprung myself on him by showing at his office when he wasn't expecting me. It went...well, it went someplace I would never have guessed it'd go. In his way, he made it obvious he missed me. That my freezing him out was rough on him. That he...he wanted to talk. It seemed like he wanted to mend fences."

"Okay."

"I told him the only way I'd consider that is if he dropped Babić as a client."

Hugger said nothing.

"This happened less than twenty-four hours ago, Hugger," I finished.

He drew in a big breath, sat back, and let it out.

"Well, goddamn," he whispered.

"That about covers it," I replied.

"What are you gonna do?"

"I think I need to have dinner with him."

"I don't know the history, babe. But seems to me he's extended one helluvan olive branch."

I nodded.

"Should I...do you think I should call him back?" I asked.

"No," he said decisively. "You should text him. Say you're processing shit. Give him something to go on about the gesture he's made. And let him know you're thinking about that dinner."

This was good advice.

I pulled open my tote to get my phone.

I then typed in, *Sorry about that. I was overwhelmed. Can you give me some time to process things? Then maybe we can talk about dinner.*

I finished typing, turned the phone around and showed it to Hugger.

"Good?" I inquired.

He read it and nodded.

I sent the text.

My attention drifted to the painting and I noted inanely, "I'm not sure I have any spit to get on with this."

I nearly jumped out of my skin when my phone vibrated in my hand.

A text from Dad.

I opened it and it said, *One minute.*

"He says 'one minute,'" I told Hugger, then asked a question he could not answer. "What does that mean?"

And he couldn't answer it, so he replied, "Don't know, Diana."

I stared at the phone. I stared at it more. Even staring at it, I jumped when it went again.

Another text from Dad.

Apologies. I had to delay a client meeting. Are you okay?

"Oh my God," I breathed.

"What?" Hugger asked harshly.

I looked at him. "He delayed a client meeting to text me."

"All right."

"Hugger, he's never done anything like that. Work is his life."

Hugger just held my eyes.

"He wants to know if I'm okay," I said.

"I think you should tell him you are," he suggested.

I nodded, bent to my phone and typed in, *Yes. You just surprised me. It was a good surprise.*

I turned the phone to Hugger. He jerked up his chin in approval. I sent the text.

It barely went before I got another one. *Are you sure? That man said you were crying.*

I was just overwhelmed.

But you're okay.

Yeah, Dad. I'm okay.

Do you have a man in your life?

Uh-oh.

I turned the phone to Hugger.

And my lungs seized when he ordered, "Tell him yes."

"But—"

"Tell him, Diana."

"We might be fixing things," I pointed out. "I can't start fixing things with my dad by lying to him. What if I decide to agree to dinner and he wants you to come?"

"Then I'll come."

Was he nuts?

"You can't come!" I exclaimed.

"Why, 'cause you don't wanna bring a biker to your dad's for dinner?"

"Don't be insulting," I snapped. "Have I once given you even the slightest indication I give a shit about you being a biker?"

A glimmer of remorse hit his eyes and he mumbled, "That was out of line."

"Uh...*yeah*," I bit out.

"Just tell him you got a man at your back. You don't gotta tell him why that man is at your back."

I was as certain about Dad not being all that thrilled Suzette and I had a posse of protection as I was that the sun rose in the east. And sadly, for Dad, that would partly be about them being bikers.

Mostly, though, it was that we needed protection at all.

"Dang and crap," I muttered and bent to my phone again.

Yes. He's kind of protective.

I turned the phone to Hugger.

"Good," he approved.

I sent the text.

Dad responded quickly.

He didn't hide that. This brings me relief. You and that young woman alone was concerning me. A protective boyfriend alleviates that.

Oh shit.

"What?" Hugger asked.

I showed him the text.

His lips in his beard tipped up.

I slapped his arm. "Stop smiling, you big lug. This is going to come back to bite me in my ass, I know it."

"I don't know how."

"Then you have not read a single romance novel where the fake boyfriend gig bit the heroine in her ass," I returned.

"No, I haven't," he agreed readily.

Ugh!

My phone went again and I looked down at it.

I'll wait for you to contact me about whether or not we'll have dinner. I hope you agree to do so. I'd very much like to know what's going on in your life and have you back in mine. Please, think hard about it, Buttercup.

Reading that last word, I lifted the phone and rapped it repeatedly against my forehead in an effort to forestall the new assault of tears that were threatening.

Hugger slid it out of my hand and read the text.

"Why'd that make you bang your head with your phone?" he asked me. "Is this his way of exerting pressure without seeming like he's doin' it?"

I shook my head. "No. It's because he hasn't called me Buttercup since I was probably twelve."

"Shit," he whispered.

I held out my hand, palm up. "Hand me my phone."

He put it in my palm.

I tapped out, *I will. I'll think hard, Dad. Please be careful.*

I didn't send it.

I considered ending it with *Love you.*

Instead, I added a little blushy-smiley emoji and sent that.

Then I blew out a big breath.

"Get your spit back?" Hugger asked.

I rolled my eyes.

"Painting's not gonna spit-shine itself, babe," he remarked.

I rolled my eyes again.

Hugger got up and returned his chair to the window. He slouched in it, put his boots on the sill, ankles crossed, and fired up his phone.

With nothing for it, considering I had a mortgage to pay, and that required me getting work done so I could earn my paycheck, I turned to the painting, reached for a Q-Tip and got to work.

7

WHEN ISN'T IT?

Hugger

HUGGER SAT across from Diana at her dining room table, knowing.

Down to his gut, he knew.

Even so, he didn't trust it.

Maybe it was because he never expected it. Maybe it was because he never really wanted it. Or maybe it was more to the point he never thought he'd get it. Or maybe it was because he knew to his soul from the moment he could cogitate he'd never have it.

But whatever.

It was happening.

Although it had been brewing since he caught her wrist in the elevator, and definitely agitating during their discussion at lunch, and what happened after it, Hugger became aware of it when they hit her pad after she was finished with work.

They walked in to see Big Petey and Suzette camped out on the couch in her living room.

Pete was watching TV.

Suzette was tucked into the corner beside Pete, coloring, adult style, with fancy pencils.

"Saw your books, thought you wouldn't mind," Pete explained for Suzette, who just looked at Diana and blushed like she'd been caught doing something wrong.

With an expression on her face like Pete had announced that some doctor had cured cancer, Diana replied, "Not at all."

Indication about how withdrawn Suzette had been, not that Hugger hadn't noticed it already.

Then came the news that Big Petey had told Eight it was chicken tacos for the night and Eight, Muzzle and Driver wanted to know if they could pitch up.

This pissed Hugger off. She didn't need to be feeding their crew every night.

It didn't piss Diana off.

"Absolutely!" she chirped. Then, without delay, she hightailed her phenomenal ass to the kitchen where she opened and closed cupboards, the fridge, dug out that pad of paper from her drawer, scribbled some things down, ripped the page off the pad and lifted it in the air, waving it and asking, "Who's going to the store?"

Pete clearly didn't want to leave Suzette, so Hugger went to her closet to grab his empty saddlebags in order that he could haul groceries on his bike.

When he was in there, it struck him, as it didn't the night before when he'd unpacked, that her closet was big, but it wasn't full. She'd given him his own space with rods, shelves and drawers, but it wasn't difficult for her to do.

After he grabbed his bags, he walked back through Diana's place, seeing the same thing everywhere.

She had her shit tight, but there wasn't much of it.

This was a life beginning.

She might have the cake to make it nice, but it was clear what she said at lunch was true.

She wasn't that woman.

She wasn't a wealthy attorney's daughter who had a ton of shit, being given it, going into debt to get it, or blowing everything she earned to have it.

She was building, doing it right, but smart.

This hit Hugger, and it did it hard, like pretty much everything about Diana did.

When he walked back to the kitchen, he saw Suzette was in it with Diana, Big Petey had a beer and retained command of the couch, and Diana had the list, which she handed to him on a smile.

Fuck.

That smile.

He felt it right in his cock. Every time.

This time, it was more.

No, she wasn't pissed a bunch of bikers were horning in on dinner, or a bunch of bikers were hanging around at all.

The opposite.

It seemed like she was in her element. Like this was exactly what she wanted to do after work on a Friday night.

She told him where he could find a grocery store. Pete told him he'd informed Eight they were in charge of bringing beer. Hugger took off and came back to a dining room table set for dinner. Diana and Suzette were in the kitchen doing shit. And Eight, Muzz, Driver and Pete were lounging in the living room, drinking beer and rapping.

"Awesome!" Diana exclaimed in his direction, coming right to the bags he put on the counter. "Okay, dinner in about twenty," she announced to the room while digging stuff out of the bags.

Hugger glanced at Suzette, who appeared to be ignoring the men in the living room while she opened cans of refried beans, but at least she was out among them.

Hugger got a beer, hit the living room, and in twenty minutes they were all around Diana's table, which had make-your-own tacos paraphernalia spread over it: meat, lettuce, diced tomatoes and onions, cheese, salsa, as well as Spanish rice, refried beans and some corn dish Diana called *elote* that was ridiculous, it was so good.

She put Pete at the head of the table and sandwiched Suzette in between Pete and herself, a cocoon of safe and familiar for Suzette to be in while she was with the rest of them.

Muzz was on Pete's other side, and Hugger took the chair next to him so he could be opposite Diana. Eight sat next to Diana, Driver next to Hugger.

Through dinner, Suzette was silent and only acknowledged Pete and Diana, but again, she was there. She was also eating. Both good things.

The rest was just what it always had been since Hugger put himself forward to Chaos.

A lot of giving shit, taking it, telling stories, laughing, talking and bullshitting.

Diana fit right in.

"Serious? You lived in England?" Driver asked Diana when the food was all but decimated and they were kicked back, shooting the shit.

She nodded. "For six months. I scored a primo internship at the British Museum. It was totally rad."

"Food suck there like everyone says?" Eight asked.

"No freaking way," Diana answered. "One word: custard. Three words: bangers and mash. Two words: English breakfast. Um, let me count...four words: steak and kidney pie. I could go on. Just their cheese is orgasmic. Don't get me started on their ice cream. Dairy products on the whole give life new meaning. And I dream of their bacon."

"No shit?" Eight said.

"None at all," she replied.

"What's different about their bacon?" Driver asked.

"More meat, less fat, more flavor," she told him. "I don't know how they do that, because the flavor's in the fat. But they do it. It's like magic."

This made the men chuckle.

All but Hugger, who simultaneously wanted to taste English bacon and watch Diana eating it.

"You go anywhere else when you were over there?" Muzzle asked.

She shook her head but said, "I did a little traveling around England. Their train system makes it easy. We should resurrect that here. It's almost zero hassle and you can get practically anywhere. And I got a weekend in Paris, also by taking the train." She shrugged. "I wished I could do more, but I didn't have the time or money."

"You'll get back," Big Petey assured.

She smiled at him. "I hope so."

In the middle of her saying that, the entire table tensed, because there was a hammering at the door.

The men looked among each other, but it was Hugger who stood.

"You got neighbors who would pound on your door like that?" he asked Diana as he made his way there.

She opened her mouth to speak when they heard a male voice shout from the hall, "Diana Elizabeth Armitage, open this door!"

Diana's eyes got big as her mouth breathed, "Holy crap. That's Larry."

"Larry! Calm down!" a female's voice could now be heard through the door.

Hugger looked out the peephole, saw a man, probably in his fifties, dark hair going gray, good-looking, built, hadn't gone soft in the slightest. With him was a tall blonde woman, also built, just a different way. She looked like she could be on the cover of a magazine, even if she, too, was in her fifties.

Ex-stepmom and sorta-stepdad, once removed, the last hearing Diana was host to a bunch of bikers, he didn't like it and he was going to do something about it.

Hugger hit the button that slid the bolt out if its anchors and then he opened the door.

The man glowered at him.

The woman stared at him, her mouth dropping open.

The man then stormed in and Hugger allowed it, because he was Diana's sorta-stepdad, once removed and he was there because he was worried about her.

After the woman strolled in, Hugger made sure the door was closed and bolted, then got into position to see Larry shoot a sizzling look toward Diana, a scowl around the men, but his face softened when he saw Suzette.

"Hey, darlin'," he said gently.

"Larry," she whispered.

"How're you doing, sweetheart?" the woman asked Suzette.

"Okay. How are you?" Suzette answered quietly.

"I'd be better, if Larry wasn't having a shitfit," the woman replied.

That caused Suzette to smile, just a little.

"Speaking of..." Larry began. "Diana, a word."

"Larry, as you can see,"—Diana swung her hand wide to indicate the table, including spent bowls, plates and beers—"we're good."

"A word," Larry gritted.

Expelling an aggrieved breath, Diana stood. "Okay, but first, this is Eight." She indicated Eightball. "He's a member of the Resurrection MC, from Denver."

Eight got up, approached and offered a hand to Larry.

Hugger had to give it to him, Larry only hesitated a beat before he took it.

"And this is Big Petey, he's hanging with Suzette during the day," Diana went on. "He's a member of the Chaos MC, also in Denver."

More handshaking, the tension started to leave Larry's frame, Diana went on with the introductions and ended on Hugger.

"Hugger keeps me safe during the day and is sleeping on the couch so we both are through the night," she finished.

Hugger found Larry's grip was firm, short, and he stepped away, appearing a little humbled.

"Do we still need a word?" Diana asked.

Larry didn't answer her.

He looked through the men and said, "No offense."

"None taken," Big Petey spoke for them all. "My girl let a bunch of strange men hang at her house after knowin' them for a few minutes, I'd ream her ass too."

Larry seemed openly relieved Pete understood.

"Want a beer?" Eight offered.

"He needs seven of them," the woman said. "And by the way, I'm Nicole, and rest assured, *I* know Di is an excellent judge of character. Though I'm pretty upset I missed her *elote*."

There were smiles, a couple of chuckles, more handshakes, and Diana said to Nicole, "I'll get Larry a beer and shake you a martini."

"I'll love you forever if you do, but I was already going to do that, so just know you have my eternal gratitude for offering that elixir after I had to deal with Mr. Overprotective for the last hour," Nicole replied.

"So you kept it from him until tonight?" Diana asked as she headed to the kitchen, Nicole following.

Hugger didn't hear Nicole's answer.

Suzette mumbled, "I'll just start clearing," then she swiftly got into doing that, but more, got out of the slew of men and found a way to get herself to the women.

"She's okay with you guys?" Larry murmured low, his eyes following Suzette, having missed her ploy with the clearing.

"She is, and she ain't," Big Petey replied, also low. "I think I got her okay with me today. She tries to pretend the boys don't exist. Mostly, I think she's out of her room, not because she's comfortable, but because she doesn't want to disappoint Diana."

"Not sure that's good," Larry muttered.

"Probably not good for her to push herself before she's ready. But it's worse, her sittin' in a dark room by herself and up in her head, where it isn't a safe place to be," Pete replied.

Larry nodded.

Diana returned with Larry's beer, grabbed some plates, and

declared, "Suze and I cooked. I'll take these in, but that means we don't clean."

And with that, she strutted back to the kitchen.

"We got our orders," Eight said, and he grabbed some shit from the table, the rest of the men following suit.

"These boys do this, can I have a word?" Pete asked Larry.

Larry assessed him then jutted his chin in an affirmative.

"Hug, with us," Big Petey ordered in Hugger's direction.

They headed to the balcony.

When they got there, Pete's eyes went right to the coffee place. So did Hugger's.

It was closed, but there appeared to be no one of concern sitting in the seating outside that place, or in any of the outdoor sections.

"Everything okay?" Larry asked.

Big Petey focused on Larry.

Hugger focused on Pete.

"You know her story? Suzette's?" Pete asked.

Larry looked surprised. "You don't?"

"Know what happened to her," Pete said. "Only got one day in with her, don't know more. Wondered if you did."

"Like what do you want to know?" Larry asked.

"She got people? She got things? She got a job? She got a place?" Pete clarified.

Larry shook his head. "Nic says she's not opening up to Di, and Di doesn't want to push it."

Pete pondered this, then stated, "She's entrenched here, man. I can't get it. Shit like what happened to her never happened to me. But I also really don't get it. Even when really bad shit goes down, not a lot of us can put our whole life on hold to hole up and figure it out," Pete noted.

Big Petey had a point.

Hugger looked into the house.

The men were in the kitchen.

Diana and Nicole were sitting in the living room, gabbing.

Suzette had disappeared.

"How did those two gals hook up?" Pete asked Larry.

Larry assumed an unhappy expression when he explained, "Diana did some amateur sleuthing, pulled some cons with hospital staff and the officer guarding the door to Suzette's room, and got in there with her. Not sure how she talked her around. Not even sure why she did, though Di's got problems with her father and some history that makes it make a kind of sense."

Hugger's neck got tight.

History that makes it make a kind of sense.

"It's been worrying me and Nic since it went down," Larry kept at it. "Di isn't like this. She likes her work. She's got good friends. She goes out and has fun. But she's been almost freakishly responsible since the day I met her when she was twelve."

This didn't surprise Hugger at all.

Larry kept talking.

"She jumped into this, and after I got over my shock she did, it took everything I had not to strong-arm her right out. But Di's got no support from her family. Her mother's a flake and doesn't live close. Her grandmother is a nice woman, but she doesn't have much of a backbone. We got years in with taking Di's back because there wasn't anyone else to do it with any strength behind it. Suffice it to say, we didn't like this situation, but the way things are for her, we didn't fight her on it."

"I get you," Pete muttered.

"Why are you asking after Suzette?" Larry questioned.

Pete drew in a breath, like he was stalling for time to figure out how to say what he had to say. He let it out and said it.

"Lived some years, man. And I think there's more happenin' here than the lowdown and dirty shit that was done to that woman," he replied, which made Hugger's neck get tighter.

So he asked curtly, "Like what?"

Big Petey shook his head. "Like I don't know, unless we can get that girl to talk. And I don't see that happenin' anytime soon."

"Me either," Larry mumbled.

"Appreciate you showin' your feeling for Diana and Suzette," Pete said to Larry. "And I get your concern. Our Club's got some worries about Babić. We got no beef with the man, no dealings with him at all, so we're tryin' to figure out why he's messin' with some of our women. Nothin' as bad as what he did to Suzette, but he's playin' with their heads and diggin' into our business, and we just don't get why. We're here to find out. In the meantime, since we got the manpower, thought we'd put it in front of those girls. They're safe with us. That's a promise. You give me your contact info, I'll be glad to keep you informed. Was a dad once, I get what you need."

Larry's head jerked at Pete's last words, and he asked suspiciously, "Was a dad once?"

"My baby girl died of cancer a while ago," Pete told him.

Larry winced then said quietly, "Still a dad, my friend."

"Yeah," Pete muttered, and Hugger's eyes narrowed on the man.

He knew about Pete's girl. Everyone did.

He just really didn't like how Pete described what he felt he'd become after her loss.

Larry was studying him closely too, but he stopped to peer over his shoulder inside, clearly feeling his wife's attention on him, because it was.

He turned back to Hugger and Pete. "Best get inside. We good?"

Big Petey nodded.

Larry went inside.

Hugger and Pete stayed on the balcony.

Hugger didn't fuck around with starting it.

"What are you thinking?"

Big Petey shook his head and shrugged at the same time. "Got a bad feeling, son."

"What kind of bad feeling?"

"There's more to that girl," Pete said. "I can understand she's terrified after what happened. I can understand she's shrinkin' into herself for the same reason. But there's something deeper. Darker."

"Like what?"

Pete looked him right in the eyes. "Like she thinks she's already dead. She just happens to still be breathin' for a while."

"Stands to reason, since it's been made plain Babić isn't gonna let her take him down," Hugger bit out, with a tilt of his head indicating the courtyard that didn't have Babić's lackeys in it now, but they both knew they'd be back.

"Yeah. Maybe." Pete didn't sound convinced.

"Diana's dad withdrew as Babić's counsel," Hugger told him.

Pete's bushy gray brows shot up. "No shit?"

"She asked him to. He's making moves to sort what's broken between them. And it seems the man isn't afraid of grand gestures," Hugger said. "I gotta talk to Eight and wanna call Rush. Diana's freaked because she thinks Babić is gonna be pissed and he might do something about it. We need men on Nolan Armitage."

Pete dipped his chin sharply in assent. "Agreed. Aces got a business to run. They can cycle men through, but if we need more, could put the pinch on 'em. We'll get on that and get some more asses down here as reinforcements."

"Can you take Eight aside?" Hugger asked. "I'll call Rush while I'm out here."

"Got you on Eight and you do that with Rush. Then you call Tack," Big Petey ordered.

Hugger's brows inched together. "Tack? Why?"

"'Cause, son, you don't know what hit you yesterday. Years ago, the same thing hit him. Took him a while to get his head out of his ass to see it, and it pissed her off so bad, she was dead set against him. He had to scramble to get back in there. You talk to him, he can give you the wisdom so you won't make the same mistake."

"What are you—?"

Big Petey lifted a hand. "Don't bullshit me, Hug. I don't give two shits Nolan Armitage stood up for a rapist and all-around piece of shit and got his ass in a sling extricating himself from that relationship. But you do. Because *she* does. And we're gonna cover him. For you. And for her. Because she's yours. And you know how that goes. She's yours, means she's *ours*."

Hugger felt his throat get scratchy on the inside.

Normally, Big Petey pulling the dad act didn't bother him. He was a good man, he had a big heart, he cared about his brothers, and he cared about Hugger's ma.

Now, though, it was ticking him off.

"Big Petey—" he started.

"Don't," Pete sighed. "Just don't, son. Promise you, if you do, you'll regret it."

"It's not what I want."

He said it even if he didn't mean a word of it, but he wanted to.

It was a mistake because it opened a door Hugger took pains to keep firmly closed.

Pete waltzed through that door and laser focused on him. "I'm glad we're talkin' about this because I never got a lock on it. What is it you want?"

Hugger told him the truth. "Nothing."

That was when Big Petey started to look mad.

He didn't hesitate to explain why.

"You know it would gut her to hear you say that."

Pete was talking about his mother.

"It's the best way to live life. Have no expectations, get no disappointments. She showed me that."

"Bullshit," Pete clipped. "She had no choice. But she gave everything so you would."

Now Hugger was getting mad. "You don't know what we were. You don't know what we had."

"I knew Jackie," Big Petey shot back. "I knew the feeling she had for you. And I know that woman in there, whose world lights up just 'cause a woman opens the cage she closed around herself just enough to color in a book, and that same woman prepares a spread on the fly for a bunch of men she barely knows and gets off on it, is a woman your mother would be doin' cartwheels is in your life. She's into you, Hug, don't fuck that up."

"We're on a mission."

"You can't multi-task?"

"Shit is real, Pete."

"When isn't it?"

Hugger didn't answer that because it would prove Big Petey's point.

"Call Rush and call Tack," Pete commanded. "And I'll talk to Eight."

With that, they were done, Hugger knew because Pete left him on the balcony.

8

TAKE THE RISK

Hugger

THE NEXT MORNING, Hugger stood on the balcony sipping coffee he made and staring straight at the assholes who were back enjoying a Saturday morning latte at the coffee spot in the courtyard.

He heard the door slide open and twisted to see Diana, her hair in a messy knot at her crown, some loose drawstring shorts hanging on at her hips, and a cropped babydoll tee tight at her tits that shared she was a fan of the Diamondbacks. It was the first time he'd seen her with no makeup.

She was just as gorgeous as she was with it on.

Christ.

It was like she was trying to torture him.

"You're awake," she noted.

He nodded and tipped his head to the courtyard. "We got company."

She did an annoyed side-eye and stuck her tongue out like she was gagging.

Fuck him, her cute was as hot as her hot.

Totally torturing him.

"Gotta use the can," he told her. "You can stay out here, but don't get anywhere where they can lay eyes on you."

"You didn't already—?" she began.

"You said not to invade her space. And I agree. She needs her space."

Soft hit her expression. "Hugger, just knock on my door, and if I'm sleeping, just go through."

"Been holdin' it a half hour, babe. Can we discuss this after I drain my bladder?"

She bit her lip and nodded.

He went inside to take care of business, returned to the balcony to see her sitting on the light-blue cushions on the couch of her patio furniture, her bare feet up on the white coffee table, a mug of joe in her hand, so he went to the pot to warm up his before he joined her.

He sat in an armchair at corners to the couch.

"Sleep okay?" she asked.

He slept shit.

She was right; he was too big for her couch, even with the back cushions off.

And he was too close to her, lying in her big king bed all alone.

But it was what it was, and it was going to stay that way.

"Slept great," he lied.

"Liar," she whispered to her mug before she took a sip. She looked to him after she swallowed. "You seen Suzette?"

He shook his head.

"She'll come out when she senses you're out here."

"Yeah," he muttered.

Her gaze drifted away. "I'm gonna talk to her today about protective custody. I forgot to mention yesterday that Dad told me he spoke with one of the cops who was keen to look after her. He also said the FBI wants to talk to her—"

Hugger sat up straight. "Say what?"

Her eyes darted to him. "He said the FBI wants to talk to her."

"Why?"

She pulled her shoulders forward but said, "Babić is a bad guy and probably doesn't curtail his felonious activities solely to the Phoenix Metropolitan Area."

"And what would Suzette know about that shit?"

"I don't..." The importance of what they were discussing dawned on her, and she sat up straight too, taking her feet from the coffee table. "Oh shit, Hugger," she whispered. "When Dad said it, I didn't put it together."

She wouldn't. Her father rocked her world yesterday.

But now, she was.

"How much you know about her, babe?" he asked.

"Not really anything."

"Tell me what you know," he demanded.

"Not really anything," she repeated. "And I'm not being cagey. She hasn't opened up. At all."

"How'd she get here? You pick her up from her place or what?"

He asked because he wanted to know where that was and break into it to see if they might find some answers.

Regrettably, she shook her head. "She called from the hospital and took me up on my offer. Told me to meet her at a QuikTrip. I did. She had a bag with her, got in Baby Shark, and we came here. That's it."

"Baby shark?"

"My car."

Christ.

This fucking woman.

"She's got a phone?" he asked.

She nodded.

"She call anyone? Talk to anyone?"

"I don't keep an eye on her all the time, but no. Not that I've seen. As far as I can tell, she doesn't have anyone. When you guys aren't here, and I'm home, she comes out of her room and hangs with me. I've tried to get in there. All I know is, she got really upset when I

SMOOTH SAILING   113

asked about her parents, so I backed off fast on that one. But she just says she's not got many close friends. She's so...you've seen her, Hugger. She doesn't invite pushing. She's so fragile, I'm afraid I'll break her if I push too hard."

He got that.

And it sucked, but they were going to have to start pushing.

"Called the president of my Club last night, babe," he told her. "His name is Rush. He's sending down another brother, Dutch. Resurrection is sending down two of theirs, Core and Linus. We're gonna add on our list of things to do making sure your dad is good."

The softness came back, but it didn't fully push out the alarm.

"And we need a meet with that detective," he went on. "Because there's shit we don't know that we need to know to keep all of you safe."

"I'll get my phone," she whispered, and hauled her ass out of the couch to do that.

Hugger pulled his own out of his back pocket and shot a text to Eight and Big Petey.

Just learned the FBI wants to talk to Suzette. Diana's dad told her yesterday. Looking at getting more info on that. Hold tight.

Diana came back, and as she made her way to the couch, she asked, "Is it cool to call him on a Saturday?"

"Let's chance it," Hugger replied, holding out his hand.

She looked to his hand, then his face, and asked, "Wait, are you going to talk to him?"

"Queue him up and hand it to me, 'cause, yeah, I'm gonna talk to him."

It took her a beat, then she did what he asked and handed him the phone.

He kept his eyes on her, and his mind went to Nicole saying she knew Diana was an excellent judge of character.

So he asked, "You trust this guy?"

"He seems solid to me, but what do I know? I'd guess a cop who was dirty wouldn't expose it to anyone, much less someone like me."

"Gut, though. Solid?" he pushed.

She nodded.

"Any of the other cops you dealt with on this give you a hinky feel?"

"There weren't many, but I'll say, all of them seemed more focused on justice for Suzette than serving justice to Babić because it would be an awesome collar. I mean, it isn't like they're not all about taking him down, but she was..." She lifted her shoulders. "You know how she was, Hugger."

He knew.

"And if any of them were faking it, they're really good actors," she concluded.

"Right." He looked down at the phone that had gone dark. "Need you to engage this again, babe."

She did, he checked the name and hit the call button.

The man on the other end didn't fuck around answering.

Guess it was okay to call him on a Saturday.

"Diana, are things good?" a deep voice asked.

"Rayne Scott?" Hugger asked back.

"Who's this?"

"Harlan McCain. Chaos MC. Denver. We're providing security for Suzette and Diana."

Nothing from Scott.

"You heard Armitage is out as counsel?" Hugger inquired.

"Yeah."

"He told Diana the FBI wants a crack at Suzette."

"I wouldn't put it that way."

"How would you put it?"

"They have some lines of inquiry they wanna follow."

"Care to share?"

"I don't know you, so no. Is Diana there?"

"Sittin' right here with me on her balcony. Two of Babić's assholes are at the coffee place downstairs. So it's safe to say, think we need a meet, but not here. Suzette is comin' out of her shell, but she's takin' her time. Don't wanna do something that makes her crawl back into it. But my guess, we both got the same goal, getting her safe and keeping her that way."

"Maybe you don't know that cops don't discuss particulars of a case with anyone but those involved in the case and other cops," Scott educated him.

"And maybe you don't know we got a vested interest in making sure Suzette survives whatever she's facin' and then gets on with a long and happy life."

"I'd love to take your word on that, but I hope you don't mind I'm not going to," Scott returned.

"Can we meet?"

"We can, but it'll be a waste of time. It's not gonna change my mind." Scott paused then said, "Listen, not sure how you got involved in this. Can't say I'm upset that Suzette and Diana have someone looking out for them. But the only thing we've got to discuss is finding a way to first, get Suzette in a more secure situation, and second, get her to open up about things she might know."

"So she wasn't some random chick he picked up to destroy her life," Hugger noted.

Scott blew out an audible breath but said nothing.

Hugger knew it was useless to keep pressing, but he did anyway. "Again, I'll point out, we got the same goals here, Scott."

Scott took a beat, two, and then shocked the shit out of him by saying, "Let's meet."

Hugger jumped on it. "Great. You call when and where, we'll be there. It'll be me, and likely a brother of mine, Eight."

"How many of you are there?"

To build trust, Hugger gave it to him. "Four out-of-towners, for now. Three more coming in, 'cause we gotta cover Armitage now. And all of Aces."

"So this is about Aces," Scott muttered, sounding like he was connecting the dots, and he probably was.

"Partially. You seen Suzette. The minute we did, it became all about her. And Diana."

"I hear you."

"Where we meeting?"

Scott gave him a time and place.

"We'll be there," Hugger said.

He disconnected and tossed the phone to Diana.

"I'll get dressed," she said, already on the move to the door.

"You're not coming."

She stopped. "Yes, I am."

"No, babe, you aren't."

"I so am. Is Big Petey coming over?"

"Di—"

"*Harlan*," she snapped.

He shut up, because even saying it annoyed, he liked his name in her mouth.

"It totally sucks your name is as cool as you," she griped.

He didn't know anyone who thought his name was cool, even himself.

"Get Big Petey over here," she bossed, then flounced into the apartment.

He released a sigh.

Then he bent his head to his phone and got down to business.

More torture, Diana on the back of his bike.

It was bad when she just had his belt loops, like now.

It killed when she was pressed to him, like yesterday.

She didn't get his Club name was ironic. She didn't get he didn't like to be touched. She tugged his shirt, held his wrist, slapped his arm, and when she needed him, pressed tight.

And he didn't give what he made others get to her. Further, it was almost painful the times he pulled away from her.

He also didn't dive into why he didn't do that nor why he felt the pain.

He'd called Rush the night before, but he wasn't sure he was going to call Tack.

He wasn't sure, because what he had to talk to Tack about—first—was not taking a trip down Tack's memory road to how he won his old lady, Tyra.

There was something else.

Something huge.

A mountain between him and a life.

A mountain between him and his Club.

A mountain between him and whatever might happen with Diana.

A mountain he'd been eyeing since he joined Chaos, and he still didn't know if he wanted to climb it.

His life was steady and predictable. He couldn't say he was happy, he couldn't even say he was content.

He could say he was breathing, he was safe, he didn't have to worry about money, and he had people he respected around him.

And with the life he'd led up to Chaos, that was better than he expected he'd get.

Scaling that mountain to see what was on the other side? Something that could be an oasis. Or it could be a desert of shit.

In his experience, the most likely vista was a desert of shit.

So...yeah.

Climbing that mountain was all kinds of iffy.

But now was now.

Big Petey had been right, there was something more with Suzette.

She knew something.

Something that Babić was tweaked about even more than being convicted of a rape that included serious physical injury, which would give the man a minimum of twenty-five years, and a maximum of life.

So it was something big.

This meant it wasn't only Pete they left back at Diana's place. Muzzle was there too. Driver was back, and he'd brought another Aces brother, Gash. They were sitting outside the coffee joint, a table away from a couple of goons.

Babić wanted to make a statement?

They were gonna make one too.

He pulled into the parking lot of some public tennis courts off a road called Indian School. Eight was already there. And for some fucked up reason, even though it was a hundred and six degrees outside, two lunatics were playing tennis.

Other than that, no one was around.

He rolled up beside Eight, parked, and Diana jumped off.

He swung his leg over after she did.

Eight eyed her, looked to Hugger and grinned.

"*You* say no to her," Hugger replied to Eight's unspoken comment.

Eight's grin got bigger before he asked Diana, "What kind of tacos are we havin' tonight?"

She huffed before she shared, "Harlan doesn't want tacos every night. I'm making white chili and serving it with Red Lobster biscuits."

"What time?" Eight asked.

"I don't know. Six?" she answered.

"I'll bring the beer again," Eight said.

"Also some wine," she put in. "White. Sauvignon blanc or a buttery chardonnay."

"Buttery chardonnay. I'll get right on that," Eight replied, looking like he was about to bust a gut trying not to laugh.

Hugger felt him.

Diana Armitage was something, and fuck him standing, all of it was good.

"We're also gonna get right on giving Diana some cake. She's not feedin' this crew without reimbursement," Hugger entered the conversation.

"I'll see to that too...*Harlan*," Eight gave him shit.

"That isn't necessary," Diana stated.

"It is," Hugger and Eight said in unison.

"It really isn't," Diana asserted.

"What it is, is not up for discussion," Hugger returned.

"Bluh," she grunted adorably, giving in.

Fucking torturing him.

"Hup," Eight uttered, jerking up his chin.

Hugger and Diana turned to see a big shiny SUV rolling in.

The thing was, they knew who was behind the wheel, so it wasn't the Phoenix cop.

"This just got even more interesting," Eight murmured.

"Who's that?" Diana asked.

"Kai Mason," Hugger answered.

"You know him?" she queried as Mason swung in and parked.

"He's from Denver. Moved down here to expand their business," Hugger shared.

"And that business is?"

He looked down at her. "Investigations and security. And before you ask, yeah, they're good. The best."

"Why's he here?" She was watching Mace walk toward them.

"Because Scott can't tell us dick," Eight said. "But Mace can."

Proof.

Detective Rayne Scott was solid.

They waited until Mace got to them.

"Eight," Mace greeted on a handshake.

"Mace."

"Hug." Mace turned to him.

They shook and Hugger said, "This is Diana."

"Know who she is," Mace muttered and dipped his chin to her. "Diana."

"You know me?" she asked. "How?"

"Try to know as much as I can in this town," he replied without really giving her anything.

Of course, Diana didn't let him get away with that.

"Precisely...*me*. How do you know *me*?" she pushed.

"Anything that Imran Babić touches, I know. Anything that he might touch in a way that will piss me off, I know better," Mace returned.

That was acceptable to Diana, because she backed off.

"All right, I got a buttery chardonnay to buy, let's get down to it," Eight called it to order.

Mace got serious.

"Suzette Snyder doesn't exist."

Diana gasped.

Eight grunted.

Hugger growled.

"At least, the woman staying with you isn't named Suzette Snyder," Mace said to Diana.

"Oh my God," Diana whispered.

"Cops don't know who she is. She had no ID when she came in, and didn't provide any before she went out. Address she gave, someone else lives there and they've never heard of her. Prints aren't in the system. She reported to the cops she was twenty-three. Doctors who treated her said they can't be certain, but they think she's no more than seventeen," Mace stated.

At that, Diana reeled, so Hugger threw an arm around her shoulders, pulled her back to his front, and locked her down by curling his arm around her chest and holding her against him.

In turn, she lifted both hands and latched onto his forearm.

"You're fuckin' shittin' me," Eight gritted.

But Hugger caught on.

"Trafficked," he bit out.

"No," Diana moaned.

"That's what the cops, and FBI, are guessing," Mace affirmed. He focused his attention on Eight. "Maybe we can talk alone."

"Whatever it is, I should know," Diana put in.

"I get you think you do, but I know you don't," Mace replied.

"If anyone's going to talk her into a safe place and get her to the point she can keep it together and help, it's me. I should know what I'm dealing with," Diana pushed.

But Hugger was studying Mace's expression.

So he gave her a squeeze and said, "Babe."

She twisted her neck to look up at him. "I should know, Harlan."

Fuck, but she'd latched onto his name stronger than she had his arm, and she had a damn strong hold on him.

"How bad is it?" Eight asked.

"The worst," Mace didn't delay in answering.

Eight made a move to put distance between them. "Let's do this."

"No!" Diana shouted. "I should know."

Mace looked at Hugger.

"Don't look at him," she demanded. "Look at me."

"Why are you in this?" Mace asked her, and Hugger's hold got tighter.

"That isn't relevant," she returned.

"I disagree." Mace stood his ground.

"Okay then, it's none of your business," she retorted.

"That I can't disagree about," he replied, looking her straight in the eye, which meant he'd made an experienced guess, and that guess was correct.

Hugger felt Diana shiver, knew what that was about, and growled to Mace, "Lay off."

Mace switched to looking Hugger right in the eye, he nodded once, then said, "Prelims on the DNA came back. Multiples."

Oh *fuck*.

Heat came at him from Eight.

Blistering heat.

Fuck.

"Multiple what?" Diana asked.

"Don't answer that," Hugger gritted at Mace, let Diana go, but took her hand and pulled her away from the huddle.

"Harlan," she complained as they went.

When he got her far enough away, he turned her toward him, bent so they were face to face, and caught her with both hands on either side of her neck.

"You don't want to know this, Diana."

"I do, Harlan."

"Baby, step back from this. Let us finish talking. Then we'll go back to your crib and you're on Suzette, like normal. And we'll stay on target and get deeper into it."

Her head jerked.

Fuck.

Her face saturated with pain.

Fuck.

She was figuring it out.

"Diana, step back," he ordered.

"Multiples," she whispered.

He moved his hands to her jaw and got nose to nose with her. "Step back."

"Multiple sources of DNA," she pushed out. "It wasn't just Babić. She was gang-raped."

"Baby," he whispered.

She pulled out of his hold, whirled, took two angry steps away, then stopped so fast, her body swayed.

She whirled back to him and announced, "I want to hurt somebody."

"Somebody's gonna hurt. Just not you gonna do it. Come here."

"I can't. I can't. I..." She shook her head. "Oh my God, she's no more than seventeen and she's been gang-raped."

He didn't repeat his command.

He went to her and pulled her into his arms, one around her head so her cheek was tucked to his chest, the other around her, so she was too.

They stood that way awhile, the sun beating down on them, her heat beating into him.

Hugger was working up a sweat just standing there, but he didn't move, and this wasn't only because she felt damn good, it was because it felt better, giving her something steady to hold on to.

Eventually, he sensed her pulling her shit together.

Only then did he loosen his hold.

But he didn't let her go.

"You good?" he asked.

She tipped her head back to catch his eyes and nodded.

"You strong?" he pushed.

"I...I don't know what you mean, but I hope so."

He examined her face, at the same time he remembered her meticulously cleaning an ugly-ass painting with a Q-tip. Remembered her being in the middle of an emotional trauma, but not letting the opportunity of a cookie slide by. Remembered her pointing at her head and snapping, "Blowout." Remembered her delight at Suzette coloring in a book. Remembered her cackling with her ex-stepmom on the couch for two hours, while her sorta-stepdad, once removed made a play at bonding with the men who were looking after a woman he had no blood or real connection to, but he considered her his girl. Remembered her trusting him to help her get through a difficult text convo with her father.

And he remembered something hazy and distant.

It was hazy and distant because he made it that way. It was hazy and distant because he buried it along with every other good thing that happened in his life, outside the honor of looking after his mother.

He remembered his mom coming home from a client to a house he'd cleaned. He remembered her smile. The bright in her eyes.

And her saying, "One day, my beautiful boy, you're gonna make a woman really happy."

And he made a risky decision.

"You wanna be in this? *Really* in this?"

"I don't know what you mean about that either, but I think so."

"You gotta know if you do. And I gotta know I can trust you. So think, Di. You in, or are you gonna look after Suzette and talk her into getting safe and chatting with the Feds while the rest doesn't touch you?"

"You're kinda scaring me, Hugger," she said quietly.

"Good," he returned.

"It's hard to make a decision about something I don't know what I'm deciding at the same time being kinda entirely freaked out."

"That's the trust part."

"I—"

"Diana, in or out."

"I don't—"

He caught her by the jaw and got nose to nose with her again.

"In or out, baby."

She stared into his eyes.

And whispered, "In."

He knew that would be her answer.

And now for taking the risk.

"Resurrection MC is known by two other names."

"Okay," she said slowly.

"They're known as the Angels of Vengeance."

Her eyes got big.

"And the Angels of Death."

Her lips parted.

"And both just got activated."

"Oh my God," she breathed.

"So, you got no part in that, but you got a part in this. You and Pete. You get Suzette talking. About herself, about what went down, about getting safe and giving up what she knows, and about why she picked you."

"Why she picked me?"

"She got away and didn't hole up. She went to the hospital. That is not a woman who's given up. That's a woman who wanted help. But she doesn't trust the cops. She trusts you. We gotta know why she doesn't trust cops. So we gotta know why she picked you."

His hands moved as her head did in a nod.

"You gonna get on that?"

She nodded again.

Okay.

"Now, this is what's gonna go down," he began. "Mace knows Eight. He knows Resurrection. He knows what switch he just flipped. I don't know his motivation. Maybe he did it on purpose. Maybe he did it to light some fires elsewhere. Scott is gonna look into things. He's gonna hear things. It's a good bet Mace is gonna tell him things. And Chaos is not about that. Neither is Aces. So we're in a race right now, baby. I got no problem with what Eight and Muzz are intent to do. But me and Pete and Dutch can't let it touch you, Suzette or Chaos. And the best chance we got to do that is get Babić in a cage and shut down his shit."

"So you're...at odds with Eightball and Muzzle now?"

"It ain't cross purposes we're at. It's just the endgame doesn't match."

"Oh. All right," she muttered, sounding confused.

"Don't worry about it. Focus on you. The decision about dinner with your dad. And Suzette."

She emitted a shocked little laugh before she asked, "Dinner with Dad?"

"This is what I know, Di. Life goes on. Suzette is important. And that's important. You threw a man a lifeline yesterday. Don't lose focus and let him drown."

Her eyes started to get bright, she sniffed rough, then nodded.

"You good?"

She nodded again.

But she said, "No more than seventeen, Hug."

"Yeah," he whispered.

Her lip trembled, she clamped down on it with her teeth, let it go, sniffed again, rougher this time, and squared her shoulders.

And that right there was why he knew he could take the risk.

That right there was what he knew yesterday, but didn't trust.

Now, he had no choice but to trust.

He let her go, took her hand and led her back to the huddle.

"You got everything we need?" he asked Eight.

"Sure fuckin' do," Eight answered.

Hugger was beginning to get a new appreciation for the men of Resurrection.

Maybe, even if it still wasn't his to do, he could forgive.

But now, he had to work beside him at the same time thwarting his purpose.

That was going to be tricky.

Diana took his mind off it by squeezing his hand. "Can we go? I want to get back to Suzette."

"We can go, babe," he told her.

"Nice to meet you, kinda," she said to Mace, and added, "No offense on the kinda part."

"Nice to meet you too, Diana," Mace replied.

"See you for dinner," she said to Eight.

"You bet, sweetheart," Eight replied.

Hugger guided her to his bike.

He got on.

She swung on behind him.

And this wasn't a belt loops ride.

Tits flush to back and chin on his shoulder.

He'd been wrong, it wasn't torture.

It was indication it might be time to climb that fucking mountain.

Because maybe, just maybe, against all the odds stacked against him since his conception...

There might be an oasis on the other side.

9

MOTIVATION

Hugger

HUGGER WOKE FEELING MORE than his usual morning rough.

Diana's dark-blue couch looked good and was comfortable to sit on, but it wasn't long enough for him. He couldn't find a position that worked, which meant he woke up constantly in search of one.

He was also wearing his clothes, something he'd done every night, and that didn't help with his comfort level.

But he didn't want Suzette or Diana to run into him wearing his boxer briefs or sleep shorts.

Especially Suzette.

Hugger wanted her at all times to feel an extra layer of protection from him.

This meant he had three nights of shit sleep in a time he needed to keep his shit sharp.

So he'd just woken up, but he needed a nap.

It was still dark, just a little sun in the early dawn leaking through Diana's many windows, but he knew he wasn't going to get any more sleep.

He pushed up to sitting on the couch, put his elbows on his knees, drove his fingers through his hair, digging the pads into his scalp, and left them at his neck, his fingers holding his hair back and still digging into the tense muscle there.

Hugger had never been a morning person. He'd always woken tough. Until he was old enough to introduce himself to coffee, that tough lasted awhile.

It did his ma's head in.

On that thought, he remembered when he was eight, nine years old, slouching and grouching through his morning prep before school, and his mom grousing, "Should fill a bucket with ice water and douse you with it every morning to snap you out of it."

From that day on, Hugger had still woken rough, but he'd done everything he could to stop slouching and grouching and get on with it so it didn't bug his ma.

Feeling uneasy about this memory, mostly that it would unearth itself at all, he shoved it aside, pushed up from the couch and headed down the hall, noting Suzette's door was firmly closed, but the door at the end, Diana's, was open a couple of inches.

An indication to him he didn't need to hold it if he had to use the john.

Damn, but she was a good woman.

Cute. Smart. Funny. Thoughtful. A little loony, but it was the good kind.

Still, when he got to her door, he grabbed the handle so it wouldn't swing wider when he knocked softly so as not to wake her if she was asleep, or do the same with Suzette.

He heard nothing, so he knocked again, and only when she didn't call out did he push in.

The early sun dimly lighting the room, he saw her lying with her back to him in the middle of the big bed. The white covers were pulled up to her shoulder. Her dark and golden hair was bunched up in a holder at the top of her head and was stark on the white pillowcase. The big, square, pale-blue velvet pillows he'd seen on her bed when it was made were stacked on the floor, the pale-blue velvet comforter folded along the end of the bed.

The walls were also pale blue, but her bed had a padded head-board and was a linen color.

He'd now spent three nights with visions of banging her in that bed, another reason why sleep didn't come easy.

The nightstands were white, and they looked classy old-fash-ioned, like the stuff they had in France way back when. The lamps on them had crystal bases. And there was a big, white, 3D flower mounted above the arch of her headboard and some shelves in an inset on a wall covered in white frames with black and white pictures in them. That was pretty much it for decoration.

He'd been wanting to look at those pictures, look at her life and who mattered to her enough to have displayed in her bedroom.

He hadn't.

He also didn't spend a lot of time standing there, staring at her sleeping, because he wasn't a skeeve.

Though he did note she had a ceiling fan, which was on, the white noise droning, and it reminded him that he slept with a fan at home, so maybe if she had one he could set up in the living room, it might help him find sleep on the couch.

And if she didn't have one, he'd go out and buy one.

He went to the bathroom, took a piss, washed his hands, brushed his teeth, splashed water on his face and toweled off.

Then he stared at the towel, which was a cool, sky-blue color.

He turned his head and saw the two towels hanging side by side on the back of the door, one white, hers, the other, blue.

His.

We don't have to paint it, Ma.

My beautiful boy is turning into a man. He needs a man's room. We're painting it.

Yet another memory of his mom came unbidden, and with it the reminder that he and his ma painted his bedroom blue when he was fifteen. She didn't ask the landlord. "It's not hurting anything," she'd said. She just gave him that, even though he knew she probably lost her deposit because of it when they moved out.

It was the nicest space he'd ever had, to this day.

Until now, temporarily moved into Diana's sweet crib, having a thick blue towel and a sink of his own.

Back in Denver, he had a little house he'd bought because he could, and he needed a place to crash. He'd moved in because it was his. And other than that, he didn't do dick with it unless something broke that he had to fix.

"Fuckin' shit," Hugger muttered, not real hip on all this shit crashing into his brain when he had to keep sharp.

More indication he needed some good sleep. A solid three-hour nap. Rest his body and mind, clear his head.

He'd normally go for a workout to do this, but he didn't want to leave Diana and Suzette, and a workout would only fatigue him more, and that he didn't need.

He was going to have to find some time to get that nap in, but he didn't know how.

He headed out, going quiet, closing the door fully when he left Diana's room, and he went direct to the coffeepot. He made coffee, and while he was waiting for it to brew, he rested his ass against the counter and moved his mind to going over what happened the day before.

When he and Diana got back to her complex after meeting up with Mace, she'd grabbed his hand in the elevator bay before either of them hit the button, and declared, "Before we go up there, we need to figure this out."

This time, he did not pull his hand from hers.

No, he curled his fingers around and held on.

He thought about it, he knew he was doing it, he knew he shouldn't do it because of what it would communicate, and he'd already communicated a lot with his touch that morning.

He held on anyway.

"Figure what out?" he asked.

"You can't tell Muzzle and Big Petey about Suzette when Suzette is around. They're gonna freak."

She was right. They were gonna freak.

"But they need to know," she continued. "And Big Petey and I have to come up with a strategy of how to get her to open up, and he and I can't have a huddle with her around. We've already taken off first thing on a Saturday, which she might find weird. I don't want her to think we're ganging up on her or something is wrong."

She was right again.

"We'll finesse sharin' the new intel and doin' it away from Suzette," he assured.

"I can keep her occupied. Maybe, if you're ready to take Big Petey and Muzzle away, you can give me a hand gesture, like this one."

She then, with her free hand, executed a hand gesture that would make any football offensive coach cream his pants it was so intricate and convoluted.

Hugger couldn't believe it after the news they'd just heard, but it took everything he had not to bust out laughing.

How she managed to con hospital staff and a cop to get to Suzette, he had no clue. It was probably less about the con, and more about her charm.

"Then I'll know to get her someplace she doesn't notice you guys are gone, or something," she finished.

"You don't think she's gonna notice me doin' whatever you just did with your hand?" he asked, and he didn't have enough left after stopping himself from laughing to control his voice vibrating with humor.

She screwed up her face in irritation.

"Well, do *you* have a plan?" she snapped.

"I'm gonna send Muzzle to Eight. Eight can tell him. I'm back, so we don't need him here right now. And Pete can learn later. Don't think it's good we're off someplace first thing in the morning, and you go barrelin' in there to get her to share all her secrets and make a decision about something as important as her safety. But you do go in there easing into it. A little more pressure, a little more attention. She's good where's she's at right now, and the FBI can wait until she's ready. This all doesn't have to happen today."

"Good call," she muttered.

"Can we go up now?" he asked.

She shot him a look he was sure she thought could kill, but it didn't, since it was cute. She then hit the elevator button, so he guessed her answer was an affirmative.

Muzzle practically bowled him over on his way out as they were on their way in, which meant Eight already called him.

Pete gave him a *What the fuck is up?* look, which Hugger had no choice but to return with a *Later* one.

Diana got the brilliant idea to keep the day chill by doing normal stuff, and she corralled Suzette into helping her with it.

This included cleaning, doing laundry, sending Pete to the store with another list and starting the white chili (again in the Crock-pot). Hugger lugged out the trash and recycling and commandeered the vacuum after Diana pulled it out. Suzette and Diana made a pie (strawberry, fucking amazing, it was better than her *elote*). And they all sat around in the afternoon and watched a hilarious British movie called *Death at a Funeral* (Diana's choice).

The boys showed at six.

They ate at the dining room table. They gabbed. Muzzle pissed him off (even though it was obviously a joke) by asking Diana to marry him after he ate her pie. And Hugger further reconsidered how he felt about Resurrection when Eight showed how pleased he was when Diana approved of the wine he brought (and he brought five bottles, though she only tasted one).

They took off a lot earlier than they did the night before. Pete went with them.

And the improvements kept coming when Suzette didn't retreat to her room but watched another movie with them even though Hugger was there.

Diana coaxed Suzette to make the choice that time. She chose a Disney movie, *Encanto*, which Hugger was surprised didn't suck, and the music was tight.

They all hit the sack after that, with Suzette speaking the first words she'd ever said to him, "'Night, Hugger."

So more improvement.

When the women had gone to bed, he'd gone out on the balcony to call Rush and Big Petey.

Pete was at the crash pad, so by the time Hugger spoke to him, he already knew.

Rush was silent for a solid two minutes after he got the update, before he said tightly, "Wash has got to know this by now, though I'm not surprised he hasn't called me. They could be fixing to go rogue. Let me talk with Wash and Buck. Might need to send down Jag and Coe to help keep a lid on things. We'll see. I'll get back to you."

That was it, and now was now.

Another day in a sweet crib with a beautiful woman, a broken girl, and a lot on his mind.

He turned to the coffeepot, made himself a mug, took it to the sofa and cleared away the bedclothes Diana insisted on tucking around the cushions to make a bed for him.

He was stowing them out of sight when his phone—resting by his gun on the coffee table—lit up.

It was a call from Big Petey.

He took it and his mug to the balcony.

When he answered the call, the sky was lighter, some women were in yoga clothes carrying yoga mats and heading to a place on the bottom level, but other than that, there was no one around.

"Yo. You good?" he greeted.

"I managed to stop Eight and Muzz from storming Imran Babić's house last night, and instead, waiting for Rush, Buck and Wash to decide how they wanted it handled. So that was a win."

It was, though Hugger reckoned it was a battle and not the war.

"Good," he said.

"You're up early," Big Petey noted. "I thought I'd be leavin' a voicemail."

"Couch as a bed is shit, man."

"I bet," Pete mumbled. Then, "Gonna hit the shower, grab some donuts and come over. Workin' with these old bones, that'll probably mean a couple of hours."

"Diana wants a huddle with you to try to figure out how to get Suzette talking. But she doesn't want Suzette seeing the huddle. So if you could figure out how to do that, it'd make her feel better."

"We'll figure it out."

Something in Pete's voice was tweaking him.

"You sure you're good?" he asked.

It took a minute for the man to answer.

Eventually, he sighed, "Too old for this shit, Hug."

Hugger couldn't disagree, but he didn't like to hear it come out of Pete's mouth.

Still, he said, "You need to head back to Denver?"

"You couldn't pry me away from those two women with a whole case of dynamite until I know down deep in my gut they're safe," Pete returned.

Hugger smiled and took a sip of his coffee before he replied, "Right."

"How you doin' with all of it?"

"Suzette said goodnight to me last night, so I think she's getting used to us. Today might be a day to push. Diana will be back at work tomorrow. It's a lot on her to work to live and then come home and have an even more important job on her hands. Her job seems cush, but it requires a lot of detail and concentration."

"Agreed. Though, gotta put out there, Suzette isn't there with me, son. Hate to say it, but we don't have the time for me to get there with her. Diana and I will talk, but this is all gonna be on Diana."

Hugger suspected that, but he still didn't like it and tipped his head side to side to release the tension in his neck before he took another sip of coffee and replied, "Yeah."

"Looks with the way you two were together yesterday like you made up your mind about her."

Fuck.

It wasn't like they were all over each other, but he for certain had broken a seal for Diana. She cuddled up to him on the couch for both movies, he let her, and not only because there wasn't a lot of room for everyone if she didn't.

He'd never cuddled in front of a movie with a woman in his life... or ever. Never had the urge. He'd witnessed others cuddling, and he didn't see the draw of it, having someone up in your space like that.

With Diana, it came natural.

And it felt great.

"Pete—"

"Though, talked to Tack and he said he hasn't heard from you."

"I haven't made up my mind about her."

"Okay, so, where you at with that?"

"Not someplace I'm willing to talk about it."

"Hug—"

"It's too early for this shit, Petey."

"Maybe. But we touched on this the other day, so I'm gonna touch on it again by saying, we got you, and we don't have you."

Hugger didn't understand. "What?"

"You're Chaos. We can count on you. But I bet I asked, not one brother could say he knows you."

Hugger felt a tightness hit his chest. "That's the way it is. It's what you give and what I return."

"Yeah. That's the other thing. Not one brother could say you know them."

Hugger was not liking this.

"That isn't true."

"Only because they give a shit ton more than you do, and you pay attention."

"You sayin' that's a problem?"

"No, son, I'm sayin', for me, that's a worry."

"For fuck's sake, why?"

"Because you got a lot to give."

"Like what?"

"Maybe ask Diana."

Hugger shut his mouth.

Big Petey did not.

"She gets to that point in healing, ask Suzette. Ask any of our brothers, you pitch up at the store and do your thing there, no complaint, when most the men hate workin' the store. Ask any brother of Resurrection, when you take their backs. Ask Tab, when Playboy got to pukin' his guts out and Shy and Rush were up in Fort Collins, Tack and Tyra were in St. Lucia, you went to the hospital to hang with her until her man and her brother could get to her."

"It's what we do."

"You're Suzette, Hug, in a different way. Just livin' until you die."

That hit so close to the bone, he could feel the blade scraping.

"We gotta talk about it," Big Petey announced.

He found his breath on that because he knew what Pete wanted to talk about.

And that wasn't going to happen.

"No, we don't."

"I've left it too long. I'm too old. Slowin' down. I need to sort this for Jackie before I kick it."

He didn't like Pete talking about kicking it either.

"Pete—"

"Not now. Too much happening now. Later," Pete said as Hugger heard the sliding glass door open behind him.

He twisted to see Diana back in her loose shorts and Diamondbacks tee. The mess of hair on her head was listing off to one side. Her eyes were sleepy. Her gait was shuffling as she made her way to him.

And she was the prettiest thing he'd ever seen.

He froze solid as she came right in, fit herself to his back, and he felt her press her cheek there as she wound her arms around his middle.

It was the sweetest touch he'd ever had.

Good Christ.

"Hug?" Big Petey called.

"Diana's up," he grunted.

"Right. We'll leave it there. Though, warning, we're picking it up later. See you in a few."

"See you," he pushed out, and the call ended.

He put his mug on the railing and carefully turned in Diana's arms.

She allowed this, then pressed to his front.

"It's super early and you've obviously been up awhile," she mumbled, even her voice sweet and sleepy. "We need to go out and get an air mattress for you."

He shoved his phone in his back pocket, then he took her by her upper arms and gently but firmly set her away from him.

She blinked up at him, her face fell, and his gut lurched at seeing it.

"I'm sorry," she whispered, the sleepy gone, horrified in its place. "So sorry. I thought yesterday...you touching my face, holding my hand, watching the movies...I thought...I..." She shook her head hard, making that clutch of thick hair bounce. "I thought wrong and I'm so sorry. That had to be weird for you."

Hugger found his mouth saying, "I don't like to be touched and I'm not affectionate."

"Okay. Yeah." She nodded her head fast and repeatedly. "Again, I'm sorry." She was looking anywhere but at him. "I'm just gonna go—"

"Diana."

Her eyes skated across his face and fastened on his ear.

"Babe, look at me," he said softly.

It took visible effort for her to meet his gaze.

She looked uncomfortable, mortified, like she wanted to be a million miles away from him.

And he couldn't stand it.

Any of it, but especially the last part.

He bent to her, caught her chin between his thumb and finger, and whispered, "I'm a problem you don't need."

"What?" she whispered back.

"I got shit no good woman needs laid on her."

"What shit?"

"Shit I was born with." Fuck him, he was giving it to her. "Shit that made me."

"Harlan—"

"You got enough to deal with, you can't be taking on my shit."

"Can you give me a hint what your shit is?"

"I already did."

"I don't—" The haze of sleep and mortification cleared, and her brows snapped together. "You mean your mom?"

He had to stop touching her, but he couldn't do it without running his thumb along the line of her jaw.

So he didn't.

Then he said, "Fuck no, Di. But think on that."

"Think on what?"

"Who's my daddy?"

Her head jerked and she asked, "Do you know?"

"Met him once, once was enough, but I know who he was. All of who he was."

"Then does it matter?"

Her words felt like a lance went clean through him, so he couldn't reply.

She threw up both hands. "Who's *my* daddy?"

"Di," he choked out.

"So, okay, he's making an effort now. But I'm twenty-nine years old, Harlan. I'm grateful for that effort, and I've decided to explore it, but that's a long time to have a dad who expected me to be his brand of perfection from top to toe, to intellect, to personality, and live with falling short and disappointing him time after time. A dad who cheated on my mom, broke her heart, and I had to watch. But even if he cheated on her, he acted like she had some horrific defect and was beneath him, and me, and everybody. A dad who didn't have a lot growing up, and wasn't a big fan of that, so he pulled out all the stops to give himself, and yeah, me, more. But that meant I was raised by nannies and babysitters and—"

She was winding herself up way too tight with this shit.

So he ordered, "Stop it, honey."

"Do you want to know why I went balls to the wall to get Suzette in my house?"

Unh-unh.

Hell no.

They couldn't go there.

"Don't give me that," he growled.

"So you guessed already that I was trigged and why."

Hugger said nothing.

"When that happened, Dad—"

Oh no.

They definitely couldn't go *there*.

"Don't give me that, Di."

"He made it so that guy—"

"I'm tellin' you, babe, don't fuckin' give me that."

"That guy—"

Fuck it.

To shut her up, he hooked her around the back of the neck, yanked her to his body, bent his head and took her mouth.

For a beat, she stilled.

Then she melted into him and her hands slid up his chest.

Given the invitation, he tipped his head to the side and touched his tongue to her lips.

She opened, Hugger slid his tongue inside and tasted toothpaste and warmth and woman and mysteries and truths and the fullness of life.

All of it crashed into him all at once.

It was crushing.

And it was fucking *fantastic*.

He angled his head even more, clamped his arm around her, leaned into her, arching her over his arm, and took the kiss deeper.

Diana mewed in his mouth and slid her fingers into his hair, her other arm tight around his neck.

She pressed close, and she gave.

And gave.

And more.

Then she took, tangling her tongue with his, darting it in to get her taste of him.

Feeling her invade, his cock jumped and a growl rolled up his throat.

Her mew came back and she pushed harder into his frame.

They held on and took from each other and gave to each other and nothing else mattered.

Nothing.

The world wasn't totally fucked. Heinous shit didn't happen to good people. You didn't have to sweat and bleed and beg for any scrap you got.

No.

The world was Diana's balcony, her soft body against his, her hand in his hair, the open promise of who she was and what she could offer more than enough to give a man motivation to climb mountains.

As that thought bolted through him, Hugger broke the kiss, but not his hold, tucking her cheek against his chest.

It was then, in his mind's eye, he saw his Chaos brother, Joker's head come out from behind the hood of a car and the look on his face when he saw his old lady Carissa walking into a bay at Ride.

He saw Shy's expression when his gaze landed on Tab when he

walked in that hospital room where their kid was in a bed with a really bad flu.

He saw Georgie giving Dutch shit, and Dutch's eyes lighting up, because he loved it.

He saw Tack where he'd seen Tack maybe hundreds of times, ass resting on the edge of Tyra's desk in her office at Ride. He didn't need to be there for work. He was just there because his woman was.

A kaleidoscope of the same from Lanie and Hop, Millie and High, Hound and Keely, Jag and Archie, Rosalie and Snap, Rush and Rebel churned through his brain, and fuck, he'd been slow on the uptake.

It had been there all along.

Right in front of his face, all around him.

All along.

What his ma wanted for him.

What Big Petey and Rush had been offering him.

Even if it was all over that FFO barbeque that introduced him to the life he could have, it was what he'd never grasped, intellectually or emotionally.

"Um…" Diana hummed against his chest.

He let her head go but wrapped that arm around her to join his other.

She tipped her head back.

Her lips were bruised, there was pink in her cheeks…

Christ.

Amazing.

"So that was a really, kinda…uh, *important* kiss. Yeah?" she asked.

"Yeah," he agreed.

He felt her body sag against his with relief.

Yeah, she was as into him as he was her.

"So maybe we should get some things clear," she suggested.

"Di—"

"I'm into you."

There it was.

She went on, "I like you. I *really* liked that kiss. And, well, none of this is optimal with all that's going on and the fact we live in two different cities in two different states."

"Yeah," he agreed again.

"But I...well..." She faltered.

"I like you," he said quietly. "I'm into you. This is shit timing, not only for the reasons you stated, but I've got things I gotta figure out before I'm good to get deep with a fucking fantastic woman I wanna get to know better."

He didn't think she could melt any more, but she practically fused with him then, a happy light sparking in her pretty green eyes.

Hugger instantly fell in love with that light. He wanted to keep it lit until he took his last breath.

But she had to know.

"Baby, the shit I gotta wade through is pretty deep and not the kind of thing you lay on a woman you just met and wanna get to know," he warned.

"Um, were you there at Sack's when I had a breakdown because my dad had demonstrated for the first time in twenty-nine years he gives a shit?"

Hugger couldn't believe it, but he grinned.

She watched him grin, then looked up in his eyes. "Yes, you were. We learn something new every day, if we pay attention. And the last few days, I learned you don't get to the pick the time you meet a guy who you want to jump his bones."

His brows shot up. "You want to jump my bones?"

"Um...*again*, were you just there for that kiss?'

He stroked her back and muttered, "Totally there, baby."

"So...what? Are we gonna kinda date while we deal with all this other stuff?"

"No, but we got no choice but to get to know each other, and I'm seriously down with doin' that."

Her eyes narrowed on him, and what she said next demonstrated she'd already started getting to know him.

"You look like you haven't slept in a week."

"Di, it isn't a big deal."

"It is. I don't like it. Can you nap during the day?"

"Who can't?"

"I can't. If the sun is up, it's impossible."

Holy shit.

"Really?" he asked.

She nodded.

"Sucks for you, babe," he mumbled.

"It does. But whatever. When Big Petey gets here, you're behind closed doors in my room, catching up on sleep."

He wanted to refuse, but he shouldn't, so he didn't.

"Pete's bringing donuts," he told her.

Her eyes lit up again, and Jesus.

Fuck.

Oh yeah.

Motivation to scale mountains.

"Awesome," she replied. "So, we're just gonna ride this however it plays out while everything else plays out, is that our plan?"

"I'm down with it if you are."

More bright in her eyes and more body contact with her pressing close. "Totally."

He cupped her jaw and stroked her cheek with his thumb, and... *damn.*

Holding her, touching her, free to do that after wanting it since he laid eyes on her, it felt fucking great.

"I'm going to text Dad and say yes to dinner," she informed him. "And if he asks you to join us, you probably should know—"

He stiffened and cut her off. "Baby, like I said, *don't.*"

Her expression grew confused. "It's not good, but you should know."

"I know it's not good. I know it's not about me. And now I know he didn't take care of you through it, which is why you two had your thing."

She bit her lip.

Mm-hmm.

"So I can't know *how* he didn't do that, because it's gonna piss me off to extremes. I don't wanna be sharing a phenomenal kiss with you one second, and losing my shit about your dad the next, and maybe freaking you. I gotta be in the right place. More importantly, *you* gotta be in the right place. And you gotta agree that is not here and now."

She scrunched her nose and muttered, "You're right."

"We just jumped our first hurdle and landed on our feet. I don't need your dad throwing a leg out and tripping me up."

"I don't want that either."

"So later on that, yeah?"

She nodded.

"Wanna take a shower before Big Petey shows with donuts, I scarf a few down and then get some decent shut-eye?"

Her eyes grew round. "Shower together?"

He felt his face get soft. "No, baby. Later on that. When we get there and you're ready. Yeah?"

She nodded again, but he liked it a fuckuva lot she looked disappointed.

He bent and touched his mouth to hers.

Those green eyes were fucking sparkling when he lifted away.

"I like this new us," she decreed.

Fucking hell, he hoped he knew what he was doing.

"I do too. Now, scoot. Pete said he won't be here for a coupla hours, but Suzette might be up any time. She's seeming more comfortable with me and being out in the common space, and we don't need to be making out on the balcony when she comes out."

Diana frowned.

Hugger smiled.

Then he turned her, put a hand in the small of her back and shoved her toward the door.

He watched her walk in, so he caught her looking back at him like she wanted to make sure he was still there and he didn't leap over the railing to escape.

He lifted his chin to her.

She grinned and disappeared.

He turned and looked down at the courtyard.

A couple more women with workout bags on their shoulders and skintight clothes were heading to another door on the first floor.

It wasn't even seven o'clock on a Sunday.

Lunacy.

He nabbed his mug and took a sip.

It had to be ninety degrees out at least, and the coffee had gone cold.

So he walked into a great kitchen in a sweet crib to warm it up.

10

PRECIOUS WEIGHT

Diana

I SAT in one corner of the couch, Big Petey sat in the other.

We'd had our donuts, and now Hugger was sleeping in my bed and Suzette was in her room doing who knew what.

I'd been riding the high of what had happened on the balcony with Hugger.

No, it wasn't like I forgot that on paper—us being in the midst of a major drama that involved gangsters and the FBI, Hugger living eight-hundred and twenty-one miles away (yes, I looked it up)—taking our relationship *there* was the last thing we should be doing.

But man...

That kiss.

After *that kiss*, and, well...just about everything else about him, I didn't care if Hugger lived on the moon, I wanted to know what more we could build together.

And I wanted that *bad*.

(We could also just say he had a body made for cuddling; best two movies I'd ever watched, bar none.)

Thus, as if enough world-rocking stuff hadn't already happened that morning (though, all of that was the good kind, I could still feel Hugger's lips on mine, and his scratchy soft beard...*dayum*), and it wasn't even ten o'clock, I was staring at Armageddon on my phone.

The least catastrophic part of my technological apocalypse was my friend Bernie demanding my attendance for a night of cocktails on Friday.

I'd been pretty much blowing everyone off because of Suzette, then of course, the boys turned up and took all my attention (especially one of them...ahem). Since Nic knew everything, and because she did, Larry did too, they helped me move Suzette in, but I hadn't been super forthcoming with my friends. Only telling them that I had an out-of-town guest staying for a while, and I needed their help putting together a guest room, getting it in the form of borrowing some of their stuff.

I wasn't sure I could do Friday cocktails. I'd have to ask Hugger.

So my answer to that was easy, *That sounds fun! I'll get back to you. Soon!*

The more catastrophic part was that I'd texted Dad to let him know I was okay to have dinner.

I thought he'd be at the gym or playing a round of golf, but his reply was immediate.

Wednesday good for you?

It warmed my cockles (and I didn't even know I had cockles) that he texted back quickly and wanted to get together soon.

But I had to ask Hugger about that too. Though, since Dad and I were both under biker protection, I assumed it would be okay.

I need to check something, but I think so. I'll confirm soon.

I then realized I'd forgotten my father's bent at control and his need to form an opinion so he could voice it, the power of this urge so strong, he'd even do this when the focus should be on us figuring out where we were at with things.

I remembered when he returned, *Feel free to bring your boyfriend.*

I just knew that would bite me in the ass.

I didn't share he wasn't my boyfriend (as such...*hmm*).

I replied, *I'll talk to him.*

Gak!

I'd barely sent my last when I got a text from my mother.

And that was when Armageddon struck full force.

The text said, *Hey sweetie! I'm going to be in town to do some shopping! Pick me up at the airport Friday around two. We'll go to Fashion Square and have a fun dinner and then spend the weekend decimating Rick's bank account.*

Rick, by the by, was her husband, who I did not refer to as my stepdad. Ever.

To which I responded, *Hey Mom. Did you already buy your tickets?*

And got back, *Yes! It's all set! Girl's weekend!*

I had to sit with that a minute (okay, it took five of them), tamping down the feelings I sometimes (okay, often) got when my mom entered the picture of my life.

I loved her. She was fun and had lived almost her entire life without responsibility (like me, she was an only child, but Gram and Gramps went the opposite way with that than Dad did for me—that being spoiling her kind of bad).

Spending time with someone who was carefree with nothing dragging on it felt freeing.

For a while.

But I *did* have responsibilities.

And as much as I didn't want to get ticked at my mom, the fact she didn't ask before buying her tickets, and she expected me to be at the airport at a time when I'd be at work, not to mention, expected me to play chauffeur at all (she didn't drive in the city, "It rattles my nerves!"), I had to admit, bugged me.

However, this time, I simply couldn't be at her beck and call when she got the hankering to spend time with her daughter (or spend time at the designer boutiques at Fashion Square where I could act as her chauffer, travel guide and bag handler, and it sometimes felt that was what I was and that sometimes (okay, often) hurt).

So I had to say, *I'm sorry, I can't Mom. I have plans next weekend.*

To which I received, *More important than a visit with your mother?*

At this point, I glanced at Big Petey, who was in the other corner of the couch. He'd taken off his boots, his stocking feet were on my coffee table, and he was watching old episodes of *My Cat from Hell* (I got this; Jackson Galaxy was the bomb-diggity).

I went back to my phone. *Yes. I have a friend who needs me.*

And I need some time with my daughter.

Oh crap.

I was getting angry.

And it was probably the current situation that made me do something I'd never done, outside of burying all this disquiet about Mom, ignoring it or making excuses for it.

I pushed back.

Okay, Mom, you know I love spending time with you. But she's been gang-raped. So maybe next time shoot me a text or give me a call to make sure I'm free or can take time off work.

And that was when I got, *Oh my God, Diana. Trigger warning next time.*

I stared at the text, something bubbling inside me like acid.

It was then I remembered I didn't tell her about my own assault.

It wasn't because I was worried her response would be like Dad's, but because I knew she couldn't handle it.

I'd protected her, my own mother, from my assault.

"Not sure, no matter how hard you frown at your phone, you can make it blow up in your hand," Big Petey remarked.

I looked to him.

"You okay, girl?" he asked quietly.

"My mom can sometimes be difficult," I told him.

He watched me closely. "Yeah. That can happen."

"She made plans to come this weekend but didn't ask."

His scraggly gray beard twitched with irritation.

"Yeah," I agreed. "And she wasn't a fan of me putting her off."

"Welp, she's got a grown girl on her hands, so she doesn't really have a choice, does she?"

No. She didn't.

I turned back to my phone.

We'll plan something later, I promised.

I was about to set that unpleasantness aside and chat with Big Petey about Suzette when my phone vibrated in my hand.

Another text from Mom.

Whatever. Rick's going to be furious we have to pay for a flight change, but I suppose we'll have to deal with it.

She would, I had no doubt, have spent tens of thousands of dollars on clothes, shoes, purses, and if she went hog wild, that ante would be upped substantially if she hit a jewelry counter.

So a flight change was the least of her expenses.

But a chill crept over my skin at understanding this happened too. Me being to blame for something Mom didn't get when she wanted it.

She'd given up custody. Didn't even fight for me. I saw her on some weekends. We'd have dinner together. Dad gave her alimony until she married Brendon (husband two of three). And that alimony wasn't stingy.

Fortunately for Dad, Brendon came on the scene quickly, and as Mom told it, even though she was heartbroken at Dad's infidelity, Brendon, "Swept me off my feet."

With the custody deal, and even after it, during the short time she was with Brendon (and when I grew older, I realized Brendon didn't last long because he was a rebound), I thought at the time she just couldn't deal because she was so brokenhearted at the betrayal then loss of Dad.

I thought this, because she told me that was the way it was. She harped on quite a lot about how Dad "ruined me and our family," and how difficult it was to be replaced and have to start "from scratch," and then when things ended with Brendon it was because "your father's treachery ruined me for all men."

As noted, Brendon came quick, well within a year of them divorcing (I didn't like him either, and he didn't like me—I'd been eight). Rick came quickly after, and she didn't blink when he moved them up to Idaho.

It was like she wasn't leaving a daughter behind.

That hurt too. Then, and now I was allowing myself to remember it.

Over the years, I just put the emotional effort in to forgetting it happened.

"Now you wanna tell me why I feel the need to go out and buy more donuts for you?" Big Petey asked.

I turned again to him. "I'm just noticing stuff about Mom that irks me and wondering why I didn't really notice it before."

Big Petey had a ready answer. "We got blinders on with our parents. We need them to be perfect, or at least as good as we can make them in our heads. They made us, for one. So they're a part of us."

He seemed to drift after he said that, doing it so bad, I got concerned. He wasn't young, but he seemed sharp.

"Well, goddamn," he whispered like he was talking to himself.

"What?" I asked.

He visibly shook it off and refocused on me.

"Nothin', darlin'. Something just occurred to me. Anyway, getting back to it. We also need to know we can count on them for answers and support. But no one is perfect, Di, and every kid figures it out sometime that their parent is just a person, figuring it out like all the rest of us."

"Seems like I'm a late bloomer," I mumbled.

"You said she made plans to come this weekend. That mean she don't live close?"

I shook my head. "Idaho."

"How long's she lived there?"

I thought about it and said, "She moved when I was ten."

"You see her a lot?"

"When I was at school, summers. Some holidays. When I graduated high school, not as much."

"Not close enough for you to get a lock on it sooner, sweetheart," he shared. "That kinda time, it's all good. Vacations and celebrations. Day to day life is a different thing."

Life was a different thing.

Like the life my dad lived where he was ambitious. He wanted to make money, make partner, make a name for himself, and he was mother and father to a daughter.

He sucked at it, but he didn't shirk it. There was never a time when he seemed pissed he was saddled with me. He lived his life. He worked. He dated. He golfed and played tennis. And yeah, in a perfect world, maybe he should have spent more time with me, and when he did, he was less hard on me.

But he stuck. He wanted to. Because he was my dad.

I was getting the supremely uncomfortable feeling I'd been too hard on him.

Big Petey cut into my thoughts by handing them back to me. "Don't be too hard on yourself, Di. You were livin' your own life too."

"Right."

"You wanna talk about that more?" he offered. "I got some livin' under my belt myself. May not have all the wisdom, but what I got, I'm good to share if you wanna lay it on me."

God, Big Petey was the best.

"I think I need to process a few things first, Big Petey. But thanks."

"I'll be here awhile, you need me."

Not that it needed to be announced, since it happened way before that moment, but...*yeah.*

I really liked these guys.

All of them.

"You wanna jump to a not-at-all less sticky subject?" he asked, lowering his voice.

I scooted closer to him and lowered my voice too. "Suzette."

He slouched to the side to get nearer to me. "Hugger says she spoke to him. Said goodnight."

I nodded. "It felt like a big breakthrough."

His face got scary. "What she went through, reckon it was."

"Yeah."

"Time to push, Di."

Ugh.

"Yeah," I repeated. "Got an idea about that?"

"I figure we gotta set priorities. Do we want her under police protection first, or do we wanna know her real name?"

"*I* want her safe. But this isn't about what I want."

"In part it is, darlin'. You put yourself in front of her as her shield, and that was your choice. But she's usin' you as a shield, and that was hers. We got you. We're here for the long haul. But I cannot say we can offer better than the US Marshalls if the FBI gets involved and they look after her. And that isn't a betrayal of what you promised. You promised to keep her safe. Did you promise how you'd go about doin' that?"

He was *genius*.

"No," I replied.

"Okay, then, if it was me, I'd give it to her. Go in her room. Say she's been here awhile and maybe it's time to talk. Tell her it'd be good to get it out. Share it with somebody."

"Big Petey?" I whispered.

"Right here, Di."

"Can I tell you something?"

His face got scary again, before it turned tender.

"I know, love," he said so gently, my nose started stinging with threatening tears.

They'd all figured it out, why I'd lost my mind and got involved with this mess.

All of them had.

I didn't mind. I wanted them to understand and not think I was a harebrained idiot.

And it was nice not to have that in the way and know they were already handling me with care, so I didn't have to worry they would.

"Should I tell her?" I asked.

"I think yes. If you got it in you to share, I think she feels very alone and that'll make her feel less of that."

I nodded.

"Go now. Get it done. Let's see where she's at so we know how big a job we got ahead of us."

I nodded again, pushed out of the couch and headed to Suzette's room.

I didn't know if Hugger was a light sleeper and I didn't want to wake him if he was. I also didn't want to invade Suzette's privacy.

So I tried to strike a happy medium, opened the door, stuck my head in, words of greeting on the tip of my tongue.

They died before they were formed when I saw her quickly drop her hand with her phone in it and tuck it under her thigh where she was sitting cross-legged on her bed.

And the look of sheer terror on her face made my mouth get dry.

I slipped in and closed the door behind me.

"What was that?" I asked.

Her eyes darted this way and that, like she was trying to form an escape plan.

I came closer. "Suzette, what was that?"

"You're gonna be mad," she said in a small voice.

"I'm not gonna be mad," I assured her.

"I think I need to go someplace else," she informed me.

My heart started beating really hard.

"Like where?"

"Somewhere away from you. Somewhere away from the guys."

I took another step closer. "Are the men frightening you?"

She shook her head and did it hard, her face beginning to crumble. "No. No. They did at first, but they're all real nice."

Cautiously, I sat on the side of her bed. "Talk to me, Suzette. What's happening?"

Her face finished crumbling and she dropped it into her hand.

God.

"Can I touch you?" I asked.

She nodded her head but didn't take it out of her hand.

I scooched closer, and careful of her injured arm, I drew her into both of mine.

She still didn't pull her face out of her hand as she cried into my T-shirt. She cried quiet, but there were big gulps and body heaves to share how hard she was doing it.

I let her have at it, and it lasted a really long time.

When it started to let up, I whispered, "Stay here. I'm gonna get some Kleenex."

I shot out of the room, hit the laundry/storage area that was on the other side of the hall, nabbed a new box of tissues, and hauled ass back.

I tore off the cardboard opening, yanked out about five and handed them to her after I sat back on the bed.

She was still weeping but she wiped her eyes.

I handed her more and she blew her nose.

"Feel better?" I asked softly.

"N-no."

Of course not.

Stupid question, Diana!

"I mean in the now."

"No!" she cried, and I jumped at the force of it.

I'd never heard her be loud at all.

"He's gonna hurt them. He's gonna hurt. He's gonna hurt *me*."

Oh, poor Suzette, sitting in this room, stewing in that fear.

"You're safe here," I promised.

"No I'm not. He knows them. *He knows them* and he *wants* to hurt them."

My blood ran cold.

"He wants to hurt who?"

"H-hugger. And Eight and Muzzle and even B-b-big Petey!"

"How do you know that?"

She yanked the phone out from under her thigh and stated, "Because when I got away, I stole his phone. He talks to me. He tells me what he's gonna do if I don't come back to him. And I just want him to do it, Diana. Go back to him. I'm so tired. So tired of...of...of *everything*. And I can't let him hurt you or...or...*the guys*."

Dang, crap, *shit*.

"I need you to give me that phone, Suzette. And then I need to give it to Detective Scott."

"I need a phone so you can get in touch with me."

"I'll get you another one. I don't want you to use his anymore and he shouldn't have any communication with you. Not any at all. And I think it's important that the police have that phone."

That seemed to stun her.

"You'll get me a phone?"

"Yes. Like you said, we need to talk."

"But phones are expensive."

I forced a smile on my face. "I can't promise to get you the latest and greatest. But you'll be able to call, text, and download some phone games."

She hesitated a second, then handed over Imran Babić's phone.

I felt dirty just touching it.

"You know the code?" I asked.

She nodded. "I saw him put it in. He wasn't being careful because he...he...well, he thought I'd passed out."

I flinched for her.

"I changed it though," she went on. "It's two, two, three, two."

"Got it. I'll be back again."

"Okay."

I left her and nearly ran into Hugger in the hall.

He'd heard her *No!* and was loitering outside Suzette's door.

"Okay?" he asked in a growl.

I shook my head, grabbed his hand and dragged him to the living room.

Big Petey was alert and sitting on the edge of the couch.

He'd heard the *No!* too.

He stood when I let Hugger go and headed right to him.

I handed him the phone.

"That's Imran Babić's phone. She stole it."

"Jesus," he murmured.

"Christ," I heard Hugger say behind me.

I ran to the kitchen, opened my junk drawer and found Detective Scott's card tucked right where I left it. I nabbed it and dashed back to Big Petey.

"Can you call Detective Scott? Tell him we have Babić's phone." I handed him the card.

"Will do."

"The code is two, two, three, two," I shared. "And Big Petey, he's been communicating with her. Threatening her, me, us."

"Motherfucker," he gritted.

Hugger said nothing, but I felt the wall of anger coming from him slamming into me.

"I gotta get back to her," I said to them both.

"Go," Big Petey urged.

I ran back to Suzette's room and went right in.

She was up against the headboard, hugging a pillow to her chest, her good arm folded around her calves, curled into herself, still terrified, clearly having taken that time to convince herself she'd done wrong.

I sat back down on the bed.

And I made a scary decision.

But I sensed I had an in.

And I was going to take it.

"I know your name isn't Suzette," I told her.

She winced and curled deeper into herself.

"I'm not mad about that either," I assured her. "I'm not mad about anything, except what was done to you. You were protecting yourself."

"I don't want them to find my parents."

"Who don't you want to find your parents? Did that man threaten them too?"

"No, not him. The police. I don't want them to tell my folks where I am."

Oh boy.

"Do you wanna say why?" I asked.

"Because I got mad at them and took off. It was stupid. And he lied to me. And it was...it was just so, *so* stupid."

Oh, this sweet girl.

"What's your name?"

"Madison," she whispered.

The tears hit my eyes. "Heya, Madison."

The tears hit hers before she tossed the pillow aside and threw herself in my arms.

I held her, stroked her hair, and cried with her this time.

Maybe she'd used up most of hers, but she stopped before I did, so I forced myself to do the same.

I held her close even as I reached for the Kleenex. We both mopped up and then I settled us against the headboard, holding her to my side, keeping the tissues at hand.

And I asked, "You wanna tell me?"

She rested her head against my shoulder, and it was the most precious weight I'd ever born.

And then she said, "Yeah."

I closed my eyes in relief.

And Madison told me.

Big Petey

Hugger was prowling the area between the living room and kitchen like a caged animal.

Detective Rayne Scott was sitting on the edge of the seat of one of Diana's armchairs, elbows to his knees, evidence bag with Babić's phone in it dangling from his fingers. His attention alternated between Hugger and the wall beyond, which was where Diana and Suzette were.

Big Petey had never thought much about cops until Tack brought a few into the Chaos inner circle. Not the brotherhood, but they were as close as that could get without a patch.

Normally, if cops stayed out of his way, he stayed out of theirs.

But he respected Mitch and Brock unreservedly.

He recognized Rayne Scott was of the Mitch Lawson/Brock Lucas bent. And not simply because the sumabitch was tall, dark and a damn fine-lookin' man.

He was no nonsense. Alert. Attentive. Concerned about the state of play in Suzette's room. And being there on a Sunday morning, obviously dedicated to the job.

Hugger stopped moving abruptly and stared down the hall. So Pete got to his feet, noticing not for the first time the dry heat of Phoenix was good for his old joints. Denver was arid too, but the cold could creep in. His body felt a full five years younger down there in the desert.

Diana showed from the mouth of the hall and went right to Hugger.

And Pete went still when Hug claimed Diana immediately by wrapping a hand around the side of her neck and dipping down to get nose to nose with her.

"You," he grunted.

She understood that word and whispered, "I'm okay."

Scott got close, so Pete did too.

Hug got out of her face and she looked to Scott.

"Her name is Madison O'Keefe. She says she's nineteen years old. She's from Lubbock, Texas. She was in school to do manis and pedis. She'd met a guy online her parents had a bad feeling about. Turns out they were right. They argued about him more than once, but the last one was really bad. She packed a bag and went to him. He took off with her, and when she expressed concern about where they were going, which was crossing over the state line to New Mexico, things went downhill."

"Damn it," Scott muttered. "She didn't mention any of this when we interviewed her at the hospital."

Pete watched as Hugger slid his hand down her back until his arm was wrapped around her waist. He then fit her right to his side, and by damn, she looked purpose-built to be right there.

This move could have knocked Pete over with a feather.

Until yesterday, Pete didn't know if he'd seen Hugger touch another human being, outside horsing around with the kids. When he was with Rider, Cutter, Nash, Playboy, Wren, Princess, Travis, Clementine, Wyatt, Raven...any of them, he was a different man.

With them, he was the man he was with Diana.

He was a man who had a life that he thought was worth living.

"He essentially sold her to Babić's boys," Diana continued, yanking Pete right out of his thoughts. "And one of the reasons she knew who Babić was is because the men who bought her said, 'Hands off. Babić always gets first crack.'"

Pete ground his teeth, he heard Hugger growl, and he saw Scott's eyes turn to slits.

"She struggled to get away at one point, and they laughed at her," Diana kept at it. "Told her half the police were on Mr. Babić's payroll, so if she went to them, they'd bring her right back."

"I'm hopin' that was bullshit to make her think she's fucked no matter what," Pete remarked to Scott.

"It's bullshit," Scott gritted.

Pete studied him carefully, and damn, he hoped the man spoke truth.

"That's what I told her," Diana said. "I think I got her ready to open up to you more. But she's had enough for today." She looked up to Hugger. "I'm going to call off work tomorrow. Give her a break for the rest of today, then I hope maybe I can talk her into going in to do a formal interview that's a lot more thorough."

While she said this, Scott was on his phone.

When she was done saying this, Scott turned his phone their way and said, "Her parents reported her missing a month ago."

And there it was, a picture of Madison next to a headline: LOCAL LUBBOCK WOMAN REPORTED MISSING.

"They're probably scared out of their brains," Pete remarked.

"Can I read that?" Diana asked. Scott offered, and she took the cell, scanned the article and her eyes got bright with tears. "They're scared out of their brains," she whispered. She returned the phone to Scott, went to her own, and had head bent to it as she walked back down the hall saying, "I'll be back."

When she disappeared behind Madison's door, Pete asked, "What we got here?"

"Babić gets up to a lot of shitty stuff," Scott said. "But we've never heard of him being into trafficking."

"That something you'd know?" Big Petey asked.

Scott nodded. "We've been dedicating a lot of resources to this guy. Though, I'm sure it won't surprise you, he has a vested interest in us not learning all we need to know. Then Madison showed and not long later, so did the Feds. They sometimes don't cooperate great with the locals, but it came clear this was part of what they were investigating. Being honest with you, it shocked the shit out of me. There's not even a rumor of it being part of Babić's operations."

"That phone gonna help at all?" Pete queried.

A slow smile spread on Scott's face. "Technically, it's stolen property. Officially, it was stolen by the victim after the commission of a violent felony, so it's evidence in a rape case, and yeah, I figure we'll find some interesting things in there."

"He's been fuckin' with her head something bad," Pete reminded

Scott of what he'd shared after the man arrived. "She hasn't replied, but he's been repeatedly issuing threats against a whole slew of people she might give a shit about, including herself, for over a week. That a felony?"

"All I know is, when it gets to trial, it's not gonna play well with a jury."

Pete reckoned he was very right. If he was on a jury and he saw those texts, he'd vote to send the man so far down the river, he'd never find his way back.

They all looked down the hall to see Diana had her head and hand out of Madison's door and she was beckoning to Hugger.

Hug prowled in that direction.

Pete and Scott watched as they had a low conversation. Hugger nodded. Diana disappeared behind the door. Hugger came back to them.

"Madison lost it again," he told them both, but to Scott he said, "She wants to know if you'll call her parents and let them know she's okay."

Being a cop and probably not getting to share good news too often, Scott was all over that.

"Fuck yeah, I will. Does Madison want to speak to them?"

"Di hasn't gotten that far," Hugger told him. "But she wants them to know right away."

Scott nodded, hit a button on his phone and shifted from their huddle.

Pete heard him say to someone, "Yeah, need you to get me Lubbock PD. Texas. And the name of whoever is dealing with a missing woman named Madison O'Keefe."

Big Petey got closer to Hugger.

"Those threats, brother…" He let that trail, because Hugger had also read them.

"I wanna be here in case Di comes out. Can you call Rush with the update?" Hugger asked.

"You got it."

Hugger turned his gaze to the hall.

Pete went to the balcony.

He filled in Rush, who told them to stay the course. Dutch, Core and Linus had hit Phoenix, and Coe and Jag were heading down that day.

Rush also shared, as they suspected, Resurrection wanted to break off with Chaos to do their thing, leaving Chaos on security for Diana, Madison and Nolan Armitage.

"Kinda feel like letting them have at it," Rush said. "We're clean and clear, and they're good at that shit."

Pete didn't disagree.

By the time he was off the phone with Rush, he'd started to head back inside when he saw Diana return, going right to Hugger. She fit herself into his side that time, but he made the way clear for it and didn't hesitate to curve an arm around to hold her there.

This meant Big Petey moved back to the railing and returned his attention to his phone.

He engaged the cell.

Because it was time.

Long since time.

So he called Tack.

11

WORTH THE WAIT

Diana

"Come in."

Early afternoon, I opened Madison's door to see her still in bed, curled around a pillow, but this time she was on her side, and instead of a self-comforting-because-I'm-terrified pose, it just seemed to be a self-comforting-because-my-shit-is-real pose.

But when I walked in, she moved, scooching and pushing up with some difficulty due to her arm still in a sling, so she was sitting against one side of the headboard, an invitation for me to take the other.

I did, curling onto a hip toward her.

She curled toward me.

"Hanging in there?" I asked.

She nodded.

"Just so you know, I told Big Petey there's an Apple store essentially across the street. I also let slip you wanted a phone. Therefore, I think we both aren't all that surprised he went right out to jump on his bike to go get you a phone. So, warning, it'll probably have all the bells and whistles."

Her face got soft and her lips curled up just a little.

"He's a nice man," she whispered.

I thought about everything I'd learned about Big Petey in our short acquaintance, particularly our conversation about my mom.

Then I responded with feeling, "Yes, he is."

Her face changed when she noted, "Hugger's nice too."

Oh crap.

Did she notice?

Right, how could she *not* notice, we were cuddled up for two movies.

"Yeah, they all are," I replied, going for blithe.

I knew I failed at blithe with what she said next.

"But I think you think he's the nicest of all of them," she stated, and it took me a second, but then I realized she might be teasing me.

Or it might be something else.

To be safe, I went with the something else.

"We were just sitting close together because there wasn't a lot of room."

It was then, Madison shocked the heck out of me when she laughed, just a little, and returned, "No you weren't. I see how you look at him."

Oh crap!

Was I that obvious?

Oh crap again, was that upsetting for her?

"Are we making you uncomfortable?"

She appeared to be thinking about that before she shrugged. "No. He's nice and he's all big and strong and tough, and you're all pretty and soft and elegant. You wouldn't normally put you two together, but it's cute."

I was surprised. Well, not the opposites attract part, that was obvious, another part.

"You think I'm elegant?"

"Well...yeah. You wear fancy shoes every day to work."

Okay then. If that was the criteria, that certainly was me.

"It's a little weird, with the timing and all that, but I like him, and he likes me. That said, we'll try not to be—" I began.

"I crashed your life, Diana," she said in a small voice. "Don't let me get in the way of it."

I inched just a little closer and replied softly, "You didn't crash my life, Madison. I invited you here. Then I found out you're awesome, and I'm really glad you trusted me to look after you."

Her face scrunched, not like she was going to cry again, like she didn't believe my words.

"I really am," I asserted.

"I'm a pain in your behind."

"You are not," I stated firmly.

She gave me a look of such disbelief, I started laughing.

"Right, well, we haven't exactly been tiptoeing through the tulips," I allowed. "But still, I'm glad to know you and it means a lot to me you're letting me help you out."

She tipped her head to the side, her blue eyes got cloudy, and she whispered, "It happened to you too."

I bent my neck so my face was closer to hers, and I whispered in return, "Not as bad, not even close, but yeah, honey. It happened to me too."

She was still whispering when she said, "I'm sorry, Diana."

"I'm sorry about you."

"We girls, we gotta be sorry a lot, don't we?"

This was a sad lesson of life, and I hated we both had to learn it.

"Yeah," I agreed. "We have to be strong a lot too, and strong comes in many ways, and I'm afraid I'm going to have to tax yours just a little bit more because I have one more tough thing to give you before we let it go and try to enjoy the rest of our Sunday."

"Di—"

I did it fast so it would be over.

"Detective Scott talked to your parents. He says they were wild with relief to hear you're okay and they want to talk to you."

That was a mini lie.

He didn't use the words "wild with relief," those were mine. He also said her mother burst into tears and her dad had to end the first call and phone back, because he was choking up too.

I wasn't going to tell her that, though.

The other thing that made my statement a mini lie was they did want to talk to her, but they also wanted to see her, and they were so intent on doing that, they reported to Detective Scott they'd be on the first flight to Phoenix.

But we'd deal with that tomorrow.

She shook her head and inched back. "I'm not ready for that."

As I'd guessed.

"I told him that was probably your response. I just want you to know what's going on." Or most of it.

"Okay," she muttered.

"Okay," I said. "Now, you wanna come out and maybe have some lunch?"

"I've been crying so much and doing that always takes it out of me. I think I need to doze for a little bit."

Tears healed. Rest healed. Talking healed. And with their response to finding where their daughter was, I was hoping seeing her family would assist in healing too.

This reminded me Hugger needed to do the same. His nap hadn't even lasted an hour.

We'd wait for Big Petey to get back from the Apple store for that.

Funny how Madison and I had been going it alone for a while, and now, even after only a few days, it didn't feel right not having the guys around.

But the simple matter of it was, it didn't.

"I'll come out later, all right?" she asked.

"Anything you need, honey," I answered. "Before I go, can I hug you?"

She looked surprised at the question then she nodded and pitched toward me.

I wrapped my arms around her and gave her a careful, but tight squeeze.

I was about to let her go when she said into my ear, "I'm glad I trusted you too."

Of course, this meant I gave her another tight squeeze.

I let her go, got off the bed and was halfway to the door when she called, "Di?"

I turned. "Right here."

She hesitated before she shared, "There's more I haven't told you."

I knew there was, and she might be a tiny thing, but she *was* strong. She was a total warrior.

But enough was enough for one day. I suspected even Alexander the Great took chill time.

That wasn't my choice, however.

"Do you want to do that now?" I offered.

"I don't think..." There was a long pause before she finished, "Today has been a lot."

"It has, and I'll take this opportunity to share that what you have is yours to give. There's no rush. Since it's yours, you can give it when you want."

She sagged with relief. "Thanks, Di."

I smiled at her. "Rest. Anything special you want for dinner?"

"Are the guys coming over again?"

"Do you want them to?"

"I feel...safe when they're here. And things seem normal."

So she felt the same as me.

Her head jerked. "Not that I didn't feel safe when it was just us two."

I laughed. "Gotta say, babe, I feel a lot safer with a bunch of bikers stomping around in their motorcycle boots too."

That bought me a kinda smile, I returned it with a not-kinda smile.

"Can we have pizza?" she asked.

"We can have whatever you want. What's your favorite kind?"

"Pepperoni."

"You want homemade, or someone else to make it for us and deliver it?"

"I like cooking with you."

I was going to have to send Big Petey to the store again.

I didn't figure he'd mind.

"I'll get on that. You get on dozing."

"Okay, Di."

I smiled at her again and left her room.

When I got to the living room, Hugger pulled his big, tall frame out of the couch.

I liked that frame. I liked the intent look in his brown eyes as they watched me walk into the room, as if he could check the state of my mental health through vision. I liked the wild of his hair and the wild of his beard.

Okay, official, I just liked him.

I went to him and was about to hug him when I remembered he said he wasn't affectionate and didn't like touch.

I hadn't had the time to turn that over in my head, especially because, since yesterday at the tennis courts, he'd been touching me a lot. But now that I was turning it over in my head, it didn't make me happy.

I'd never thought about that when it came to me, and I guessed I wasn't touchy either. At least not over the top.

But I did like physical touch with my guy when I had one, and not just the sexual kind. And I couldn't say I shied away from it with other people, I just wasn't overly demonstrative.

But if Hugger didn't like it, then I'd have to deal with it.

Somehow.

So I just got close and shared, "She's not ready to talk to her parents. She wants to rest after letting out all that emotion, and I don't blame her. She also wants the guys to come over for pepperoni pizza tonight."

"She *wants* the guys to come over?" Hugger asked, not hiding his surprise.

"She says she feels safer around them."

His lips in his beard thinned before he said, "Probably shouldn't be surprised about that."

"And she likes that life feels 'normal' when they're around."

"Then I'll make a call and get their asses here," Hugger stated.

Jeez, this guy was so awesome.

"I'm going to have to send someone out for more groceries," I muttered.

"Make a list. I'll take off when Pete gets back."

Hmm.

This was another thing with Hugger.

When we were cleaning yesterday, he commandeered the vacuum and had at it, and he didn't even have to be asked to take out the trash. No hiding on the balcony or pretending to fiddle with a faucet that wasn't actually leaking to get out of doing housework.

I hadn't thought about that at the time, either.

But now that I was, although the not touchy or affectionate thing was in the con column on the pros and cons list of Do I Want to Explore This with Hugger, that was definitely a pro.

Neither of my long-term boyfriends helped out around the house, and I'd lived with both of them. There were excuses—tee times, ball-games, trips to Lowe's to pick up stuff to fix things I wasn't sure were broken, and when they pitched in, they did a shitty job at it.

When I heard the term "weaponized incompetence" it rang the top bell for me with both of them.

Hugger didn't just run the vacuum here and there to make a show of doing something, he actually *vacuumed*.

And he tidied the couch every morning, putting the toss pillows back like I liked them and everything (and I didn't have to ask him to do that either).

Now, he was offering to go to the store, and it was partly because I couldn't, but I was thinking it was mostly because that was Hugger.

Yes, this was definitely a pro.

Even so.

"I could also order them online so Pete doesn't have to go back out," I suggested. "You need to try to catch more sleep."

"We'll talk about it when Big Petey gets back."

I agreed on a nod.

"Now let's talk about you. How are you doin' with all of this?" he asked.

"I'm thrilled to pieces she cried. I'm thrilled to pieces she got the chance to get that emotion out, I think that will help start the healing, and I don't think she's been anywhere near doing that. I'm further thrilled to pieces her parents know she's okay, or at least she's still of this world and they know where she is. I'm also thrilled this is moving forward, she obviously trusts me and she feels safe with the guys being around. Last, I'm thrilled to the absolute beyond I know her name."

"Yeah," he murmured, then asked, "Is it fucked that I'm glad she's nineteen and not seventeen? I mean, it's totally heinous, what was done to her, no matter her age. That's not what I'm sayin'. But—"

I shook my head and really wanted to touch him, since he appeared so awkward, saying what he was saying, and it was sweet and cute, but no one liked to feel awkward.

"No," I cut him off. "I think back to when I was seventeen and when I was nineteen, which was when my incident happened to me, and I can say it would have been way harder to deal if it happened earlier."

His voice was deeper, rougher when he asked quietly, "You were nineteen?"

"Mm-hmm,"

His lips thinned again and there was a scary air charging out of him, and again, I really wanted to touch him.

"I'm okay, Hugger. And I kneed him in the balls before it got too far, and when he was dealing with that, I punched him in the dick so I could be sure to get away."

Hugger did a slow blink. "You punched him in the dick?"

"Well, yeah. I had to make sure he was incapacitated when I ran to get the RA."

Abruptly, his hand darted out, caught me at the back of my head and slammed me face first into his wide chest.

That chest was shaking, and so was his voice when he said, "That's my girl. Don't leave a job half-finished."

I couldn't believe it, considering the subject matter, but I was laughing too.

And it felt nice he called me "my girl," not to mention he was touching me.

He one-upped his own self when he pulled me onto the couch, curling me into his arms and holding me close.

"You been through a lot this morning too," he remarked.

I loved he understood that.

Still.

"Really, I'm okay."

I snuggled deeper anyway, because if my chances at this kind of time with Hugger were going to be limited, I was going to take full advantage of them when I had them.

"You don't always gotta be going hell bent for leather to take care of everyone, Di," he stated. "You can take some time for yourself too."

"Well, we need to talk about that, because not only does Dad want me to come over for dinner on Wednesday, he's invited you too, and warning, this is so he can size you up, judge you and find you lacking."

Hugger did a masculine eye roll at that, and if you don't know what that is, it's mostly a side-eye, but his eyeballs were aimed upward too.

It was kinda funny and kinda hot.

I didn't have time for either. I had to smack him with the fullness of honesty about Dad.

"I will share, this will be about you being a biker. But it wouldn't matter if you weren't, he wouldn't like you. He never liked any of my boyfriends."

"Dads have a knack for bein' like that," he said. "Don't know if I'll win him over. Do know, I don't care if I do. The only person who's gotta like me is you."

I'd been resting my head on his shoulder, but I lifted it to look at him.

"You're going?"

"Yeah, because I don't want you alone with your dad this first visit when he's been a dick to you in the past."

Man, he was just *so sweet*.

"And yeah, because I wanna make sure you're safe in other ways too," he concluded.

Totally another pro for Hugger.

All the same.

"I don't really want to eat dinner with Dad being a dick to you."

"I got tough skin, Di. Don't worry about me."

I wanted to know more about why he had to have tough skin, but I didn't get into that. We were getting to know each other, but we didn't have to do it all in one day.

"My friend Bernie also wants me to go out to cocktails on Friday."

"We can arrange that too."

"Would you like to come to that?"

His lips tipped up and he replied, "Not a cocktail guy, babe."

No surprise.

"And feel it'd be more of a trial by fire to pitch up with your friends than with your dad."

He was right about that.

My friends weren't judgy, but we didn't accept just any pretty face when it came to who we were dating.

"They know about Madison?" Hugger asked.

"No."

"They know about you?" he asked more gently.

"Yeah."

"You wanna tell me why you didn't tell them about Madison?"

"Because I didn't want them to talk me out of doing something totally insane."

He chuckled, and it sounded and felt nice.

"So I can say yes to Dad and Bernie," I summed up.

"Yeah."

"And now I need to make another list. So I need to know what your favorite pizza is."

He answered readily. "Not a fan of soggy onions, and if there's a pizza in this house with pineapple on it, I'll throw it over your balcony."

I started laughing.

Through my laughter, he went on, "Other than that, I'll eat anything. But if I was ordering just for myself, it'd be sausage and mushroom."

"So pepperoni for Madison and sausage and mushroom for you."

He gave me a squeeze. "And what about you?"

"What's my favorite pizza?"

"Yeah, I wanna know that. But I also want you putting your favorites on the list. Gonna repeat, it isn't all about everyone else all the time."

"I fear you might be getting the wrong idea about me, my man."

Me saying "my man" got me another squeeze, even if I didn't mean it that way.

I liked what that squeeze meant, though.

"I'm not always this selfless," I warned him.

"We'll see," he muttered.

"I'm really not," I stressed.

"Okay, I believe you," he openly lied.

I smiled at him.

His eyes dropped to my mouth and I saw up close how they heated.

"Prettiest smile I've seen," he murmured.

Ohmigod!

Nice!

"You think it's safe to make out?" I asked.

His eyes came to mine, and now I saw regret.

"No," he answered.

"Just a little?" I pushed.

That was when I saw close-up his eyes glimmered with humor.

"You think after that kiss this morning we could make out 'just a little?' It wasn't easy to stop then. Now that I know how good it is havin' that mouth, not sure that's in the cards."

I frowned as I was forced to concede, "I see your point."

He chuckled again, I liked the feel and sound of it again, so I took a chance and snuggled closer.

His arms tightened even as he noted, "You got a list to make."

"Yeah," I mumbled.

"We can order pizza, Di."

"Madison likes to cook with me."

His body started shaking and it took me a bit to realize he was laughing.

"What's funny?" I asked.

"Tell me again how you're not selfless all the time."

I smacked his chest.

He caught my wrist, lifted it to his mouth, and I felt the brush of his whiskers along with the softness of his lips when he touched them on the inside.

And the all-over happy wiggles were back with a vengeance, because not only feeling that, but watching him do it was a massive turn-on.

"Go get the pad and bring it back," he ordered. "We'll do a big-ass shop. Make a menu or somethin', so you're not always havin' to write out lists, and we're not always havin' to leave you with only one man on you when we go to the store."

I thought this was a great idea, so I broke from his hold and zipped to the kitchen to get my pad and a pen.

When I returned, for a second I wasn't sure what to do. Since he instigated cuddling, could I go back to that? Or did I need to give him space?

Hugger decided for me by taking my hand and tugging me to the couch where I was close.

"Let's make hot fudge sundaes tonight for dessert," he suggested.

"I'm so in love with that idea, I could cry."

Now those fabulous brown eyes were twinkling.

"You're a nut," he joked (though, as we all knew, there was some truth to that).

"Not a bad one, though," I said.

"No, baby," he whispered, looking right in my eyes. "Not even a little bit."

God, I *needed* to kiss him.

"Are you sure we can't make out?"

My heart soared when he dipped in and touched his lips to mine.

Then he pulled back.

And I narrowed my eyes at him.

"Tease," I accused.

"Whatever," he replied. "Put ice cream on the list. And a jar of hot fudge, a can of whipped cream, not that Cool Whip stuff, nuts and cherries."

"You're hog wild when it comes to sundaes," I noted with deep approval.

"We could say I'm an aficionado."

Now he was totally teasing, and it was totally sweet, so I laughed out loud.

Hugger curled an arm around my shoulders, tucked me close and ordered, "Woman. List."

I got down to scribbling.

Hugger helped with menu selections.

Big Petey came back with Madison's phone, and we decided he'd go to the store because he didn't have any problem taking Baby Shark and neither of their bikes could cart that amount of groceries.

Hugger stayed with me, chilling, chatting and starting up *My Cat from Hell* episodes until Big Petey got back with the groceries. He helped put away (another big one for the pro side) before he returned to my room to try another nap.

Madison came out not much later, and was so happy to have a phone, she actually gave Big Petey a hug.

He wrapped her close in his arms, looked over her head and met my eyes.

Mine were wet.

And his were too.

PIZZA, hot fudge sundaes, copious beer and wine consumed, the men were gone, Big Petey going with them.

Madison had turned in early, probably still drained from her emotional day (though, I had the sneaking suspicion she was also giving me time alone with Hugger).

This I was taking, not cuddling on the couch.

Oh no.

We were both stretched out on it, Hugger to the back, me along his front, our arms around each other and our legs a little tangled, totally in make-out position (and more), just without the making-out part.

He had a weird way of not being affectionate and touchy.

I wasn't going to say a danged thing.

As noted, we were not snogging, but Hugger was busy inscribing a number of pros on the Do I Want to Explore This with Hugger List.

These included being hella skilled with delivering a butterfly kiss (I mean...*yum*), having awesome powers using his hands to smooth and sooth and not get a girl hot and bothered (or not *too* hot and bothered, I was both just being so close to him, feeling his warmth, smelling his scent, having his attention), and playing footsie.

Yes!

Playing footsie.

See?

He was totally cute under all that big, strong, burly, whiskered *man*.

"So do you have a minimum rating on the hotness scale to allow bikers into your brotherhood?" I asked.

He blinked once, fast, and chuckling, asked back, "What?"

"Dutch is amazing-looking."

Yes, I'd met Dutch.

And Eight had dragged Core and Linus along with the rest of them, so my table was so full, I'd had to borrow chairs from my neighbor. Although Madison didn't natter away with all the boys, in her cocoon with me, Pete, Hugger, Eight and Muzzle at one end of the table, she did open up.

Core was Hollywood handsome. Linus not far away from that, but he was younger and hadn't grown into his good looks yet, that being, exuding the confidence that Core did.

And Dutch was what I said.

Amazing.

There was just something really beautiful in his eyes, like a universal empathy with all the woes a human could face. It was a sight to behold.

"You think Dutch is hot?" Hugger asked, like he thought Dutch was the dictionary definition of fugly.

"You don't?"

"Can say we don't have a minimum rating because we don't notice that shit."

"It's hard to miss. I mean, I'm scared to meet Jagger and Roscoe when they get here. My retinas might burn out."

Another chuckle and, "Get ready. Jagger is Dutch's younger brother. You think Dutch is hot, they look alike, so there you go. I don't got a vagina, so no clue what women think of Coe. Though, can say he's got no problem with getting himself some."

"I'll let you know when I meet him," I offered.

"I'll be waitin' with bated breath for that, babe," he teased.

"So Dutch is very married, considering how big and shiny his wedding band is," I noted as a prompt to get him talking about his brothers.

"Yeah, Georgie. She's the shit. Jag's hitched too, to Archie. She's also the shit, but in a different way. Georgie is a journalist. Archie owns her own store, and I don't shop, but it's pretty kickass."

"Two brothers are married to two women with men's names?"

"It just happened that way."

A good reminder that life could offer some fun surprises sometimes.

"Dutch seems..." I didn't know how to describe it. "Like he's super-tuned into what's going on. Almost more than Big Petey is with his age and experience and wisdom."

"Dutch's dad was murdered when he was a little kid."

My body froze and I stared.

"I met his dad when I was a lot younger," Hugger continued. "Too young to be able to form an impression outside of knowing I dug him. He liked kids."

"Ugh. I hate that for Dutch."

"You experience something like that, watch your mom grieve your dad's death for two decades, it informs you on tragedy. We do what we do with Resurrection in part because of Dutch. Men were gettin' antsy, that was a thing, but Dutch knew the Club just as good as any brother who'd had their patch for decades. He was restless, others were too. Now we wade in, if we want."

"Knew the Club?"

He rolled to his back, pulling me partly on him and up, so we were face-to-face.

"Our president, Rush's old lady, Rebel, she's a movie director. She made a documentary about Chaos." He took a beat before he concluded, "I think you should watch it, Di."

Oh, I was so totally doing that.

"How cool," I said.

"We used to be outlaws."

Hmm.

I wasn't so sure about that.

"What does that mean?" I queried carefully.

"Ran guns. Ran security for shipments of illegal shit. Ran a stable of whores. My mom was one of Chaos's girls."

Holy crap!

"Harlan, I...that doesn't..." Ulk! "Whoa."

"Yup," he agreed with my stunned stammering.

"That isn't a problem for you?"

"Most the brothers didn't want to be messed up with that shit. They got out. They took care of all of their girls when they did, at least they did that as best they could. Took 'em a while to extricate themselves, and it was dangerous, but they did it. By the time I was with the Club, they were clean."

I was beginning to get it.

"But they used to be adrenaline junkies, and to get a fix of that, you all hooked up with Resurrection."

"Not exactly," he replied. "In making the statement they were no longer outlaw, Resurrection went outlaw the other way, becoming vigilantes."

Ummmmmmmmm...

Holy *crap*!

Though, this shouldn't surprise me too much, considering Hugger and Big Petey showing up to do what they were doing for me and Madison.

Nonetheless, providing security for a couple of chicks and looking into why some criminal madman had targeted your club was a lot different than being a vigilante.

"Not what you're thinkin'," Hugger told me. "We just kept our patch clean. That's it. No drugs, prostitutes, any a' that shit around Ride, our store and the garage we run. We ran out of enemies, we stopped doin' that, and now we leave it to the cops. That said, anything like that gets close to the store, we shut it down. But we minimized our patch to a couple a' blocks around the store, not miles around it."

"Right."

He was studying me closely while advising, "You need to watch the documentary."

"I totally do. Wanna watch it now?"

He sounded surprised when he asked, "You wanna watch it with me?"

"Are you in it?"

"No."

"Do you not want to watch it with me?"

"No, actually"—he tucked some hair behind my ear (and he was skilled at that too, I knew, considering the charge of electricity that sizzled down the side of my neck when he did it)—"that'd be cool."

"Want me to make some popcorn?"

"Babe, you made four pizzas, a huge-ass Caesar, and we went through two gallons when we made the sundaes. You can put down some popcorn?"

"Is that a no?" I asked testily, never a fan of anyone commenting on what I ate (we could just say, Dad did that a lot), and definitely not a man I liked doing it.

"No, it's not a no. I'm just impressed."

I relaxed and grinned at him.

"I'll get a brew and top up your wine, you deal with the popcorn," he said.

"Do you want microwave or oil popped?"

"You choose."

"Oil popped with melted butter and tons of salt."

Hugger slid his hands up my spine, murmuring, "Perfect."

Though, the way he was looking at me gave me the sense that word had two meanings.

And damn, that felt good.

Sadly, it didn't last long because Hugger curled up, taking me with him, and then we were on our feet.

We both headed to the kitchen.

He helped by melting the butter (another pro for the Do I Want to Explore This with Hugger List).

We cued up the movie and sat snuggled together with the popcorn bowl between us, watching the documentary of his Club that I would have thought was kickass even if it wasn't about Chaos.

This Rebel chick had some serious chops as a filmmaker.

I couldn't say some of it wasn't scary, it was.

I could say I loved that Hugger was so open about it, not hiding anything, but also that the Club had made it to the other side.

Oh, and Dutch's dad was just as amazing as he was, and that wasn't just his looks. The man had a beautiful smile and clearly loved his wife, kids and brothers, something that made me sad, but I was glad he'd created two sons to carry on that goodness before he was lost to the world.

When the movie was over, it was late, and after a couple of lip brushes and some squeezes, Hugger sent me to my bed.

It was on the tip of my tongue to offer for him to come with me. Not jumping too far too fast, but he could sleep over the covers, me under them, and he'd get better rest.

I didn't offer because, after butterfly kisses and footsie and popcorn, and the brutal honesty he shared so openly with that documentary, I didn't need the temptation.

So I went to bed alone without even a mini make out session to see me through.

It sucked.

But honestly, all that Hugger was giving told me he was going to be worth the wait.

12

AIR MATTRESS

Diana

My hip was moving, and I wasn't doing it.

I opened my eyes to early morning sun, turned my head and saw Hugger looming over me.

Well then.

Good morning to me.

"Hey," I whispered.

"Fucks me to wake you, babe, but Scott's been on the phone and shit's going down."

I sat up so fast, I nearly crashed heads with Hugger.

"What's going on?" I asked.

He sat on the side of my bed. "First, Madison's people are at the police station. Probably not a surprise they're being vocal about wanting to see her."

"Crap," I mumbled.

I'd hoped to have at least the morning to break the news to her and talk her into seeing them.

"And Scott told me something else."

All sleep gone, I focused hard on him. "What'd he tell you?"

"That phone is not Imran Babić's."

Wait.

"What?" I asked.

"It's his son's. Esad Babić."

Wait.

"*What?*"

Hugger shook his head. "Don't know, Di. But Scott really wants to talk to Madison."

There's more I haven't told you.

Maybe she didn't mean what I thought she meant with that.

"Di?" Hugger called.

"I don't know what to do with that."

"I don't either, but Scott told me something else."

Fantastic.

"That being?" I asked, even if I wasn't sure I wanted to know.

"There was a call during the time Madison had the phone from a number programmed in as 'Otac,' which apparently means 'father' in Bosnian. The call came in the morning after she showed at the emergency room and lasted fifteen minutes."

"And this means she had the son's phone, but talked to the dad."

"I don't know what it means, honey. I just know Scott told me that call came before the police interviewed her. So shit is now convoluted, because she named Imran Babić as her rapist, and they arrested him for that crime, but she's got his son's phone and shared yesterday it was the phone of the man who assaulted her."

I made a face. "Father/son tag team rapists? Is this guy *that* gross?"

"Again, I don't know, but Scott needs to, so as they investigate this, it doesn't get fucked."

Damn, crap, shit.

I pushed back in bed, reaching for my phone on my nightstand, mumbling, "I'm gonna call Scott."

"You want me to bring you coffee?"

I stared at him while mentally unfurling more of the scroll on which I was writing the pro side of the Do I Want to Explore This with Hugger List.

If you're keeping track, it was only the not-touchy thing that was on the con side, and he kept being touchy, so that was written in pencil.

"Would you?" I asked.

"'Course," he muttered, bent in, touched my forehead with his bristly lips (another pro!) and then he left to get me coffee.

Were all bikers like this?

I really wanted to know.

I tried to decide if brushing my teeth or calling Detective Scott was my top priority and settled on the detective by a narrow margin because morning mouth was icky.

He picked up right away.

"Diana?"

"Hello, Detective Scott."

"As I keep saying, you can call me Rayne."

He had a really nice name to go with a really nice face.

In fact, before Hugger, he was totally my type.

But I bet he didn't vacuum.

"Harlan filled me in," I shared.

"Right."

"So now I need to know what to do with Madison. I mean, can you come to us, where she feels safe? Or should I figure out how to get her to you?"

"Optimal for my purposes, if we can get her to open up, I'd want her in a room where I could get what she says recorded. But if we can get her to open up, I don't care where it happens."

"Gotcha on that. What about her family?"

"That's your call. She's not living in my space. But I'd urge you to make that happen soon. They know what happened to her and they're coming apart at the seams."

Damn, crap, shit.

Hugger came in with my coffee.

"Okay, give me a half an hour, and I'll call you back."

"Appreciated."

"Later."

"'Bye, Diana."

By the time we disconnected, Hugger had handed me my coffee and was sitting again on the side of the bed.

I took a moment to sip and enjoy the view.

"Where we at?" he queried.

"Scott says it'd be better if the interview happened at the station so they can get it on tape. But I think we should let her family come here to see her."

"We?"

I nodded while taking a sip.

"Di, baby, this isn't my house," he told me something I knew.

"We're in this together, aren't we?" I asked.

His lips curved up, taking his beard with them, and I liked that look.

"We are that," he agreed.

I sensed his assent had a double meaning, and since mine did too, I was totally down with that.

"Speaking of my house, how did you sleep?"

"All good."

"Liar, liar, pants on fire."

A sharp, but quiet, bark of laughter escaped him, and I liked that too.

What I didn't like was that it also sounded rough, like he didn't laugh all that much.

With no other choice with all the stuff that was brewing, I had to let that go.

For now.

"Have you talked to Big Petey?" I inquired.

"Called him before you. He's probably on his way by now."

That was good. Madison had definitely bonded with him, and it seemed her gift of the phone cemented that.

"It'd be good you could get her to the station," Hugger remarked. "We can get you there, and you'll be safe there, since I got news from Big Petey that Wash is also in Phoenix. He showed last night. He wants a meet, and we're guessin' that meet means he's gonna try to scrape Chaos off so they can go it alone. We'll take security, and they'll deal with the Babićs."

"Wash?"

"Prez of Resurrection."

Oh.

"They probably should know which Babić they're dealing with," I noted.

"I don't think they care."

Eek!

"Okay, so our plan is, you get the bathroom first while I sip coffee and call my boss to tell her I'm taking a personal day," I stated. "Then I'll do the bathroom thing, I'll wake up Madison, and get her good with her parents coming over, while also getting her good with going in and being re-interviewed by the police."

"Good plan."

"So, nothing much, except moving some minor mountains before eight in the morning."

Hugger smiled. "Yeah, nothing much, except that."

Gulk.

"You got this," Hugger stated before coming right in to press his lips tight to mine.

Coffee and morning breath was a no go for me to offer up for a kiss.

But I'd take a tight press from him any day.

He got up and headed to the bathroom.

I sipped my coffee and scrolled on my phone until I found Annie's number.

And when I hit go, I hit go on making the effort to move a mountain.

***

"THEY'RE GONNA BE REALLY MAD."

The time was imminent, and by that I meant Hugger had gone down to escort Mr. and Mrs. O'Keefe up to see their daughter.

Rayne was with them.

I was with Madison and Big Petey in my living room.

Big Petey was providing support and presence. Madison was not fretting as much as she was freaking.

She'd agreed to this after I told her about the crying and choking up and needing a second phone call because they were so overwhelmed with emotion.

But I could tell she was having second thoughts.

"I don't like how they go, they're out," Big Petey stated.

Madison and I looked to him.

"Hear me, girl?" he asked Madison.

"I caused all this being stupid, Big Petey, and I got myself—"

"Garbage," he cut her off sharply. "You didn't do that first thing to yourself, Maddy, darlin'. Put that shit right outta your head. Now you hear that?"

"Yes, Big Petey," she said quietly.

"They blame you, they'll answer to me before I put them out," Big Petey threatened.

Christ on a cracker, this was killing me, because it felt like I had to fight crying about five hundred times a day.

This time was because I wished my dad had acted like Big Petey after what happened to me.

Madison didn't have a chance to respond to his threat.

We heard the front door open and Big Petey moved to stand in front, and just to the side, of Madison.

Worth a repeat, I really liked these men.

I moved into her, taking her hand.

She held mine tight.

Hugger rounded the wall to the dining room first.

He stepped to the side and two people came in after him.

It was then I saw Madison was a carbon copy of her mom. She was a wee thing with lots of blonde hair and big blue eyes.

Her father gave Hugger competition with bulk, though Mr. O'Keefe's was softer (so Hugger won, then again, obvs, he'd win anyway).

Both their eyes were pinging everywhere until they landed on Madison, and then they stopped dead.

I squeezed her hand.

She squeezed mine back.

Rayne came up the rear and halted behind the O'Keefes.

No one said anything, no one even moved.

Until Mr. O'Keefe's guttural "My baby girl" sounded.

Then Mrs. O'Keefe's sob sounded.

And then Madison let me go and flew across the room to her dad.

He wrapped his arms around her in a hug so big, he pulled her off her feet.

Mrs. O'Keefe burrowed in, and he held his daughter aloft even as he let her go with one arm to hold his wife.

Oh yeah.

Totally weeping.

Damn!

Hugger came to me, and the supposedly not affectionate new man in my life pulled me into both of his arms and tucked me to his side.

This group hug lasted a long time and included some murmuring I made a point not to hear.

I was wondering if I should lead everyone to the dining room to give them space right before the group hug came to an end.

"Torture, not knowin' where you were, baby girl," Mr. O'Keefe grunted. And yes, before that, I had no idea anyone could grunt an entire sentence, but he did.

"Daddy, I'm so sorry," Madison wept into his neck.

He gently put her down but didn't let either of his girls go.

Though, he looked confused. "What are you sorry about?"

"I was stupid. You told me—"

"Stop it right now, Madison Renee O'Keefe," Mrs. O'Keefe snapped.

I pushed closer into Hugger.

"Mama—"

"Not another word like that, Maddy," she warned. "Not one more word."

"Okay, Mama," Madison mumbled, though she didn't do it chastened, she just agreed.

Mrs. O'Keefe, who might be diminutive, but I was beginning to sense she was a force to be reckoned with, pulled from her husband's arm, straightened her tidy but pretty blouse and spoke again.

"Now, who are these people who've been lookin' out for our girl?"

Madison tucked herself into her father's side, a father, I noted, who wouldn't have let her go if she tried get away.

She didn't.

"That's Hugger. He keeps us safe all the time, even sleeping on the couch to do it," she introduced. "And that's Big Petey, he bought me a phone yesterday, and donuts." Her voice lowered. "And that's Diana, she rescued me."

I sniffed, wiped my face (glad I hadn't had time for mascara), pulled away from Hugger and moved to the O'Keefe family.

"I didn't rescue her. She rescued herself. I just offered her a place to stay," I explained.

Then I had no choice but to emit a startled cry because I walked too close to the claws of a mama bear, and no hesitation, she sunk them into my shoulder (the woman had really long nails), yanked me into her arms and gave me the tightest hug I'd ever experienced.

"Never be able to repay you," she whispered into my hair.

"You never have to," I whispered back.

She snuffled, let me go as abruptly as she snatched me, and moved to shake hands with Hugger and Big Petey.

Mr. O'Keefe stayed with his daughter, deciding on verbal greetings, which he used.

Proving my theory correct about the force Mrs. O'Keefe was, once that was done, she declared, "Now, we got this. First, we're gonna go to the police station, because Detective Scott has some questions for you." She said this direct to Madison. The rest, she said to the room at large. "Then we got ourselves one of those Vrbos. It's got a pool that's also got a Jacuzzi. We're gonna stick around until Detective Scott has all he needs, and then we'll go home."

Through this speech, I noticed Madison's face getting paler and paler.

Oh shit.

"Um..." I started, but I didn't know what to say.

Fortunately, Rayne did.

"I explained a few things to you at the station, Mrs. O'Keefe. If Madison doesn't stay here, with the protection Diana is offering her through Harlan and Pete, then Madison needs to go somewhere where the Phoenix police have her covered."

"We couldn't bring a gun on an airplane," Mrs. O'Keefe returned. "But we know how to buy 'em, and you can read from that, Elias here isn't afraid of using 'em."

"We'd rather no one had to discharge a firearm for safety and protection within city limits," Rayne noted.

"What Emmylou's sayin', son, is that we don't wanna be away from our girl and we're hopin' you understand that and can figure out a way to respect it."

"I'm safe here," Madison said softly.

"Baby, your daddy and me are here now," Emmylou replied.

"I know, Mama, but I'm safe here, with Diana and the guys. It isn't just Big Petey and Hugger. There's Eight and Muzzle and Dutch and Core and Linus."

Both the older O'Keefes turned our way.

"You can stay with us too," I offered. "We'll move the dining room around and get an air mattress."

"You and those fuckin' air mattresses," Hugger said under his breath, but he sounded amused.

Even so, I shot him a look.

"Not gonna have Maddy's parents on the front lines, someone gets in through the front door," Big Petey stated.

"You think I won't have it covered?" Elias shot back.

"I think Hugger should be in with Diana, you take the couch, and Emmylou here sleeps with her daughter," Big Petey returned.

Oh my *God*.

I could *kiss* Big Petey.

Perfect solution for a variety of reasons.

"Pete," Hugger growled.

"It's set," Emmylou decreed. "If you're sure you don't mind, Miss Diana."

"I don't mind, Mrs. O'Keefe," I assured. "Not at all."

"Call me Emmylou. Or just Emmy," she invited. She then turned to her daughter. "Ready to go talk to the police?"

Before Madison could answer, Pete ordered, "Hang tight. Want you to have an escort. We got boys patrolling the complex. Gotta give 'em a heads up they need to get to their bikes."

"All righty," Emmylou agreed, apparently not perplexed in the slightest that Madison had a small army of bikers looking after her.

Seemed that Rayne did a lot of updating at the station.

"Anyone want coffee while Big Petey sets that up?" I asked.

"I'm fueled up, darlin', but thank you," Elias said.

"I need coffee, hon. Didn't sleep a wink last night," Emmylou said.

"Oh, Mama," Madison groaned.

Emmylou whirled on her daughter. "Girl, I'll sleep like a baby tonight, you sleepin' beside me. Now let's have coffee and get this done so Detective Scott can get on with his job."

I was seeing good things with the addition of Emmylou. I hadn't gotten around to talking Madison into going to the police station yet.

Now I didn't have to do that.

I made coffee in to-go mugs, just in case it didn't take long for the boys to hit their bikes.

As I did, both Hugger and Big Petey were on their phones, and my guess was, Hugger was on his to set that meet while we were at the police station.

He then came to me and murmured, "I'll go out and get one of those mattresses so I can sleep on the floor in your room."

"You can get one for Mr. O'Keefe so he can be comfortable. You aren't getting one for you."

"Babe."

"It isn't like you don't know I want to sleep with you."

"I do know that, and I want the same, but—"

As he was speaking, I was casting my gaze around, and no one was paying any attention to us, but still. I didn't live in Buckingham Palace where the rooms were the size of football fields. They might hear even if they weren't listening.

Thus, I cut him off. "We'll talk about it later."

"Di—"

I skewered him with a look. "Harlan, we'll talk about it later."

His mouth got tight.

I got up on my toes to kiss it.

It stopped being tight.

There you go.

Another pro.

Give the man a quick peck, he might not get over it, but he won't belabor it.

With that accomplished, I walked a travel mug of coffee to Emmylou.

13

GOODNIGHT

Diana

I'd hit my limit.

I wasn't proud of it, but it couldn't be denied.

This was why I was lying curled up on my bed.

I told myself I was giving time to Madison, Elias and Emmylou, who were out in the living room, re-bonding.

But really, I just needed space from all the crap I'd learned that day.

Emmylou might have given every indication she day-to-day steamrolled her family in her role as matriarch of the O'Keefe clan, but Maddy exhibited some Emmylou Mini-Me characteristics when she put her foot down she didn't want either of her parents there when she was interviewed.

She wanted me.

So she got me.

We weren't in a room with a table and chairs like you see on all the true crime shows.

Detective Scott put us in a room with a couch and some

armchairs. They were utilitarian, but more welcoming and comfortable.

Though, that was the only thing that was comfortable.

Hugger had phoned in the midst of this, and I couldn't pick up the call, so he texted that they weren't going to be able to escort us back home, but he was making other arrangements.

When it was all done, we had an Aces High escort, including Ink, Driver, Cruise, Gash *and* a police escort.

Whatever the boys were talking about was taking some time, because the interviews (yes, plural) took hours, and Hugger and Big Petey weren't back yet.

On this thought, I heard the door open, lifted my head and saw Hugger coming in.

I wasn't prepared for the wave of relief that hit me just seeing him.

But I couldn't deny a wave of relief hit me, or how huge it was.

I started to push up on an arm, but he took one look at me and ordered stonily, "Don't fuckin' move."

Surprised at his tone, I didn't fucking move.

I watched as he walked to the end of my bed and then I watched as he toed off his boots, put a knee to the bed, and last, I watched as he crawled up it.

I was in no mood for anything as hot as that.

Still, watching Hugger prowl toward me on my bed like a big cat was so good, a miracle happened, and I got in the mood.

He settled behind me, assumed the position of the big spoon and commanded, "Relax."

I lay back down, and with his arm around me, he pulled me close.

He then kept being bossy.

"Talk to me."

Okay, now I got his tone, and indications were I shouldn't play poker.

One could say I dug a spoon, and I'd just discovered Hugger did it better than any other.

I still squiggled around so we were in our position of the night before, face to face, legs slightly tangled, and I tipped my head back to look at him.

The instant our eyes met, he smoothed a large hand up my spine and whispered, "Baby."

Nope.

Shouldn't play poker.

"I've felt the urge to murder," I replied. "Genuinely. I'm being serious."

"Fuck," he muttered.

I drew in a breath and let it out speaking. "So, this is what the police are putting together. Esad Babić went rogue from his daddy's nefarious dealings. He decided to set up his own. He works with recruiters, like the one who located Madison online, in order to lure young women into their clutches and sell them to people like Esad. After they were...done with her—"

Hugger pulled me closer.

I skipped forward in the story.

"They thought she was unconscious and left her where she was. Madison, who seems to have made an art of hiding how strong and smart she is, pretended to be that way in the hope they'd do just what they did and she'd be able to get away. After all they did to her, Harlan, she had the presence of mind—"

I gulped.

"Di, honey, maybe we shouldn't go over this," Hugger murmured, now stroking my back.

"No, I need to get it out, if you'll listen."

"'Course I'll listen, baby. That's why I'm right here."

How in this shitty, *shitty* world, where such hideous things happened to such good people, did Harlan "Hugger" McCain corner me in an elevator, and in doing so, become a part of my life?

I shouldn't question it.

I should savor it.

I did that as I went back to sharing.

"As we know, her ploy worked, she grabbed Esad's phone and got the hell out of there. A good Samaritan picked her up and took her to the nearest emergency room."

"Right," Hugger said.

"They're surmising Esad found her and his phone missing, and knew his ass was in a sling, so he came clean to Daddy so Daddy could cover for him. Daddy went into action, calling Maddy on his son's phone the next morning, giving her instructions. Tell the police it was him who did the deed. If she didn't, he would not rest until he hunted her down and shared his displeasure. He advised Maddy she wouldn't end that episode breathing, and she wouldn't be the only one. He'd go after everyone she loved. Unsurprisingly, that threat worked and that was what Madison did."

Hugger appeared confused.

This was my reaction too.

Hugger voiced his confusion.

"Why didn't he just threaten her to keep quiet? Why would he put himself in that spot?"

"Rayne talked to me after," I began to explain. "He said they think that the senior Babić did this because none of the DNA would come back to him. He'd be exonerated, she'd be discredited. After falsely reporting, even if she did eventually point the finger at Esad and his boys, a good defense attorney would have a field day with her on the stand. And according to Rayne, that's one way Babić gets his giggles. Messing with the police. And if he can make them and a witness appear incompetent, all the better. So it was a twofer for ole Imran. He gets his son off, and he gets to play with the cops. Win-win for him."

"And now?" Hugger asked.

"Now, the Feds are pursuing this network of recruiters and their buyers. I guess they're transporting these girls everywhere. So they've got an arrest warrant for Esad, and from mugshots, Madison has identified the two guys that were with him, so they have warrants for them as well. And the Feds sat down with her. She couldn't give them much, though she was very thorough with her description of the man who groomed her and was able to identify him from a photo array too. She was scared sick at the time, so she didn't pay a lot of attention, but she did say she saw other girls there. Though she didn't know how many, she just saw two. And between Maddy, who doesn't know Phoenix at all but gave a description of where she was taken, and the good Samaritan, who gave a thorough report at the hospital, they've got a vicinity of where this place is."

"Some good news."

I nodded. "And there's more. Esad's phone was a huge get. It's been a treasure trove for them. And if they can pull in Esad and his boys, and they can get one of them to talk, they think this is going to be huge and the pins of that organization will start toppling."

"Okay, yeah. That's good too."

It was.

"They took her phone," I noted. "Esad and his assholes took it, and her purse, so she had no identifying information. But she packed a bag before she took off on her folks, that bag remained with her, and she grabbed that too when she escaped. I get why they took her phone and purse. But I think it's weird that they wouldn't take her belongings from her."

"Don't know how these clowns work, babe. But at least she had her own shit with her when she got away from them. Maybe that was a comfort?" he suggested.

I hoped so.

Now, for the rough part.

"They're taking them," I whispered.

"What?"

"Maddy, Elias and Emmylou. They're getting everything sorted, and tomorrow morning, they're taking them into protective custody, at the very least until this Babić situation is sorted. But maybe even longer, if Maddy has to go into WITSEC. Either way, I'll lose contact since she can't talk to me. That might just be for the interim, or it might be forever."

"Di," he murmured tenderly.

I shoved my face in his throat and burrowed into him.

"I know it's better for her," I said to his skin. "I know it. But I don't want her to go. And WITSEC? Her entire life was turned upside down, now it's gonna be turned upside down again?"

"It's what's best for her, what's safest."

"Yeah," I grumbled.

He was right, of course.

I just hated that she'd been through so much, and now she had to go through more.

"Scott was seriously forthcoming about shit," Hugger observed.

I pulled my face out of his throat. "He was. But I also sat in on the interviews because Maddy wanted me to."

He stopped stroking my back in order to hold me tight, whispering, "Babe."

"It's okay. I'm okay. I was honored she asked."

He got a funny look on his face before he said, "We're gonna have to talk about your bent to sacrifice yourself to be all you need to be for other people."

"I survived, Harlan."

"Never forget the look of your face, and of you, curled up in here, hiding away so no one will see you lick your wounds. Yeah, you're a survivor, but how much you gonna make yourself take before you realize how much it's taking out of you?"

Instead of answering, I shoved my face in his throat again.

He returned to stroking my back.

So I guessed I answered him.

I decided a change of subject was in order.

"Emmylou is taking over. I've learned in the Texan way of doing things, there are gender differences in making sandwiches. The boys got ones with three inches of lunchmeat. Me and Maddy only had two inches."

Hugger chuckled.

I pulled my face out of his throat again in order to look at him. "Two inches is a lot of meat, Hugger."

He got a certain look on his face and kept chuckling.

And he said, "Not really."

During this awful day, was I really going to laugh?

I couldn't help it.

I laughed, even as I bossed, "Get your mind out of the gutter."

"Right," he pushed out through his continuing amusement.

"Ink, Driver, Cruise and Gash did their manly best, but I feared a wafer-thin-mint moment was going to happen."

Hugger's brows drew together. "Wafer-thin-mint?"

"That scene in the Monty Python movie where the guy eats so much, he explodes."

"Haven't seen it."

"You must. It's a classic."

He slid a hand over my hip (nice). "Maybe we'll do that our next movie night."

Our next movie night.

Nicer.

"Also, you'll probably be pleased to know, Emmylou is using the cubed beef we bought so I could craft my fabulous shredded-beef tacos to make beef and noodles tonight. She needs numbers of who's coming to dinner."

"I'll get those for her," he replied.

"Your turn," I said.

He sighed before he dropped to his back and pulled me on top of him.

This wasn't a better or worse position with Hugger.

They were all *just right.*

His big, long, burly frame was just so *snuggly.*

"I need to report all this shit to them," he shared. "But even when I do, I don't think their mission will change. Aces and Chaos are out, Resurrection is gonna deal with the Babićs."

"As a law-abiding citizen, I see why this is concerning. As a person who likes you, and they're your friends, I see why this is concerning. As a person who likes them, again with the concern. After all I heard today, I don't have enough left in me to give a shit about the Angels of Death going after these assholes." I tipped my head to the side and asked, "Where are you with that?"

"Goal is to defeat the enemy. Better goal is to defeat them and humiliate them," Hugger replied. "I don't think they'll like what Resurrection has planned. I think they'd hate it more, rotting in a prison for the rest of their lives."

I saw his point.

"That means?" I queried.

"That means we hope the cops pick up Esad and his bros. Also that they nab Imran, for whatever they can pin on him, and do this before Resurrection gets messy. But when they do that, we're always out. After learning what was done to Maddy, they refuse to back down. When they find out there's a racket going on, they're gonna go all in until they dismantle it. So bottom line, no matter what we think of their intent, we're out."

An unhappy thought occurred to me right then.

"With Maddy going, and Resurrection taking over, does that mean you're leaving?" I asked.

He shook his head, and the tension that had begun winding through my body subsided.

"The last few days, Buck's been trying to reach out to Imran for a parlay. He's not responding. Part of what Buck wanted to talk about was to be certain you and your dad were off their radar. Since Imran isn't gonna sit down for a chat so we can get some shit straight and set some ground rules, we gotta keep you and your dad covered until we know neither of you is in play."

"So you and Big Petey are staying?"

This time, he nodded. "And Dutch, Jag and Coe. Eight, Muzzle and Linus are going under."

I hoped those boys were safe after they went "under."

"What about Core?"

"Core has a woman. He's heading back to Denver. Once a brother of Resurrection claims a woman, Wash assigns them duties that won't get their asses arrested or dead."

Eep!

"Okay," I forced out, deciding to sidestep that particular discussion.

"Though, just sayin', you and me are doin' this, so even if things were copacetic with you and your dad when it comes to the Babićs, I'd be staying so we could see to this."

On his *this*, he gave me a squeeze.

My mood shifted immediately, I smiled big and repeated, "Okay."

"Now we need to talk about the sleeping arrangements for tonight."

Another mood shift. "Harlan—"

"Babe, we're not there."

"No, but you need some good sleep and the situation at my place demands you do it here, and you're not going to do it on the floor when there's a bed in this room big enough for two. I talked with the boys, and both Ink and Cruise have air mattresses. They're delivering one for Elias."

I took a chance with his no-touch policy (that still included a great deal of touching, which reminded me I needed a new list, one of things to talk to Hugger about) and stroked his beard.

It felt great, and he didn't quibble, so I kept doing it and returned to speaking.

"It'll be hard, I know, but I figure we can keep our hands off each other for one night."

"Hard enough getting sleep knowin' you're down the hall. Probably impossible with you right beside me in a big, soft bed."

I really didn't want to do it, but the situation warranted it.

I smirked.

Hugger moved his hands to my waist and squeezed.

"You getting off on knowing what you do to my dick isn't helping matters, babe," he noted.

"Sorry," I lied.

He sifted his long fingers into the side of my hair, tucking it behind my ear, adding a nuance to the touch he'd given me last night, which I liked, making it better, which I loved.

"I don't want you thinkin' I'm taking advantage," he said softly.

I blinked.

I stared.

I shoved my face in his neck and did it hard.

Who was this man and what did I do in this life to deserve being cornered in an elevator by him?

"It's Big Petey's idea," he went on. "Not yours. And you got a heart the size of Alaska, and it's so golden, it's blinding. You want me to get good sleep. And you constantly put everyone else in front of yourself and—"

I lifted my head at the same time I rested my fingers on his bearded lips.

"I wanted to offer it to you last night," I told him. "I was ecstatic when Big Petey made that suggestion. And yes, that's about you, and me wanting you to get good rest. But it's also about me, because I like you, I'm attracted to you, I'm loving getting to know you, and I foresee, eventually, you being here anyway."

This time, he pulled a bunch of my hair over my shoulder and started twirling it.

Reluctantly, I shifted my fingers from his lips.

"And it'll be nice, not having to be alone on the last night we have Maddy with us," I whispered.

With my hair still in his fingers, he stroked my jaw. "Then I'm in here with you in your bed tonight."

How did I know that was what he'd say?

Seemed I wasn't the only one with the bent of putting others before myself.

"Can you take tomorrow off too?" he asked. "Give yourself some time to deal with losing her."

My boss was a hands-off person in the sense that she pretty much didn't notice anything going on except what she was in the middle of doing.

Annie would notice if I didn't get work done.

She wouldn't notice if I didn't show up for three days, and when I returned, she'd say something like, "I thought something seemed off at the workshop."

It was good she wasn't a professor, or she'd be the example that proved the stereotype.

"My boss is pretty cool. I'll call her, because that's a good idea."

"How 'bout doin' that now, getting it out of the way, and we'll go out and spend some time with Maddy so you got that before she has to go away."

This was a good plan, so I moved carefully to reach for my phone without losing much contact with him.

I then hit go on her number.

She answered probably half a second before it went to voicemail.

"Yes?"

"Hi, Annie. It's Di again."

"Hello, dear."

"Listen, I'm sorry. I need to take tomorrow off too."

"You're not here?"

See what I mean?

"Yeah. Remember? I called you this morning asking for a personal day."

"Yes, yes. I forgot," she mumbled.

"So is it okay if I take tomorrow off? I'll explain when I come into the office on Wednesday."

"Of course, Di. Whatever you need. Wait. Where are you with the Galligan's painting?"

"Still working on it. But I'll have it done by the time you promised it to them."

"And the Harris's icon?"

"That's up next."

"Fine then," she said distractedly. "See you Wednesday."

And then she proved how distracted she was by hanging up on me so she could get on with whatever she was doing.

I tossed my phone aside and announced, "I'm good at work."

"All right. So are you good to go out there and get some time in with Maddy before she goes?"

I was, absolutely, and I wasn't, also absolutely, but the latter bit was only because we'd have that time knowing she was going.

"Let's go out."

Hugger cupped the back of my head so he could bring it down to his for a bristly lip brush and then he rolled us both out of bed.

"You think Emmylou will make me a man sandwich?" he asked as we walked hand in hand to the door. "I didn't get lunch."

"I think Emmylou would craft an entire Thanksgiving dinner in half an hour if one of the men who looked after her girl asked for it."

His deep voice held humor when he agreed, "I think you're right."

He opened the door and the scent of sugary goodness wafted down the hall.

"See?" I asked Hugger upon being assaulted by that smell.

He smiled down at me.

Damn, but he had a great smile.

We hit the living room to see Big Petey gabbing with Elias in the living room, and Emmylou and Madison in my kitchen, making cookies.

And sandwiches.

"Pete says you two didn't have lunch, Hugger," Emmylou called. "Dinner is only a couple of hours away, but I'm making you boys something to tide you over."

"Obliged," Hugger replied on a beard twitch.

"What kind of cookies are those?" I asked.

"Mama's famous almond cookies," Maddy answered.

"Oh my God, I love almond," I told Emmylou.

"I aim to please," Emmylou murmured as she carted two plates weighed down by massive sandwiches and such big piles of chips they covered the sandwiches, which I suspected would "tide over" Hugger and Big Petey quite nicely.

Hugger sat with Pete and Elias in the living room to eat his sandwich.

I went to the kitchen to help with cookies.

"WHAT'S A YURT?" Emmylou asked Jagger.

Bit of news: Jagger was, indeed, as handsome as his older brother. A little less intense, but no less good-looking.

Roscoe was also cute, if bikers could be overtly cute, though Roscoe proved they could, and he wore big, black-framed Buddy Holly glasses, which made him cuter.

We were all sitting around the dinner table, munching on cookies after scarfing down Emmylou's insanely good beef and noodles.

I needed to get her recipes before she left.

"It's a round tent that doesn't have a center support," Jagger told Emmylou. "And I only know that because my wife has an adventurous spirit. She had a hankering to stay in a yurt. I got her to one and I can't say it sucked."

"Where all have you been?" Elias asked.

"Better to ask where they haven't," Big Petey butted in. "The weather's good, they're off somewhere all the time."

"Only young once," Emmylou stated. "Get the wanderlust out of you, hunker down and create your family."

"Think when we have 'em, Arch is gonna strap our kids to her and me and get us on the road anyway, Miss Emmylou," Jagger replied.

"To each their own," Emmylou stated. "Children need stability, but that comes in the form of their parents, and the rest doesn't matter."

I looked to Maddy to see how she was dealing with all of this.

She was biting into a cookie with a little smile on her face aimed at her mother.

There it was, more healing.

She had a long row to hoe, but at least now she had the people she needed around her to do it.

Eight pushed his chair back.

"Best get goin'," he declared.

The rest of the boys followed suit, so we all got up.

There were handshakes, claps on the back, murmurs of farewell, lower murmurs of gratitude from the two older O'Keefes, and I got hugs too, particularly long ones from Eight and Muzzle.

But like they'd been doing since they showed days ago, they kept their distance from Maddy.

Until they were at the door and Eight had it open, ready to walk out.

That was when Maddy cried, "Wait! That's it?"

All the men stopped and looked back at her.

No one said anything.

Then Maddy burst forth, hit Eight on the run and wrapped her arms around him.

I knew, by the look on his face as he curved his tall body over hers and returned her hug, that whatever he was going to get up to, if you agreed with it or not, it was his calling.

"Thank you," I heard her whisper the first words she said to him.

And the new look on Eight's face both gutted me and restored my faith in humanity.

"My honor, little one," he muttered.

Oh shit, it was happening again.

I was going to cry.

I jumped when Hugger slung an arm around my shoulders and tucked me to his side.

We watched as she did the same with Muzzle but with Linus, Core, Dutch, Jagger and Roscoe, who she didn't know as well, she just waved.

Muzzle was the last out the door, but he left his head inside it and said to Maddy, "Every second you live good and strong, babe, you beat them. Keep kicking their asses, Maddy. You got this."

Maddy emitted a soft sob.

Elias wrapped his arms around his girl.

Muzzle disappeared from the door.

HUGGER and I were at our respective sinks in the bathroom, each of us brushing our teeth.

Why did I love looking in the mirror and seeing Hugger at my side with toothpaste foam in his beard?

"Di?"

At Maddy calling my name from the bedroom, I turned to look at Hugger in person, before I spit, rinsed, wiped, and left the bathroom.

Maddy was standing just inside the door.

"All good?" I asked, going to her.

"Can I ask you to do something?"

"Anything."

When I said that, something washed over her face, something warm and wonderful, and sad and sorrowful, before she reached out and took my hand.

She fiddled with my fingers while she watched.

But she didn't say anything.

"Maddy, you okay?" I asked.

She lifted her head. "Don't get up and say goodbye to us in the morning."

I felt like I'd been punched in the sternum.

"Maddy," I whispered.

"I can't say goodbye to you, Di."

Damn it!

I'd managed to hold them at bay when the guys left, but I wasn't sure I could do it this time.

"We go to sleep, like normal, except Mama and Daddy are here," she stated. "Then you wake up, and I'm gone."

"Honey," I pushed out.

She latched onto my hand hard. "Don't make me say goodbye to you. Just say goodnight and we'll pretend I'm not going away."

My voice was croaky and my throat hurt like crazy when I asked, "Can our goodnight include a hug?"

Her answer was to walk right into me.

We held on to each other for what was a long time but felt like seconds.

A million words came to my mind when she broke free, but I couldn't get any of them out of my mouth.

She stopped at the door, looked back at me, and I committed to memory her peaches and cream skin, her pretty blonde hair and her beautiful blue eyes.

"Goodnight, Di," she said.

I was losing it, but I managed to get out, "Goodnight, Maddy."

She shot me one of her little smiles and disappeared behind the door.

I dropped my head in my hands and almost went to my knees.

What stopped me from doing the last was Hugger swinging me up in his arms and carrying me to bed.

Once we were there, I burrowed again and used all the rest of my energy to stop myself from breaking down.

"Let them go," he whispered.

"Tomorrow," I choked out.

"Okay, baby," he agreed.

He kept hold on me as he rolled side to side to turn out the lights on the nightstands.

I belatedly realized his chest was bare, and hairy.

I didn't have it in me to process this. I just had it in me to feel Hugger yank the covers from under us and pull them over us.

"I'm never gonna get to sleep tonight," I told him.

"Good you got the day off tomorrow, then," he replied.

"Yeah," I mumbled.

Hugger twined his long legs with my shorter ones and held on.

I listened hard for signs of life in my house.

There weren't any.

I kept listening.

And, held safe in Hugger's arms, I fell asleep doing it.

WHEN I WOKE, Hugger was the big spoon again.

I knew he knew I was awake when his arm around me pulled me deeper into his body.

And I knew he knew I heard the noises beyond my bedroom door when he kept holding tight.

Eventually, there was silence, and my body, tense from toes to top of my head, remained that way.

There was a quiet knock on the door.

I didn't move.

I felt Hugger lift his head before he called, "Yeah?"

"They got our girl. She's all good," I heard Big Petey say quietly.

"Thanks, brother," Hugger replied.

The door snicked shut.

I turned in Hugger's arms, pressed close and let the tears go.

Hugger tangled his fingers in my hair, held me tight with his other arm, and let me.

14

SOLITAIRE

Hugger

An alarm went off that sounded like birds tweeting.

Jesus, Diana woke up to tweeting birds.

Hugger was partly on his stomach, partly on his side.

Diana was tucked to his back.

He felt her shift, the softness of her lips pressed to his back, the softness of her voice ordering the alarm to stop, and then she rolled out of bed.

He opened his eyes and saw his gun on the nightstand.

He moved his gaze and watched her ass in loose shorts covered in daisies disappear behind the closed door in the bathroom.

He rolled to his back and lifted both hands to rub them over his face.

When he was smoothing down his beard, he saw Di's 3D white flower hanging over the bed, and he felt her soft sheets and perfect-mix-of-firm-and-soft mattress.

"What the fuck am I doing?" he muttered to himself.

He heard the shower go on and his morning wood made itself known.

"Christ, what the fuck am I doing?" he repeated, again on a mutter.

Yesterday, the day they woke up without Maddy, had been a chill day.

Even so, Diana had moped through it, and Hugger found he liked she didn't try to hide her upset Maddy was gone.

She didn't make a drama about it, but he and big Petey knew she was suffering. They didn't have to guess, and they didn't have to worry she was tamping down shit that would explode at some future time and bite everyone around her in the ass.

Hugger had never had a relationship that lasted over two months. He'd never lived with a woman, outside his mother.

But his mother had moods.

Then again, he did too.

Whenever he'd hear a man bitch about a moody woman, he didn't get it. Like, that man didn't have emotions too, and show them? Like a woman was supposed to float through life singing, smiling and twirling like fucking Sleeping Beauty?

Sure, it sucked when his ma got pissy.

Though, she didn't like it much when he did either.

Also the day before, Hugger felt a weird warmth hit his gut at witnessing how Di let Big Petey look after her.

The man was a brother's brother. When it came to his Club, Pete was not skimpy with his experience or wisdom.

But he was a woman's man in the sense he set himself up as dad, uncle or grandpa to every female he met in order to offer them what they needed.

Hugger reckoned that was a father who only had one daughter. If you were a good man, and Big Petey was the best, that's just what happened when you made a girl.

So Pete was in his element with Di.

In fact, the last few days, Big Petey had seemed more himself, and more content, than he had in a long time.

It went further though, because Hugger knew Di sensed it, and she gave him that.

Because she was Di.

All about giving.

Late in the afternoon, they got news from Scott that Maddy and her family were safe and settled.

Scott also shared Imran, Esad, and Esad's boys were proving hard to find, and in the raid they conducted on the house where the suspected activity was happening, they discovered it had been cleared out. Though, there was evidence of recent occupancy, and it was not the kind of evidence that pointed at a nuclear family living there.

They believed they also discovered Maddy's crime scene, and what they found there indicated it was the scene of many other crimes, so they had a lot to process.

All that was moving forward, which was good, just not very fast, which was expected.

The last thing about the day before was Hugger had let Di con him into sleeping beside her again.

Truth, it didn't take much.

And she copped to what she was doing right away.

All she said was, "Warning, incoming emotional manipulation." She then made her pretty green eyes all soft and sweet and begged, "Please don't make me sleep alone tonight."

Yep, that was it.

Again, it didn't take much.

Now, Maddy was gone and life was going to go back to normal for Diana. Although they were keeping her covered, with Maddy out of the picture, the Babićs had no beef with Diana, so no reason to fuck with her.

Armitage was a different story. But Hugger guessed you didn't make it far, even in the criminal world, by wasting your time and resources on someone who mildly inconvenienced you.

That meant they'd likely find out soon there was no reason for Hugger to be in Phoenix anymore, except to be with Diana.

It also meant there was nothing in the way of them exploring what they had either.

This made Hugger uneasy.

He had his Club. A job he did so he could do his bit for the Club, but he couldn't say he liked it. What he could say was that it passed the time. He had a house he didn't give a shit about. A bank account that was healthy, because he rarely spent any money.

And that was it.

Di had friends, family, a job she did that she dug and a stylish pad that had her stamp all over it. They were having dinner with her father that night and she was having cocktails with her friends on Friday. This meant she had more social engagements in one week than Hugger had in the last six months. And the only one he had was a Chaos hog roast, so that was about the entire brotherhood and their family, he could go or skip it, it didn't matter, so it wasn't about Hugger.

She had a life.

He had an existence.

That wasn't a lot to offer a good woman.

On that cheery thought, he angled out of bed, hit the guest bathroom to do his business, then hit the kitchen to make coffee.

While it was brewing, he went back to the bedroom to check his phone.

Like he'd been getting the last twenty-four hours, not overwhelmingly, but there had been more than just one, there was another call from Tack.

Hugger had been avoiding those calls, and had reason.

Now, he didn't really have a reason.

He still didn't call the man back.

He returned to the coffee and saw it was brewed. He poured himself a cup, and one for Di.

He took them back to her room and called through the bathroom door. "Babe, you decent? Got coffee."

Within half a second, the door flew open, and he saw her standing there with her hair twisted up in a weird towel, a short robe covering the rest of her body.

Her face looked slimy.

For a second, she seemed suspended in motion, her eyes locked to his bare chest.

His morning wood was gone, but her staring at his chest like that was making it threaten to come back.

Before he had to say something to snap her out of it, like warning her if she didn't quit looking at him like that, she'd find herself fucked for the first time by him on her bathroom floor with her face shiny and her hair in a weird towel, her gaze shifted to the mug in his hand.

"Oh my God, you just *rawk*," she declared, taking her cup of coffee, leaning in for a quick kiss of his beard, then turning to go into the bathroom to her sink, which had makeup spread all around it.

He went to his own.

"Sleep good?" Diana asked, her ass shaking as she rubbed what seemed like more slime on her face.

He took the toothbrush out of the fancy cup she had on her counter and answered, "Yeah."

"Me too. I'm surprised. But I felt a lot better when Rayne called and said they were safe."

He spread toothpaste on the brush and replied, "Yeah."

He started brushing as he watched her start to do shit to her eyelids as she babbled, "So, Dad wants us over at six thirty. I think I should bring something. A sort of 'I come in peace' gesture. But he's a dude, so I don't think flowers, even though he's got fresh flowers all over his office. He drinks gin, so maybe a bottle of Hendrick's. But he can afford his own gin. Though, it's the thought that counts, right?"

Hugger had brushed, spit, rinsed and was about to splash water on his face, but when she asked her question, he said, "I think all he gives a shit about is you bringing is you."

He splashed water on his face.

"Right," she muttered.

He was toweling down when he turned to her, and now she was at it with a thin brush.

She also didn't seem to have any problem with him standing right there.

"You live with a man before, baby?" he asked quietly.

Thin brush pointed to her eyelid, she turned her head his way. "Yes. Twice." She shifted her attention back to the mirror. "The first one I caught texting *and* sexting his high school girlfriend, who'd moved to Virginia. They weren't doing the deed physically, but they were totally doing it mentally. I broke up with him. He acted like that was the end of his world, but within a month, he'd found a job in Virginia and moved there to be with her."

She switched brushes, grabbed a long, narrow box off the counter, flipped it open to expose a bunch of eyeshadows that were a bunch of colors in the same shade, and went at it again.

"They got engaged," she continued. "A month before the wedding, he found her schtupping the guy she dumped to be with him, because, yes, when they were texting *and* sexting, she was with someone too. They were doing it in the bed he shared with her. The wedding wasn't called off. She just married the other guy during it. My ex was so humiliated, he came back to Phoenix. He tried to start it up again with me, but that was definitely a no-go."

Hugger was now leaning a hip against her bathroom counter, arms crossed on his chest, watching her put on makeup and listening.

"Wild story, babe. But sounds like you dodged a drama bullet."

"Yep," she agreed. Then, all Diana what seemed to be all the time, she kept giving it. "The other guy, well, we just weren't meant for each other. It was crazy, but we both kinda figured out we were going through the motions at the same time. He asked if we could have a quiet night 'to chat' the same day I was going to go home and ask him to have a 'chat.'"

She shrugged and switched up makeup shit.

And she kept talking.

"We're still friends, mostly. I mean, if I ran into him, we'd be nice to each other. We don't hang out or anything."

"Right," he muttered.

"You?" she asked the mirror.

"What?"

She turned to him. "Have you ever lived with anybody?"

"My ma. A coupla roommates. No woman," he shared, feeling some discomfort in doing it.

Her brows drifted up. "How old are you?"

"Thirty-five. And just so you know, never had a woman in my life for more than a coupla months either."

Now she was staring at him. "Really?"

He nodded.

"You're sweet. You're protective. You're insanely hot. You bring a girl coffee. So the question must be asked, why on earth not?"

It felt good, all those things she said about him.

Damn good.

But that was an excellent question.

The one who he had, Mandy, was solid. Great smile. Good in bed. Had her shit together.

Though, if it had lasted with Mandy, he wouldn't have a shot with Diana, so he was glad it didn't.

"Harlan?" Diana called.

He focused on her and said quietly, "Think that's part of the shit I didn't want to lay on you, baby. And we gotta talk about that, because, now we're without any distractions, we gotta figure out what this is and how hard we wanna fight for it."

"I think I already know how hard I wanna fight for it," she declared.

Now he felt even more uncomfortable.

"Babe—"

She shook her head and turned to the mirror, interrupting him. "This isn't a conversation for now. Let's have a normal day, the dinner with Dad notwithstanding. We can make a date to talk about serious stuff later. I'm thinking Saturday. No, we should have a fun day Saturday. Let's do it Sunday."

Hugger felt his lips curl up. "Right. So we got a date to do that Sunday, four days from now when we're essentially livin' together and I'll be going to work with you, so we got all sorts of time to talk."

She was at her cheeks with a bigger brush. "But we're talking about that stuff on Sunday."

"Right," he repeated.

"Do you want me to take my makeup to the bedroom to finish this so you can shower?"

"I can shower in the guest room."

She pushed closer to the mirror to get a better view of what she was doing, which tipped her fine ass up, and she did this while mumbling, "Okay, honey."

He liked the sight of her ass tipped up like that in her short robe. He liked that she called him honey. He also liked that she seemed totally cool with putting on her makeup while he brushed his teeth beside her, in her nice bathroom with the handles on her sky-blue drawers and cupboards being glass with gold hardware. The blue, gold and white wallpaper on one wall being both a geometric design, but there were also flowers. More flowers, these fake but looking real, a small bouquet of them between his sink and hers.

This space, like all her space, was her. Sharp, smart and sophisticated, but full of personality. Attractive. Welcoming. And he felt good in it.

What he didn't like was knowing he was a man without a lot to offer, and she was a woman who should have it all.

But they'd talk about that Sunday.

Now, he needed to get a shower.

In the small parking lot outside her work, as necessary, Diana popped off the bike before he swung his leg over.

He did this with his eyes on her, coming off liking what he was feeling, Di on the back of his bike with him, to liking what he was seeing.

She was wearing a pair of brown pants with wide legs and a wide black belt through the hoops, a tight black top that had no sleeves, and shiny black pumps that had a strap over the top of her foot.

Hugger never in his life found a woman dressed like that for work, entirely—no, almost excruciatingly—fuckable. And it wasn't (only) about how hot it was that Di jumped on his bike in that getup like she'd been riding behind him on it for the last decade.

But since Maddy left, he was finding everything about Di fuckable. Though, deep down, he knew, before Maddy left, it was just that all the shit going down with Maddy could take his mind off it.

Right now, he had a job, though, and he wasn't doing it watching Di's tits move while she slung her big black bag more securely over her shoulder.

He'd scanned the area when they drove in and he scanned it again as he went to her, took her hand and walked to the front door.

He felt her hand twitch in his when he took it, so he looked down at her.

"All right?" he asked.

"For not being a guy who's touchy"—she squeezed his hand and gave him a bright smile—"you're kinda touchy."

He wasn't.

But he couldn't keep his hands off her.

"That cool with you?" he asked.

"Yes, honey, it's very cool," she murmured, still smiling big as she pushed through the door and took them into the tidy and small reception area of Di's work.

When he'd been in the space before, it felt unused.

Now, there was a woman behind the reception counter looking like she was rifling through the place in order to steal secret documents.

Hugger was a biker. This meant he was a live and let live kind of guy. Before that, he'd been a bouncer.

He'd seen it all.

But the woman behind the counter made him do a double take.

She was whip thin, short and wearing a black turtleneck. She had steel gray hair, and a part of it at her forehead was tucked under in one of those big, 40s-style curves. The rest was held back with a wide black headband to fall in soft curls at her shoulders. And either by nature, or by design, there was a long, black stripe of hair running through that gray above her left eye.

She had black-framed glasses perched on her nose, the lenses circles that seemed too small to be useful in correcting vision.

The slash of red that was her mouth shone stark against vampire-white skin he could see was made that way by her natural color and whatever makeup she put on. Her skin was beginning to wrinkle in places, showing her age, and she seemed down with that. And she had those black eyeliner things women were doing these days that kicked out the sides of her eyes, but hers were pronounced almost cartoonishly.

Against the odds, she worked those too, along with all the rest of it.

She didn't have anything near a "normal" vibe, part of why Hugger instantly dug her. The other part was she looked like the kind of woman you'd want to know.

"Hey, Annie," Diana called. "Looking for something?"

Annie's head shot up like she didn't hear the front door open and two people arrive. She then stared at them as if she didn't know what human beings were (though, it could be she couldn't see them through the tiny round lenses in her glasses).

Total blank for Hugger, and the same for Diana, who was on her payroll.

Something cleared, and Annie said, "Oh, hi, Diana."

Di tugged him to the opposite side of the receptionist counter. "Looking for something?"

The woman appeared massively confused. "I am?"

Diana gestured to the reception desk.

The woman peered down at it like she was supposed to see something there, but she saw nothing there, not even the desk.

Jesus Christ.

Di had warned him her boss was "a little vague," but damn.

"Oh!" Annie exclaimed. "Right. I'm out here looking for the Bernardi invoice."

"I sent that last week," Diana told her. "It's on the spreadsheet."

Annie raised her tiny-lensed glasses to Di. "Did they pay?"

"I don't know. They pay by check. I sent it on Thursday and I haven't been here for two days."

Annie's attention listed to the door and she mumbled, "I forgot to get the mail."

Shocker.

"I'll get it," Di offered.

"I'll get it," Hugger declared.

She looked up at him. Annie looked up at him.

Di noticed Annie noticing him so she said, "Annie, this is Hugger. There's been a situation with one of my father's clients. A possible threat. Not a credible one," she said swiftly, even though Annie had zero response to the mention of a threat. "So until we know that isn't an issue, Hugger is going to hang with me. I hope that's okay."

"Will you go get the mail?" Annie asked him.

What she did not ask was about this "situation" or anything about the fact her only employee needed a bodyguard.

Damn, this bitch was a trip.

"Yeah," he answered.

"Great," Annie said then dropped her attention to the desk again. "Now, what was I looking for?"

Holy fuck.

He heard Diana stifle a laugh.

Time to get past Annie being a total ditz.

"Where's the mailbox?" he asked Di.

She went around the reception desk, opened a drawer, got a key chain with a small key on it and handed it to him. "It's on the outside of the building, to the right of the door if you're facing it."

"Gotcha," he muttered and took off.

By the time he got back with the mail, Annie was gone, and Diana had lost her bag and was at the door to her studio waiting for him.

He walked to her, and she lifted a hand for the mail when he got close, so he handed it to her.

"How does that woman run a business?" he asked as he followed her into her studio while she sifted through the mail.

"Not very well, before she hired me. I've had occasion to have a gander through her personnel files and she had a lot of other me's that didn't last long, likely because she drove them batty. She drove me batty too, at first. Then I offered to take over the admin, if she upped my salary a bit to add paying me for those responsibilities. I got what was fair for taking on more work, she doesn't have to worry about it, the business runs smoother, and I like the autonomy her being scatterbrained gives me."

There it was again.

Di taking care of someone.

But at least she got paid for it this time.

She stopped sifting through the mail and headed across the space, still talking.

"We have a spreadsheet we share about projects, so I know what she's working on, samesies with me, progress, target completion dates, estimates of work, invoices sent, invoices paid. This way, if she remembers to check, she knows I'm getting work done, and we're getting paid. She has a bookkeeper, so I don't have to deal with money, outside depositing a check or making sure we got the PayPal or Venmo payment. I don't have set hours. I have set projects. And I dig that."

"Sounds cush, babe," Hugger replied, watching her sit at a small desk facing out at a diagonal in the corner, away from all the mess of easels, tables, lamps, pots, jars, jugs and instruments.

But he was feeling even more shit because she wasn't only doing what she liked doing, she was free to do it without a lot of hassle and someone breathing down her neck.

Sure, the woman he just met in the reception area was flighty as all fuck, but if she mostly got on with her thing, and let Di get on with hers, that, to Hugger, was the perfect work situation.

He knew, because that was his work situation.

Di had grabbed a letter opener, and she was slitting open the mail.

Hugger headed over to the chair he'd put by the window.

He settled in, boots up on the sill, eyes aimed out the window, and he stayed that way until Di left her desk and went to the easel that held the painting she was working on.

"I thought we'd got to Taco Chelo for lunch today," she stated.

Of course she thought they'd go for fucking tacos.

He felt his lips tip up, but he stopped doing that when he turned his attention to her.

"How long you worked here, babe?" he asked.

"Four years," she replied to the painting. "Since I quit school because of the situation with Dad, it took me an extra year to get my bachelor's, even going to summer school. With the internship, it added another six months to getting my masters. Annie's my first job in my field."

So she had a master's degree.

Shit.

"Landed on your feet," he muttered.

She stopped rolling a Q-tip in her mouth and smiled at him.

"Got it made," he stated.

She bent over the painting with her cotton swab.

"Not really. Though Annie pays well, since she takes private commissions from people who can afford it, the holy grail of conservation work is getting a position at a museum. I keep my eye on PHAM's career page, but alas, nothing has come up."

"PHAM?"

"Phoenix Art Museum. Outside of going somewhere like The Met, or one of the Smithsonians, which would be a dream, locally, that would be where I'd want to be," she stated. "Don't get me wrong, this is good work and I love it. But the diversity of work I'd have access to, the things I could learn, and the collegiality is missing here." She shot him another smile. "Not that Annie isn't collegial. Just that she's, well...Annie."

That woman was definitely...Annie.

"You'd take a hit to your salary if you went to a museum?" he asked.

She was rolling the other end of the swab in her mouth.

She took it out and went back to the painting, saying, "Yeah. So it honestly might not be in the cards. Things are steady for me, but if I took a pay cut, they'd get tight."

Not if she halved her expenses by having a man.

He turned to the window again, thinking the Denver Art Museum was supposed to be awesome. He'd never been, but he knew where it was, and it was his favorite building in the city. It looked like a gray spaceship. It was the total shit.

"If I'm not doin' a job like this, I work as a sales associate at Ride Auto Supply Store, the Club's business," he told the window. "And I got a two-bedroom crackerbox house I furnished all at once from a charity shop."

When Diana had no reply, he turned to her to find her looking at him.

"Sunday," she said.

Okay.

Yeah.

But she had to know what she was working with on Sunday.

"Babe, the brothers share profits equal across the board, and we got a slew of auto supply stores, and the builds from the garage bring in a shit ton. I'm not hurtin'. But I don't live like you do."

"So, if you wanted to live like I do, you could, because you have the money to do it. You just aren't really bothered, so you don't."

"Honestly?" he asked.

"Absolutely," she answered.

"I never had good like you got, so I didn't really think about it, even though a lot of the brothers, especially the ones with old ladies, got it pimp."

"Do you like it pimp?" she asked quietly.

Her pad?

The scent of her hair and her perfume on her soft sheets?

A home-cooked meal every night?

Fuck yeah.

"Definitely gonna look at some rolls of wallpaper when I get home," he joked.

She gave him another smile and went back to the painting, asking, "What did you want to be when you grew up?"

Hugger returned his attention to the window.

He wanted his mom safe and out from under the thumb of some asshole pimp.

Enter Chaos for the second time in her life, they got her free of the last asshole pimp she had, set her up so she could manage her own clients, and she went freelance.

After that, he just hoped he didn't grow up to be like his father.

"Harlan?" Di prompted.

"Never really thought about it," he said to the window.

He felt the air get heavy and he let it be.

Because, yeah.

On Sunday, she had to know what she was dealing with.

They were in the zone they hadn't had much time in, so when they talked on Sunday, if this wasn't going anywhere, she wouldn't feel like she wasted time on him.

In the meantime, he got to have her for the next four days. Have her time. Her smiles. Have her back when she sat down with her dad.

And he decided in that moment that was good for him.

Hugger hadn't had a lot on his life, and it was no joke that what he had with Di the last six days was the best he'd ever had, bar none, and he hadn't even banged her yet.

So he'd take what he could get of Diana Armitage, then he'd take off out of her life when she realized he was a hassle who wasn't worth it.

On a thought that was unhappy, but not unusual for Hugger, he pulled out his phone to play solitaire while she spit-washed an ugly-as-fuck painting.

At lunch, they went downtown to a place that made excellent tacos using freshly rolled and grilled tortillas, and Hugger noted, in a city that seemed to be nothing but a never-ending succession of strip malls, they had damn good food.

On their way back to her work, they stopped at a Total Wine so she could buy her dad a bottle of gin.

She returned to the painting.

And he went back to something familiar.

Solitaire.

15

SOMETHING BIG

Diana

"You don't have to change!" I shouted down the hall. "I'm not changing."

We needed to leave imminently for dinner.

I was in the kitchen, trying to fashion a bow around Dad's bottle of gin.

Maybe the bow was overkill, but I was nervous.

I didn't want Dad to be a dick to Hugger, for one. That would end the night real soon, because I wouldn't put up with it.

I didn't want Dad to be a dick to me, either.

Of course, that would suck for me, but I wasn't sure how Hugger would respond to it. Though, I did know neither Dad nor I wanted to find out, but Dad might want it less than me.

I was also nervous about Hugger.

There'd been a change in him since Madison left.

There was something almost fatalistic about him.

Sure, I could see how we'd started was weird. We hadn't had a date. We'd had one kiss. Police and the FBI were a part of our lives.

And we were living together and sleeping together without the fun sex parts that came with those.

And onward from all of this, our road was pretty rocky.

Hugger would have to go back home.

I would have to stay here.

I could say the emotion I felt was hate at the knowledge that, eventually, he was going to leave.

Just that. Him leaving.

This was how used to having him around I'd become.

And how much I liked it.

It got worse thinking we'd have to try to get to know each other over phone calls and texts, and figuring out times for visits, and then there was the expense of that.

I didn't know a thing about motorcycle clubs outside what I learned when watching that documentary about Chaos, but I suspected, if you were in one, they wanted you to be *in it*, not living with some chick in another state. And what I learned in that documentary pretty much confirmed that suspicion.

As for me, well, it wasn't like jobs in art conservation and preservation were a dime a dozen. They were pretty damned thin on the ground.

I was set here. I'd lived here my whole life, outside the time I spent in London.

But I'd really liked the time in London. The different food, weather, people.

Oh, God, I was becoming one of those women who searched for reasons to uproot her life for a man.

And the man for whom I was searching for these reasons I hadn't even known a full week.

"You also look good and have a nice outfit on," Hugger's voice came at me, so I looked up from not quite tying the bow to see him walk into the kitchen.

He had nice jeans on, a caramel-colored button-down that did great things for his tan skin, blond-brown hair and brown eyes. And his shoulder-length hair was back away from his face, not hanging in it, like usual. It didn't look like there was any product in it. It appeared dry, but it stayed away from his face, and there were cute flips at the ends.

At the sight of Hugger's version of cleaned up, I clamped my thighs together and prayed the padding of my bra was doing its job.

"Don't meet a woman's dad lookin' like a bum," he finished, coming to a stop beside me.

"You never look like a bum," I retorted.

"You know what I mean," he said.

I did, and it meant a lot he made an effort.

Hugger, I had absolutely not failed to note, was all about effort, bringing me coffee, pitching in with the dishes, making the bed (really well, I fell into a thirty second freeze of shock that morning when I saw how, while I'd been doing my hair, he'd made the bed exactly like I did).

I was stunned he'd never lived with a woman. He acted like a man who'd been trained.

Then again, it was clear his mother had meant the world to him, so maybe it was her who did the training.

If so, I thanked her, because by all evidence gathered thus far, she did a phenomenal job.

Cautiously, because he didn't hide anything (not a thing), but still, I could tell he sometimes felt awkward with some of the things we'd talked about that day, I asked, "Have you met many parents?"

"Dated a lot in high school," he stated freely. "Dads of high school girls tend to want to meet the boys their daughters are hanging out with. So yeah. Also met Mandy's folks."

"Mandy?"

"The woman who lasted a coupla months."

"Ah."

"You ready to go?" he asked.

Guess we weren't talking about that anymore.

"I need to tie this bow," I answered.

He looked to the bottle. "Why?"

Excellent question.

I pulled the ribbon off and grasped the bottle.

"Ready to go," I told him.

He smiled right before he frowned.

I understood his frown when he said, "Probably need to take your fuckin' car."

I burst out laughing.

When I was done, I said, "I think we just need to be us for Dad. We can take your bike."

"It fucks me to say this, and I'll deny that I did until my dying breath, but I didn't do shit to my hair to have it fucked up on a bike ride to your dad's."

I burst out laughing again.

And boy, one could say it warmed many parts of me, mostly around my heart, that it was clear he wanted to make a good impression on my father.

Hugger grabbed my hand, led me to my tote, let go of my hand and gave me the tote. I threw it over my shoulder. He claimed my hand again, and we walked out.

"I'm drivin'," he said when we were in the elevator going down.

After he made that declaration, before I knew what he was about, he reached and pulled the keys out of my fingers. I'd dug them out of my tote in order to fob us to the parking level.

"You don't know where Dad lives," I stated the obvious.

"You got a mouth. You can direct me," he returned.

"Women have been driving since there've been cars," I pointed out.

"I know," he said as the doors opened.

He said no more.

He simply grabbed my hand again and pulled me out.

"Can you explain then why I'm apparently not driving my own car?" I asked after he pushed through the vestibule doors and led us into the garage.

He stopped and looked down at me. Since we were attached, I stopped too and looked up at him.

"No. Got absolutely no rational explanation for that."

Well, that was honest.

He kept going.

"What I can say is, I've never had a woman of my own, but I know there are some things that are gonna go down if I do."

Oo.

Interesting.

"And what are those things?" I asked, trying not to sound too eager for this information.

"I drive."

I frowned.

He grinned and added, "And she won't take out the garbage. Ever."

Hmm.

I liked this.

I wasn't sure anyone enjoyed taking out the garbage, but what I knew was, I didn't.

"Unless she's got some knowledge of them, any vehicles we own are my domain," he went on.

I liked this too because I had no knowledge of them, but also because the maintenance and purchasing of them was a pain in the ass.

"I don't do yards, but she's not gonna either. We'll hire out," he continued.

"What if she likes doing yards?" I asked, regardless of the fact that I'd never done yardwork in my life, and I hoped I lived the rest of it not doing any.

He narrowed his eyes on me. "You like doing yardwork?"

"I've never done it, but even so, I feel I can safely proclaim that I do not."

"So in this context, does the answer to your question matter?"

"Kind of. I mean, if she likes mowing and trimming and all of that, would you not let her do it?"

He thought about this.

And then he said, "Yeah, but then I'd have to do it with her."

"Why?"

"Multiple reasons."

"Name two," I challenged.

"One, because she might like doin' it, but it's still work. Shit can get under your skin, you think you're carrying more than your share of the load. So I'd pitch in so she didn't think she was carrying me."

That was a ridiculously good answer.

"Two," he carried on, "because my guess is, if she's my woman, I like spending time with her, so even if you don't dig everything she digs, you find ways to spend time together."

Oh my fucking *God*.

That was a ridiculously good answer too.

How was this guy *all* that was *this guy*?

"We done with your interrogation?" he asked.

"I'm not interrogating you," I declared.

His head tipped to the side and one side of his lips hitched up.

I rolled my eyes and tugged his hand to get us going again, admitting, "Okay. Minor interrogation. Relax. I didn't pull out the thumbscrews." I paused for maximum comical effect. "This time."

He chuckled and beeped the locks on my car.

I got in the passenger side of Baby Shark, a seat I'd never taken.

It was comfy.

As I put on my belt, Hugger adjusted the driver's side before he even attempted to fold in.

It seemed he did it without too much trouble, however, he looked squeezed in once he closed the door.

And now I was considering buying a new car...for a man. Even if it'd be my car and only sometimes would he be driving it.

Yeesh.

I had it bad.

The thing was, deep down, I didn't really care.

No.

I was pretending to care because I felt like I was supposed to, even though it felt totally right having it bad for Hugger.

"Are you comfortable?" I inquired while he was latching his belt.

"No. Because I'm scared as fuck one of Phoenix's desperado drivers is gonna make us become one with this scrap of metal."

That was when I chuckled and leaned forward to program Dad's address into the satnav so Hugger could get us there without me having to direct him.

We headed out.

"Do you only own your bike?" I asked.

"Nope. We get weather in Denver, so I also got a truck."

"What color is it?"

"Silver."

"Do you like snow?"

"Lanie and Hop got a place up in Vail. They let anyone use it if they aren't up there. I like to head up when it snows. Their place is away from the slopes. Peaceful. Seems more of that when snow is on the ground."

I could see that.

"Don't like drivin' in it," he continued. "I know how. Others don't. They're the problem and you got no control over it."

"I've never driven in snow, and I need a jacket if it gets close to seventy degrees," I shared.

He busted out laughing.

I reveled in it because I was noticing he didn't laugh all that much.

There were smiles, chuckles, but not much laughter.

Through it, he asked, "Seventy degrees?"

"I've got desert girl blood."

"I guess so," he murmured, and chuckled anew, saying. "Seventy degrees. You must have been in hell in London."

"Oddly, no. I grew to form a great appreciation for jumpers and boots."

"Jumpers?"

"What they call sweaters."

"Why do they call them jumpers?"

"No idea. Though it was fun learning all their different words for things," I told him, then asked, "Have you been out of the country?"

He took a turn on Lincoln Drive. "Nope."

"Ever want to go?"

He shifted his ass in his seat and said, "Never really thought about it."

He "never really thought about" what he wanted to be when he grew up either.

I found that alarming when I learned it, as I thought it alarming that he hadn't thought about vacationing outside the US.

If he said, "Nothing I want to see outside this great country," I would get it, even if I wouldn't agree with it, because I wanted to go everywhere. It was part of who I was. It was part of why I became who I became.

"I'd already been to London," I shared. "Dad took me when I was, I don't know, I think thirteen. We also took a cruise down the Rhine when I was fifteen. It started in Amsterdam and went through Germany, Belgium and Switzerland. And for my sweet sixteen, he gave me an Italy trip. Rome, Milan, Florence. Seeing the architecture, going to the museums was why I decided to do what I do for a living."

"What was your favorite place?"

"Probably Florence, for the art. But Switzerland is crazy gorgeous, so there for the landscape. Lucerne seriously is downright magical."

"Would you go back, or would you want to try something new?"

"Both. Though, the new stuff first." I took a beat then asked, "Would you go?"

"Fuck yeah," he said. "Hire a bike, ride through Europe. Reckon that would be the shit."

I relaxed.

Because yes.

That would be the shit.

"Did you have fun with your dad on those trips?" he queried.

I thought about it, then it was me shifting in my seat.

"Yeah," I said, realizing I'd been so busy holding my grudge, I'd forgotten something important. "He's a different man away from the office, and he loves to travel. His family wasn't destitute, but they didn't have a lot, and he'd always wanted to go places and see things. I mean, part of it was Dad being Dad. He wanted me to experience stuff that wasn't my every day, so there was a lot of urging to try foods I wasn't sure I wanted to try, and no matter how much I loved it, he could spend years in museums, and as a kid, that got tired. But he says a mind narrows when a person narrows their world. Like they don't travel. They don't try different foods. They don't expose them-selves to different things, like music or theater or whatever. We used to have this—"

I stopped speaking abruptly because I forgot about this too.

And I'd loved doing it with my dad.

Hugger held his hand my way, palm up.

I placed mine in it.

Once he'd curled his fingers around and rested it on his (very hard, though I'd discovered that already with all our snuggling) thigh, he asked gently, "You used to have this what?"

"Monthly movie night," I croaked out, then cleared the sudden emotion that clogged my throat. "It was sacrosanct. Even if he had a big case happening, he carved out two hours to watch a movie with me. One month was his choice, and I had to watch whatever it was. One month it was mine, and same. We did that for as long as I can remember. Even before he and Mom divorced. And that was the last thing we did together, the night before we moved me to school. It was our thing."

"He pick good movies?"

"It's how I know about Monty Python. So, yeah."

His fingers closed tighter around mine. "Baby, people fall out. We're headed to dinner with him. All isn't lost."

I hadn't told him about my mom's texts, or my conversation with Big Petey, and I hadn't had the time to dive into some of the weirdness I was feeling around that.

I didn't have the time now, because Hugger was turning right on Tatum, so we were maybe five minutes from Dad's place.

But I had to focus on the present because he was right.

All wasn't lost.

Man, I really hoped my dad wasn't a dick to Hugger.

Though, since we had this getting-to-know-time, I wanted to go over one more thing.

"So, I saw it in the documentary, that insignia tattooed on your back. That's Chaos, right?" I asked.

"Yup. Chaos's mark. All the guys got 'em."

Ah.

"And the one under your shoulder at the front?" I continued.

"Chaos history. A lesson. All the brothers have it too. You saw the story in that doc, though Rebel kept some stuff that's personal to us, like that tat, just for us. What it means is, we lost Black, Dutch and Jag's dad, we almost lost Cherry, or Tyra, but Tack calls her Red, and this happened when the men were messed up in seriously stupid shit. But it isn't play stupid games, win stupid prizes. It's, be stupid and do stupid shit, lose what matters."

That tat was a scale, with one side saying BLACK with a grim reaper type figure floating above it, and the other side saying RED with blood dripping off it.

It was way cool, but a little scary.

Now I understood why.

"No other tats for you?" I asked.

Since I'd seen most of his body, but not all of it, I was just checking.

"I'm not a tat guy. Wouldn't have these if it wasn't for the brotherhood. I don't mind it, but I don't have a hankering to get more." He glanced at me. "You got any?"

"Nope."

"Not a tat gal?" he queried.

"Tattoos are art, like yours are, so I like them. I just guess I never had a hankering for one either. Though, if I do, I won't hesitate."

"Yeah," he murmured and flipped on the signal to indicate our turn into Dad's community.

His community was gated, but he left our names at the gate, thus the attendant let us through with no issue.

The reminder of the gate, however, made me wonder how Hugger's brothers were looking after my father when he was home.

"Might not have grown up with much," Hugger began, "but he found his way to it."

He had, and the mini mansions in Dad's neighborhood screamed it.

Not long later, Hugger pulled into Dad's hacienda style home on a low whistle.

"You okay?" I asked as he parked.

He turned to me and asked in return, "You mean, am I intimidated by the fact the man who owns this home doesn't have to have a big dick?"

I burst out laughing again.

I stopped when he drew the backs of his fingers down my jaw and said, "No, babe. Learned a long time ago, I am who I am, I got what I got, and if people think shit about it, fuck 'em. Also, no good comes from wanting what you haven't got. If you want it enough, get it. If you don't get it, you either didn't want it bad enough or it wasn't yours to have."

Okay, we were in my dad's driveway, a place I hadn't been in a decade, and the imminent dinner was anxiety-inducing, to say the least.

It didn't matter.

I let my seatbelt fly and leaned across the short expanse to press my lips to Hugger's.

He caught me at the back of my neck, so I tilted my head and opened my mouth.

He angled his head and accepted my invitation.

And I had Hugger's tongue back, his taste, the darkness of it, the manliness of it, the thrill of it.

All of it was sublime.

Fortunately, he ended the kiss before I crawled into his lap, which was what I was keen to do, but I figured dry humping Hugger in my Fiat in Dad's driveway might not lend to us having a successful mending-fences dinner with my dad.

"Let's do this," he whispered.

I nodded.

He touched his mouth to mine then got out of the car.

I took hold of the gin, my tote, got out, rounded the hood, and there was no hand holding as we walked to the front door.

Nope, Hugger threw his arm around my shoulders and guided me there. He also hit the bell.

We didn't stand there for very long before Dad, wearing casual gray trousers and a silvery-blue long-sleeved polo shirt, opened the door.

He looked at me first, smiled, then looked up at Hugger, his smile vanished and his eyes got huge.

Oh boy.

"Hey, Dad," I greeted.

Dad tore his attention from Hugger and looked back at me.

"I got you some gin," I announced, then pushed the bottle his direction.

Dang, I was nervous.

He stared at the bottle.

He glanced at Hugger.

Then he looked at me with such relief and warmth in his eyes, my legs nearly buckled.

He took the bottle from me like it was priceless crystal and bid, "Come inside."

We did, but I did it shakily due to Dad acting like Hendrick's was priceless.

I mean, he lived in a seven thousand square foot pad in Paradise Valley, he could afford better than Hendrick's, even if Hendrick's was great.

"This is Harlan," I said, indicating Hugger with a weird, restless flick of my hand. "Harlan McCain. Harlan, this is my dad. Nolan Armitage."

Dad offered a hand. "Harlan."

Hugger took it. "Nolan."

"Let's get in and get you some drinks," Dad invited when they broke.

As we followed him, I noticed Dad had added a few pieces to his collection of art, but other than that, the home I shared with him when we moved into it when I was fifteen hadn't changed much.

We hit the back family room, which was close to the kitchen, and on the other side was the dining room, all of which had views to the beautifully landscaped courtyard and the equally beautifully land-scaped pool in the backyard, and Dad offered, "What can I get you to drink?"

I wanted to mainline vodka, so I said, "A dirty martini."

Dad nodded and turned to Hugger.

"I'm drivin', so nothin', unless you got a pop," he said.

"I've got Coke and Sprite," Dad told him.

"Coke'd do me," Hugger replied.

Dad went to the built-in bar, saying, "Make yourselves comfortable."

God, this was so strange.

I kinda grew up here. This had been my home. And as far as I knew, a person's childhood home, no matter they moved into it when they were a teenager, and moved out of it still as a teenager, was always their home.

But I felt like a stranger here, and it made it worse when Dad urged me to make myself comfortable.

Hugger pulled me to one of two white couches facing each other perpendicular to an adobe fireplace.

We sat, doing it close at Hugger's physical command, and Hugger remarked, "Nice house."

"I'm thinking of downsizing," Dad said from the bar.

That sorta hurt.

Why did that sorta hurt?

"It's a lot for one man," Hugger noted.

"Precisely," Dad agreed.

Okay, the strange quotient kept climbing, considering Dad hadn't even roused himself to look askance at a big dude with long hair and an unkempt beard wearing nice jeans and a shirt, but doing this with motorcycle boots.

Dad approached with a fancy tall glass filled with chipped ice and Coke and gave it to Hugger.

"Thanks, man," Hugger muttered, taking it.

Dad returned to the bar asking, "How did you two meet?"

"In an elevator," I said quickly, glancing sideways at Hugger.

He was smiling into his Coke.

Dad had no more to say, even when he came to me with a filled martini glass that included a silver pick stabbed through four fat olives.

I took it from him with murmured gratitude and tried not to down it in one.

He made his own martini (with the Hendrick's) and moved to sit opposite us.

Now the strange quotient was off the charts, because my father was sitting opposite me, but I had no clue what to say.

"How is Suzette?" Dad asked.

"She's been moved to protective custody," I told him.

Was it me? Or did his shoulders slightly slump with relief?

"I think that's wise," he remarked. "Was she okay with it?"

"She's with her parents, so yes," I said.

Dad's brows drew together. "She's with her parents?"

"Actually, her name is Madison. She was abducted in Texas, trafficked, purchased by Imran Babić's son, who was the one, along with a couple of his buds, who violated her," I shared.

Dad winced.

"Imran got in touch with her, threatened her, forcing her to make a false report," I went on. "All that's straightened out now."

"In the end, you should know, I was pleased you encouraged me to drop him as a client. I can't say all my clients are angels, but, particularly, Babić is not a good man," Dad proclaimed.

I didn't exactly *encourage* him.

But if he wanted to look at it that way, I'd take it.

Dad kept going.

"His son is..." a long hesitation before he finished, "worse."

I'd never met the guy, didn't want to, but I knew he was definitely...*worse.*

Dad then looked to Hugger. "Thank you for looking after my daughter and, erm, Madison through that."

"My job as her guy," Hugger replied smoothly before sipping from his Coke.

I bumped him with an elbow.

He made no show I did it except I caught an upward twitch of his beard.

"All right," Dad said, suddenly talking in his booming lawyer voice, which made me jump.

Hugger slid an arm along my shoulders.

Dad kept talking, and he did this directly to me.

"I'd like to get past this first part as it might be something that will make you annoyed, but it must be done, so let's do it and move beyond it."

Here we go.

Before I could waylay him in possibly being a dick, Dad kept going.

"I've set up a trust with what I'm assuming was your tuition, and also rent and an allocation for food and sundries," he began. "This for both your undergraduate and graduate degrees. There will be tax implications for any income and distributions you get from it. But you don't have to pay taxes on the principal. If you have any questions about any of that, you can speak to my accountant."

I sat very still and said not a word.

Because I very well knew that if he was covering those expenses, that trust had to be well over a hundred thousand dollars.

"I would really rather you not attempt to refuse it, Diana," Dad stated. "It's yours. It was my privilege as your father to offer it to you. I didn't get that chance, and I understand why. This is simply me, in part, rectifying my mistake."

When the silence stretched so long after he stopped talking, I forced myself to say something.

"I, uh...Dad, that has to be a lot of money."

"It was set aside for you already," he returned. "At least for your undergraduate. I just added to it when I heard you got your master's."

I was processing a lot, but...

Hang on a second.

This wasn't the first time he noted stuff about me that he shouldn't know.

I mean, he said he had friends who were clients of Annie's, but, although I was on Annie to update her website, which was barely functional outside giving people contact info and a list of services, she did not have bios of staff on there. And as far as I knew, she didn't hand my CV to current or prospective clients.

In other words, this was fishy and gave me a funny feeling.

"Who told you I got my master's?" I asked.

He sipped from his martini before he murmured, "Your mother delighted in keeping me informed of all I'd been missing."

Uh-oh.

Color me still raw about the situation with Mom and her defunct visit, but I was getting mad.

And freaked.

"She didn't tell me she did that," I noted.

Dad said nothing.

"Why would she do that?" I asked.

Dad took another sip from his martini, and again said nothing.

"Dad," I prompted.

Dad sighed.

"I'm sorry for it, been sorry for it nearly your entire life, Diana," Dad said. "But me and your mother not getting along is not something you're unfamiliar with."

"You've been divorced for over two decades," I pointed out. "She's remarried, lives in another state, and I'm grown. There really isn't any reason you two should be speaking at all."

"I was glad to have the updates."

"I can see that. But Mom knew we had a falling out, and the way you said she shared intel about me makes me think it was something she was lording over you."

Hugger's arm around my shoulders tightened.

"I should have chosen different words," Dad murmured.

"But she was lording it over you," I stated.

"She didn't make it a secret she was pleased we weren't speaking," Dad allowed.

"And she told you stuff that, if I wanted you to know, I would have told you. Topping that, she didn't mention once in ten years she was keeping you apprised of my life."

"Diana—" Dad tried.

"She bought a plane ticket to come down here and have a shopping spree this weekend," I announced.

Dad's lips thinned.

Mm-hmm.

Hugger moved his hand so it was wrapped around the back of my neck.

That was sweet, supportive, but still.

"And she didn't ask me. I told her she couldn't come. I didn't know we'd have that breakthrough with Maddy and get her safe. She wasn't pleased."

"Your mother tends to like to get what she wants when she wants it, this isn't something you don't know either, Diana," Dad said.

I made another announcement.

"Nicole encouraged me to mend fences with you."

Dad looked to his crossed knee and muttered like Hugger and I weren't sitting right across from him, "Now, Nicole was a good woman, and I fucked that up."

"Are you serious?" I asked.

His eyes came to mine. "Diana—"

"She said there was something I'm now old enough to know. What is that?"

Dad's face blanched.

Oh God.

It was something.

Something big.

"What is that?" I demanded.

"Baby," Hugger whispered.

"What is it?" I pushed Dad, ignoring Hugger.

Dad looked me right in the eye and asked, or more like pleaded, "Can we have a nice dinner, Buttercup, catch up and leave the harder stuff for later?"

The "Buttercup" was a good touch.

But...

No way.

"Let's get it all out there," I suggested.

"I'm not sure you want your man hearing this."

Now I was less mad and more freaked.

Because...

Hearing what?

"Dad—"

"Diana, really—"

"Dad!" I snapped.

Hugger made a move to get up, which meant he let me go, and I didn't like that at all.

"Maybe I'll just—" he began.

"No." I was still snapping. "You want to know me, you get to know this."

"Diana," Dad bit.

I stared Hugger in the eyes and whispered, "I need you, honey."

A sort of manly wonder washed over his handsome face, a look I instantly adored.

It was quickly followed by a rush of warmth, and I adored that look too.

After gifting me with those, Hugger settled back in.

"Harlan and I are very honest with each other. We don't hold anything back," I declared to Dad, and I realized then we didn't, and that was awesome.

"Fine then, maybe we can get into it later," Dad replied.

"Is it something big?" I asked.

Dad took another sip of his drink.

Avoiding the question.

"Dad, is it something big?"

Again, my father locked eyes with me and he said, "Your mother was having an affair with Brendon Malley well before I began things with Nicole."

I gasped so hard, I nearly choked.

"In fact, I'd already obtained a divorce attorney and had asked her for a divorce by the time I started things with Nicole," Dad continued.

My mouth dropped open.

"Brendon came from family money," Dad kept at it. "We were raising a daughter on one income and scraping together the money for me to buy in as an equity partner, and as such, I had to say no to Margaret too often for her liking. Brendon didn't say no."

The single most sucky part of this?

I believed it.

Every word.

"She cheated on you first?" I whispered, and Hugger's hand was back at my neck, warm and snug.

I wanted to feel better with his touch, and I did.

But my father just rocked my world.

"She did," Dad affirmed.

"She told me you did."

"I know."

Oh my God.

I jumped from my seat and shouted, "Why didn't you tell me?"

Dad stood too, as did Hugger.

Hugger's hand lighted on the small of my back and immediately commenced stroking.

Dad spoke. "Why would I do that?"

"*Why?*" I all but screeched.

"Diana—"

I slammed my glass down on the table between me and my father, thankful it didn't shatter, and straightened, saying, "She made you out to be the bad guy."

"And what was I to do?" Dad asked. "Cast your mother in that role?"

I threw out both hands and cried, "Yes! Since she earned it."

"When you have children, sweetheart," Dad said quietly, "you'll understand."

"You protected her," I whispered.

"No. I protected you."

Holy *shit*.

I turned into Hugger and he wrapped his arms around me.

I was not going to cry.

I was *not*.

Instead, I deep-breathed as Hugger smoothed his hand up and down my back.

It was like he felt I was getting a lock on it because I'd just started doing that when he bent and murmured into my ear, "Not sure it's me you should be hugging, baby."

I looked up at him.

Then I turned to Dad. "Were you going to tell me when I got old enough?"

Dad shook his head. "I was never going to tell you."

"I always blamed you for the divorce."

"I know, Buttercup, and you always loved your mother unreservedly. Girls need their mothers like that."

"They need their dads too."

Dad's face fell and he said, "Maybe I mishandled it."

"No," I said fiercely. "No. No, Dad. You didn't mishandle it at all."

And with that, I walked around the coffee table and threw myself in my father's arms.

He caught me, of course.

He'd done that all my life.

I just didn't know.

And when I did know, I either didn't notice or didn't give him credit for it.

That was about the time I got mascara all over his shiny, silvery-blue polo shirt.

Dad didn't mind.

16

BEST THING I EVER DID

Hugger

WHEN THEY RETURNED to her pad that night, Di was definitely in another mood.

But this time, she wasn't talking.

All the way home, up the elevator and into her place, she was silent.

Hugger stopped at her kitchen bar, threw her keys on it, and watched as she walked right to her bedroom, her movements stiff and jerky.

He saw the lights go on in there.

Hugger really wanted to call Joker, or Shy, Dutch or Jag and ask what to do when your woman just got emotionally gutted from belly to gullet. They'd all been through it, some worse than others, but they had.

He didn't have time to do that.

As ever, he was on his own. This time, he was trying to figure out how to be there for her now.

After Di had her crying jag on her dad's chest, there were only two further sticky moments during dinner.

The first came when Di took off to fix her face, leaving Hugger alone with Armitage.

The man didn't beat around the bush.

"You the reason why I have bikers following me everywhere?"

In order to provide visible presence, his brothers had decided not to go stealthy, but it was still interesting Armitage noticed.

"Di was worried for your safety after you kicked Babić to the curb," he explained. "So I got my brothers to give you some cover."

That openly mollified him, the same with pleasing him, which Hugger thought was a shocker. Though, considering what it said was that his daughter was worried about him, it made sense.

"Are you in a Club?" Armitage asked.

"Yeah. Look it up. Chaos MC. We own and operate Ride Auto Supply Stores and our garage does custom builds. You can find an article in *Wilde and Hay* about our Club and builds. It's still on their website. Also got a documentary about our history. It's streaming. It's called *Blood, Guts and Brotherhood*."

"That's forthcoming."

"Got nothin' to hide."

Armitage glanced in the direction Di had gone, then came back to Hugger.

"You seem to care deeply for her."

Without hesitation, Hugger gave Diana's father the fullness of it.

"My ma did the best she could do, but we didn't have it great. So with all she is and all she gives, Diana is the best thing that's ever happened to me in my life."

Armitage stared at him for several long beats before he confessed, "I did wrong by her."

"You mean not telling her about her mother?"

"No, something else."

Hugger made an educated guess. "You mean not handlin' it like you should when she got hurt."

"That," Armitage forced out in a strangled voice.

"Man, if you don't know your daughter's got a heart of gold by now, start paying attention. I don't know what went down because I asked her not to tell me before I met you seein' as I didn't want to hate your guts before that happened. What I know is, she's here now. She misses you. So fix it. And advice, you're not gonna do that if you act like she's a guest in her father's house."

"Of course," Armitage murmured, his attention acute on Hugger, sizing him up with this new information, before he jerked up his chin to indicate Di was returning.

The second sticky part happened twenty minutes later, when a huge-ass order of Indian food showed. Apparently, it was all Di's favorites and from Di's favorite Indian joint.

She nearly lost it again, having this demonstration her dad remembered something that mattered to her, but she held it together.

They ate it around the kitchen island, like family, not in the dining room, even though Hugger saw the table was set.

Di relaxed and caught up with her dad.

There was a lot they talked about that made Hugger feel out of place.

They were both highly educated and well-traveled, with Armitage sharing he continued to tour the world the years Di wasn't in his life, hitting Sweden, Poland, Australia, New Zealand, South Korea and Japan.

Di told him all about her internship in London and her "museum vacations" to Washington DC, New York City, Chicago and Los Angeles, and her "beach vacations" to St. Thomas and Aruba.

Hugger didn't have a lot to offer, and fortunately, they were so into catching up, that was neither noticed nor expected.

Though Di, being Di, made sure he wasn't left out, touching him, smiling at him, leaning in to bump him with her shoulder to indicate she hadn't forgotten he was there and making sure his plate was piled high.

They ate a gut-busting amount of food, and Armitage still unearthed a caramel apple pie he'd bought that made Di sniffle, telling Hugger that was another favorite, but again she held it together.

She said she was going to host her dad for their next dinner, and Armitage jumped right on that.

They set it for the next Wednesday.

The mood came over her the minute they hit the car.

And now he had to do something about it.

He just had no clue what.

He walked down the hall to her bedroom just in time to see her standing on her side of the bed, her phone to her ear, obviously in the middle of leaving her mother a message.

"...acting like a child. Stop pouting. I had dinner with Dad tonight, and you and I have something important to talk about. *Call me.*"

She stabbed her screen then looked at Hugger.

"I'm such an idiot," she decreed.

Shit, he was glad she was talking.

Even so, he didn't like what she was saying.

"You are not," he growled.

"All my life, I've been ignoring what a spoiled brat she is."

"She's your ma. That's shit you don't notice."

"Well, Dad wasn't like that. Nic wasn't like that. So how didn't I notice?"

"Because she's your ma."

She stared at him a beat before she teetered, landing face first in the bed.

Christ, the last few weeks she'd been put through the gamut of emotions.

And still, she could be cute.

He toed off his boots before he got in the bed on the other side, claimed her under her arms and hauled her up to his side.

He then went still when Diana shifted so she was on her hip and she could flip off her pumps. She then immediately shifted again so she was straddling his hips, collapsed her chest on his and dug her forehead into his neck.

"There's more with Dad," she announced. "Stuff we have to talk through. But I think I'm getting it."

"Getting what?"

"Why it felt like he was so hard on me. Okay, not felt like, he was hard on me. But maybe he was like that so I wouldn't turn out like Mom."

Hugger had his fingers wrapped around her waist. She felt too good astride him, her weight on him, her smell everywhere. All of that was so fantastic he didn't trust himself to move his hands.

So he kept them where they were and asked, "How was he hard on you?"

She pushed up so she was resting her forearms in his chest, which wasn't better or worse on the effect she was having on his cock, though now he could see her beautiful face and fantastic hair, and that was definitely worse.

Fuck, he had to get his shit tight. She was going through something and all he could think about was banging her.

"I had to get good grades, as in, a B was unacceptable," she said. "Extracurricular activities, and a lot of them, so I could have a well-rounded experience in school and didn't 'waste my time,' Dad's words, on something useless like TV. I had chores around the house. I had a reading list that was not school mandated, but Dad mandated. He opened a joint checking account for me when I was sixteen, and I had to keep it balanced monthly and show him my work. He had firm opinions about how I wore my hair, and my clothes, lecturing about how they represented me, but also him. He was also pretty intense about me not gaining weight. He's a fit guy, and into healthy living, and he pressed that on me in a big way."

Listening to all of this, Hugger treaded cautiously. "So, essentially, he was a dad."

"It was a lot, Hugger, and maybe as a man, he didn't get how being judgy about how a girl ate and her weight and appearance are really, *really* not good things. But more, I never got a 'well-done.' It was more, 'okay, you did that, this is what you need to learn next.' His disappointment was pretty extreme when I put a foot wrong, and he didn't hesitate to share it. It felt like he wanted me to be a Stepford kid. Part of it was suffocating, most of it was that it sucks to disappoint your dad."

She shut her mouth with a snap and her eyes got big.

She explained this by saying hurriedly, "This must all sound pretty stupid to someone like you."

He didn't get what she was saying. "Why?"

"I had a dad who gave a shit and maybe was a little too tough on me, probably because he didn't want me to grow up spoiled and so selfish, it was more important for me to get my hooks in a rich man who would take care of me as I wished to be taken care of, than it was to retain custody of my only child. And you haven't shared, but you must have—"

Hugger's fingers moved, not of their volition, and they did this to dig into her flesh.

"Your mom gave up custody of you?"

"Yeah. From the beginning, Dad had full custody, and she didn't fight it. And when she met Rick, she moved to Idaho to be with him."

Hugger tried to digest that.

He couldn't digest it.

He then tried to come to terms with it, because that had to have destroyed Diana when it happened.

It was impossible to come to terms with and he hoped like fuck he never met her mother.

"Harlan," Di called.

"Against all the odds, my ma kept firm hold on me," he told her. "We were never rolling in it, but I always had a roof over my head, and it was a decent one, food in my belly, and plenty of it, and clothes on my back, and she made a big deal out of getting me new at the beginning of each school year and tripling down on that at Christmas and my birthday. No kid in school ever knew what my mother did, and they never knew we didn't have a lot. She made it that way, so people wouldn't think shit and kids wouldn't be assholes to me. She let me go only when she was dead, and she didn't even want to do that. She died with her hand in mine, too weak to curl her fingers around, but she was still holding on. And her last words on this Earth were, 'Best thing I ever did was you.'"

He watched bright hit her eyes, and she whispered, "Those were her last words?"

"Lookin' me right in the eye until the light blinked out in hers."

She pushed up so she could drop her forehead to his. "Oh, Hugger."

Fuck.

Fuck.

That felt good.

All his life, they'd been alone...

He'd been alone when he lost her.

He wasn't alone now.

Fuck.

"You are, you know," she said.

His voice sounded funny, scratchy and strange, when he asked, "I am what?"

"The best."

Fuck.

It was wrong, it wasn't the time, but Jesus, he had to kiss her.

He was wrong. It was the time, because Di kissed him.

He'd thought a lot about it, too much, but he knew their first time he wanted to take it slow, lead them both to savoring it, making it a memory that lasted forever.

The instant his tongue touched hers, that plan flew out the window.

He rolled her to her back and he couldn't seem to get enough of her. His hands were everywhere, his mouth devouring hers.

She met him with intensity and exceeded it, heaving to push him to his back so she was on top again, breaking the kiss, lifting up and yanking off her top.

She was wearing a little black pushup bra, no frills, but the swells of her tits over the top of her bra made his dick jerk.

He sat up and went after her neck with his lips, down her chest, as she went after the buttons on his shirt.

He was nearly to her tit, intent to take the nipple through her bra (before he took off her bra) when she pushed him to his back and bent to his chest, shoving his shirt aside, scraping her fingers through the hair, finding his nipple with her mouth.

He wasn't sensitive there, but he felt it, it felt good, and it felt even better when she kept using her nails as she trailed her lips down, down, until she was edging the waistband of his jeans with her tongue and going for his fly with her fingers.

Oh no.

Hell no.

He got first taste.

She cried out in surprise and excitement when he lifted her clean off him and tossed her to her back, and he felt the sound she made in his dick too.

Then he got out of bed, tugged his shirt off his shoulders, heard her gasp, took hold of her ankles, dragged her to him and heard her gasp again.

With her green gaze searing into him, he went after her belt, her button, her fly, and dragged her pants and panties down her legs.

Seeing her, mostly bare for him, he almost came in his jeans.

"Harlan," she breathed.

He dropped to his knees beside the bed, hauled her ass to the edge of it, pitched one of her thighs over his shoulder, the other one, heard her whimper, saw her pretty, slick, pink pussy right there for him.

And he buried his face in it.

Christ, heaven.

If he was in his right mind, no matter how wet he found her when his mouth hit her, he would have given her a lot more foreplay before this point.

But the instant she felt his touch there, she arched her back, digging her pussy into his mouth, her heels into his back, and she moaned, so he took a break from licking to smile against her cunt, because she was right there with him.

Always, Di was right there with him.

Hugger learned quick that he could eat her for a lifetime and not get bored, especially after she clenched her hand in his hair to hold him to her.

He knew she was about to go with the noises she made, the way she was clenching and unclenching her fist in his hair, the way she was ramming her pussy into his face and wriggling.

So he got to his feet.

"Harlan!" she gasped.

He wiped his mouth with the back of his arm, bent to yank off his socks, pulled out his wallet and grabbed a condom. He tossed the wallet on the nightstand, clasping the edge of the condom packet in his teeth as he went after his jeans, his focus on Diana. Her face flushed. Her hair all over the white covers. Her eyes hot, her lids heavy.

She was life. She was heart. She was goodness. She was everything, ready and primed and waiting for him in her bed, her eyes locked to his.

That was, they were locked to his before he pulled his down jeans, then they were locked to his dick.

Her face got pinker, her eyes got hotter, she started to move, and he grunted, "Don't even think about it."

She stopped, and her gaze was even hotter.

Done with the condom, Hugger bent and wrapped an arm around her, digging the sweet little intake of breath he heard when he pulled her deeper into bed.

Having her where he wanted her, he settled into her. He curved one of her legs around his ass, the other around his thigh, took hold of his dick and guided it to her.

"We doin' this, baby?" he whispered against her lips.

"If we don't do it *right now*, I think I'll never forgive you."

He smiled and nudged her opening with the tip.

"Stop playing, Hugger," she ordered.

"You gotta have time to adjust," he explained.

"I got an eyeful, honey. I know that. But I'm tougher than you think."

He knew she was tough, but he was never going to be the one to make her be that way.

He gave her an inch and saw her eyes round then get lazy.

"Nice," she whispered.

She said it, but he felt it.

He gave her another inch, and, Christ, she was tight and so hot, it was killing him to go slow.

"Nicer, honey." She was still whispering, her hands roaming and desperate on his heated skin.

He gave her another inch.

She whimpered, and he got her nails.

Fuck yeah.

"You with me?" he groaned.

"Oh yeah," she gasped. "More, Hugger."

Slowly, he slid all the way in to the root.

She was correct.

Oh yeah.

"Good?" he grunted.

"Great," she breathed.

He kissed her, and he'd wanted to slow things down, give it to her long and good, but she tangled her tongue with his, the kiss went wild, her hands and nails on him were wilder, her legs tightened on a demand, and she gave him no choice but to bang the fuck out of her.

So he did.

She got off on it, arching and grasping and scratching.

He got off on it because he'd been right.

She was everything.

Proving that, Diana came loud against his mouth, doing it clutching a fistful of his hair, a handful of his ass and her pussy around his dick.

He came quiet, groaning into her neck and pumping hard into her cunt.

It was quiet because it was the biggest load he'd ever shot, the longest he'd ever gone, and the sweetest he'd ever had, and his body needed the energy to give it to him.

He had just enough presence of mind to keep his weight in his forearms as he collapsed on her.

And he knew he was done.

This was it.

She was it.

He might not have much to offer, but even if it killed him, he'd find a way to hand her the world.

"Okay, that was…" He felt her chest expand with a big breath. "Freaking *fantastic*."

He lifted his head to look down at her, cheeks still flushed, lips swollen, eyes hazy.

Damn, she was perfect.

"I wanted to go slower our first time," he shared.

"For heaven's sake, why?"

He felt his lips curl up even as he explained, "I wanted to make love, not bang."

"Making love is for movies and romance novels. Banging is where it's *at*."

Still buried inside her, he burst out laughing.

He'd never done that with a woman, and it felt phenomenal.

"Your beard and the head you give, baby," she purred, running her fingers through his hair before she scraped her nails through his beard. "*Damn*."

"You a blow-by-blow after type of girl?" he teased.

"Not until now. But I think we should go over every second of that and how awesome it was so we're sure to commit it to memory."

Fuck him, he was laughing again.

But he didn't need to go over it.

He'd remember every second until he died.

"I'm losin' you," he murmured, brushed his lips against hers, and went on, "Gonna go deal with this rubber and be back."

She nodded.

He kissed her, meaning it to be quick and light.

Instead, they made out and it took a while for him to disengage and hit the bathroom.

When he came out, she had his shirt on, drawn end over end at her front, and she was sitting cross legged in the middle of the bed.

He stopped dead on sight of her.

In his shirt, in her fancy duds, in her cute little sleep shorts, all made up, makeup-free or slime all over her face, she was the most beautiful woman he'd ever seen.

Though, he really fucking dug her in his shirt.

Her eyes roved over him.

His did over her.

And yeah.

Fuck yeah.

Whatever it took, Diana Armitage was gonna be his woman.

Hugger came unstuck and moved the rest of the way to the bed, pulling the covers down. Di adjusted as he did, so when he got in, she could tuck herself to him, and he could yank the bedding over them.

"Fuck hair looks good on you, babe," he observed.

She giggled, actually girlie giggled, and rubbed her face in the hair on his chest.

Totally everything.

She lifted her head and said, "It does on you too."

His response to that was tugging his shirt up at her back and clamping a hand on her ass.

Then he got serious.

"How you feelin'?"

"Exceptional. Awesome. Amazing. Fantastic. Do you need more adjectives?"

He couldn't stop himself smiling at her, but he had to say, "I mean about the other shit."

Another big breath where her tits dug into him, something that felt really fucking nice, and she let it out, saying, "It'll be interesting to hear what Mom has to say about lying to me my entire life. But I think tonight actually went well, especially after Dad stopped acting like the Princess of Wales was over for a martini, and it became a family night."

So he called that right.

Good.

"And it might have been a bumpy ride, but the ride I got after dinner totally made up for it," she added.

He couldn't stop his chuckle, either.

And he felt relief, because it seemed he'd played it right.

"How many condoms do you have?" she asked.

"Only that one."

Her lips turned down. "This is not good hot-biker-guy planning, Hugger McCain."

"I'll swing by a CVS tomorrow."

"What are we gonna do until then?"

At that, he burst out laughing.

Then he rolled her to her back and murmured, "We'll figure it out."

"I'm one hundred percent certain we will," she whispered, slipping her arms around his neck.

He kissed her.

Di, being Di, gave it right back.

17

BORN THAT WAY

Hugger

"Babe," he warned, his voice guttural.

Diana, kneeling between his spread thighs, his legs bent at the knees, his head and shoulders against her headboard so he could watch, kept blowing him.

If forced to make a choice, say, with a gun to his head, that he'd only have her mouth or her pussy for the rest of his life, he'd pick her pussy.

But it'd be a tough decision.

"Di," he grunted when he felt his balls draw up.

He was about to blow.

She slid him out, he got her eyes, but her tight little fist around his dick kept pumping him, and she used the nails of her other hand to drag them down his inner thigh.

This meant he closed his own eyes, dug his head into her headboard and shot all over his stomach.

She milked the last gushes out with a gentler hand, and he was far from over it when she landed on him like she wasn't bothered the least about lying on a puddle of cum.

He forced himself to focus on her and saw her smiling huge.

"Well, that was fun," she said.

Hugger grunted again, but it was just a sound, no words this time.

"I'm glad I did my hair yesterday so I'd have an extra half an hour to go down on you this morning," she shared.

He'd woken rough, as normal, but got over it pretty damn quick when Diana went at him right away.

He was back to rough, and more, realizing he had a woman on his hands who was chipper in the morning.

Not to mention thrilled she got to give him a blowjob.

"Give me a second to recover, and I'll return the favor," he mumbled.

"That's not necessary."

He squeezed her with his arms. "Babe, I come, you come."

"Is that a rule?"

"It is for me. For us."

"I overwhelmingly accept this as a rule for us, though with caveats, like rainchecks when I have to get up and get ready for work."

"I thought you could pretty much come and go as you please."

"I like to be disciplined about it so if Annie tunes into the real world, she doesn't think I'm taking advantage."

He rolled her, stating, "You're gonna be late today."

"Harlan."

He slid his fingers between her legs.

"Harlan," she whispered.

He smiled.

Then he kissed her.

Then he went about negating any bullshit about rainchecks.

Hugger was in his chair at the window, he had his phone out, and he was looking at the careers page of the Denver Art Museum.

They had three openings.

None of them in Di's field.

Di had finished with the painting the day before, and now she was sitting at the big table in the middle of the space, bent over a tiny square of wood, peering through a big stationary magnifying glass, working on it with some brushes.

It was mid-morning.

And this was when Annie wandered in.

She stopped, looked at Di, then to Hugger, then to Di, and Hugger, back to Di.

Di's head came up, and when Annie just stood there, she called, "Hey, Annie."

"Hey." She took another step in. "Is your father okay?"

Hugger straightened, taking his feet from the sill.

"I think so," Diana said slowly. "Why do you ask?"

"You said there was some threat."

Hugger relaxed.

Seemed it took approximately twenty-seven hours for Annie to process shit.

"We're just being cautious," Di told her. "Everything should be fine and Hugger won't have to be with me every day."

Annie looked to Hugger. "Are you a professional bodyguard?"

"No, I'm a biker."

Annie nodded like this made perfect sense to her.

She then looked to Diana. "I'm having brunch this Sunday. Would you and your bodyguard like to come?"

Hugger did not miss the *Oh shit!* look on Di's face before she hid it and said, "Full disclosure, Annie. Hugger is also my guy."

Annie appeared confused. "Your guy?"

"My boyfriend," Diana explained.

They hadn't had that conversation, but it was good to know she knew where they were at.

Annie's gaze drifted to him. "Oh, how lovely. You're looking out for your girlfriend."

"Yeah," he said.

"Very gallant of you," Annie remarked.

"Thanks," he replied.

"Do you like brunches?" Annie queried.

"I've never been to one," he said.

Annie's eyes got about two times bigger than her round lenses. "Really?"

"Really."

"Never?" she pushed.

"Bikers aren't big on brunches," Diana butted in.

"Well then, you must come. You're missing out." She turned to Diana. "My place. Ten. See you then," she said like they wouldn't be working in the same building for the next two days.

And with that, she wandered out.

Hugger looked to Di. "What was that 'oh shit' look you had when she invited us to brunch?"

Di glanced at the door then waved her hand at him in a *come here* gesture.

He hauled his ass out of his chair and went there.

"Three possibilities," she whispered like Annie might overhear. "She'll remember she asked people to brunch, and when we all show at ten o'clock, she'll be prepared to host a brunch. Or, she'll remember, just too late, so we'll all sit around for two hours while she prepares brunch. And we'll all do that constantly reminding her she might want to go back to the kitchen and finish what she started. Or, she'll totally forget, we'll show, and she won't be there because she decided to spend the day in Sedona."

He grinned at her. "This doesn't surprise me."

"There is a fourth possibility, that being we'll show to find she burned her house down while preparing brunch."

He laughed softly before he said, "We'll go prepared and have donuts before."

"You're good with brunch with Annie?"

He needed to un-narrow his world, and he was starting now.

"Sure, why wouldn't I be?"

"Because she's Annie, and she might forget who you are by Sunday."

He laughed again, bent to touch his mouth to hers, and when he pulled away, said, "I'll weather that blow if it happens."

She smiled brightly up at him, and damn, but he liked her smile.

"See things have progressed while I been away."

They both turned to see Big Petey strolling into Di's workshop.

"Petey!" Diana cried, like he'd been away years, not days.

She got up from her chair and raced around the table to throw her arms around him.

Hugger watched Pete's eyes close as he enveloped her with his arms and gave her a tight hug.

When they broke, Di asked, "How've you been keeping?"

"I ain't been eatin' as good, that's for sure."

"So obviously that means you're coming over for dinner," Diana stated.

Hugger wanted some just them time when she wasn't at work or getting over dealing with heavy shit.

But for both Pete and Di, he'd deal with it.

Pete gave him a glance, and when Hugger gave him a nod, he turned back to Diana.

"Sounds good."

"Awesome," she gushed.

"Here to check in and give you two an update."

"Let me drag another chair over," Di said.

"Don't you move," Hugger ordered.

Di looked to him.

But Hugger just walked to his chair, dragged it over, her chair, and rolled it over, and the chair behind her desk, and he rolled that over too.

They sat and Pete launched in.

"Resurrection has some assets that are good with findin' shit out. And they found some shit out. Part of that was Imran put Esad's and his bros' asses on a plane to Costa Rica two days after Maddy took herself to the hospital. Imran himself jumped bail four days ago, and he went to Bolivia. Costa Rica has an extradition treaty with the States. Bolivia does too, just not a functioning one."

Diana sat back in her chair. "They ran?"

Pete nodded. "There's reasons they ran. Feds are deep into this trafficking ring. So deep, Maddy's statements were just icing on a cake they been baking. Could be weeks, or maybe just days, before they moved in with warrants. Esad's involvement in this, something they already knew about, turned them on to Imran, and they started gathering shit on him too. They know they all fled, so they stepped up shit and did a series of raids yesterday. Rounded up a lot of Imran's army he left behind, not to mention a bunch of other stuff that means he best keep his ass in South America or it'll get nailed."

"What does this mean?" Di asked.

"It means Imran is one stone-cold motherfucker, because it's clear his boy isn't the brightest bulb in the box, and either the cops, or Resurrection, are gonna track his ass down. And if it's the cops, they'll haul it back here and none of them are gonna breathe free air for the rest of their lives." Pete sucked in a breath and further shared, "They found the other girls. There were three. And they got no one threatening them to talk smack to the police, so they're singing. Esad and his boys are fucked."

"So Imran's...what? Sacrificing his son?" Di asked.

"Ain't gonna let his boy lead anyone to him. Easier to go on your own. Less expensive too," Big Petey said.

"I really don't care what happens to Esad, but if you consider minimum accepted parenting protocols, that's gross," Diana declared.

Both Hugger and Big Petey chuckled.

"That all you got?" Hugger asked.

Big Petey nodded but said, "Rush wants us to stay down here on

Di and Armitage. They haven't rounded up the entire army and Rush wants to make sure it's all good before he pulls us."

Diana was smiling, but she had nothing to worry about.

Until he nailed things down with her as to where they were at, and where they were going, he wasn't going anywhere.

Big Petey kept talking.

"Rush is chatting with Lee, and Lee is chatting with Mace, who's keeping on top of all of this. Mace's crew down here is new, but they're making some inroads, got some informants, and he thinks they'll know if Imran left anyone with any orders we won't like."

"Good," Hugger muttered.

"Who's Lee?" Diana asked.

"Lee Nightingale," Pete said. "The firm that Mace runs down here is called Nightingale Investigations and Security. Mace is a partner, and they got three offices in three states."

"Ah," she murmured.

"Good you're here," Hugger said. "You can hang with Di while I run an errand."

"I can also run the errand for you," Matchmaker Pete offered.

He loved the man, but he wasn't going to task him with buying condoms.

"I gotta do this myself," he said. Then requested, "Walk me to my bike?"

Big Petey pushed out of his chair saying, "Sure thing."

Hugger got out of his own, rolled it back behind Di's desk, and she was standing with Pete when he returned.

He dropped a kiss on her hair and earned her tipping her head back to catch his gaze.

"Get a mondo box. *Mondo*," she instructed.

He grinned at her again, dropped another kiss, this one on her lips, then he turned to Pete, who was watching them, grinning himself, and they strolled out.

He waited until they were standing by his bike before he started.

"Got shit I gotta work out with the Club," he announced.

"Right," Big Petey replied, regarding him intently.

"Tack's been callin' me."

"That's because I told him it's time you worked your shit out with the Club."

Hugger crossed his arms on his chest.

"Don't be pissed at me," Pete ordered. "You're there now so you know it's time."

He couldn't argue that.

"I see you and Di got yourselves sorted," Pete observed.

"We do," Hugger confirmed. "Though there are issues."

"Those being?"

"Man, I don't gotta say them because they're obvious."

"Since I asked, you can take it that they aren't."

"She's got a master's degree. She's traveled to places like Lucerne. She's got a good life here."

Big Petey narrowed his gaze on Hugger. "You not been payin' attention, son?"

"Pete—"

"Lanie owns the top advertising firm in Denver. Millie owns the top party-planning company."

"Pete—"

"Georgie's an award-winning journalist," Pete kept at him.

"Yeah, and Hop, High and Dutch got a lot more to offer than I do," Hugger shot back.

Big Petey was getting mad. "How's that work out, Hug?"

"I..."

Hugger shut his mouth because he didn't know what to say.

"Yeah, that's about how it works out," Big Petey bit off and stepped closer. "Listen, Hug, love isn't a weight. One person doesn't get into it with more on their side of the scale so the other has to catch up. Love just *is*. It's the air we breathe. It's the beat of a heart. You fall in love with a woman, the only thing that's important that you got to offer is *you*, and if she doesn't take you as you are, then she isn't the woman you should give your love."

Hugger had nothing to say to that.

Big Petey got even closer.

"Lanie loves Hop because *Lanie loves Hop*. Millie fell in love with High the first night she met him. Georgie and Dutch were livin' together before you could blink. Joker and Carrie fell in love in high school, were torn apart, and now they got five kids."

"Joker is genius at building a chopper or anything with an engine," Hugger reminded him.

"Carrie don't love Joker because he builds killer cars and bikes. Joke could dig graves for a living, and he'd be her life."

This was completely true.

Hugger's gaze drifted to the window he sat at in Di's studio.

"I'll tell you something, brother," Big Petey said, regaining his attention. "There's a lot that goes into making us who we are. Yeah, part of it is our parents, and I don't think I'll get an argument from you that you had the best mom on the planet."

"You won't get an argument with me on that," Hugger said low.

Pete nodded once. "Yup. And she provided the guidance to make you the man you are. And we can just say that woman had more than enough of putting up with men, so she knew how to guide you to be the best you could be. You took it from there. And I can guaran-damn-tee you, that woman in there"—he jabbed a finger at Di's work-shop—"sees every lesson Jackie taught you, every gift Jackie gave you, everything you sucked up from the life you led so you could give good to the woman you claimed as yours. And Di wants that, and she wouldn't care if you dug graves either. She just wants *you*."

Hugger suddenly realized he was having trouble breathing.

"I'll tell you one more thing before I go back to your girl," Big Petey stated. "If I hear you even remotely runnin' yourself down to me, I'm an old bastard, but I'll find it in me to kick your ass. I get you. I get what you gotta work out. I get that you gotta get past that and I'm pissed as shit I didn't push it so you could get past it a lot earlier than right now. But you'll get past it, with your Club at your back, because you got him in you, but you'll learn *you are not him*."

You are not him.

Yeah, fuck.

He couldn't breathe.

Pete wasn't done.

"Di doesn't care what books you've read or what countries you've visited or what job you do. She cares that you ran the vacuum. She cares that you made her dad safe. She cares that you made *her* safe. She cares that you held her when she lost Maddy. She cares about the way you look at her, you treat her, and you touch her. That's all she cares about. You've known her a week and she knows you better than you know yourself, brother. You can decide to stay home while she gallivants around the world, but she'll always come home to you and be happy as fuck she did."

Hugger stood still as Pete got up on his toes to get right in his face.

"Pay attention, son, she's been givin' you that from the very beginning. Don't put your own damned self in the place of missing it, which might mean you'll miss out on the best thing that's ever come into your life, because I promise you, you'll hate yourself for the rest of it if you do."

"Relax, Pete. I already decided I'll do whatever it takes to make Di mine."

Big Petey rolled back on his feet and muttered, "Well, all right."

"Do me a favor and look after her so I can buy us a mondo-sized box of condoms."

Pete narrowed annoyed eyes at him, then blew out a breath.

After that, the man turned and stomped back to Di's workshop.

Hugger got on his bike and rode to a CVS he'd noticed while taking Di to work.

Before he went in, he pulled out his phone and texted Di to see if she needed anything.

He'd nabbed the prophylactics and was heading to the cashier when she texted back *Twizzlers cherry licorice bites.*

This text meant he was smiling, even after he'd cashed out.

He was on his bike, ready to start it up and roll out, when the urge hit him.

It was the type of urge that had only hit him once before, last night when he didn't know what to do to help Di.

But now he had time.

His first instinct was to fight it.

His second was to set it aside and think about it later.

His last was to just fucking do it.

So he called Dutch.

"Yo, Hug," Dutch answered. "All good?"

"Yeah, Pete's with Di and I'm running an errand, but you got a second?"

"Got lots of 'em. Jag and Coe are on the dad and I'm kicking back at the rental until you get home with Diana. Then I'll be keeping an eye on the complex. What's up?"

"You and Georgie hooked up fast and put down roots just as fast."

"Yeah."

"How'd you..." Jesus, this was tough. "How'd you know with her?"

Dutch chuckled and said, "Man, at first, I didn't. She was a major bitch when I met her. Then she wasn't, and I said some stupid shit and nearly blew it. But then she was just her, and I just knew."

"That was it?"

"You know Georgie?"

He did.

And yeah, she was a damn fine woman.

"I see your point," he muttered.

"Not lost on any of us you got your eye on Diana," Dutch said leadingly.

"She's problematic in the sense she gives everything she's got to pretty much everyone she knows."

"Sounds like a match."

Hugger stared at his fuel tank as he asked, "What?"

"You're the first to volunteer on missions. You're the first in to open the store. You're the first to raise your hand when someone needs something covered. Hop said we gave you the wrong Club name. He said we shoulda called you Shaky, since that's the opposite of Steady."

Hugger lifted a hand to rub the back of his neck, which was getting scorched by the sun, but that wasn't the heat that was concerning him.

That heat was happening in his gut.

"Hug?" Dutch called.

"You know who my dad is?" he asked abruptly.

"No," Dutch replied. "I know whose seed made you. I also know he wasn't even close to bein' your dad."

"I still was made from his seed."

"Brother, you know Joker's story. Now, is Joke one thing like that shitheel who made him?"

Fuck.

"No," Hugger pushed out.

"And word got out about what Core grew up with, what happened, what his dad did. Core veered hard off the righteous path, but he pulled out all the stops to drag himself back. Hellen thinks he hangs the moon and ushers in the sun. He strayed, but he got his shit tight and earned the love of a good woman and lives a life doing good things for people who need it. In the end, he's not one thing like the seed that made him."

Hugger knew Hardcore's story too.

And again.

Fuck.

"Listen," Dutch said. "You need to talk to Tack."

"I'm gonna."

"Right, then in the meantime, don't let that shit stand in the way when you find what you want. Hell, when you find what you deserve, man. Just don't."

"She lives in a different state, brother."

"I'd follow Georgie to Kazakhstan if she had to move there for a posting, and I don't even know where Kazakhstan is."

Hugger chuckled, but he was surprised at hearing this.

"You would?"

"Definitely."

"What about the Club?"

"Club's not going anywhere. My patch will still stand. I'd just be wearing it in Kazakhstan."

At that, Hugger felt the sun scorching at his neck and he wondered if he could put up with it for a long haul.

"Thanks, Dutch. This was cool."

"Anytime, you hear that?'

"Yeah."

"No really, Hug. You hear that?"

The heat came back to his gut and his voice was low when he said, "Yeah, Dutch. I heard it."

"You got a lotta love, brother. You just gotta open yourself up to us giving it."

That was when Hugger dropped his head.

And he repeated, "Yeah."

"Good to let you go?"

Hugger lifted his head. "Come up for dinner if you're patrolling the complex. Diana would be pissed you were close and she didn't feed you."

"Tell me the time, I'll be there."

"Gotcha. Later, brother. And thanks again."

"My pleasure. See you tonight."

They disconnected, and before he could talk himself out of it, he made another call.

He put the phone to his ear, listened to it ring twice, and then he heard the connection.

"About time," Tack said.

"I need something, brother, but I don't know what I need," Hugger admitted.

"You good with me seein' to that with your brothers?"

"No, but it's time."

"Why the no?"

Because he was shit scared, that was why.

"It's about her and you. Jackie and Harlan," Tack's gravelly voice growled. "It has never been about him. You were legacy because you were Jackie's, Hugger. Now when you get home, that will be confirmed. I'll sort it. You got me?"

You were legacy because you were Jackie's.

"I was legacy because of Ma?"

"You're ours, Hug. Born that way."

Ours.

Born that way.

"You got me?" Tack repeated.

"I'm gonna be down here awhile," he warned Tack.

"Yeah. Pete said you're connecting with Diana. Glad for you, brother. 'Bout time on that too. You got a lot of good to give a woman."

Okay, he had to end this because it was messing with his head.

Sure, that was happening in good ways.

But Hugger was discovering a man could take only so much good at once.

Especially if he wasn't used to it.

And he was living right in it with Di. It was all around him all the time, so he could say now it was getting to be too much.

"Bring her up. Introduce her to the family," Tack urged. "And we'll sort this shit out so you can let it go."

"Right."

"Right."

"Man, I just..." Goddamn it. "I never thanked you for lookin' out for Ma. Back when and Chaos paying for her medical shit when she got sick."

"Appreciate the gratitude, Hugger, but I see we been fallin' down on the job. You don't thank family for taking care of family. Now, win your woman and bring her up here so the other women can perform the initiation ceremony. Just be aware she'll go back with about fifty pairs of shoes."

A bark of laughter escaped Hugger because he had not missed the old ladies, all of them, liked their shoes.

"I don't think she'll mind."

"They don't."

"I don't think I'll mind."

"I hear you. Red in her skirts and heels do things to my dick even after I gave her two kids and got well over a decade in with her."

"Good to know."

"You find the right one, that never goes away. It might mellow for a spell. There'll be highs and lows you gotta ride. But one way or another, it doesn't go away."

"Good to know that too."

"We good?" Tack asked.

"Always," Hugger answered.

"Remember that, because it's the bottom-line truth," Tack stated.

Then he hung up.

Hugger shoved his phone in his back pocket.

Then he fired up his bike, backed out, and rode to Di's workshop so he could hand over her licorice.

18

MISSION

Diana

"That's me and Georgie when we got hitched," Dutch said, turning his phone my way so I could see what was on the screen from where I sat across from him at my dining room table.

It hit deep when I saw the picture of the fabulous-looking Dutch Black looking even more fabulous in a tuxedo *sans* bowtie, his collar open.

He was standing next to a model-gorgeous woman with shining brunette hair. Her wedding gown was bodycon with lots of ruched tulle, in a mermaid style, with a princess neckline and cap sleeves made of lace. It was understated but hella elegant with a nod to girlie. A miracle of execution. I dug it entirely.

And she was curvy.

I'd now seen Hugger's body top-to-toe naked. It was sheer perfection, without an ounce of body fat. The furred boxes of his abs were mouth-watering. The delectable V indents at his hips were life-affirming. The bulges of his biceps, veined sinews of his forearms, definition in his shoulders and back, power in his quads (you get me), were proof there was a God.

This was nowhere near what I offered up, and although Hugger gave absolutely no indication he had a problem with my ass, thighs and belly, seeing how happy Dutch and Georgie were, with an obvious underlining of sheer contentment, made something in my heart settle.

Dutch took his phone away, slid his finger on the screen, turned it around and said, "This is Jag and Arch at their shindig."

Whoa.

The woman in that photo was also beautiful, but slender, wearing a strapless sheath of ivory satin with a color-matching circle scarf of soft chiffon that fell from her neck down her back. Her hair was up with no adornment, and there were some fancy chandelier earrings made of pearls falling from her ears. That was it. It was utter simplic-ity, and so freaking cool, it made me rethink the wedding dress confection I'd always dreamed of wearing at my own "shindig."

"Looks like you boys have good taste," I remarked.

Dutch turned the phone around and studied the picture, "Yeah. Arch is the shit." He aimed a smile at me. "And obviously, Georgie was the most perfect bride there ever was."

I returned his smile. "Obviously."

"I got some," Big Petey said from the head of the table, and I turned to my right to see him also showing me his phone.

On it was a picture of an adorable little boy with an equally adorable little girl, both of them dark-headed and smiling.

"That's Playboy and Princess," Big Petey said as he reached over the phone to slide the next picture where a ridiculously handsome, lanky man, with dark hair and green eyes, was holding the little girl from the earlier photo on his hip, another less-little but still little girl on his other hip, and he was standing next to a stunning brunette with sapphire eyes who had the little boy's hand in hers. "Shy and Tabby's kids."

I turned to Hugger, who was sitting beside me, and asked, "You don't have a hotness quotient your brothers have to meet before they become members?"

He grinned at me.

I heard Big Petey and Dutch chuckle.

I turned back to Big Petey who was shuffling through pictures on his phone.

"Playboy and Princess?" I asked.

"Nicknames," Pete grunted. "Real names are Landon Kane and Caroline Tyra. Their middle girl is Wren. Their son is named after Shy's brother and Tab's father, and their last girl is named after Shy's ma and Tab's stepma. Wren is pure wren, our pretty little bird."

"Ah."

"This is Joke and Carrie's brood," Big Petey said, turning the phone back to me.

And yes, you guessed it, Joker was ludicrously good-looking, and his woman, with blonde-red curls, reminded me of a cheerleader. They were surrounded (and one might even say *besieged*) by children.

"Travis, Clementine, Wyatt, Raven and Dakota," Big Petey said. "They were gonna go for another one but thought instead maybe they should let the kids get a little older and adopt one who's older, 'cause they're harder to place. Or they might foster."

He turned the phone his way, slid his finger across the screen, then showed it to me again.

When I saw the picture on it, I felt something I'd never felt before.

My womb clutching with unadulterated yearning.

This was because it was a photo of Hugger with Raven on his back. She had her little arms wrapped around his thick neck. She appeared to be whispering something in his ear, and he appeared to be taking whatever it was seriously.

"Thick as thieves, those two," Big Petey announced. "Uncle Hug's all the kids' favorite, 'cause he's got all the time in the world for them."

"Pete," Hugger warned low.

Big Petey ignored him. "But think sometimes Rave gets lost in the mix with all the kids. Not just her own brood, but all a' Chaos is crawlin' with little ones. She's a shy little gal. Hugger is her safe place."

Slowly, I turned my head to Hugger.

His full lips in his beard were thin in annoyance at Big Petey laying it on kinda thick.

But I *loved this*.

"Uncle Hug," I whispered.

"Shut it," he whispered back.

I smiled huge at him.

Hugger sighed then stood, announcing, "Di cooked, so Dutch, we're gonna clear."

Dutch, who was grinning madly at his lap, muttered, "Right," and stood up, grabbing plates.

Hugger nabbed some of his own and the two men left Pete and me alone.

When the men had gone, I turned to Big Petey.

"Can I see that picture again?"

Pete handed me his phone and I stared at Hugger and Raven.

"They're super cute together," I murmured my understatement.

"Wait until you get a load of them in real life," Pete said.

I couldn't.

I simply couldn't wait.

I also couldn't wait for other things. And seeing that photo made me hope even more than I already was that I'd get them.

Hugger and Dutch came back to get more stuff, then they returned to the kitchen.

I leaned toward Pete, handing his phone to him.

"I think you get we're together now," I whispered.

Pete leaned toward me, his lips tipped up. "Oh, I get that, darlin'."

"He's different." I kept whispering.

"Different how?" Pete asked.

"After Maddy left, he seemed to be pulling away. I mean, not really, but it was like he thought something would happen so we wouldn't. Even before Maddy left, it seemed like he was holding something back. But today, it's not like that at all."

"That happens when a man who's fallin' in love quits fightin' the fact he's falling in love."

My breath caught.

Falling in love.

We heard washing-up noises coming from the kitchen.

"He's got some shit it's his to give you, Di," Pete said, then he warned. "It's heavy."

"Heavy like me working things out with my dad and finding things out about my mom that rocked my world, and Hugger was at my side through all of that?"

Big Petey's brows shot up. "What'd you find out about your mom?

I told him.

"Well, shit," he said, collapsing back in his chair when I finished.

See?

Heavy.

"Harlan told me he had this stuff, I'm not going in blind, Petey," I assured. "But it isn't like he's balked when all my stuff was coming at me. We can't decide how life is going to go, and it's for sure what's going on with him and me isn't out of a storybook. What I can say is, I totally like it like that. Trial by fire, then maybe we'll have smooth sailing."

"Hope you do and glad for you," Pete murmured. "Glad for you both."

I smiled. "Me too."

"Now about your mom..." he trailed off so I'd jump in.

And I did.

"I called her. Left a message. Asked her to call me. She hasn't.

Since then, I've texted twice. She left them on read. I think she knows I know and she's avoiding me."

"What are you gonna do when she stops doin' that?" Pete asked.

Hugger and Dutch came back with the tin of almond cookies as I answered, "I haven't decided. I want to hear what she has to say."

"What're you talkin' about?" Hugger asked.

"My mom," I told him.

His lips thinned again.

"Whatever happens, it'll be okay," I promised, stroking his forearm.

"Mm..." he hummed.

Mm...I so liked Hugger's deep, rough *mm*.

"Parents gotta make all sorts of decisions that are hard," Big Petey announced sagely. "But it's good you know all you had with your dad, no matter what happens with your mom."

"This is true," I murmured, then turned to Dutch. "Speaking of Dad, he lives in a gated community. I was wondering how you guys were looking out for him there. Not that I'm questioning you," I added hurriedly. "Just wondered."

"Darkness covers a lot of shit," was Dutch's answer.

He said no more, but I decided from what he said, they had it covered.

"Pass me that tin," Big Petey ordered.

I slid the tin his way.

He took a cookie, bit into it, and with mouth full, stated, "I hope someone got this recipe off Emmy before she left."

"Don't worry, I totally did. And her recipe for beef and noodles."

Big Petey shot me twinkling eyes. "'Course you did, darlin'."

Hugger draped his arm around the back of my chair, repeating, "'Course you did."

And...yeah.

I liked those cookies, the guys liked them, but Hugger loved those cookies so much, it was a wonder any of them were left.

So of course I did.

ONE COULD SAY it was hard as hell not to climax just riding my big guy with his big dick, his beautiful chest, handsome face, thick hair all over my pillow, thick beard mine for the tugging, all of that being all I could see.

Somehow I managed it.

I watched his eyes darken (more), felt the pads of his fingers dig into my hips, and I was pretty danged pleased I was about to take him there when suddenly I wasn't bouncing on his big cock.

I cried out as he pulled me off and put me on my knees in the bed beside him.

Then he knifed up, moved in, and with his body at my back, he forced me to walk up the bed on my knees, before he tipped me toward the headboard, dipped, positioned, and drove up inside me.

My hand flew out to brace against the wall.

Lord.

So good.

Hugger kept pounding.

My head fell back to his shoulder.

God, I loved, loved, *loved* being tossed around and positioned by my guy. Hugger was a man who knew what he wanted in bed, and didn't hesitate to take it. It was so freaking hot, it was beyond next level hot. It was fifty levels above next level hot.

Scorching.

No, *sizzling*.

Both his hands cupped my breasts, his calloused thumbs rubbing my nipples.

Okay, and I loved riding Hugger, but this was better.

His face buried in the side of my neck, he fucked me, I took it, I adored it—no, *revered* it— and I knew it was getting serious when one of his hands left my breast to trail down my belly and dive between my legs, his finger hitting my clit.

My body jerked as licks of flame shot through it.

"Yeah, honey," I breathed my encouragement.

I met his thrusts, lifted my ass to get more of him, dug my head into his shoulder, and reached behind me to hold on to his hips as he drove into me. It'd been building for a while, but suddenly, it exploded, engulfing me, carrying me away where the only hold I had on anything was being fucked by Hugger. And it was the only hold I wanted on anything.

I was coming down, feeling his finger leave my clit so he could wrap his arm around my belly and hold me steady for his drives.

I got off on that, turning my head so I could get off on hearing his harsh breaths, the soft grunts that shifted to groans, until he plunged deep, squeezed my tit and tightened his hold on my middle as he came.

Hugger was quiet during sex, unlike me. He made noises, but they were soft and belied the effort he put in to making it (super) good for us both.

It was as much of a turn on as everything about Hugger.

He shifted my hair away from my neck with his chin, an effort doomed to fail as I felt it get tangled in his beard, but he kissed my neck through the tangles.

Then he slid out, shifted us back, gently placed me in bed, touched his lips to my forehead and got out of bed so he could deal with the condom.

I adjusted the covers so they were over me and stretched, languid and chill and happy.

Oh yeah, definitely yeah.

Hugger was different that day, not entirely different but different.

It was like he'd been with me, at the same time protecting me from something.

Now, it wasn't like that.

Now, he was just *with me*.

I didn't know what happened, and I wanted to know, but if he never shared, I didn't care.

I was just glad whatever he was holding between us he'd set aside.

He's falling in love.

If any of my closest friends, Bernie, Charlie, Mel, told me they were falling in love with a guy after knowing him a week, I'd have concerns.

But here it was, I was in it.

So was Hugger.

And zero concerns.

This was my happy thought when I noticed the light go off in the bathroom and then Hugger coming out in all his glory.

That glory was glorious, but the look on his face was not.

I was perplexed as he walked around the bed to my side, more perplexed when he took my phone off the charge, and even more perplexed when his annoyed expression turned into an out-and-out scowl when he glanced at the screen.

He put the phone back on the magnet, lifted the covers, moved in and lowered his bulk right on top on me, flicking the covers over his hips once he settled.

At least that felt good (really good).

"What's up?" I asked.

"Your mother still hasn't texted."

I relaxed beneath him, smoothed my hands up his back and mumbled, "Honey."

"It's pissin' me off," he stated.

"I can tell," I said. "But there's nothing we can do about it."

"Yeah," he grunted.

"Can I ask you something?" I requested.

He focused on me. "You can ask me anything."

Okay.

Um.

Yeah.

Totally falling in love with this guy.

And he was totally now all with me.

"You told me earlier you don't like touch and aren't affectionate."

"I don't and I'm not."

I blinked.

"Can't keep my hands off you, though," he muttered.

I pressed my lips together so my smile wouldn't blind him.

"And love your hands on me, even when we aren't fuckin'," he went on.

I pressed my lips tighter.

Once I had a lock on it, I noted, "You seemed pretty affectionate with Raven."

"She's a little kid, and Pete was right. She's bashful. Gets lost in the mix of a lot of rowdy and big personalities."

I stroked his beard and asked gently, "Do you feel a kinship with her with that?"

His head ticked then he said, "Guess so, yeah. Never thought about it, but makes sense."

"Do you, uh...want kids?" I asked cautiously.

He got that expression on his face that he always got when he was about to say "I never thought about it."

Then the look cleared and he said softly, "Yeah."

I thought I was pretty loose under him, but when he said that, I got looser.

"You?" he inquired.

"Yeah."

"How many?"

"Two."

"Two's good. Wouldn't know, but I heard that middle child shit ain't real fun."

"I wouldn't know either, but I heard the same."

His eyes got soft and he went in to rub his nose against mine.

Dang, I loved it when he did that too.

Since he was being so forthcoming (not that he ever wasn't, but still), I took a chance and noted, "You seem different today."

"That's because I decided we're doin' this."

I emitted a surprised pip of laughter. "You just decided that today?"

"No. Decided last night when I found out you were a fantastic lay."

My mouth dropped open.

"Rounded out the perfect package," he stated.

"Well, thank God I didn't disappoint you in bed," I muttered.

"Not sure you can disappoint me in anything, babe."

Holy crap!

I mean, seriously.

Was he for real?

"I was letting my shit get in the way of our shit," he explained. "You took the hit of Maddy, stood strong. Took the hit from your dad about your mom, same thing. Nothing shakes you. We'll be good."

"You wanna tell me what might shake me about you?" I asked.

"That's for Sunday, baby," he said quietly. "Will say, what was fuckin' with my head was that I wasn't good enough for you."

My mouth dropped open again, but this time it did not only because I was surprised, but because I was angry.

"Are you joking?"

"No." He caught my mood and cupped the side of my head with his hand. "Babe, you got a master's degree."

"So what?"

"I've never been out of Colorado except to hit Vegas a coupla times and come here."

This shocked me.

Even so.

"So what?" I repeated on a snap.

His head went back several inches. "You don't see where I'm comin' from with that?"

"Not really, seeing as what it says is that you think I'd eventually think I was better than you."

His voice shared he was getting pissed when he stated, "It wasn't that."

"Then explain what it was," I demanded.

"I see your face when I tell you I never expected anything out of my life, never even thought about it."

"I fear this discussion might be difficult not having what I need, and instead having to wait until Sunday to get it."

He moved abruptly so he was holding my head in both hands, and his face was in mine.

"Never dreamed, never wanted shit, because I knew I couldn't have it," he growled. "Then I follow this gorgeous woman with sass to spare into the sweet crib she created, and I started wanting shit. Thirty-five years old, woman, first time in my life I saw what I wanted. All of it. All of what I'd need for the rest of my life. It tweaked me. Scared the absolute fuck outta me. You don't want, you don't get disappointed. I see now that was what I was doin'. Protecting myself. Because all of a sudden, there it was,"—his hands put gentle pressure on my head—"*all* of it, and I knew, I...*fuckin'*... *knew* how deep it would cut if I didn't get it."

"Harlan," I whispered, overwhelmed. Feeling so much it felt like it was clogging my throat, my pores, the entire room, but even so, it was an excruciatingly beautiful feeling.

"So I know my bathroom at home is shit," he carried on, "and I brush my teeth in your swank bathroom beside you with your mass of fantastic hair and your sweet round ass tipped as you put on mascara and your outrageous supply of makeup at hand—"

"My makeup supply isn't outrageous."

"Watched you tidy up after yourself two days in a row, babe, and you got three drawers of that shit."

So...

All right.

My makeup supply was outrageous.

"We come from different worlds," he continued, "and I want you in my world, but I want more to be a part of yours."

Oh, he was going to be a part of mine all right.

"So, what you're saying is, this last week you've been coming to terms with the fact that you might finally get what you deserve, and it freaked you," I summed up.

"Don't know about deserve, but yeah, it freaked me."

"Harlan, prepare, my gorgeous man, for me to pull out the big guns when I ask, what would your mother say to you thinking you don't deserve a good life?"

He winced.

Mm-hmm.

And mm-hmm again.

Because now I had a goddamned mission.

I didn't know where we would land. I didn't know what was in store for me on Sunday.

What I knew was, he was going to have a great fucking bathroom, a great fucking bedroom, a great fucking *everything*. And he was going to be a part of creating that—with me—but he was going to have his say and get what he wanted so he could live in the dream he never allowed himself to have.

That was my mission.

And I was going to best it.

I wrapped my arms around him, lifted my head off the pillow and touched my mouth to his before dropping my head back.

"Sunday, you can lay it on me," I invited. "But for now, we haven't had a lot of time together, so I haven't had the time it might take to make you realize you deserve a swank bathroom and whatever else it is you might someday realize you want. But know, I've taken on that job and I'm not gonna stop until you're where you were always supposed to be."

He swept his thumb along my cheekbone as he kept his gaze to mine, but he didn't say anything.

"Did you hear that?" I demanded.

"You're cute when you're handing out shit."

"Harlan!" I snapped, at the same time slapping his lat.

He grinned. "Starting with brunch, you gonna show me the world?"

"Absolutely."

"Think I wanna start with Japan. I like sushi and their gardens are the bomb."

Excellent news he liked sushi, because I was an aficionado of that too.

"Our first vacation," I declared.

My body started shaking because his body was shaking since he was laughing.

"You find this funny?" I asked tartly.

"Babe," was all he said.

Ugh.

He kissed me and rolled us so I was on top.

Oh well.

Whatever.

He'd see.

But we had a mondo box of condoms on hand, so first things first —we'd see about what was going to happen next.

Spoiler: what happened next was *awesome*.

19

I LOVE HIM ALREADY

Diana

THE NEXT EVENING, I walked down the hall while putting in my last earring, hit the living room and saw Hugger slouched in the couch, his eyes on the TV.

When I showed, he turned his head to me.

Then I watched with a good deal of interest as every inch of his long body went alert.

"This is the first time I've worn this," I announced, raising my arms at my sides like that would show him the LBD I was wearing better.

It was pretty simple, as LBDs should be. One long sleeve, one shoulder bare, skintight, a short skirt that hit several inches above the knee, slit on one side.

I'd convinced myself I could pull it off at the store when I tried it on.

I wasn't so sure now.

"Does it work?" I asked Hugger.

"How?"

His question confused me. "How what?"

"How do you want it to work?"

I looked down at myself, saying, "Well, I have kinda wide hips, and then there's this." I put both hands to my little belly.

"Come again?"

I was even more confused, so I turned my attention to him. "It's so tight, you can see my pouch."

"All I see is my woman in a dress that's makin' my dick hard."

Hmm.

"Really?"

"You wanna feel the evidence?"

I shivered at the invitation, but had to say, "I fear that would make us late."

"Your hand gets anywhere near my cock, especially right now with you in that dress, we'll be late, baby," he decreed.

I really, *really* wanted my hand near his cock.

But I'd been blowing off my friends, and late was rude.

Damn.

I bit the side of my lip in indecision.

Hugger chuckled as he pulled himself out of my couch.

"Let's get you to cocktails," he said, taking my hand.

Before he could tug me anywhere (not that I could go anywhere except my closet, I still had to switch out purses), I held strong to his fingers and asked, "You don't mind that I wear my dedication to cookies and tacos on my ass and belly and elsewhere?"

His expression changed to irritable.

And as ever with Hugger, he didn't make me wait to understand his emotion.

"I now see how your dad dicked that up."

"Yes, but you're super fit," I pointed out.

"Because we got a gym on Chaos and all the brothers take advantage of it."

"On Chaos?"

"Our flagship, with the first store, the garage, and the Club

Compound is referred to like an island. You're there, you're 'on Chaos.' Don't know how that came about, just know that's how it is."

"Oh."

Now I didn't know why I loved knowing that about his Club, but it was just how it was.

"Was a bouncer before I became a brother," he went on. "Pay was shit, but I was good at it. You can't do that unless you know what your body can do and you can take care of business. To know what your body can do, you work out."

"Right."

"Became a habit, and I dig it," he stated. "Clears my head."

"I took a Pilates class downstairs once and couldn't move for two days."

He smiled.

"When the heat goes off the Valley, I like to take walks. However, with the heat on or off the Valley, most of those walks happen in a mall."

His smile got bigger.

"Pretty much, I get my exercise by cleaning my house once a week," I finished.

He got closer and tucked his chin in his neck to keep his eyes on me.

"I give you any indication at all I don't love every inch of you?" he asked quietly.

"No," I answered honestly, and yes, a little breathlessly.

"Get that shit outta your head, then. Only person who needs to feel good in that dress is you. But just sayin', you look beautiful. You always look beautiful, but you pulled out all the stops tonight."

Well then.

Fuck it.

I got up on my toes, threw my arms around his neck, pressed close and kissed him, hot, wet and heavy.

Hugger backed me to the arm of the couch and we toppled over.

So when we finally left, we were late.

"WHAT THE FUCK?" Hugger asked as we turned the corner from the hostess station at 36 Below.

I stifled a laugh, because this tiny bar in the basement of a coffee place had miniscule orange-velvet padded stools around nearly-as-miniscule tables, and green-velvet barstools around the bar. It also had screens all around showing an animated landscape of a fairy world complete with lots of toadstools, a water wheel, woodland animals skittering about and floating glitter. Further, it had people drinking out of mushroom-shaped glasses set on moss-covered slabs of bark-circled wood or lit glass lanterns dangling from fake-flower-festooned iron hooks.

Not a biker hangout in the slightest.

You had to have a reservation, and we had a close-to-miniscule table with four stools, so Hugger was only there to meet the girls and then he was going to chill upstairs, keep an eye on the entrance, and probably drink coffee.

Pulling him to where my girls were (they hadn't all gone LBD, Bernie was in an LBD, but the "B" stood for electric blue, Mel was openly wishing for autumn in a short, bodycon, green turtleneck sweater dress, and Charlie, our hippie girl, was wearing a sleeveless, boatneck maxi dress made of cream gauze, with a high side slit and line of diminutive bells on the full skirt that I knew would jingle when she walked—she was seated, but I knew about the slit and bells because I'd been with her when she'd worn that dress before).

As we made our short way to them, they were all staring at me and Hugger with identical expressions of astonishment mixed with extreme interest.

"Hey, sorry I'm late," I said when we made it to the table.

No one replied.

They were all now just staring at Hugger.

"This is Harlan," I indicated him. "He's dropping me, but I wanted you to meet him."

They continued their silence and stared at Hugger.

"This is Bernie, or Bernice," I indicated Bernie. "And Mel, or Melissa," I went on with another flick of my hand. "And Charlie, or Charlotte," I concluded.

"Odd woman out, you don't got a guy's nickname," Hugger remarked.

"And it's too bad Jagger and Dutch are taken, because it would seem all my girls would have been candidates," I noted.

Hugger shot me a smile.

I heard Charlie gurgle.

I got that totally: his smile with his white teeth in that multi-colored beard was the best.

"Leave you women to it," he said, then angled his head and bent to kiss my neck. When he caught my eyes after that awesome maneuver, he bid, "Have fun." He turned to my friends. "Nice to meet you."

"Yeah," Bernie choked.

"You too," Mel breathed.

Charlie just waved at him.

Hugger strolled through the small space like he owned it and disappeared around the wall to the stairs.

I nearly tumbled off my high-heeled black sandals as Charlie yanked on my wrist. Fortunately, against all the odds, my ass landed on a miniscule orange-velvet padded stool.

All of them leaned toward me in unison.

"Who the hell is that guy?" Mel demanded.

"Okay, don't get mad—" I started.

"I'm not mad. I'm jealous as all hell, but I'm not mad," Charlie said. "I mean that guy is like...*whoa.*"

He was definitely *whoa.*

"Why would we be mad?" Bernie asked. "Except for the fact you were persona non seena or hearda for weeks, and now you show up with beefy hot guy who kisses your neck before he leaves you."

Bernie, by the way, was slim, Black, had no small amount of back, but definitely a small chest, so everything looked good on her in every color, and she changed her hairstyles more often than I changed my purses, and I changed my purses all the time.

Now she had very long, thin braids, half up, half down, with the up part being in a fabulous knot with braid ends sticking out at the back of her head.

She was kind of shy, kind of quiet, but not with her girls. When she was with her girls, she was outspoken and no nonsense.

Mel, on the other hand, was white, auburn-haired, petite, and totally together. She was the only one of us who had a guy, Gerard, who was Scottish and really into her (as far as I could tell, half the time, I couldn't understand what he was saying, his brogue was so thick).

Charlie, as noted, was our hippie chick. She was a wedding photographer and keyboardist in an ambient music band (if you could call them that) who played tunes that I guessed worked, because they put me to sleep, though that wasn't what you were supposed to do when you went to one of their gigs to hear them play.

Still, we all went to see her all the time because she was Charlie.

The waitress showed, and I saw on the table there was a mushroom, a lantern and a green vase with some spiked leaves sticking out of it along with an apple slice and some floating almonds, so I went for the Solis, because it was yummy, but it was served in a goblet, and I figured that would round it out.

Once the waitress left, I said, "Okay, so a lot has gone down."

"Ya think?" Mel asked, and jerked her head of luxurious tresses toward where Hugger disappeared.

"Are your hatches battened?" I asked.

"Oh boy," Charlie whispered.

"Hatches battened. Spill," Bernie ordered.

I spilled.

And I kept doing it through receiving my cocktail, and it went on until I was halfway done with it.

"Holy Mahoney," Charlie muttered when I finally shut up, indicating that by sucking another quarter of my cocktail up my straw because all I'd just shared warranted it.

"Bad guys might be after you?" Bernie asked.

"We don't think so, but maybe. They used to hang out in the courtyard of my complex to provide a threatening presence, but we haven't seen them in days. Though, Hugger isn't taking any chances," I replied, putting my goblet on the table.

"He's in a motorcycle club?" Mel queried.

I wasn't certain about the look on her face, but I answered firmly, "Yes."

"Why didn't you tell us all this was happening?" Bernie asked the million-dollar question.

"Well, first of all, a lot was going down, so I didn't have the time," I explained.

"I see that," Mel mumbled.

"And second, so much was going down, with Maddy, Dad, Hugger, I didn't have the headspace to get into it, because there was so much of it." I spread my hands over the table. "But now, I'm getting into it."

"I think we should start with your mom," Bernie said.

"I think we should start with this guy who lives in Denver," Mel countered.

"I think we should lay off because, like Di said, this is a lot," Charlie shot at Mel and Bernie across the table.

"Well, for all of that, there's nothing more to give about Mom," I told them. "She still hasn't replied to my voicemail or any of my texts."

"Sorry, babe, but lame," Mel declared.

Forgot to mention, Mel was pretty no nonsense too.

Though in this instance, like many, she was right.

"Agreed," I replied. "The longer it takes her to reach out, the more all of it is pissing me off. And it's super pissing Hugger off. He had a really great mom. I think this totally confuses him, but more, he had that, so he hates what I have. It's also stupid, because it's giving me plenty of opportunity, which I'm taking, to shuffle back through my memories and notice a lot of stuff that really isn't good."

"Like her giving up custody without a squeak?" Bernice offered.

"And her taking off to Idaho like she didn't birth no babies, when she did, and that baby she forgot she birthed was you," Mel put in.

"And like she shows when she shows, and you or your gram have to drop everything to be at her beck and call, but she won't stay with either of you. Nope. She's got a bungalow at the Biltmore and you have to go get her and traipse around Phoenix at her whim," Charlie added.

Welp!

It seemed my girls had my mom's number before I did.

"And straight up, she had the means to help you out when you were busting your back to get your degrees," Bernie started, "and she didn't. I can't believe your dad put all that in a trust and gave it to you. Along with him dropping that mobster client because you asked him to, that's a seriously stand-up thing to do."

Dad and I had not come to terms about the trust, but Bernie was right. It was a stand-up thing to do.

"It isn't Mom's money," I pointed out.

"She sells one Birkin bag, she pays an entire year of your tuition," Mel returned.

Sadly, I couldn't argue this.

"More stand-up from your dad, that he took the hits he took all your life," Bernie stated. "What I don't get is why your mom would pull what she pulled."

"Well, it isn't like, in front of Di, Nolan and Margaret are gonna have a chat about who cheated first," Mel noted.

"That's the worst part of this," Charlie said. "The Big Lie."

"Victims gonna victim," Mel replied. "Can't get everyone to kiss your feet and make life easy for you if you don't convince them they should."

I stilled.

Victims gonna victim.

Dad cheated on her (when he didn't).

Brendon gave up on her (but did he?).

Rick forced her to live in Idaho where she had to drive all the way to Seattle for good shopping, or fly down to Phoenix (but she went up there with him without a peep).

Rick went out hunting, and left her "all alone" (when, for God's sake, people had hobbies).

Rick got mad because she didn't like to ride in his speedboat because it messed up her hair and "doesn't he understand about a woman's hair?!" But she rode in it and bitched about it, like taking a ride in a speedboat on a beautiful lake in God's country was akin to being stretched on the rack.

Nothing was Mom's responsibility.

Nothing went Mom's way.

But she lived a damn good life.

I didn't even know how she spent her time up there, except she always had perfect nails, an immaculate pedicure, no roots in her hair, and she often went to spas.

I'd wanted to do it on my own, getting my degrees, but I'd wanted to do that to show Dad.

That said, it had been all kinds of hard work.

I'd met all of my girls our first year in college. They knew everything about me. They went through all of that with me. Hell, Bernice's parents gave me a waitressing job at one of their restaurants. I'd worked there for three years.

And they were right. Mom and Rick gave me big checks at birthdays and Christmases, but they weren't *that* big.

She could have helped.

She could have at least offered.

She didn't.

She never even asked about it, and truth, she still gave me those big checks, though now I was seeing them as guilt checks, if she could feel that emotion.

What they weren't were presents.

Even when I was a kid, Mom gave me money on those occasions.

Like, she was a superior shopper, and she didn't bother to know me enough to buy me an actual present that I might want.

"Di?" Bernie called.

I focused on her.

"Oh shit," Mel mumbled when she caught sight of my face.

"It really hurts," I whispered.

"Okay, now we're gonna lay off," Charlie decided.

Bernie reached across our nearly miniscule table toward me.

I took her hand.

"It sucks you have to come to terms with this, but I'm glad you are, because you give that woman a lot when she demands it, and she doesn't really deserve it," Bernie said.

"Bernie!" Charlie snapped.

"No," I cut in, giving Bernie's fingers a squeeze and letting go. "She's right."

"Do you know what you're going to do when she calls?" Mel asked.

"I think...I need to talk to Hugger about it," I said.

"Hugger?" Charlie asked.

"No offense, but I..." I smiled. "He's kinda become my touchstone."

"Perfect segue," Mel muttered.

Yep.

Now was the time to get into Hugger.

"He vacuums," I announced.

"Sorry?" Bernie queried.

"Maddy and I were cleaning last Saturday, I got out the vacuum, he took it from me and vacuumed my whole house."

"Yowza," Bernie said.

"Has Gerard ever done that?" Charlie asked Mel.

"Once, and he did it so badly, he's never done it again," Mel told her.

Bernie and Charlie rolled their eyes at each other.

"Excuse me, but he has other attributes," Mel said saucily.

"Yeah, he knows what to do with his dick," Bernie murmured.

And we knew all about that.

"And he can make a woman come just by talking to her with that accent," Charlie added.

There was that too.

"There's that," Mel spoke my thoughts. "And he cooks and does the grocery shopping, and I don't like to do either."

"He's a good guy, really," Charlie assuaged. "But he could say, 'I don't wanna vacuum, let's figure out the allotment of chores,' rather than just doing a shitty job vacuuming so he can get out of doing it."

"I read he doesn't like doing it, so now I do, and he didn't have to say that because I have a mind to my man, and just to say, he has a mind to me and that's why he cooks," Mel returned.

"Let's get back to Di," Bernie urged.

"He grew up with his mom, just those two," I shared. "And I think he had to pitch in, so it's just a part of who he is. Like, he makes the bed in the morning *just like I do*."

"Holy shit," Mel whispered reverently.

"I know," I said. "He listens. And he's smart. And he gives good advice. He says he's not affectionate, but he's really demonstrative with me. It feels mega nice. He likes my pouch and big ass and doesn't even glance askance at me when I eat a third cookie. Or a fourth."

"Wow," Bernie said.

"And he's been at my side through all of this, and honestly, I don't know if I would have gotten through it if he wasn't."

"Aw, Di,"—Charlie patted my hand—"you so would."

"And you had your girls," Mel reminded me.

"I know, but he was there, and he stuck, and because he did, he made it easier."

"So he isn't hard on the eyes, and he's got no issue being supportive," Bernie brought it to a fine point.

"Yes, and more," I said.

"Please say that big man with that big body does big things for you in bed," Charlie begged.

I smiled. "He's very...take charge."

Charlie rolled her eyes back and moaned.

Bernie and Mel smiled at each other.

Charlie recovered, tipped her head to the side and asked, "So... Denver?"

I shook my head. "We haven't gotten that far. We're going to have the big chat on Sunday. But until he knows I'm safe, he's not going anywhere."

"Sweet," Charlie whispered.

"And when's that gonna happen?" Bernie asked. "You knowing you're safe?"

"It's doubtful I'm not, they just want to make sure."

"So...Denver?" Mel brought us back around.

"I don't know. I don't want him to leave. I'm not fired up about a long-distance thing. I don't want to think about moving, because I love my life here, and before you say anything, I know it's way too soon for a decision like that. So it's going to sound wild when I say, I just know whatever happens, we'll figure it out."

"You really know that," Charlie said, watching me closely.

"Know what?" I asked her.

"Know you'll figure it out," she explained.

I smiled. "Yeah, that's one thing in all this mess I definitely know." I took them all in. "He's my guy. I can't explain it, because there'd never been an explanation for it. I just know it." I patted my hand over my heart. "Deep in here."

Charlie put both arms around me and gave me a fierce squeeze. "I love that for you."

Bernie and Mel were giving me soft, happy faces.

Shoo!

They got it.

Then again, if I thought about it, I knew they would.

"Do you all want another cocktail?" The server was at our table.

Bernie looked at her watch. "Damn, our time is almost up."

You got allotted timings at 36 Below. You had to drink up and go.

"I don't want another," Charlie said.

"Me either," Mel said.

I shook my head.

"I'll get your bill," the waitress mumbled and walked the single step to the server station.

I grabbed my glass to suck down more drink.

"I think we need to go someplace where Hugger can sit with us," Bernie decreed.

"I'm in," Charlie chirped.

"Totally," Mel said.

"He's not going to drink. When he drives, he doesn't," I warned them. "But he'll probably have a Coke."

"I love him already," Bernie decided.

And I loved her.

I loved all of them.

"I'm sorry I didn't tell you guys any of this stuff," I said.

"Yes you did," Mel returned. "Just now."

"All good," Bernie put in.

Totally loved all of them.

The waitress came back with our bill.

"Let's sort this and go get Hugger," Charlie said, reaching for the bill.

This wasn't about them sizing him up.

This was about them getting to know him.

So I uttered not a peep as I opened my clutch to get my credit card.

"WHAT THE FUCK IS AN 'AMBIENT JAM'?" Hugger asked.

I busted out laughing.

It was after drinks at the Linger Longer Lounge, which included late-night scarfing of fried bologna sandwiches. We were a little over-dressed (well, Hugger wasn't), but it was the Linger Longer and it was Phoenix, so anything went.

It was after incredible sex.

We were in a zone that was coming to be familiar, me on my back in bed, Hugger on me, both of us under the covers, happy, limber, warm post-coital and chatting.

And Charlie had invited us to her gig the next weekend.

An "ambient jam."

"We'll need to down two dirty chais before we hit it, trust me," I replied.

"What?" he asked.

"She's in a sort of band. And I don't say 'sort of' to be mean, it's just not like any band you've ever seen, though they play instruments. Charlie's keyboards, there's someone on a drum machine, there's a lead guitar and a bass guitar. But it's all very..." I searched for a word. "*Moody*. They have some recordings, and I have them on my phone. I'll play one for you tomorrow."

"I'm not sure I'm looking forward to that."

I smiled and ran my fingers along the whiskers at his jaw. "It's really nice, if you're in a mellow mood at home, coloring in books and drinking wine or whatever. It's a little...shall we say, awkward when you're out at a gig."

"But you go," he noted.

I shrugged. "Charlie wants us there, so yeah."

"So yeah," he repeated quietly.

We weren't going to get into how selfless I was again, because right then, I was feeling cozy good and nicely tired without being exhausted, and we had something else to go over.

"Did you like them?" I asked.

"They're great."

I smiled again.

"Mel, Charlie and I had a conversation while you were pissing me off going to the bar with Bernie to get more drinks."

I beat back a snicker and said, "They were getting uncomfortable with you buying them all."

"Whatever," he muttered.

"What did you chat about?"

"They said you had an epiphany about your ma."

Gluh.

"It was a good night, I'm pleasantly tired, can we leave that for later?" I requested.

"Only if you tell me you're good."

I ran my fingers through his beard and whispered, "I'm good."

"All right."

That was Hugger.

Everything with him was all right.

With that, he moved to turn off both bedside lamps, then he snuggled me close, front to front, in the dark.

"Glad you had a good night, baby," he murmured.

"Glad you liked my friends, honey," I murmured back.

Hugger gathered me closer.

I tucked my head under his chin, closed my eyes, and for yet another night, fell asleep snug and safe in my guy's arms.

20

ABSOLUTELY ADORABLE

Diana

A BUZZER WAS BUZZING.

I half-woke, not in the position I normally did, spooning Hugger or tucked to his back.

No, this time he was spooning me.

Nice.

The buzzing stopped.

My eyes opened then drooped as I fell back to sleep in the warm curve of Hugger's body.

The buzzer went again and this time it stayed pressed.

My eyes popped open.

"What the fuck?" Hugger groused.

My man, I'd noticed, was not a morning guy. I'd learned a blowjob or sex could stave off his haze, but it returned after his orgasm and stayed until he was at least halfway through his first cup of coffee.

It was adorable.

So as he threw back the covers and angled out of bed, I glanced at the bedside clock to see it was barely seven thirty, which was early for a Saturday, especially since we stayed out late last night, and as such, total Haze Time for Hugger.

I saw him stop at the wall panel beside the bedroom door.

Stark naked (hot!), he hit a button and demanded, "What?"

"Who's this?" my mother's voice came through the panel.

I shot to sitting in bed.

"It's me you're buzzin', woman. Who's this?" Hugger growled.

"Mom," I whispered.

Hugger's head whipped my way, and truly, with all that was holy, I hoped to God I never personally earned that look on his face.

"I'm looking for Diana Armitage," Mom said.

"Someone will be down," Hugger grunted, hit the button to let her into the elevator vestibule, but not the one to let her up to my unit, then he prowled to his jeans on the floor.

"Harlan—"

Bent to get his jeans, his head snapped back, and he skewered me with his eyes.

"Fuck no, baby. *Fuck no.*"

That was all he said before he stepped into his jeans and yanked them up.

He'd buttoned his fly and was pulling on his tee when I realized I needed to get my ass in gear.

I flew from the bed.

We slept naked, not something I'd ever done. It was just something that happened with us.

So I had to race to the hooks in my closet where I'd put my PJs while Hugger prowled to the hall.

"Shit, shit, shit, shit, *shit*," I chanted as I tugged on my sleep shorts commando, nabbed the bralette (because the girl below could be free and breezy for a spell, but the girls up top needed contained) and struggled to put it on, then grabbed the tee.

I was pulling it over my head as I left the closet and heard a knock at the door.

Hang on.

How did Mom get up the elevator? She didn't have a fob.

I sprinted down the hall.

Hugger wasn't in the living room, so I dashed to the dining room just in time to see him opening the door.

Mom was there, with Gram (explaining the fob, since Gram had one, and a key), probably because Mom made Gram get up early to come pick her up and bring her to my place.

I knew then she didn't change her flight plans, she just enlisted Gram to play chauffeur and tour guide.

Both of them were staring up at Hugger in shock, but it was only Mom who spoke.

"Who're you?"

"Your worst nightmare," Hugger replied.

Eek!

Mom's face froze.

Gram's head ticked in surprise.

"Do not do shit to piss me off," Hugger warned them, then walked away from the door so it started closing and Mom had to throw out a hand to catch it before it slammed in her face.

Hugger stalked to me and right beyond me.

Woodenly, I turned so I could watch as he kept going down the hall and disappeared in the bedroom.

"Diana! Who is that man?" Mom demanded.

I turned to see her and Gram both standing inside the door.

Mom was blonde (fake, she'd had my color hair, but I suspected she was silver or gray now). We had the same body type and height, but she was a good thirty pounds lighter than me, if not more. She was wearing slim-fit brown trousers, a white blouse with a pretty brown leaf design on it and billowy bell sleeves. She was holding a suede jacket, even if the temperatures had cooled, but it was still ninety-eight degrees during the day. And on her feet were suede, high, block-heeled sandals with a wide crisscross at the front.

Gram's hair was all silver, so it was glorious. We got our frames from her, but she was probably thirty pounds heavier than me, and as far as I was concerned, she worked it. And she was wearing cropped jeans and a man-style button-down, French tucked (go Gram!) in a soft peach.

"Diana!" Mom called sharply. "I asked you a question."

"That's Harlan, my boyfriend."

"You have a boyfriend, doll?" Gram asked, her confusion clearing and her eyes lighting with happiness.

"Yes, you have a boyfriend that you didn't tell your mother about?" Mom demanded, her eyes flat with rebuke.

"Listen, you woke us up and—"

"So is that what was really happening?" Mom cut me off to ask. "And it wasn't some girl who was harmed. You have a man in your life and you drop everything, including your mother, so you can give him all your attention?"

Could heads explode?

I needed to know so I could warn Hugger to get out the mop.

"Maggie," Gram whispered, now a startled expression was falling over her face as she gazed at Mom.

"How could you make up a story like that?" Mom snapped at me.

But Hugger was there, he had his phone in his hand and murder in his expression.

"You're gonna go downstairs and have a coffee and wait until Di calls to say you can come back up," he commanded my mother and grandmother.

"Of course," Gram agreed.

"I think not," Mom retorted.

"This isn't gonna happen until Di and I have a second to shake the sleep off," Hugger returned.

"I'm sorry, I don't even *know* you, so I'm not going to take orders from you," Mom shot back.

"Maggie," Gram whispered again, but it was sharper, more alarmed. "It's obvious we woke them up. I told you it was too early to surprise Diana on a Saturday. Let's give them some time."

Mom slung an arm in our direction and said to Gram, "They're awake now."

Gram's head jerked yet again in surprise.

"Mom, really, just half an hour. Okay?" I requested.

"I think it's my due to know what's going on with my daughter!" Mom's voice was rising.

Hugger made a scary noise that had to come from deep in his chest.

But I demanded, "Are you joking?"

Mom pointed straight-armed at Hugger. "A man I do not know opened my daughter's door."

"Get your ass to the coffee joint," Hugger growled.

"No!" Mom bit. "Maybe *you* can absent *yourself* while I have a chat with *my daughter*."

"Not gonna fuckin' happen, lady," Hugger returned.

Mom's torso swung back in affront. "You speak to me with that language?"

Hugger opened his mouth...

But I was done.

"This is *my* home where *I* pay the mortgage, so it's *me* who says what happens here, and what does *not* happen is *you* getting into my man's shit."

"Diana," Mom breathed in injured astonishment.

"You wanna do this now, we will," I clipped.

"Baby," Hugger murmured.

"But I suggest you go have a coffee so I can cool off," I finished.

"Let's go get a latte, hon," Gram urged.

"Cool off from what?" Mom ignored Gram and asked me.

Had she not been here the last five minutes?

And had she not listened to my voicemail or actually read my texts?

"We can talk about that when you get back," I stated. "And by the way, when you come back, you can bring me a dirty chai made with oat milk, Hugger a double espresso, and bring up two cheese Danishes."

"I'm not a waitress," Mom hissed.

"You're not much of anything," Hugger said under his breath.

"What did you say?" Mom demanded to know.

"You don't wanna know," Hugger told her the truth.

She glared at him then turned that to me.

"I can't believe you're letting your boyfriend disrespect me, Diana," Mom said. "But I suppose I shouldn't be surprised, since he clearly lacks even the most basic of hygiene."

"Maggie!" Gram cried.

But I was seeing red.

No.

Scarlet

No.

Vermillion.

I started to launch myself at her, for what purpose, I had no clue, but Hugger caught me around my belly and pulled me to his front.

"Take a breath," he said in my ear.

I opened my mouth.

"Take a breath," he repeated.

Fuck!

I took a breath.

"Maggie, I could use a coffee," Gram said cajolingly, the way she talked to my mom a lot. "Let's give them some time to get dressed. It's just downstairs."

"You better be in a different frame of mind when I get back, missy," Mom threatened me, then she flounced to the door, tugged it open, and flounced out without holding it open for her own mother.

"I don't know what's going on, but I'll talk to her, doll," Gram said to me.

I just nodded my head jerkily.

The door closed behind Gram.

It was then Hugger frog-marched me, still held to his front, to the living room and only let me go when he got me there.

"I'll make coffee," he said when I turned to him. "You go do your thing so you'll be ready."

"Did you call someone?" I asked.

"Yeah," he answered.

"Who'd you call?"

"I called Pete, and told him to haul ass here, but before he did, I told him to get your dad's number and tell him your mom is here so he should haul his ass here too."

"How's he going to find Dad's cell phone number?"

"Trust me, he'll find it."

With the way he said that, I believed Big Petey would.

But I deflated. "Hugger, I don't know—"

He took my jaw in both hands and dipped down to me. "This showdown is gonna happen, baby, because you need it. But you need to have your family at your back when you do."

Oh my God!

I was so falling in love with this guy!

I face-planted in his chest.

He wrapped his hand around the back of my head, kissed my hair, and said there, "Go. Brush your teeth. Do what you gotta do."

Needless to say, after I relieved my bladder, and halfway through my tooth brushing, Hugger showed in the bathroom with a mug of coffee.

He set the mug beside mine and went to his own sink.

I mentally went through my wardrobe to see if I had a Showdown with My Mother Outfit.

I did not.

While adding a thin veneer of armor to my face, including foundation, concealer, powder, blush, highlighter, single-toned eyeshadow and mascara, I figured it out.

So once I spritzed and deodorized, I hit the closet and put on my rosy-pink T-shirt dress with the wide V-neck. It hit right below the knee, had kickass pockets, and a wide same-color satin ribbon belt that elevated it, gave it shape and made it feminine.

I felt good in it, comfy and together.

So it was perfect.

I went back to the bathroom to fashion a messy bun in my hair with some tendrils falling around my face.

I headed back to the closet to put in the diamond earrings Dad bought me for high school graduation, and in my other piercings, some little bars with baby diamonds along the line that the girls gave me for my birthday a couple of years before. I added the diamond drop necklace Dad gave me for my sweet sixteen for the final touch on my moral jewelry support.

I walked out barefoot to find Dad in my kitchen with Hugger, both of them sipping coffee.

Dad looked unhappy.

Hugger's eyes did a top to toe and he smirked.

Proof I called it right with the outfit.

Glad I put some panties on.

A knock came at the door.

"That'll be Pete," Hugger said, put his mug down and moved to the door.

I moved to Dad.

"I like your man," Dad said.

This surprised the heck out of me, but I loved that he did.

"Are you missing a tee time to be here?" I asked.

"The course isn't going anywhere."

That meant yes.

I moved again, right into his arms.

"Harlan told me what's already happened," Dad said into my hair.

"Yeah, it wasn't good."

"If you don't want to do this, I can go down and send her away," Dad offered.

I tipped my head back. "She's here. Face to face is probably better."

"I don't want this for you, Buttercup," he murmured.

"Well, it is what is it is. And I have to say, with all the garbage that's been going on, I'm glad for the chance to just get it done."

Dad nodded, then turned us both, keeping an arm around me, because Hugger was back with Big Petey.

"Nolan, this is Pete Waite, brother of mine, friend to Diana," Hugger introduced.

Big Petey came forward, shook Dad's hand then looked at me.

"You doin' okay, sweetheart?" he asked.

I nodded (nonverbally lying).

"You ready?" Hugger asked me.

I nodded again (still nonverbally lying).

"Text your grandma, baby," he murmured.

Shit.

I went back to my room and grabbed my phone.

I texted Gram on the return trip to the kitchen.

When I got there, I got a reply from Gram, *Just getting your coffees and be right up!*

The chipper bent to her text said Gram was doing what Gram did a lot for Mom. Trying to smooth things over.

I wondered if Gram had calmed Mom down and talked some sense into her.

I doubted Gram calmed Mom down or talked any sense into her.

"They're coming up," I announced.

Pete got himself some coffee, topped Dad up, Dad watched with unhidden interest as Pete moved around my kitchen with open familiarity, and fifteen minutes later, the knock came at the door.

Hugger went to open it.

I tensed.

He walked in first, but when Mom followed him, she stopped dead so Gram, holding a bag that probably had the Danishes, and paper coffee cups in each hand (because of course Mom didn't help her carry the stuff up—how was I so blind for so long?) ran into her as she came in after.

"Oh, so I see this is going to be an ambush," she accused, scowling at Dad.

"Margaret, I suggest you keep quiet and listen to what our daughter has to say," Dad advised.

"The time you get to tell me what to do is long gone, Nolan," Mom bit back.

Dad sighed.

Gram looked about ready to cry.

Then again, she was all love and goodness, wasn't comfortable around confrontation, and she adored me and her daughter. Thus, this open enmity that would seem very sudden to her was undoubtedly killing her. She probably thought they were showing up to take me along on their day. And I could see Mom hadn't explained while they were having lattes that she'd been getting some peevish communications from me.

It sucked huge I couldn't help her with that, but at that moment, I couldn't help her with it except to suggest, "Gram, maybe you might want to go out on the balcony for a little bit?"

"I think I'll stay here, doll," Gram replied uncertainly.

Mom ignored this exchange and pointed to Big Petey. "Who's this man?"

"A friend of mine," I stated.

She regarded Pete derisively and mumbled loudly, "Why am I not surprised?"

Patience, Diana, patience, I told myself.

"I don't know, since you don't know me at all, so how you could be surprised about anything about me is, in itself, surprising," I said.

Mom homed in on me as I walked around the kitchen bar to the living room.

We were going to have a showdown?

Time to take my position.

"I can't believe you just said that to me," Mom whispered, full of hurt.

"What's my favorite color?" I asked.

"I—" She cut herself off, and to save face about the fact she didn't know, she demanded, "Is this going to be some kind of test?"

But...*damn*, that cut to the quick.

It *was* a test, and she failed.

My mother didn't know my favorite color.

"What color is it?" I pushed.

"Blue, doll, it's all over the place," Gram chipped in fake perkily.

"Don't help her, Shannon," Dad said.

Before Mom or Gram could say anything, I did.

"Dad never told you to do anything, did he?" I asked. "At least, not successfully."

"What are you—?" Mom began.

"Though, he tried, so that's why you turned to Brendon," I stated.

I watched the color drain from Mom's face.

I'd believed Dad when he told me, but seeing that, I knew.

I knew.

"What?" Gram asked.

"So many questions," I said. "The normal ones, like how could you cheat on your husband and the father of your child? And the unusual ones, like how could you have the audacity to tell everyone he was the one who cheated on you?"

Gram rounded Mom. "What's Di talking about, Maggie?"

"I see he's telling you lies," Mom said.

Before I could reply, Dad did.

"You broke my heart."

At the frank emotion in his voice, my stomach clenched so hard, I thought I'd hurl.

Gram's eyes flew to Dad.

Mom's face got color, and fast, but this time it was red.

Dad moved out of the kitchen and did it talking.

"I loved you so much. I was so immensely destroyed by what you did to me, I found a good woman after you and messed it up. Lost her too. But that was my doing."

"Hardly after," Mom said shakily, because the jig was up.

"Should we call Nicole?" Dad suggested. "See how her timeline matches up?"

"She'd lie too," Mom snapped, finding her groove and sticking there.

"Margaret, what's going on here?" Gram asked.

"Nothing, Mom. Nolan's at his games again," Mom stated.

"So you didn't cheat on Dad with Brendon?" I requested clarity. "Dad hadn't asked you for a divorce before Nicole and he became a thing? That didn't happen? Even though you married Brendon within a few months of the divorce being final."

"It was a whirlwind romance," Mom said.

"You are honestly standing there lying to me in my own damned house?" I asked.

"Of course you believe him," she complained. "It was always him and you against me."

"No, it was always you and me against him, because you made it that way. What I failed to realize was that *he was there for me* and *you were not!*"

Okay, dang.

I was shouting.

But I couldn't stop.

"You didn't fight for custody! You didn't help me pick my prom dress! *You were never there for me!* So I'm supposed to believe you were true to Dad?"

"He ruined our family!" Mom shouted back.

"Then why was he the one who kept us together after you left? Why were he and I still a family without you?"

"I didn't have the means to look after you," Mom sniped.

"You had healthy alimony. It would have been more with child support. You weren't incapable of finding a job. You were in your thirties. You could build a life with your daughter."

"It's seems so easy when you say it, Diana," she retorted. "It's never that easy."

I swung an arm out. "Look around, Mom. Do you think what I built here was *easy*? Newsflash, *it wasn't*. But I did it anyway. Answer Dad. Should we call Nic and ask her how it went down? Maybe call Brendon, ask him?"

"Don't you dare speak to that man," Mom snapped.

"Why, because you hate him because he figured you out and scraped you off, or because he'll verify Dad's story? Or both?"

"I don't need to put up with this," Mom declared, turned on her expensive heel, and saw Hugger blocking the entrance to the dining room. "Step aside," she demanded.

"Not until Di's done with you," Hugger replied.

"*Step aside!*" she shrieked.

"Margaret, look at me," Gram demanded.

She did, to whine, "Tell this man to move, Mom."

"Did you do what Diana said?" Gram asked.

Mom threw up both her hands. "Not you too."

"Answer," Gram demanded.

"Of course not," Mom returned, not quite meeting Gram's eyes.

"Dear Lord," Gram gasped, and now the color was draining from her face. "You did."

"I didn't," Mom bit off.

But Gram's attention was slowly moving toward Dad.

"Nolan," she whispered, and it hurt like hell to hear the utter disappointment, regret and sadness in her voice.

Mom turned again to the room. "So now *everyone* is against me? As usual. My ex-husband takes my daughter from me when she was just a baby and then he does it again—"

Fuck that noise.

I cut her off, "I wasn't a baby. I was cognizant at the time, Mom, speaking full sentences, reading, doing math. I remember you didn't fight for me."

"I didn't have the means," Mom retorted.

"Excuse me, Margaret Ann, your father and I offered you those means," Gram stated.

This was news.

Interesting.

"I couldn't ask you for money, Mom," my mother replied.

"Why not? You did it a lot while you were growing up," Gram shot back. "And this particular time, it would have been for something important. My *granddaughter.*"

Mom put her hand to her chest. "It was me who was destroyed by what Nolan did to me."

"You got over that quickly, marrying that sonuvabitch," Gram retorted.

Whoa.

I felt my eyes get big.

Gram never cursed.

She also never stood up to Mom.

Maybe she was pissed she had to get up early to play chauffeur.

Or maybe she was fed up, like me.

"You can't help when you fall in love," Mom said.

"*Hogwash,*" Gram hissed, and God bless him, I didn't know how he did it, but Big Petey sidled in and took the coffee and Danishes from Gram even as Gram ranted on. "I cannot believe you're standing there, humiliating yourself, and me, *again. Twice in one morning.* Rude to Di's young man. Rude to Di, your own child. Rude when you returned after I spent forty-five minutes talking to you at the coffee place."

Mom pointed at me. "Well *she* lied about some poor girl who was gang-raped in order to spend more time with her new boyfriend."

"Watch it," Hugger warned.

Mom whirled on him. "You are not in this."

"Her name is Madison," Big Petey said, and Mom whirled again, this time on Pete, where he was standing at the kitchen bar, the coffees and Danish bag on the counter in front of him. Gram turned to him too. "She was abducted from her home in Texas, sold to traffickers, and assaulted by three men. Your daughter provided her safe harbor, found a way in to get her talking to the police and FBI, and got her into protective custody."

"That's preposterous," Mom decreed.

"Perhaps you'd allow me to escort you to the police station to talk to Detective Rayne Scott," Dad offered. "He can corroborate Pete's story."

"How are you even here?" Mom demanded. "For years, Diana wasn't even talking to you."

I got there before Dad did. "That's not your business."

"How is it not my business? I'm your mother!" Mom shouted.

"It's not your business, because Dad and I had a thing after I got sexually assaulted in my dorm room."

Gram gasped, then moaned, and finally reeled, throwing out a hand to catch the kitchen counter.

Big Petey got close to spot her.

Mom stared at me.

Dad moved nearer to me.

But as much as I felt for Gram, and it was a lot, I was in this too deep, so I was all about Mom.

"But I didn't even tell you about it, Mom, because you're so goddamned fragile, I knew you couldn't handle it," I went on. "Except I realized the truth recently. I didn't tell you about *my* assault because I knew deep down inside somehow, you'd twist it, and you'd make it about you."

"That's a terrible thing to say," Mom whispered.

"I know it is. I even *feel* it is, because it's true," I returned.

"Diana," Gram choked.

I looked to my grandmother, and the expression on her face wrecked me.

"I'm okay, Gram. It was ten years ago. I'm good," I promised.

"Why didn't you tell me?" she asked.

And...yeah.

I didn't tell her and Gramps either, because Gramps wouldn't have been able to handle it (he was super protective of all his girls, a boon (for me), what would become a burden (because...*Mom*)) and Gram would have told Mom.

"Because you would tell Mom, and I couldn't handle dealing with what had happened and dealing with her too." Tears filled her eyes, so I said softly, "I'm sorry."

"That's why you quit school," she surmised.

"Part of it, yes."

"You don't have to apologize to me, doll. It was me and your grandfather who let you down," Gram said.

"No, you didn't. You let me move in with you."

"We could have done more."

"There wasn't more," I told her. "You did what I needed."

"Well isn't this marvelous?" Mom cut in sarcastically. "Everyone is all good and cozy, except you all are angry at me when I didn't even know what was happening."

"Maggie, your daughter just shared—" Gram began.

"*Save it, Mom!*" my mother screeched.

"Do not talk to her that way," I warned.

"Speaking like that to your own mother," she bit at me, like she hadn't just screeched at hers.

Seriously.

I'd had enough.

"Are you actually my mother?" I asked.

It was a low blow, and it landed.

Mom let out a noise like she'd been gut punched.

Gram flinched.

Dad whispered, "Diana."

But Hugger?

Hugger grinned at me.

And Pete?

He winked.

"I see how it is," Mom said, her voice mortally wounded.

But no.

Oh no.

She wasn't the victim here.

"In essence, you took my father from me," I said with deceptive quiet. "You lied to me and made me believe things that weren't true about my own father. You drove a wedge between us when he loved me, he provided for me, he was there for me. But your lie was always between us. He knew it, and he sacrificed what we could have had to give me you."

Gram made a sobbing sound.

Mom stared at me.

"I don't know if I can forgive you for that," I stated honestly. "What I do know is you coming to my home, speaking like you did to me, Harlan, Pete, Dad, Gram, is not the way to guide me to that."

"I suppose you can go to *Nicole*, who's always been there for you, and cry on her shoulder," Mom returned.

"I know I can, because you're right, she's always been there for me," I replied.

Gram made another weeping noise.

Mom turned to Gram. "I want to go back to the Biltmore. I need to rest and process all of this before I go to my spa appointments."

Good God.

"Do you hear yourself, Margaret?" Gram asked, clearly so shocked by her daughter's statement, it shocked the tears right out of her eyes.

Which was not shocking because Mom was a huge-ass *brat*. And not the good kind.

"I think I've been treated abysmally, so you can't be surprised I need some time to—"

"For goodness' sakes, stop talking," Gram sighed. "And order up one of those Ubers. I'm not taking you back to the Biltmore."

"Mom!" my mother snapped.

"Loved you to bits, did you wrong," Gram muttered.

"Mother!" Mom shouted.

"I'm shattered, Maggie," Gram whispered. "You might not have been here for all that just happened, choosing, as ever, to live in the fantasy world in that head of yours, but *I was*. Order a damned Uber."

"I'll call for one," Dad offered.

"I don't want anything from you," Mom snapped at him.

"Fine," Dad murmured.

"So this is it?" Mom asked me.

"That's up to you," I said.

"Well, I certainly won't come all the way down from Idaho to be treated like this again," Mom warned.

"I think all that needed to be said was said," I stated. "It's up to you to apologize and—"

Mom interrupted me. "Apologize?"

"Call the Uber, Maggie," Gram ordered, still my mother's mother, and even as shattered as she was, she was trying to stem the flow of disaster.

"I won't be coming to visit you either," Mom sniped at her.

Gram's face fell.

"Christ, you're a piece of work," Hugger muttered loudly.

"Like I give a shit what a man like you thinks about me," Mom retorted.

Uh-oh.

Hugger just shrugged and moved out of the way to her exit.

By the time I got used to the fire burning in my belly and searing its way through my veins, Mom was moving.

"Stop," I demanded.

Mom turned to me.

"No contact," I said.

Dad made an alarmed noise.

Hugger started moving to me.

"What?" Mom asked.

"That's the term they use when you cut yourself off from a member of your family. You go no contact. I'm blocking you on my phone. We're done."

Hugger stood at my back as Mom stared and whispered, "What?"

I shook my head. "You don't get it. None of it. You never will. And your finale was to talk shit to my guy, *again*, like that's quite all right. Well, it isn't. You talked shit to Dad, to Gram, to Big Petey, and I let it slide. Hugger, no. Absolutely no. That was the last straw. Like I said, we're done."

Mom's face grew haggard before she asked, "You can't be serious."

"Deadly," I replied, my stomach sinking and twisting.

But we were here.

This was going to suck. I loved her. I really did. Even with all of this.

But she was by no means healthy for me.

Or anybody.

She kept staring awhile before she straightened her shoulders and said, "You did the same thing with your father, so I don't suppose this will last."

"We'll see in ten years," I remarked.

Mom went pale again.

"Do you have the Uber app? Because going now would be good," I prompted.

"I cannot believe you're doing this to me," Mom whispered.

"And that's the problem," I returned. "I'm not doing anything to you. You brought this all on yourself."

She looked at me. She looked at Dad. She looked at Gram.

Then she sniffed, and pure Mom, no matter what was going down, she'd perfected the art of the flounce, and that was what she did into the dining room, disappearing.

No one said anything as we waited to hear the front door open and close.

And no one said anything after it did.

I broke the silence.

"Gram, you okay?"

"N-no," Gram stammered.

I walked to her and gathered her in my arms.

"I'm so sorry you had to be here for all of that," I said softly.

"I'm sorry for you, doll," she replied, holding tight. "Your mom—"

"Please don't make excuses," I whispered my plea.

"Okay, Di," she whispered back.

I gave her a squeeze, kissed the side of her head, then moved to her side, still with an arm around her, and looked at Hugger.

"I guess our fun Saturday is a wash," I remarked.

"Oh no," Gram mumbled.

But Hugger just stared hard at me.

And then he said, "Don't know, babe. Your family is here. I think we can figure a way to rally."

So...

Totally...

Falling for my guy.

I smiled at him.

His beard moved as he blew me a kiss.

First time for that.

And oh yeah.

It was absolutely adorable.

21

CLOSURE

Diana

HUGGER GOT his first brunch a day early.

This was because we all went to Prep and Pastry after Mom stormed off and I calmed Gram down.

One could say, after two decades of Gram thinking Dad was a prick, and now you could tell she felt awful about it, on top of being staggered by all she'd learned that morning, brunch was not all smiles and laughter, mostly because Gram looked and acted like she'd been hit by a truck.

Though, Dad was super cool with her, Big Petey was good at keeping conversation flowing, no matter how stilted it was in some arenas, and in the end, I got the impression Gram was pleased to have the opportunity to start to make amends for something that wasn't her fault.

Hugger, by the way, was mostly quiet throughout all of this.

Then again, I'd learned the night before that Hugger was just a quiet kind of guy.

Oh, he talked to me and gave it openly and honestly.

But in social situations, he was an observer.

He didn't seem uncomfortable in this, it was just who he was, and since Hugger was always just who he was, that was it.

Like everything with Hugger, I found it incredibly attractive.

After brunch, it killed me we had three men in our midst, what with Nordstrom's shoe department only a two-minute walk away from Prep and Pastry.

However, Gram looked like she'd aged five years since she showed at my door that morning, and no matter she was rocking the style of a French tuck, she wasn't young anymore and that scene with Mom had been crazy. I knew she wasn't in the mood to try on shoes (or play with makeup at the makeup counters).

Thus, Hugger and I walked her to her car. I promised to have her over to dinner sometime soon, gave her a kiss, she gave Hugger a distracted smile and a mumbled, "So lovely to meet you, son, wish it was different circumstances," got in and started up her car.

"On your cell in half an hour to check up on her," Hugger ordered as we watched her drive away.

Also incredibly attractive.

I forsook Nordstrom (devastating!) and we went back to my pad so I could give Dad an official tour. This included not only taking him through every nook and cranny of my place, but also taking him around the complex, showing him the pool, the exercise room, and the clubroom.

Hugger and Big Petey gave us time to do it alone, but I suspected they did that because Dutch, Jagger or Roscoe were keeping an eye on the complex.

"This is incredibly impressive," Dad said when we were walking back to my pad.

What he meant was, this was pretty high-end for a twenty-nine-year-old.

"I placed a massive bet on black thirteen at Talking Stick, and the ball landed on thirteen black."

Dad stopped dead and stared down at me.

Several expressions battled to take over his face. Surprise (because that was a surprising thing for me to do). Reproach (because that was totally something Dad would strongly advise me not to do). Confusion (because even with those winnings, this was a high-end place, and I hadn't mentioned Gramps's contribution).

And then he burst out laughing.

God, it was awesome to see Dad laugh.

And it came to the fore what I'd known all my life.

He was really handsome.

Totes, my dad still had it.

"I'd won most of that on an amazing roll of video poker, so I was feeling sassy, took it to the roulette table and let it ride," I shared. "I cashed out right away and I've never been to another casino again."

He put his arm around me and guided me through the courtyard toward my elevator bay. "Although I would never advise my daughter, who was working to build her life, or anyone, to lay down big money on a single-digit roulette bet, you certainly invested it well."

Dang, I felt like preening.

I didn't think I'd ever preened in my life, but I felt like doing it then.

I fobbed us into the bay, and as we were waiting for the elevator, Dad said, "You handled yourself well with your mom, Buttercup."

I scrunched my nose.

"She'll take you back in an instant, you decide to change your mind on your decision to go no contact," he assured.

The elevator doors opened, we walked in, I fobbed my floor and turned to my father.

"We both know she'll put me through the wringer, twist it until I'm apologizing to her, and things will go back to the way they were, which isn't healthy."

Dad decided not to say anything.

"It's going to suck and I'm going to miss her, but, Dad, I told her I'd been assaulted. Gram nearly passed out, but Mom had zero reaction except about what was happening to her."

"Indeed," he muttered miserably.

Sadly, I couldn't do anything about his misery; I was too busy dealing with my own. And in the end, we were both going to have to learn to live with it.

We got off the elevator and he took my hand.

I stopped and looked up at him.

"You and I need to talk about that," he said carefully.

"No we don't," I disagreed. "You didn't handle it well at the time. I made that abundantly clear and held my grudge too long. Honestly, do you think you haven't made up for it?"

"I hope so."

"So can we just move on?" I requested.

His fingers tightened around mine. "I'd love that."

"And it isn't about the money in the trust, though we should talk about that too."

This time, his hand squeezed mine. "Diana, you shouldn't refuse it."

"I'm proud of what I did."

"I'm proud of what you did too, sweetheart. But you could drain that trust and remortgage your condominium, and significantly reduce your payments."

Hmm.

"Or you could let it sit and have a very nice down payment when you decide to move up the property ladder," Dad went on.

Hmm again.

"Or you could deduct the interest every quarter and do something nice for yourself," he continued. He squeezed my hand again. "I worked too hard and too many hours when you were growing up. I see that now. But what I want you to see is this is precisely why I did. Your mom told me you managed to get through two degrees without a single loan. But you worked impossibly hard to do it. Now please, allow me to do what I worked so hard to do. When it was time for my daughter to get serious about building her life, give her some financial peace of mind."

Man, having Dad back so freaking *rocked*.

"Okay, I'll accept the trust," I gave in.

His smile was so blinding, I didn't know why I considered turning it down.

"I don't want you to sell our house," I blurted.

Dad blinked.

"I'm sorry," I mumbled. "That was selfish."

"It's only me there," he said gently. "It's a lot for just me to ramble around in that house."

"You could find an appropriate woman," I suggested and wished I'd skipped the "appropriate" when he flinched. "Sorry again. I shouldn't butt into your love life."

He hooked my hand around his elbow and started us walking down the hall.

"I've been thinking quite a bit since you came back into my life," he said as we went. "And I've noticed something else. I sabotaged myself in relationships, I did the same to the women I was with, so I wouldn't get hurt again."

"Oh, Dad," I whispered.

"I regret the hearts I played with," he muttered.

"When your own is wounded, you probably kinda can't see past that," I said.

"Don't make excuses for me, Di," he replied.

I pressed my lips together and nodded.

"I'll think about keeping the house," he said.

"You don't have to. I shouldn't have mentioned it."

"Maybe I'll keep it for a while, so you can have some time in it," he suggested. "*We* can have some time in it, be a family there again."

I smiled. "That'd be great."

He covered my hand at his elbow and gave it a pat, then he let me go so I could let us into my place.

We did some chitchatting before Pete and Dad left.

It was then, Hugger ordered, "Text your girls."

I nearly lost it laughing, because my man was making it clear he was going to be all over me seeing to Gram (I'd texted her, she'd lied and said she was fine, but at least she knew she was on my mind) and not getting so lost in the drama that had become my life, I lost one of my lifelines (my girls).

And thus commenced me getting into a half hour marathon text exchange with Mel, Bernie and Charlie.

They were all very sad for me that I'd had to make the decision I did, but they were all in agreement that I'd made it.

I did this futzing around and cleaning, including grabbing some of Hugger's and my clothes to take to the laundry room and loading the washer.

But I was flat on my back on the couch when the text marathon was petering out, so I was prime real estate for Hugger to stretch out on top of me.

(By the way, in the midst of my texting, he helped me strip the bed and change the sheets, and he'd taken the vacuum out to both balconies to suck up the Phoenician dust on the decks, rugs and furniture—and I didn't even ask!)

I tossed my phone on the coffee table, gladly accepting his weight, and curved my arms around him.

"Got something to say," he announced.

"And I have ears, so have it," I invited.

He smiled, but it died when he went on carefully, "Don't like anyone doing my laundry, babe."

Oh.

"I did laundry for me and Ma," he explained. "We didn't have much, so what we had, we took care of it. Got in the habit of bein' particular about how it's done. You see how I do it, you're good with me doin' it for us both, then I'll do yours. If not, we can each do our own."

Well then.

This suddenly became a very Planning Our Lives Together Conversation.

And I was totally there for it.

"If you keep taking all the chores, I'll gain fifty pounds eating bonbons and doing my nails while watching *Real Housewives*," I warned.

His brows shot up. "You watch that shit?"

"Absolutely not."

His brows went down and he kissed me.

When he lifted his head, I said, "Okay, I'm too dressed up to do a deep clean. I can do that sometime tomorrow. So what do you want to do for the rest of our fun Saturday?"

Before he could say anything, I listed his options.

"You mentioned Japanese gardens, we have a great botanical garden in Phoenix which is fun to walk through and has a fabulous gift shop. We also have an actual Japanese Friendship Garden, though 'actual' is that it's in that style. Obviously, it's not in Japan."

His beard twitched.

I kept going.

"Or we could walk Papago Park, which is incredibly beautiful. Or the movie theater is literally a block away, and they have fantastic recliner seats, if you want to go see a movie. There's also Talking Stick Casino. I've tried my luck as far as I'm going to with that, but you said you've been to Vegas. If you dig gambling, we can go, and I can watch you have fun. Then there's the Biltmore Mall. It's shopping, but it's an outdoor mall, it's pretty and they have great restaurants there. We could have a late lunch at Blanco or Zinburger, then get a gelato at Frost."

"Babe—"

"The Farmer's Market downtown is lush, but I think it's closed by now," I blathered on. "And I can check the *AZ Republic's* event site to see if there's a festival happening or something. We're getting close to Oktoberfest, and the state fair is on."

I stopped when I felt my body rocking because he was silently laughing.

"What?" I asked.

"Trying to sell me on Phoenix?"

Oh shit.

I totally was.

I gave him big eyes and belatedly kept my mouth shut.

I got another kiss and he again lifted his head.

"Too hot for my blood to walk outside. I'd do a movie but would prefer to watch that Monty Python flick with you here," he said, but added, "Though, if there's any of that shit you want to do, I'll do it."

"How about we watch a movie here, then go out and get something to eat later," I proposed.

"Works for me. You want popcorn?"

He asked his question as my phone vibrated on the coffee table.

He reached a long arm to it, and we both saw NIC CALLING on the screen.

He handed it to me, went in to kiss my neck, muttered, "I'll get on the popcorn," and then he got off me.

I sat up and took the call.

"Hey, Nic."

"Oh, hon," she said with feeling. "Your dad phoned me."

Wow.

He did?

"Really?" I asked.

"He wanted me to know what happened between you and your mom."

Holy crap.

"How did Larry take Dad calling?" I asked carefully.

Larry wasn't the jealous possessive type, and still, Larry was kind of the jealous possessive type.

I mean, it didn't work between Dad and Nicole, but she'd been really in love with him. No doubt Larry knew that, and any man who knew that wouldn't be real hip on her ex calling out of the blue.

"At first, he wasn't a fan, but as he heard what we were talking about, he got over it," Nic said.

"Well, that's good."

"Do you need me to come over?" she offered.

She was so awesome.

"No, Nic. Thanks. Um…" I glanced to the kitchen to see Hugger plugging in my popcorn popper. "I kinda hooked up in a serious way with one of the bikers."

Hugger's head turned my way and he grinned.

I grinned back.

"Please tell me it was the big, bearded, teddy bear one," she replied.

It was indeed, though I'd never in a million years refer to Hugger as a teddy bear.

Sure, if you didn't know him, maybe.

But I'd seen him naked.

And I'd also seen the look on his face when Mom showed early on a Saturday morning.

He was more like a grizzly bear. He looked cute and you wanted to pet him, but if you messed with him, someone he cared about or who was under his protection, he'd maul you to a bloody pulp.

"Yes, Harlan. Hugger. It's…"

Should I go out to the balcony?

No, it was all out there between Hugger and me.

"It's something, Nic."

"I love that for you, honey."

That was Nicole, supportive all the way.

"Anyway, he was there, and he knows all that's going down. I'm fine. Not *fine* fine, but I'll live. In the end, I think it'll be better. There isn't a lie festering between us anymore. And I have Dad back."

"Gotta say, I'm really glad you worked it out with your father."

"Me too. So it's all good, and Hugger and me are about to watch a movie."

"Oh. Okay then. I'll let you go."

There was something in her voice I couldn't place.

"Are *you* okay?" I asked.

There was a long hesitation.

I waited silently.

"I knew all about this, Di, and I didn't tell you," she eventually admitted.

My sweet Nicole.

"Dad made you promise," I guessed.

"Yeah," she confirmed.

"It wasn't yours to tell, Nic," I assured her.

"No," she replied.

"Please don't feel badly about it," I begged. "It really wasn't yours to tell. I mean, what were you supposed to do?"

"I guess...what I did."

"Yes. What you did."

"You should know how far your dad is going with all of this," she began.

Oh boy.

I'd taken a lot that day, so I braced, because I sensed I was about to get more.

"He apologized to me," she shared. "He told me he was very much in love with me, but so broken by what Maggie did, he didn't trust it."

I dropped my head in my hand, ravaged for the both of them, and moaned, "Oh, Nic."

"I know," she whispered. "It was devastating hearing it. How heartbroken he was."

Gah!

"Yeah," I forced out.

"It also felt nice, knowing what I felt was real, when I thought I'd read it so wrong."

I felt Hugger's big hand wrap around the back of my neck.

I lifted my head out of my hand, looked at him, and mouthed *I'm all right.*

He studied me a second, then nodded once and returned to the kitchen.

To Nic, I said, "I hope that helps."

"I found Larry after Nolan and I were over. I did more than okay.

Which makes me even happier you and Nolan worked things out so he isn't so...alone."

Ugh.

"We're definitely working things out," I promised. "Did you tell Larry about that last?"

"I don't keep anything from him, Di, so I did. He knows I worship the ground he walks on, which I see sometimes is a mistake I let that out."

I laughed.

"So he knows Nolan is no threat," she continued. "It was a long time ago. In the end, I think Larry was happy there was some closure, and it was the good kind. And considering how we all share you, maybe, if we can get to that place, we can all be a loose sort of family for you."

Oh my God!

Would the people I loved stop testing the boundaries of my tear ducts?

Argh!

"Well, yay Dad for being big enough to reach out to you," I said instead of bursting into tears.

"It's a lot for all of us, especially you, but we're getting through it," she said. "And Nolan also updated me about Suzette, who was really Madison. I'm pleased she's somewhere safe and with her parents."

"Me too."

"Have you heard from her?"

"I know she got where she was supposed to go, but other than that, until the threat has passed, I won't."

"Right."

"I'll let you know if she gets in touch, though," I said.

"Good. Such a little thing to have to be so strong. I hope she comes to understand her strength."

I hoped she did too.

We ended the call and rang off around the time Hugger returned with a massive bowl of popcorn.

"Good?" he asked when he settled beside me.

"Dad told her about the showdown this morning. He also told her he loved her and fucked it up."

Hugger's brows shot up again.

"I know," I said. "But she's okay with it, and I think it was something Dad needed to do in order that all of that could be laid to rest."

"I like him. He loves you. He's honest. He's a standup guy. Your mom had serious issues with you having bikers in your life and let fly about that, no qualms. Your dad didn't even blink."

"I have to admit, I found that surprising. But it was a good surprise."

"Yeah. So, since I know the man he is now, you wanna tell me what he did to you back then?"

It wasn't a good time, but it'd never be a good time.

And I didn't want Hugger to change his mind about Dad.

But he was ready to hear it, so I told him the whole story.

"As fucked up as that is, baby, he's not the only one who thinks like that," he said quietly after I finished my sorry tale. "Especially people of his generation. Even women think that stupid shit."

"I know. I was too hard on him," I muttered.

"Diana, get me, I didn't say that," he stated in a flinty voice. "I see, with extremely faulty logic, he thought he was doing right by you. But it's not only that he wasn't. Sounds to me he got a problem laid in his lap, and in the course of his busy life, he just moved to fix it without thinking about it or the fact that *it* happened to his girl and taking a second to talk to you about what you wanted done about it. That was seriously bad. Then, he let ten years go by before he found you and told you he fucked up royally. In the end, he didn't even find you, you found him. That's not okay. He's twisting himself into knots to make it right now, but although I'm pleased as fuck he's putting that effort in, it doesn't change the fact that he screwed the fuckin' pooch with you...and huge."

Oh man.

I *loved* it that he thought that way.

"He's like a different guy, Hug," I told him, watching his eyes warm when I shortened his name like his brothers did, so I made a note he didn't mind it coming from me, and a further note to do it often. "He openly says he's proud of me. He's open...about every-thing. We even talked about the shitty choices he was making with his relationships."

"Babe, if I lost you for a decade because I acted like a twat, I got a shot at getting you back, I'd think real hard on everything and get my shit straight too."

Oh my God!

"Can we bang before we watch the movie?" I asked.

He did a sexy half smile, but replied, "The butter on the corn will get congealed."

"Do you care?"

"Not even a little bit."

Hugger put the popcorn bowl on the coffee table.

I attacked him.

We had sex on my couch for the second time.

It lasted longer than the first, but it was a tossup of which was better.

The popcorn wasn't gross when we returned to it, but it wasn't as good as fresh.

Though, the sushi we got later at Sushiholic was a whole lot better.

So, in the end, even with a hella rocky start, it was a fun Saturday with my man.

22

ALL IN

Diana

Hugger stopped us the minute we stepped inside Annie's house the next morning.

I knew why.

There was a vague smell of burnt food.

However vague it was, you couldn't miss it.

This meant, when we made our way into Annie's house, Hugger was chuckling, and I was pleased as punch because he was doing it.

Regardless of the smell, when we hit the dining room, the table was covered with food, and none of it looked burnt.

After a brief search, we found Annie out by the pool.

She was talking to someone, so we stood just a bit away, waiting for the moment to greet her.

We were doing this even though the person with her glanced at us five times, all of them smiling, and he did it to try to get Annie to cotton on she had new guests.

And we continued to stand there until she finally turned to us (on the dude's glance number six), she blinked and said, "Oh, you're here."

"Yeah, we are," I replied, and offered her the bottle of Veuve we bought her.

She took it, gazing down at it distractedly like she'd never seen a bottle of Champagne before.

"How lovely," she mumbled.

"Thanks for asking us for brunch," I said.

She nodded and turned to Hugger, looking him up and down.

"You clean up nice," she remarked.

He was back in his caramel button down.

"Thanks," he muttered.

"I prefer the T-shirts," Annie said.

Hugger's lips twitched. "Right."

"They have more personality," she explained (and I agreed, though he looked fab in his button down).

"Right," Hugger repeated.

"And there's great art put on T-shirts," she went on. "Album and rock art are forms of that medium that are often overlooked. Annie Leibowitz, Robert Mapplethorpe and Andy Warhol have all done cover art for rock albums. But Storm Thorgerson and Audrey Powell of Hipgnosis were pioneers of album art and created iconic images that are even better known than Warhol's Campbell Soup pieces."

"Can't argue with you on that," Hugger said. "*Dark Side of the Moon.* Zepplin's *Houses of the Holy.* 10cc's *Look Hear?* The Wings' *Band on the Run.*"

I stared at my man, because I was impressed.

Annie was too. "You know your album art."

"Yup."

"Can I talk to you a moment?" she asked.

Although her gaze was aimed at Hugger, as was her conversation (so why she was asking was a mystery, since she was already talking to him), and considering she shouldn't have anything to talk to Hugger about, except album art, I queried, "Me?"

"No, your young man." She tucked her arm in his. "Come along."

And off they went, leaving me behind, with them rounding her pool to the other side while I watched.

I continued to watch as, surprisingly, Annie did most of the talking.

Hugger, unsurprisingly, said nothing. He just listened while looking serious.

In the end, he nodded. Annie tucked her arm in his again and returned him to me.

"You can have him back now," she declared.

Then she wandered off, seeming to have forgotten she was carrying a bottle of Champagne.

I looked up at Hugger. "What was that about?"

"She told me she has clients who have 'connections.' She then said if I hurt you, she'll call on them to show me the error of my ways so I'll wish I didn't."

This stunned me.

"What on earth?" I whispered, my gaze drifting to Annie.

"It was hilarious as fuck," Hugger said, and I turned my attention to him. "And kinda cute. Though, I didn't let on it was either."

Annie had...

Wow.

When it hit me what just happened, I latched onto his arm, leaned all my weight into him and said, "I think she likes me. She really, *really* likes me."

He smiled down at me. "Yeah, babe, she really likes you."

Although I kinda knew that.

Still.

It felt *great*.

"I didn't know any of our clients had 'connections,'" I remarked.

"They probably don't. She just made that shit up so I'd do you right, and she knows a little chick who always wears black with her hair rolled at her forehead like she's Betty Grable is not gonna have me quaking in my boots when she lays a threat on me."

"Gotta admit, Annie is the least threatening woman I know, outside my gram."

"Your gram still laid your mom out yesterday," he reminded me. Then he advised, "Never underestimate a woman. Most of them might not have the brute strength of men, but they find a way to get the job done. Like just now."

I adored that he knew that.

So I shot him a beaming smile.

Hugger bent his head and kissed it off my face.

"You have enough room after our donuts to get some food?" I asked after he pulled away.

"Sure," he replied.

We went into Annie's house, which was located in Arcadia Lite and was decorated in All Annie (that being monochromatic in blacks, grays and whites, the perfect foil to showcase her Jeff Koons magenta balloon swan and her Ashley Longshore pop art portrait of Linda Carter as Wonder Woman that included the words ROLL THE CREDITS).

Along the way, I waved at people I knew and made note to introduce Hugger to them. Though, this was a bigger smash than Annie normally put on, and I wondered how she remembered all the people she met in order to invite them to her pad.

After having a donut earlier, I went directly to a mini quiche to balance the levels in my stomach of sweet pastries with a savory one.

Hugger grabbed a plate and nabbed a small stack of little pancakes, skewered with a long pick through a blackberry. It was a cool idea to lay them out like that, turning pancakes into finger food, and I made note should I ever create a brunch buffet.

He poured some syrup on them, and holding the plate under it as he went, he was raising the stick to shove them in his mouth when a woman standing close cried, "Don't!"

Too late, he'd bitten down.

Then he turned to me.

At the expression on his face, I immediately dashed to a stack of paper napkins and gave one to him.

He turned his head and spit out the pancakes.

The woman leaned in after he straightened and said, "We think Annie put salt in them instead of sugar. But everything else seems okay, erm...so far."

I started giggling.

Because...

Annie.

"How do you know Annie?" she asked.

"I work with her," I told her.

"Oh, that means you must be Diana."

Hmm.

Annie spoke of me.

"Guilty," I said. "And this is my boyfriend, Harlan."

"Hi there," she said to Hugger.

"Hey," he replied.

"I'm Wendy. Me and my husband have known Annie for ages. We live down the street. She talks about you a lot. All good. She thinks you're just great."

If the threat of Hugger's broken kneecaps (or other) wasn't warming me enough, that did it.

"She says you're the best employee she's ever had," Wendy continued.

And more warmth.

"Wow, that's nice," I replied.

She leaned in again and whispered, "My husband says she'd be out of business without you. She's sweet as sugar and would do anything for someone she cares about,"—yes, like the threat of busted kneecaps (or other)—"but she isn't the type to be a savvy businesswoman."

Hugger grunted.

I tamped down laughter. "No, she's a great boss, and I really like her, but she's not that."

"I..." The woman sniffed and her brow wrinkled. "Do you smell something—?"

A loud beeping filled the house.

"Fuck," Hugger grunted a word this time, then he dumped his plate and the napkin, and he was on the move.

I followed him to a kitchen filled with smoke.

I noted where it was coming from, dashed to the oven, opened it, and more smoke billowed out, making me cough. I waved at it, and after some of the smoke dissipated, I saw some kind of casserole that was put directly under the top coils had caught on fire.

Hugger saw it too, I knew, because he yanked me back and went in himself.

"Hugger!" I cried.

He turned off the oven, grabbed some oven mitts, and ordered loudly to be heard over the fire alarm still going off. "Do something about the alarm, babe."

I ran to a window, opened it, then raced to a dish towel and started waving it at the alarm as Hugger used the oven mitts to pull a casserole dish out of the oven. He dropped it with a clatter on the stovetop, then used those mitts to beat out the fire.

After flapping the dish towel about a dozen more times, the alarm stopped sounding.

Thank God.

What a racket.

The kitchen reeked of burnt food.

I suddenly sensed we had attention, so I turned to the doorway of the kitchen, which was jammed with people.

And just then, Annie pushed through to the front.

She was still cradling the bottle of Champagne we gave her.

She looked at me, Hugger, the casserole, Hugger, me, and back to the casserole.

"Oh, did I make bread pudding?" she asked no one and everyone.

That was when it happened.

One of those golden moments of life.

And I got to watch.

This being the fact that Hugger didn't only bust out laughing...

He was taken over with it so bad, still holding a singed oven mitt in each hand, he leaned his ass against Annie's kitchen counter, bent double, and his whole big body shook with amusement so strong, he had to brace his hands (and the mitts) against his knees so he could continue laughing and not topple over.

In that moment, watching Harlan "Hugger" McCain laugh that hard, I knew I'd love Annie forever.

But I'd love my guy for eternity.

HUGGER RETURNED from the bathroom after disposing of condom number two of the afternoon.

I lay naked as a jaybird on my stomach at a diagonal on my bed, and barely had it in me to jump when he lightly slapped my ass and asked, "I finally do you in?"

As I knew well, and lived that knowledge, you learned something new every day.

What I learned that day was never wrestle a biker.

And definitely don't do it in bed.

And further, absolutely don't do it naked.

What got into me, I didn't know. My man was take charge, and I liked it like that.

Though, if I tried to take charge, something else I'd just learned, he took it as a challenge.

It was an awesome challenge and one I oh-so-one-hundred-percent didn't mind that I lost in a massive way.

But it was a challenge.

He got in bed properly and tugged me so I was draped down his side.

"Next time we wrestle, you have to have one arm tied behind your back," I mumbled.

"I'll still get you on yours and fuck you stupid."

"Ulk," I gagged, though I had no doubt this would be true, and it would be awesome, like what just happened was.

He chuckled (he knew it was awesome, then again, how loud I was and how hard I came couldn't be missed).

I lifted my head so I could watch his humor, and made the mammoth effort to move my hand so I could sift my fingers through his beard as he experienced it.

"I could look at you for days," I whispered. "Especially when you're happy."

"Di," he whispered back, scooching down in bed and turning to me so we were face to face.

"I don't want to scare you, but in a theme for our day, you should know, I like you. I really, *really* like you," I confessed.

"That's good, 'cause I feel the same."

I relaxed into him. "Thank God."

He smiled gently at me. "Thought I made that pretty plain."

"Nice to have the words."

"So noted," he murmured, then came in for a peck of our lips.

"I think it's time we had our chat," I said.

"Yeah, about that."

Uh-oh.

I wasn't sure that was a good beginning.

"When we know you're safe, I need to go back to Denver. Work some shit out with the brothers," Hugger declared.

Oh boy.

"What shit?" I asked cautiously.

He was quiet for a spell, then he pulled me closer.

"My father was a Chaos brother."

"Oh," I breathed, because I wasn't expecting that. He loved those guys, and they loved him, but no mention until then of his father being one of them.

"He did some nasty shit. Seriously nasty, to the Club, to a bunch of other people. It takes a lot, once you're in, for your brothers to turn on you. They all hate him, Di. And there's a lot to hate. He did them so dirty, anytime I think about it, it turns my stomach. He was an absolute waste of space along with being a total piece of shit."

I hated this for him.

"Harlan."

"I never really knew him. Only met him once. Just knew of him."

"How did you know all of that then?"

"I asked Ma. She put it off until I was older, after he came to me, tried to get in there with me, mostly so he could use me, probably so he could use me against Chaos. She told me so I'd know and wouldn't buy his bullshit. And so you know, he did her dirty too. It was back in the day when the Club had lost its way. Mom was in their stable. This guy, he conned her. Sweet-talked her. Told her he loved her. Told her he was gonna get her out of the life, marry her, give her a house, kids. She fell for it. She fell for him. If he hadn't done that, she'd never have let him have her ungloved so they'd make me."

"Oh God," I groaned, hating that his mother got her heart broken through a betrayal like that.

"Yeah. He was full of it. He just wanted freebies."

I pushed closer. "God, Harlan. What a..." I didn't know what to call the man because that was such a down and dirty shitty thing to do, I didn't think there was a word for it.

"Yeah, not many words strong enough to describe what a complete dick he was."

I grimaced.

Hugger ran his thumb under my eye then continued sharing.

"When Chaos got out of all that business, she tried to go it alone. Tried to set up a client-only situation so it'd be safer. But she got strong-armed by a pimp who was a total asshole. He wanted Ma under his thumb, but after what my dad did, she didn't want to be under anyone's thumb. He wasn't taking no for an answer, beat her to shit more than once."

This just got worse and worse.

I pressed even closer and the only thing I could think to say was, "Honey."

"Yeah," he agreed to all the feeling I put in that one word. "About the third time that happened, she went to Chaos. Took me with her, because he threatened me too, all so he could take his cut of the money she earned off her back. Literally. She told Chaos, they found this guy and put him out of business forever."

I felt my eyes get big. "You mean, they killed him?"

"No, I mean they did a number on him, and he was so shit scared of them after they did, when they told him to get in a different business, he did."

"Oh. Right," I muttered.

"Then they got her set up. It took a while, but after that while, she never walked the streets again. Had a client list. Took referrals and ran checks on them before she took them on. In the end, a lot of them were just regulars who got in the habit of visiting her, they did the deed, but mostly they just wanted company, someone to talk to, and Ma was familiar."

It hurt my soul he knew this about his mother's business.

I wondered why she didn't try to do something else.

Then again, single moms now had it rough. Thirty-five years ago, it had to be worse.

And it was something she knew how to do.

"Chaos also paid for her cancer care," he continued. "Chemo. Radiation. Then eventually hospice. She didn't have insurance. I was bouncing then, I sure as fuck didn't have much to help her out. They got her the best Denver offered." His voice dropped so he whispered his last. "Luxury death care."

My heart heavy with his loss, I smoothed his hair back off his forehead, and kept running my fingers through, because as much as I wanted to wave a magic wand and change this for him, there was nothing for me to say.

"Last, they paid to bury her," he finished.

Official, with a stamp, a gold seal and everything.

I totally loved those guys, and I hadn't even met half of them.

"God, honey. I don't know what to say," I admitted.

"Nothin' to say. It was our life. It wasn't good. It wasn't bad. What I know is, I had a great mom. It wasn't about her keeping me fed or clothed, she was just a great mom. In our house, you wouldn't know what she did. We were normal. She gave me that against some pretty slanted odds."

They weren't normal, with what he knew about all of this.

Then again, I'd lived a protected life. So protected, I was even protected from my mother.

So maybe they just lived an honest life.

"What do you need to do with your brothers?" I asked.

"Figure out why my ma worked so hard to give me a good life, show me the way, but I let a man who done her wrong, a man who I only met once, drag me down into thinkin' I didn't deserve shit. Set me on a path in life where I was just breathing, and not really living."

I would very much like Hugger to get a handle on that.

"Will they be able to help?" I asked.

"Kinda already did. Had a conversation with our ex-president the other day. He was the one who guided them out of the fucked-up crap they were doin'. He knew my dad."

"Biological father," I corrected.

His lips tipped up slightly. "Biological father," he repeated and ran a finger along my hairline. "Do you ever worry you'll turn out like your mom?"

"No. I worry that I didn't give my dad the credit he deserved for how hard he worked to make sure I didn't."

"He didn't want you to know that, babe," he reminded me.

"I know. And I have to get past it. I will. But we aren't talking about me now."

"I asked the question."

I gave him a soft smile. "You're right. You did." I moved us along. "Do you worry you'll be like your bio-father?"

"I did. Maybe still do. It's haunted me."

I could imagine.

"So this ex-president?" I prompted. "Is he going to help with that too?"

"Tack. Good man. Solid gold. Loving father. Loving husband. Loyal brother."

"Okay," I said when he stopped talking.

"Chaos recruited me. They came after me. I didn't get that, not with who my..."—his lips curled up—"biological father was. But they told me my mom wanted it for me. I see it. She trusted them. And what Tack made of the Club, she knew it was a safe place for me. Somewhere I could be when she was gone with people looking out for me. So I became a prospect, but I did it for her."

"I wish I'd met her," I said fiercely.

"I do too, baby," he whispered. "She would have loved you."

"I hope so."

"No, baby, get this, she would have really loved you."

Fuck, I was going to cry again.

Fortunately, Hugger let that go and carried on, "What I didn't get was what Ma really wanted me to have when it came to Chaos. Even though they told me from the beginning. I didn't get it. Until recently."

"What's that?"

"Family."

I closed my eyes and tucked my face in his throat.

He wove his fingers in my hair.

"I had one, and then she was gone, and it was just me," he said quietly, like it was a confession. "But I'm understanding now, I've been grieving her something fierce. I been thinkin', and I reckon that's why I fell into just getting through one day at a time. It was always just her and me. Didn't have any grandparents that I knew. Home wasn't good for her growin' up, she never went back. That meant I never lost anyone that meant anything to me. After she was gone, I didn't know what I was feeling, so I couldn't know how to deal with it."

God, he was just *killing me.*

Sensing why his mom had to do what she had to do to get by.

How alone they were.

How alone *he* was after she was gone.

How much he loved her and how much he lost.

And that he had enough trust in me to be this beautifully honest.

Yes.

Totally killing me.

Hugger kept going, and I knew by the change in his tone that it was about to get even worse.

"She would listen to this song," he whispered. "And sometimes, she'd sing it to me."

"What song, honey?" I whispered back.

"'You and Me Against the World.' Heard it?"

I shook my head while swallowing, holding back tears, because just the title of the song done me in.

"That song..." He took a second, then he said, "It was like she was preparing me for when she wouldn't be there."

Oh God.

"I wanna hear the song," I croaked.

"I'll play it for you later, baby," he murmured.

"Okay."

He pulled breath into his nose and kept giving it to me.

"So, yeah. I got so stuck in the grief, when Chaos took me on, I didn't realize what was all around me. What she wanted for me. What Pete and Rush went out of their way to find me and give to me. What all the brothers and the old ladies and the kids gave me from the get-go."

I loved he was understanding what he had with his Club.

I *loved it.*

But I had a sinking sensation in my stomach because of what he was saying.

His family was in Denver.

And mine was in Phoenix.

With the life he lived, I couldn't take that from him. Especially not now when he was comprehending the fullness of what his mother gave him.

Even though I just lost some of mine, I got the important parts back.

Still.

So Hugger could have his family, I was going to have to move to Denver.

"Di?" he called.

I tipped my head back to catch his gaze. "I can't contain my joy that you're figuring it out, Hug. I haven't met them all, but the ones I've met are awesome. And I can tell by the way they treat you they think the same about you."

"Yeah."

"So, if that was what she wanted, your mom would be happy you're with them?" I asked a question I knew the answer to.

"She totally would."

God.

I was going to have to move to Denver.

"You get one parking spot with this unit, or two?" he asked.

I blinked slowly, not following his change of subject. "Sorry?"

"Your parking spot come with the property, or you rent it?"

"It comes with."

"Just one?"

"No," I breathed. "There are two. And, um, a big storage room. I mean, not humungous, but it fits my Christmas tree and other stuff. Though, I don't have a lot of other stuff, so it's mostly empty."

"Mm," he hummed.

"Why did you ask that?"

"'Cause, I move in, I gotta have somewhere to park my truck so I don't have to get in a fuckin' oven whenever I use it."

My body went completely still.

"Now, this is the way I see it," he went on.

Suddenly, even if a second prior I would have told you I could take no more, I could not wait to find out the way he saw it.

"I'm all ears," I practically panted.

He smiled at me, rolled to his back, pulling me on top.

He then gathered my hair at my neck and held it there in both hands, resting his forearms on my bare back.

"I go home. I figure shit out. Won't take long, but it's gotta be done. You come up for a weekend, meet the brothers, their women, the kids. I show you Denver. If you fall in love, sweet. If you don't, I talk to my brother Snap. He owns a ton of properties. Rentals. He buys 'em, fixes 'em up, rents 'em out. He'd help me do that to my pad. I rent it out, I got income."

"I—"

"I move in with you when I move down here."

When I move down here.

I melted into his body.

He kept speaking.

"Already seems we do okay with that, I mean living together, but we're new. Might just be first blush of all we got going. Lots going down, we haven't really gotten to real, day-to-day life shit. We conquer that and we're good, we're golden. We don't, I move out, we get to know each other the normal way, I move back in when we're ready. We got a plan?"

My voice was hoarse when I asked, "What about the Club?"

"I don't need a lot, so I got a good amount saved, though gonna have to use some of it to fix up my place. I won't feel good takin' my cut if I'm not doin' my bit for them, but I'll have to have that discussion with them. Although all MCs have rules and regs, a hierarchy, none of them are about puttin' a man in chains. Or not any I know of. Though, what I know right down to my gut is my Club will not stand in the way of me having you."

"Maybe we should talk about Denver," I forced out.

"Denver is a great city. You're gonna like it. But it doesn't have your dad, Nicole, Larry, Charlie, Bernie, Mel, Annie. A job you love. And—"

"And Phoenix doesn't have Big Petey, or Dutch, Jagger, Roscoe, this Tack guy, and all the rest of them."

All of what his mother wanted him to have.

He rolled us again, so he was mostly on top, and he got right in my face.

"Here's the bottom-line deal," he announced.

I held my breath.

It was a good call.

"I don't give a fuck where I am, as long as you're there."

Once he said that, I wasn't sure I'd ever breathe again.

But he was far from done.

"I'll rent my place, got the investment in it so that'll always be there for us, and it'll keep growing. I'll also have whatever it rents for, which'll help us out." He smiled. "But I'm not the kinda guy who can sit around watching *Real Housewives*. I need something to do. I'll figure it out. Aces has a home improvement store in north Phoenix, and I bet they'd take me on. I got store experience, practically run Ride, so it won't be like they won't get a good man who'll do them right."

"Hugger—"

"I don't know how much you make, but I'll contribute. Half and half, across the board. I like your crib. It's the shit. Covered parking. Secure. No yardwork. You don't wanna make coffee, you go down and get yourself some. We get on to making those two kids, babe, we're gonna have to have bigger. I'll carry my load with that too."

"Hug—"

"It's hot as fuck here, but I checked, and the weather will be crap from June to September. Four months of twelve, I can work it."

He had checked.

He'd checked!

He kept going.

"And I like snow, but you got mountains here, not far away, same as Denver. I get a hankerin', we can drive to it." He gave me a gentle shake on another smile. "And I'll do the driving. Just like in Denver, you gotta take a road trip to get to the good kind of snow in the mountains, but here, you never have to live in it, which is all right with me."

"No, you don't have to live in it. But, Hugger—"

"In the end, Denver is a two-hour flight or a one-day drive away. It's a haul, but you can do it in a day. Ain't that far. We can go back and be with my family whenever we want."

I waited to see if he had more to say, and when he didn't, I tried again.

"This can break couples," I noted.

"What?"

"You giving up something so huge for me."

"And what are you giving me?" he asked.

I wasn't sure of the question.

"I...I don't know."

"Brunch in a hip pad with a kickass Wonder Woman painting in it that fortunately didn't go up in smoke today."

I wanted to smile at his quip, but with what we were discussing, there was too much at stake, so I didn't have it in me.

He kept going.

"You can have your cocktails in a weird bar with animated fairies flyin' around on the walls and drinks served in weird glasses. I could tell that wasn't for me. But that other bar was the shit. And their fried bologna sandwiches can't be beat."

I ran a hand over his shoulder and whispered, "Hugger."

"You're all that's you, babe, and I think I made it clear I want all a' that."

Oh, he did that for certain.

"But you're opening up my world," he continued rocking mine, "and I never knew I wanted it, but now I know I do. More, my ma would want it for me, and she'd love you're giving it to me."

My "Honey" this time was trembling.

He rubbed his nose against mine before he said, "I think you get, if I had a shot at havin' my mom back, I'd take it."

Yeah, I got that.

"And you just got your dad back," he continued. "No way in fuck I'm takin' that away from you...or him."

"It's not the same thing," I pointed out.

"No, not entirely, but it still kinda is."

I couldn't argue that, so I repeated, "And you just figured out what the Club really means to you."

"My Club, my family, they're not goin' anywhere, Di. They'll always be there. Another thing I learned recently 'cause Pete put it up in my face, and then Dutch did, and finally Tack did...they want me to be happy." His arms tightened around me. "You said it earlier, babe, but I don't think you get it. It's you that makes me happy, Di, and they want that for me. They've all said it, about you, direct. Even Tack, and he hasn't even met you. Just told me to get you up to meet the family."

"He did?"

"Yup."

"Whoa."

"Yup."

"Does Big Petey have a big mouth?" I asked suspiciously.

"Yup."

I didn't find this surprising.

"Okay," I stated.

"Okay what?"

"Okay, I'll go up to Denver. I want to see it. I want to meet everyone. I'll talk to Annie about scheduling a vacation, sometime really soon, spend a week up there. I still have a week of vacation left. I'll go up there, get a really good look around so we can decide. I might love it. Who knows? But I want the experience I'll need to make an informed decision. If it doesn't seem for me, then we can do it your way."

His lips started to spread into a grin.

I put a finger to them before it fully formed.

"But I want you to promise to communicate with me," I demanded. "If the heat gets too much. Or you don't like working at a home improvement store. Or you just miss your family."

He pulled my hand from his mouth and said, "I can promise that."

"And I don't want any long-distance stuff."

"Come again?"

"You need to go up there to deal with whatever you have to deal with, laying your issues with your biological father to rest, okay. But when you come back, you bring your truck, haul your bike, fill your truck with your stuff, and we're doing this."

He rolled further into me so he was totally on top of me.

And man, oh man, I freaking *loved* the look he had on his amazing face.

"We're doing this?" he asked.

"All in," I declared.

"You totally fucked out?" he asked.

"Yes, I am totally fucked out," I answered. "And seeing as that's all your fault, if you're in the mood to bang me again, you have to do all the work."

"Like I don't do most of it already," he teased.

"You will note that earlier, I *tried* to take control, you just didn't let me."

His hands were moving on me, and as ever, my body was reacting.

"I did notice something like that," he muttered on a sly grin.

"How could you miss it? I practically fell off the bed twice."

He dipped his head and said to the skin on my chest, "Definitely noticed that." He trailed his mouth to my nipple. "Not where I wanted you."

"Well, you did something about it," I returned, going for fake-irritably, and failing since it came out all breathy.

He flicked my nipple with his tongue.

My clit contracted.

It was like he knew it, because one roaming hand glided over my hip and in, and when I said "in" I meant "*in*."

I mewed and ran my nails lightly up his spine.

"Always so fuckin' wet for me," he said against my nipple, before he sucked it between his lips.

I fisted a hand in his hair and arched into his mouth.

He paid attention to my nipples (both of them) and my clit, until I was writhing under him and pumping my hips into his hand.

Hugger brought his mouth to mine.

"You on the pill?" he asked.

"No."

"You gonna get on the pill?" he pressed.

"Yeah."

"Both of us tested, ASAP. Get on that."

"Okay, honey."

I thought he'd reach for a condom.

He didn't.

He slid down my body, threw my legs over his shoulders and went down on me.

I came against his mouth, and I came again a little while later around his cock.

It was then, something else was official.

I was fucked out *and* orgasmed out.

I had no idea either could happen, but there I was.

I'd also found my man.

And he was an amazing man.

Perfect.

He was mine.

He was coming to me.

He was moving in with me.

We were figuring this out with no long-distance crap pulling us apart.

We were doing this.

Both of us.

All in.

And even though, when Hugger left me in bed to deal with the condom, I literally couldn't move (I certainly couldn't do the happy jumps and cartwheels I felt like doing), I was ecstatic about it.

Abso-freaking-lutely.

23

CAREFREE

Hugger

Hugger moved out of the shadows at the side of Di's grandma's house when he heard the front door open and the two women saying goodbye.

It was Tuesday after their epic weekend of shit stuff and great stuff, and Di felt the need to check in on her grandmother. Hugger took her, but he thought it best they have some alone time, therefore he kept watch outside while they had a glass of wine.

He met the women on the stoop.

"Oh, now you're here, you should come in for a quick drink, Harlan," Shannon invited.

She didn't know he wasn't there for a pickup, he'd been there the whole time, because she didn't know he wasn't just Di's boyfriend, but also her bodyguard.

"'Preciate it, Shannon, but it's getting late, and I need to get my woman home so she can relax. She's got work tomorrow," Hugger replied.

"Such a good boy," Shannon muttered, and Hugger nearly smiled.

He hadn't been called a boy in a very long time.

He didn't smile because he wasn't a big fan of the expression on either woman's face.

Di went in for a hug from her gram, Hugger gave the woman his hand, and Shannon took it but did not shake it. She patted it, and never having a grandma himself, so never feeling anything like what came through her touch, he couldn't deny those pats felt sweet.

When the woman let him go, he slung his arm around Di's shoulders, felt hers snake along his waist, and they walked to his bike.

It was nine thirty, eighty degrees outside, deep in September, and there'd been no weather at all since he'd been down there that would keep him off the back of his bike.

Maybe Phoenix wasn't going to be so bad, even in the shitty months.

He stopped her at his bike and turned her to his front.

He was going to speak, but she got there before him. "I see what Dutch meant about the dark."

"Come again?"

"You materialized out of the night like a shadow taking shape. So I see what Dutch meant. I'm impressed."

She was teasing, but he wasn't buying it.

So instead of replying to what she said, he asked, "How'd that go?"

It took her a beat before she shook her head, planted her face in his chest a second, pressing the rest of her to him with both arms rounding him, and then she tipped her head back.

That was something he hadn't felt before either, or he hadn't let it penetrate.

And, damn, it felt good to stand strong when his woman needed to lean on him.

"She's called Mom to chat every day since the incident," she told him. "Even when Mom was still in town. Mom's ghosting her."

Christ, that woman was a total bitch.

He didn't say that.

"You think she'll cave?" he asked.

"I don't know. No one has ever called Mom on her shit in that grand of a fashion. We're in uncharted territory."

His phone at his ass vibrated, he ignored it, and kept his attention on his woman.

He did this because they hadn't had a lot of time in, but he still knew his woman.

"You gonna wade into that?"

She bit her lip.

Just as he suspected, Di giving everything to everybody else, sometimes at the expense of herself.

She didn't know it, but her mother played a part in Di being like that. Diana had been dancing attendance on that woman since she'd taken her first breath, it was all she knew.

It was good that Di could twist it so it could be worthwhile for people who mattered.

And it was good she had him now, so he could make sure she didn't use herself up.

"Di—"

"Ugh," she grunted. "I can't. No contact means no contact. And seriously, Mom's so good at her games, she might be doing this to Gram for the sole purpose of making me wade in."

"Yeah," he agreed.

"So I can't."

"Yeah," he agreed a lot more firmly.

"Ugh," she repeated.

Hugger bent to touch his lips to hers, and when he moved away, murmured, "Let's get you home."

"'Kay," she mumbled.

They let go, he got on his bike, she swung on behind him, plastered herself to his back with her arms around his stomach, chin to his shoulder, and that didn't feel as good as her leaning on him, but it still felt damn good.

They took off, and like he felt it, she probably felt his phone vibrating at his ass again.

When they stopped at a red light, he yelled over the pipes, "Grab that, will you?"

Di shifted enough to reach into his back pocket and get his phone after the call had ended.

"Dutch," she said in his ear.

"Show it my face, then call him," he ordered, reminding himself to give her his passcode later.

She activated his phone, pointed it at his face, and kept hold with one arm around him as he took off when the light went green.

He heard her shouted conversation with Dutch, so he already guessed what was coming before she ended the call and said loudly in his ear, "He wants you at the crash pad as soon as you can get there. He says I can come too."

Hugger changed lanes.

Something else to be said about Phoenix, a city that was built nearly entirely on a grid system with numbered avenues (west) and streets (east) with a central road dividing the two called Central made learning the way around super fucking easy.

Twenty minutes later, he rolled up the driveway behind several other bikes, and he felt his eyes narrow on them because it wasn't just Dutch, Jagger and Coe's bikes and Big Petey's trike, and one or two of them should be on Armitage, Eight and Muzzle's bikes were there, and parked at the curb was one of the NI&S SUVs, a flashy truck, and a sleek Jaguar.

Diana swung off, he came off after her and stopped when he caught her look.

"What?" he asked.

"This is a crash pad?" she asked back, tossing her arm to the long ranch house on the side of a hill that had a fantastic view of the Valley. It also had four bedrooms, four and a half baths, a swimming pool with a waterfall into a Jacuzzi and an air hockey table.

"Resurrection owns some dispensaries in Denver," he explained. "They got cake."

She just stared at him.

So he continued, "And Ride's got shops and garages all over Colorado. They do good trade, even better now after the millennials and Gen Z decided it was important to shop local. And our custom builds sell for hundreds of thousands of dollars."

"So as well as playing bodyguards and part-time vigilantes, you're all biker entrepreneurs," she noted.

He slung an arm around her shoulders again and muttered, "Something like that."

He led her inside and immediately saw all the players.

Yes, Eight and Muzz were back. Also there were Mace and Cap Jackson, another member of the NI&S team, and Sylvie and Tucker Creed, two local PIs with ties to Denver seeing as Sylvie used to work for Knight Sebring, an ally of Chaos. And last, a woman he met at their only other Phoenix meeting, a meeting that all of these folks drifted in and out of, providing information and advice, which was why that meet had lasted so long.

She was called Sixx. She was gorgeous, he had no idea what her occupation was, but whatever it was, it was badass, and if he were anybody else other than him, she'd scare the shit out of him.

He didn't get the chance to introduce his woman to the new people, because Diana cried, "Oh my God! Guys!" and dashed straight to Muzzle.

She gave him a big hug, and Muzz, being part asshole, held her close and gave her a visible squeeze at the same time he gave Hugger a smirk.

Fucker.

Hugger just crossed his arms on his chest and watched.

Di moved to Eight, and Eight didn't bust his balls, but he did give her a tight hug.

When she popped away from Eight, she asked, "What are you guys doing back?"

"That's what we gotta talk about," Eight said.

This commenced Di getting intros to Cap, Sylvie, Tucker and Sixx.

After that, Mace said to her, "Hang with the guys for a few while we steal your man?"

Di, not stupid in the slightest, Hugger already knew had figured shit with the Babićs had or was coming to a head.

But she didn't argue as Jagger approached and said, "Your choice. Beer or air hockey."

"I only get one?" Di returned.

Yup, that was his woman.

"C'mon, darlin'," Big Petey urged, holding a hand Di's way. "We'll get a game started while Jag sets us up."

Di headed toward Big Petey and the air hockey table as Jag went to the fridge.

Hugger followed Eight and Mace to the den situated at the front of the crib. Sylvie, Tucker, Cap and Sixx followed them.

Cap closed the door behind them.

Eight took a tablet from the desk in there, woke it up, and handed it to Hugger.

Hugger looked at the picture on it and sucked in a sharp breath.

The picture showed three men on their asses on the ground, backs propped up against a wall, but still falling into each other.

That was because they were filled with holes, covered in blood and very dead.

Resting on their laps were two big pieces of paper. One said I'm and the other said Done.

One of the men was Esad Babić. The other two were his bros.

"This is what the Costa Rican authorities found when they caught up with Esad," Mace shared.

Hugger locked eyes with Eight.

Eight shook his head. "Not us. We were down there, working

with some connections to procure firearms, but we were too late. Heard word the deed was done, got back to the States late this afternoon."

"So who?" Hugger asked. "And what does 'I'm done' mean?"

Sixx came closer. "Imran hasn't left Bolivia. That doesn't mean Imran can't call a hit. And word is, Imran called three hits from his hacienda in Bolivia."

Hugger was shocked as shit. "He gave the order to have his own son whacked?"

"Imran is a lunatic," Sylvie chimed in, "but he's a shrewd businessman. Cops and Feds have been all over his properties here in the Valley, and elsewhere. They found nothing to tie him to anything but his legit dealings. Imran's problem was they had Esad's phone, which was a big get. Though, when they searched Esad's house, they found his laptop, something the moron left behind, which was an even bigger one. It held a wealth of information, not only about the crap he'd been doing, but about his dad's interests. They also got Esad's car, with his address history in his navigation system. Led them to known and unknown stash houses, safehouses and warehouses of the Babić empire. There was quite a bit of connecting the dots of shell companies and known associates, still more to do, but all of it so far, with all the shit in it, has been connected to Imran." She paused and finished, "They're cooked."

"As in 'done,'" Tucker added.

Hugger couldn't believe this. "His boy programmed stash houses and safehouses in his satnav?"

"Yep," Tucker confirmed.

Christ, that guy was one stupid motherfucker.

"Cops and Feds have rounded up most of Imran's army," Mace put in. "Not all of them, but most of them. None of them are talking. Either because of their code, or because they're terrified of Babić, considering he'd call a hit on his own son, and the aforementioned fact he's a lunatic."

Cap took it from there, "Some of his soldiers are still breathing free, but they've scattered. A few of them headed to Bolivia. Most of them crossed the border into Mexico."

"In the wind?" Hugger asked.

"For now," Cap answered.

"There's more," Sixx said.

"What's that?" Hugger prompted when that was all she said.

"Babić got word to someone who would get word to me," she replied. "This was so I could tell Mace, Sylvie, Tucker or someone who would get that word to you boys since he didn't know we'd been introduced. He shared he has no beef with either Nolan or Diana Armitage, and he never did."

His son dead at his order, Hugger thought this was too good to be true.

"We believe that?" Hugger pushed.

"We do," Sixx said.

"There a reason he didn't just tell Buck this info when Buck tried to reach out ten fuckin' times?" Hugger groused.

"Unfortunately, there is," Sixx told him. "He thought it was hilarious, how much effort you all were putting into keeping safe two people he didn't give a shit about."

What an asshole.

But that was something he could believe about this guy, and at least it meant Di and Nolan were safe, and Dutch, Jag and Coe could go home.

He was sticking in Phoenix, at least for a while.

"And Maddy?" Hugger kept at Sixx.

"Maddy isn't his problem," Sixx replied. "She was, when he was trying to keep his son from tanking himself and the family business. She's not anymore. There's nothing that links Imran Babić with that trafficking ring. And the Feds have decimated it. They have the testimony of a good number of women, not to mention several players who are making deals. Madison might not even have to testify."

Well, that was a huge fucking relief.

Hugger turned to Eight. "Any word on what his gig is with the clubs?"

Eight's eyes darkened and he said, "Yeah. Back in Denver, Core and Brain got hold of an informant, that bein' an informant of Babić's. They did their work and found out that somehow, Babić learned about the situation with Chaos and Resurrection and Benito Valenzuela."

Valenzuela was a name out of Chaos's history books, just like Hugger's bio-father was.

And like Hugger's bio-father, the story wasn't a fun one.

Therefore, Hugger didn't have a good feeling about this.

"So what?"

"So, seems like Babić got it in his head he didn't like the fact that two motorcycle clubs bested one of his kind," Eight informed him. "For shits and grins, because this guy is one twisted motherfucker, thought he'd bump up against us and see how that shook out."

Fucking hell.

Hugger studied Eight closely. "How much he know about Valenzuela?"

Eight's voice went low. "Enough, but not any of that. No one knows anything about any of that."

Hugger relaxed.

Only slightly.

"His army decimated, his business in ruins, is he maybe rethinking making that play?" Hugger asked.

"Would be hard," Mace said. "Unless he smuggles himself back into the country, any point of entry he tried, he'd be arrested immediately. He could call the shots from South America, but without any soldiers left, not sure who he could trust that he'd reach out to for an operation that would have to be intricate and well-managed."

"Men like him find their way to get around," Hugger pointed out.

No one had a response to that.

"He'd also have to rebuild," Cap added. "We suspect he's living off hidden money, but he had bank accounts here, all of them healthy, now all of them are frozen, and as those wheels turn, no doubt they're gonna get seized, along with all his property. So he doesn't have near the resources he used to."

"Not to mention, he made a mistake picking Bolivia," Mace put in. "The extradition treaty we signed with them hasn't been fruitful for the US, to the point it's like it's not there. Last person they allowed extradited was in the mid-nineties. They're not fans of extraditing Bolivian nationals. But he's not a Bolivian national. He got American citizenship in 1998. They've been made aware he's there, the US government is in talks with them about extricating him, so he might need to make another move and do it soon."

"So he's gonna be on the run," Hugger deduced.

"Maybe preoccupied with that, you boys are in the clear. Maybe his message of 'I'm done,' is bullshit to take you off your guard. But at least for now, he's not going to be an immediate problem," Sylvie said.

This meant they weren't assured the Babić situation was sorted, but Nolan and Di were safe, and they had some breathing room and a warning they were on the radar of a lunatic who had the urge to dick with them.

"We'll keep an ear out," Tucker added.

"Bottom line for now, Di and her dad are good," Eight stated.

"You goin' back to Denver?" Hugger asked him.

"Linus is already headed up there, tomorrow Muzz and me will too. Roscoe is going with us. We got this house until the end of the month, so apparently, Georgie and Archie are coming down for the weekend before the Black brothers head back."

That'd be good, Di could meet them.

"So this is done," Hugger summed up.

"For now," Eight said.

Yeah.

For now.

But he'd take that with knowing Di was safe.

The rest, they'd see.

AFTER TALKING to her dad to let him know all was good with Babić, Hugger saw her enter her bedroom.

He was stretched out in her bed with a book he pulled from her shelf (*Mother Daughter Murder Night*, sounded up his alley, even if he'd never been a reader—he was trying new things, and since Di had a big bookshelf filled with books in her living room, he'd helped himself).

He watched her walk to him in her tight cropped tee and loose drawstring shorts.

He quickly put the book aside as she collapsed on top of him.

"Your dad good?" he asked.

She nodded. "He wants to throw a pool party on Saturday, since Georgie and Archie will be here."

Hugger hadn't owned a pair of swimming trunks since he was at least eight.

"I'll have to warn Dutch and Arch so the women can pack suits."

"Okay."

"And we'll have to go out and get me some trunks."

She grinned at the idea of shopping. "Okay."

He dug his fingers into the hems of her shorts and up into her panties. "Why the fuck you put on pajamas?"

Di assumed a fake severe expression. "Excuse me, Harlan 'Hugger' McCain, you have the wrong impression about me. I am not easy."

That was when he grinned, flipped her to the back and proved her wrong.

HUGGER WAS DOING Di on all fours, curled over her, one hand to the bed, one hand between her legs, finger to her clit.

And he was almost there, so she needed to fucking get there.

On that thought, her head, which had been bent, flashed back, slammed into his shoulder, her soft hair coasting all over his face and tangling in his beard, making his balls draw up in warning, and she came...loud.

Thank fucking God.

He glided his finger away, wrapped his arm around her hips, held her stationary for his thrusts, and eventually shoved his face in her neck, shot his load, and as usual with Diana, he did it hard.

He was still using condoms. She had a doctor's appointment the next week. He had one the week after up in Denver.

He cruised slow inside her as he lost the hard, then pulled out, kissed her shoulder, lifted up, gently pushed her to her side in the bed, and he left her there, flicking the covers over her as he moved to get rid of the rubber.

When he got back, he stretched out beside her, and she snuggled close.

"That gig was bizarre, babe," he declared.

She started laughing.

"I nearly fell asleep," he went on.

She kept laughing.

Fuck, but he loved to make her laugh.

She looked up at him. "So the ambient jam is not your style?"

It was late night Saturday. They'd gone to Charlie's gig that night, and they'd done it not only with Mel and her man Gerard (who seemed a decent dude, more so when Mel had to elbow him because he actually did fall asleep), Bernie, as well as Dutch, Georgie, Jagger and Archie.

Dutch and Jagger kept shooting him *What the fuck?* looks through the whole thing.

Georgie appeared to be near laughter through the whole thing.

Archie seemed to dig it, or at least she pretended a lot better than the rest of them that she didn't think it was as totally whacked as it was.

"No," he answered Diana's question.

"You don't have to go again," she told him.

"You go to all of them?"

She nodded.

Of course she did.

"They don't happen very often," she explained, "because, I mean...obviously, they don't have a big following and there aren't a lot of venues longing to have a band that will put their clientele to sleep."

He had noticed not many tables in that bar were filled, and some had emptied after Charlie and her crew got started.

"Charlie doesn't care, she just likes to play," Di continued.

"How often do gigs happen?"

"Maybe once every couple of months. They go up to Sedona and Flag to play more than they do here. Sometimes we go, because those places are fun to hang in. Sometimes we don't."

"We'll see when it happens again."

She gave him a soft look, stroked his beard and changed the subject.

"I like Georgie and Archie. They're both totally rad."

His lips tipped up. "They're definitely...*rad*."

She stopped stroking his beard to slap his pec and demanded, "Don't give me shit."

Hugger smiled fully.

Warmth hit her eyes as she watched him do it, but he felt her mood shift.

"Babe," he said quietly, "it's gotta get done."

He was talking about the fact that he knew what her mood was about.

He'd told her he was riding back up to Denver with Dutch and Jag on Wednesday.

"I know," she mumbled.

"Snap's in to help renovate my place," he reminded her. "He texted today and said Hound's already been over there to start gutting the kitchen."

Her eyes rounded in surprise. "Really?"

"Hound likes to destroy shit."

Her mood shifted again as she started laughing.

"Earned yourself a Club name," he muttered, loving the fact that she had down to his bones.

Both Georgie and Archie started calling her "Blue" the minute they hit her pad that night when they all met up to go have something to eat before the gig.

Her mood entirely shifted as she beamed at him. "I'm official."

"Already were, baby," he murmured.

That bought him a kiss.

He gave that back before he ended it and rolled her this way and that to turn out the bedside lights.

He was tired, he'd come hard, and they had a big day the next day. They had to get some shuteye.

They cuddled front to front, like every night. Though, he usually shifted, and they woke up with her tucked to his back, or sometimes, she shifted, so he was curved to hers.

But they started connected and ended connected.

Every night.

Hugger didn't think about it, not once, not since the beginning.

Because this was Di.

So he didn't think about it then, when he felt her drift asleep in his arms, and he followed her.

And he didn't think about it hours later, when he woke, curled into her back, holding her close.

THAT AFTERNOON, Hugger pulled himself out of Nolan's pool, shook the wet from his hair and grabbed one of the thick beach towels from the stack that had been put out so he could towel down.

He then walked to the gigantic cooler filled with beer and helped himself to one.

He twisted the cap, tossed it in the trash bin sitting near, and turned to take in what was happening in the pool.

There was semi-loud music playing, and thankfully, it wasn't ambient. To fit his generation, and theirs, Nolan had set the music to nineties grunge, which worked for both.

Di was riding a pool noodle wearing a sweet red two-piece that had a halter top with a little ruffle, and it plunged way low in the front showing a good amount of her tits. The pants came up high at the waist, had some gathers at the belly and showed nice ass cheek.

It was sexy as fuck.

They'd hit the mall that morning and got him some extra-long board shorts in army green. Di had wanted him to buy a red pair, but he wasn't a red guy. Now he was glad he pushed back on that, or they'd match, and that'd be goofy as shit.

But he reckoned this was why she pushed for the red, so they'd be goofy, she'd be cute, at the same time a pain in his ass, something he also found cute.

Mel, Charlie and Georgie were riding noodles too. Bernie was sitting next to Nicole on the edge of what Di told him was called a Baja bench in the pool. The women all had melting frozen drinks in their hands in fancy, but plastic glasses and they were forming a huddle.

Jagger appeared to be asleep on a float that looked like a massive pillow. Dutch and Gerard were in the lounge chairs set on the Baja bench, drinking beers and rapping. Pete was completely conked under a lounger at the side of the pool, and he had company. Shannon was reading a romance novel in the lounger next to Pete's.

So, yeah.

Another plus for Phoenix, that view right there.

Larry hadn't come. He apparently was all in for Diana to have her family around her, so Nicole had shocked the shit out of both Di and Hugger when she showed, but it'd probably take a while before Larry was fully down with partying at his wife's ex's house.

Said a lot about the man that Nicole was there, though, just as it said a lot about Nicole.

Grudges will fuck you up, it was best to avoid them.

Though, Hugger hoped Di kept hers against her mother for the next twenty-five years.

When he heard the door open behind him, he turned and watched Armitage stroll out.

The man looked to the pool, his face went soft, then he looked to Hugger and came his way.

He got his own beer and stood beside Hugger.

"You're not a man to mess around," Hugger noted, tipping the neck of his beer bottle to the pool.

"It would appear you aren't either," Armitage replied, then took a drag from his beer. "Diana tells me you're moving down here."

"Yup."

"That's quite a sacrifice," Armitage remarked. "Takes you away from your family."

"My brothers will get it. And Di doesn't live in New Zealand."

"No," Armitage murmured to his bottle of beer. "She doesn't." He then took another drag.

Hugger took his own and went on, "Anyway, I lost my ma, she found her dad. And that woman who's her mother is playing games with her grandma. It'd kill her to be away from either of you right now."

He felt the man's eyes, so he turned from watching Diana smiling at something Archie was saying to look at her father.

"You lost your mother?" Armitage asked.

"Yeah."

"I'm so sorry, Harlan," Armitage said quietly.

Hugger took another drag and said, "Happened a while ago."

"You never get over it," Armitage said.

His gut clenched but he didn't say anything.

"I had a wonderful mother," Armitage told him. "She and my dad worked hard all their lives, died too young and didn't get to enjoy all they worked for. They were both in their sixties when they went, but still, it was too young. I miss them every day, and I hate that for them every day. I would have wanted them to leave this earth having had time to enjoy being on it without expending a lot of blood, sweat and tears."

Hugger remained silent, feeling this in the marrow of his bones, because it was the same for him.

Armitage's attention was acute on Hugger when he said, "That's their due, what they earn from us, not to be forgotten. They live on in us, as long as we have their memories."

"Yeah," Hugger grunted.

But he liked that.

It was what his ma told him in that song.

She'd be gone, and her memory would get him through.

And she was with him, maybe just in his thoughts, but every day, whenever he needed her, he could call her up, and she'd be right there.

His attention was taken when female cackles rent the air, and both men focused on the women in the pool, seeing all of them lost in laughter.

"With what Margaret did, there was always something, like a blanket smothering our happiness as a family, Di's and mine," Armitage said as he watched the women laugh. "Never seen her so happy and carefree."

Hugger felt his throat close.

Because what Armitage just said...

That was for him.

The man was giving him that gift.

Armitage turned to him. "Thanks for that, Harlan."

Christ, *that was for him.*

"You can call me by my Club name, Hugger or Hug," Hugger pushed out.

Armitage smiled and murmured, "Honored." Then he walked to

the edge of the pool and asked, "Anyone ready for me to put the burgers on the grill?"

Pete woke for that and yelled, "Fuck yeah!"

"Want help, Dad?" Di called.

"I'd love it, Buttercup," Armitage answered.

Armitage glanced at Hugger with a dip of his chin as he took his beer back into the house.

Diana paddled her way to the Baja bench, listed off the noodle and pulled herself out of the pool.

Dutch and Gerard got off the loungers, Dutch going to sit on the edge of the bench, Gerard commandeering Diana's noodle and floating in the pool.

Jagger lifted his glasses off his nose, looked at Hugger and grinned.

And Hugger set his beer aside and toweled off some more so he wasn't dripping.

Then he went into the house to help Di and her dad with the burgers.

24

THE ISLAND OF CHAOS

Hugger

Two weeks later...

HUGGER STOOD in his house in Denver and decided (all the shit that meant anything to him packed and sitting in High and Millie's basement, waiting for him to load it up and drive down to Phoenix, all the rest of it, furniture, kitchen shit, whatever, taken to the dump), the place looked better than it ever had.

The rooms with carpet had been stripped of it, the kitchen and bathrooms gutted, the wall that separated the kitchen from the living room had been torn down so they could create a great room.

There was a corner of the living room filled with boxes and loaded pallets. Another stacked with tools. They were waiting for the kitchen cabinets that had been picked by Rosalie and Tyra (and approved by Diana) to arrive. But they were ready to roll on the bathrooms.

That work was going to start tomorrow.

He'd be glad to have it done, renters in, income coming in.

It had never been a home. But now it would be something.

Something that would feed into making a good life with Diana.

He left the house, setting the security alarm that was the first thing put in because now there was something in it that had worth, and locking up.

He hopped on his bike and headed to Chaos.

When he hit the forecourt, he saw all his brothers' rides parked in a line outside the Compound.

Hugger parked at the end, shut her down and got off.

He was headed to the front door to the Compound when something pulled him another direction.

Even though he knew the men were waiting for him, he found his feet taking him to the back door of the store. He punched in the code, pulled open the door, strolled through the meticulously organized storeroom (his doing—before him, that room was a pit), and hit the store.

It felt funny, walking through it, knowing where every fanbelt was hung, every jug of wiper fluid was shelved, every can of motor oil was stacked.

It was then he realized he got off on being the first one in to open. He got off on being the man they could ask if they had a question about some shit at the register or how long it might take to get a special part from a certain vendor.

He got off on being that guy for his brothers.

It was then, he knew he was going to miss it.

He'd tell Di about that, after he was moved in and settled. She was already tweaked enough about what he was "giving up" for her. He wasn't going to add to that until she knew he was good, and they were solid.

His phone went with a text when he was leaving Ride to head to the Compound.

Since it was from Di, he stopped to read it.

Maddy just phoned! She's home with E&E and looking into starting up classes again!!!!!!!!

She added about a dozen double pink hearts and smiley-faces with hearts surrounding them and ended with about two dozen women dancing.

He was hepped up about what was about to happen, but even so, at that news, he grinned and returned, *Great news, baby. She phones again, tell her I said hey.*

He got, *Already did that*, when he was halfway through the Compound on his way to the meet room.

He stopped moving again and sent her a blowing-kiss face.

After he did that, he looked around.

The curved bar. The beat-up leather couches. The pool table.

His mom had to find places for them to live where the landlord would take cash and not ask questions. These kinds of people weren't steady, and often weren't law-abiding, so they moved often.

Therefore, it was then he realized for the first time in his life, this was home.

It didn't just feel like home.

It was his *home.*

The Compound.

The island of Chaos.

This was never gonna go anywhere.

This was never going to change.

This was going to be his, a part of him, a safe place, until he died.

No matter where he was.

But leaving it was going to suck too. Leaving the place, leaving the brothers behind, and he finally understood why Diana was so concerned about him moving.

It didn't change his mind.

She was his woman.

She was his happiness.

She was his future.

But this was his sacrifice, and it was going to cut.

He shook off his thoughts and focused on what was up next.

They were meeting...for him.

They were meeting to help him exorcise his bio-father.

And he was going to tell them he was moving to Phoenix.

Hugger squared his shoulders and walked the rest of the way to the meet room.

He opened the door and saw they were all there, seated around the big table with the cutout in the middle covered in Plexiglas and filled with the first-ever Chaos flag, their insignia in the middle, their motto, the words WIND, FIRE, RIDE and FREE surrounding it.

The only one not sitting was Hound, who never sat. He always stood, arms crossed on his chest, shoulders and the sole of his boot against the wall, the brothers' guard dog, always on alert.

Rush was at the head of the table, and Hugger had to pause when he saw a tall stack of plastic-folder-covered-bound paper, like some kind of reports, sitting on the table beside him.

He didn't know what those were, but considering why they were all there, that stack made him uneasy.

"Good of you to show," Boz gave him shit for being late.

Hugger went to his chair, one that was situated between Dog and Snapper.

Only when he was seated did he flip Boz the bird.

Boz grinned.

"Right, we're all here," Rush said and brought down the gavel.

Hugger tensed.

This was it.

Fuck.

"We got somethin' to talk about and we all know what it is, but business first," Rush declared.

With that, Rush stood and started sending those plastic-folder-covered reports flying down the center of the table. Hands shot out to grab them, pass them around, until everyone had one.

Hugger looked at the cover of his, and there was some logo, some firm name under it, and it said:

MARKET RESEARCH SURVEY
EXPANSION PROJECT
RIDE AUTO SUPPLY STORE AND GARAGE
PHOENIX, ARIZONA

Hugger felt his throat close tight.

"Have a look at what it says, but I'll sum up," Rush began. "Phoenix is growing. One of the fastest growing cities in the US. It's a biker haven. Also lots of interest in vintage rides and restoration. Good mix of income levels, good mix of generation levels, which means money to spend and people to spend it. They got some factories going up and plenty of housing development underway or planned. Both are only going to mean more growth. It's ripe for investment and expansion. Also, state tax code is advantageous."

He turned to the remaining stack of plastic-folder-covered papers and sent them sailing.

The men caught them, handed them out, and before Hugger could look at the cover, Rush was speaking again.

"Looking at three lots. Two are empty. One, if we decide to do this, and pick that one, there'd need to be some demo. The two empty lots are huge, way bigger than what we need, but that's because Aces High has approached for a partnership. They're ready to expand too. They want to open another store and they'd be willing to hitch up with Ride if we go for it. Good opportunity there for cross marketing."

Fighting to breathe and hiding he was, Hugger flipped through the real estate report.

He didn't know the exact addresses, but because his woman was as she was, while he was in Phoenix, he'd had ample opportunity to get around, so he had a sense of where they were, and they were good spots.

"Obviously, before we get down to talking about property, we need to decide whether we're gonna expand out of Colorado into Arizona," Rush said.

"Millie's folks are getting on in years, and they live down there" High piped up. "She was already talking about us getting a place so she could have somewhere to land when the time comes they need more attention. And Cleo's got her heart set on the nursing program at U of A. Zadie will go where her sister goes. So reckon we'd be looking at having someplace down there sometime soon anyway, if not movin' down full stop. Millie won't want me far away from my girls."

What High left unsaid was, since Millie was thick and thieves with her stepdaughters, she wouldn't want to be far away from them either.

"Red's done with snow," Tack chimed in. "And the boys are gonna be out of high school in a few years and wreaking havoc on Denver, so she'll want it not to be easy to get to us for bail money." There were some chuckles, but Tack spoke over them. "Won't be full-time, not leavin' my grandbabies, and Red won't want to either, but for the winter, need to get my woman out of the snow and cold."

Hop threw in then, "Where Tyra goes, Lanie will wanna follow. And I'm good with any place I can ride all year long. We got a longer wait for Nash to be done with school, though."

"Gonna get a winter place down there," Big Petey added. "That Phoenician sun was good to these old bones. Seize up completely if I gotta spend another four cold months here."

"Renae good with that?" Snapper asked after Pete's old lady, who was also Snapper's mother-in-law.

"Yeah, son," Big Petey answered. "She was beside herself at the thought of not having to scrape another windshield."

"I'm good to be down there all year," Boz announced. "Not the snow, a fresh menu of pussy."

There were some groans, and Hound threw his market report and hit Boz in the side of the head with it.

Boz's angry gaze shot to Hound, who just grinned.

But before anything could come of that, Rush asked, "You men wanna read the report, or are you good to vote?"

"Obviously I'm in," High said.

"In," Tack grunted.

"In," Hop added.

"Totally in," Big Petey declared.

"Aye," Shy said.

"Aye," Dutch and Jag said in unison.

"Wouldn't mind movin' down there either," Roscoe announced, looking at Hound. "And don't throw shit at me, but seriously, down there, you don't have to put up with five months of women covering themselves up in big sweaters and bulky coats and shit."

Joker, Snapper, Dog, Chill and Saddle all gave their ayes.

"Already talked to Brick, Arlo, Tug, Bat, and Speck, and they're good with it," Rush said. Those were the members who'd moved to the other locations to see to business there. Then he looked Hugger in the eye. "You haven't voted, Hug."

He hadn't, because he couldn't talk.

When he left Denver for Phoenix, no word they were looking at expansion.

He knew what this was.

They were doing this for him.

This was *for him*.

So he wouldn't lose his family.

So he wouldn't lose his home.

So he would know precisely what made him.

"Hug?" Tack prompted.

"Aye," he forced out.

Tack nodded.

"Looks like Ride is headed to Phoenix," Rush decreed. "Now, have a look at those properties. We can decide on that later." Rush turned again to Hugger. "Gonna task you with being our man on the ground down there. You good with that?"

Hugger had to clear his throat before he said, "Yeah."

Rush switched his attention to Dog. "Brick's in to help, but also gotta ask if you will too. You two have the most experience opening new shops. Hug's gonna need some brothers at his back."

"You got it," Dog said and grinned. "Anway, Sheila will be all over trips down to the Valley. She can spend time with her brother and spoil her nieces and nephew to shit."

Sheila was Buck's sister.

"Good. That done?" Rush asked.

"It's done," Tack stated.

Rush brought down the gavel.

Hugger felt like his chest was going to explode.

Rush looked to his dad.

Tack didn't hesitate.

"Now, we gotta talk about Chew," Tack stated.

"No," Hugger pushed out.

At Hugger's word, the room went deathly quiet.

He had to clear his throat again and he did it staring Tack Allen straight in the eye.

Because his son was president.

But Ride in Phoenix was Tack's idea.

"No, we don't. Do we?" he asked Tack.

"Up to you, brother," Tack replied like he didn't give a shit one way or another.

And he didn't.

Because Chew wasn't worth a shit.

But he did.

Because they just proved beyond doubt that Hugger was.

"Did what just happened, just happen?" Hugger asked a question that didn't need answering.

"It happened," Tack confirmed.

They were buying a huge-ass commercial lot in an entirely different state and setting up a business so Hugger wouldn't lose his family.

"Then I reckon we don't have to talk about my bio-father," Hugger said.

"That mean you get who you are?" Tack asked.

Hugger nodded.

"Say it, brother," Hop urged quietly.

"Jackie McCain's son," Hugger said.

"And?" Hound pushed.

Hugger looked to Hound.

"And I'm Chaos."

"Damn straight," Hound grunted.

It took sheer strength of will to keep his head held up on his shoulders, the beautiful weight of all they were doing, all they were saying, was crushing.

Fuck, he wished his ma was still alive.

Fuck.

"We gotta perform some ceremony, like pulling the legs off a tarantula or something, to finally be rid of Arthur Fuckin' Lannigan?" Hound asked.

Arthur "Chew" Lannigan.

Ex-Chaos.

Total motherfucker.

Hugger's bio-father.

"Millie'd kick your ass if you hurt a tarantula," High stated.

"One of her spike heels up your backside would sting, brother," Jagger razzed his step-dad (that being Hound).

"Hugger," Big Petey called.

He looked at the man and thought, maybe he was wrong.

Maybe it wasn't Tack who orchestrated this.

Maybe it was Big Petey.

Or both.

But in the end, it was all of them.

So it didn't matter whose idea it was.

"Man's dead and buried," Hugger stated.

The room went quiet again, like everyone was taking his pulse, trying to get a bead, trying to make certain that the words that came out of his mouth were words he believed deep into his soul.

The quiet ended when Dog clapped him staunchly on the back.

"We done?" Rush asked.

There was a chorus of "ayes," and Rush slammed down the gavel.

All the men got up, preparing to leave the room, go home to their old ladies, go to the common room to shoot the shit and have a beer, get on with life like they didn't just change Hugger's in a way he'd never be able to repay.

But he didn't have to.

Because...

Goddamn.

This was family.

He started to move but didn't get very far when Snapper was up in his space.

Hugger stiffened, but it didn't stop Snap from wrapping an arm around him, bumping chests, pounding him in the back with the side of his fist, and stepping away.

But once Snapper stepped away, he didn't move away. He immediately made eye contact, and it felt like Hugger's body emptied, becoming a shell, and then filled up again with what that contact was saying.

Hugger's bio-dad had called a hit on Snap. If that had succeeded, Snap wouldn't be there, Rosie wouldn't be happy, living with the man she adored, and they wouldn't be making babies.

And Snap was saying that had nothing to do with Hugger.

"Yeah?" Snapper asked if he got it.

"Yeah," Hugger confirmed.

Only then did Snap fully step away.

Rush came in next and did much of the same thing.

Hugger's bio-dad had done the worst thing he could do to Rush's mom, and it wasn't just that he held her at gunpoint. Rush wasn't tight with her, she was a tough woman to love, but she was still his mom, and no woman deserved what his biological father did to her.

Rush ended it by thumping him on the shoulder with his fist

three times, his gaze locked to Hugger's, and he didn't move until Hugger jerked up his chin.

Dog came in next and did much the same thing, without the eye contact at the end.

Jagger followed Dog, Roscoe followed Jag, Dutch followed Roscoe.

They all came in for a hug, except Hound, who took him by the side of the neck and swayed him forward and back before slapping him there, letting go and walking out of the room.

And Tack, who didn't give him a hug.

He caught Hugger's head on both sides and smashed their foreheads together so they were nose to nose.

Eye to eye.

The intensity of Tack's blue gaze bore into his, like if there were any remnants of Arthur Lannigan left haunting Hugger, that fierce blue stare would banish them forever.

No, it wasn't "like" he was doing that.

When Tack let him go, that was what he did.

Chew Lannigan's ghost was gone.

And all that was left was Harlan "Hugger" McCain, Jacqueline McCain's boy, and brother of Chaos.

In the end, the only ones left in the room were Hugger and Big Petey, who hadn't left his seat at the table.

"You orchestrate that?" he asked the old man.

"Does it matter?" Big Petey asked in return.

"Reckon it doesn't," Hugger muttered.

"You got love, Hugger," Big Petey said.

He knew that.

Oh yeah, he knew.

"Yeah," Hugger grunted.

"Love you, son," Big Petey said quietly.

Goddammit, fuck him.

He looked Pete square in the eye.

"Love you too, old man," Hugger replied.

Big Petey's lips tipped up, he pushed away from the table and got out of his chair.

"Now, let's go get a fuckin' beer," Pete said.

A week later...

HE TOOK Diana direct to Chaos after picking her up at the airport.

He'd never been nervous when he met his high school girlfriends' parents, because, he now knew, his mom set him up to give good boyfriend.

But he'd always been nervous when his mom met his girls, not because he worried what his girls would think of his ma, but what his ma would make of his choice in girls.

And even though Di was all Di was, and Hugger reckoned she could charm a snake, that was the uneasy feeling he had when they walked into the door in the Compound. The same one he had when he'd introduce one of his girlfriends to his mom.

When they walked in, Di was to his left, and she looked left, taking in the pitted walls covered in pictures and stuck-on stickers, the scarred couches, nicked and scratched tables and chairs and pool table.

Hugger looked right, to the bar, where Tack and Hop were both behind it, resting their asses against the back counter, and Hound, Big Petey, Joker and Dutch were sitting at it.

His attention returned to his woman when she exclaimed, "Oh my God! This place is *so lit!*"

She took another step forward, turned right and squealed.

She then raced to Big Petey, who, like all the other men, had come off his stool. To do it, she ran right by Hound, who had a look that many people would take in and think twice about getting close to the man, and she hit Pete like a bullet.

Hugger started at Big Petey taking that hit, as did all the other men, a telltale sign that all of them were aware that Big Petey was slowing down.

But Pete just went back on a foot and stood strong, folding his arms around Di as she did the same.

After a tight hug, she leaned away and said, "Our dining room table isn't the same without you."

When she said that, Hugger glanced at the other men, and that was when he saw it, plain as day.

Diana Armitage had just passed muster.

"Did Maddy call?" Di asked Big Petey. "I gave her your number."

"Yeah, we've had a coupla chats, darlin'," Big Petey told her.

"Of course you did," Di said softly, the same kind of look on her face.

The door behind him opened and Tyra, Elvira and Millie came dashing in.

They all listed to a halt a couple feet inside the door. And they were all winded.

"Any a' you break a heel on your sprint over here?" Tack asked them.

Tyra gave her husband a killing look.

But yeah, they saw Hugger pulling in and didn't waste any time racing across the forecourt from Tyra's office at the garage in order to get a load of Diana.

Diana, though, wasn't noticing this.

She was hugging Dutch.

When they broke, she cried, "Holy crap! You have to come back down! Charlie has another gig in a couple of weeks. Ambient jam-a-palooza!"

The look on Dutch's face nearly made Hugger bust a gut laughing.

"What the fuck is an ambient jam?" Hound asked.

"You don't wanna know," Hop, who used to be in a rock band, answered.

But Di just slapped Dutch's arm and said, "Just kidding. I'll tell Charlie that you said you're sorry you were going to miss it, though."

Relief hit Dutch's face, and he replied, "Obliged."

At that point, Diana turned and took in the rest of the men, just when High, who was probably with the women in the office, but he hadn't sprinted across the forecourt, walked in. So Di got a look at him too.

She then turned right to Hugger, arched her brows, put her hands on her hips, and demanded, "There isn't a hotness quotient your brothers have to meet before they prospect? Bullshit. And it looks like the women have to meet it too."

That was when the entire room exploded with laughter.

Elvira strolled further into the room. "Girl, please tell me you drink tequila." She jerked a thumb at Hugger and went on, "Someone melted this mountain of snow, we gotta do celebratory shots."

Diana gave him a look like she'd fallen toward a ravine and certain death, saved herself with a spike, and made it the next day to the peak of Mount Everest.

Hugger just shook his head and smiled.

She turned back to Elvira with an expression of regret, "Sorry, I'm not a fan of tequila."

"Girl, please tell me you drink vodka," Elvira amended as she rounded the bar and headed toward the bottles of liquor.

"Fireball?" Diana suggested.

Elvira shot straight, turning her gaze to Diana, the light of approval in it dazzling the entire room.

Di bellied up to the bar and asked Elvira, "Which brother do you belong to?"

"He's another kind of brother," Elvira replied while pulling the Fireball from where they kept it, out of their ice bin. "His name is Malik. He's a cop. I'm not an old lady, but I've been adopted."

Diana shot Hugger a happy smile then said to Elvira, "Cool!"

Tyra and Millie approached. Hugger did too, in order to do the introductions to the rest of them, and in the next hour, as word got 'round Di was there, everyone showed so they could size her up.

He was the only "mountain of snow" on Chaos, but still, Di had the chops, so she melted them all within seconds of meeting them.

Yeah, he should never have been uneasy.

He should have known with all that was Di, she'd have them eating out of her hands.

Because Di was Di.

And by the end of the night, she was also Chaos.

Two days later...

HUGGER WAS ass to a stool in the Compound when they came in.

Tyra, Lanie, Tab, Rosalie, Carrie, Millie, Keely, Rebel and Elvira.

The women dispersed to the men who belonged to them, except Elvira, who, as noted previously, was an honorary but treasured member of the old lady crew.

Elvira made her way behind the bar.

So that meant Diana came to him.

"'Bout time, woman," he said after she cozied right up to his side and gave him a quick kiss.

"We won't miss our slot," she replied.

"How much damage you do?" he asked.

Her eyeballs studied her hairline.

Right.

"Di," he prompted.

She blew out a breath. "So I bought five pairs of shoes. Haven't you heard? I've recently become a trust fund baby."

Christ, she was cute.

"That it?" he asked.

"And maybe some makeup."

"You got any more room in your drawers for that shit?"

"I can use your drawers."

She could.

She wanted a warehouse of makeup, he'd find a way to get her one.

So he was done talking about that shit.

"You ready?" he asked.

Her eyes lit and she nodded.

He slid off his stool and took her hand.

"You need us to bring anything for later, Millie?" Di asked as he guided her to the doors.

"We're covered, babe," Millie called.

His house gutted, at Millie's insistence, even though he had a room at the Compound where he could crash, he was staying with Millie and High in their massive house on the hill in the Highlands.

But now that Diana was there, since the guest room at that castle was a whole lot better than his room at the Compound, they were definitely staying with Millie and High.

Diana had fallen in love with Millie's cats, so Hugger reckoned there was a pet in their future.

Though, he'd fucked her in his room at the Compound. Yeah, he for sure didn't let that opportunity slide by.

Millie and High were throwing a shindig that night for everybody.

"See you later, Di," Rebel yelled as Hugger pushed open the door.

"Yeah, later," Carrie cried.

"'Later, babes!" Di called back.

It was clear she got along with the women, but he expected that to happen, because she was Di, and those women were the best there were.

She was the perfect addition.

He had to admit, though, it settled him to see how well she did it.

There was a nip in the air, so they weren't on his bike, they were in his truck.

He loaded his woman up, closed the door on her, rounded the hood and hauled his ass in.

He hit the ignition, pulled out and headed downtown.

Di gabbed about the brunch with the girls she had that day, and shopping, and how Elvira was a hoot, Carrie was sweet, Rebel was cool as all hell, etcetera (this was a lot of what he was hearing from her about all of his family the last two days), and how it was too bad Archie had to be at her store and Georgie was on a story, and they couldn't come.

She did all of this through the drive and him parking. She kept doing it as they walked to the building and inside.

They went to a counter, he showed the tickets on his phone, they got some recorder machines with headphones and were shown the line waiting for the next timeslot to enter.

When they got in line, Di kept hold of his hand and pressed her tits tight to his arm.

He looked down at her to see she was lit up like a Christmas tree with excitement.

"This is *insane*," she proclaimed. "So cool! A whole exhibit of Norman Rockwell. We're going to get to see *The Problem We All Live With* and *Girl at Mirror* and the *Four Freedoms* series *live and in person*. I can't believe it!"

He smiled down at her.

The doors opened and their group was ushered in.

Di put on her headphones and tinkered with the machine.

Hugger followed suit.

And at the Denver Art Museum, with Diana, Hugger walked through the first art exhibit he'd ever seen.

It was the absolute shit.

The Problem We All Live With was powerful.

But as he discussed it with Di on their way to the Highlands after they left DAM, he shared his favorites were *Saying Grace*, *Before the Shot* and *The Lineman*.

25

TAKE IT FROM HERE

Big Petey

Several years ago...

THE PLACE WAS quiet as a tomb, and Big Petey didn't like to make that comparison, but there it was.

It was dark, late-ish, but there were still lots of staff and visitors, people taking time, eking out the last dregs, trying to make a miracle by making what was proved finite, last longer.

He found her room, he also found her alone.

He wasn't expecting this, he thought for sure Harlan would be there.

When Jackie noticed him loitering at the door, she raised her hand to him, and since it looked like it took a lot out of her to do it, he rushed forward and held it.

"Pete," she whispered.

"Hey, pretty girl," he whispered back.

"Thank you...for coming," she pushed out with some effort.

"Anytime you need me, Jackie. You know that."

She gave him a ghost of a smile.

He glanced around the room then down to her. "Where's your boy?"

"Asked him to go out and get me some DQ."

It was Pete's turn to give her a ghost of a smile. "Bet he got right on that."

"Didn't want to." Her weak voice came at him. "Didn't want to leave me. But you're right, he went right out to get it." She gave him a feeble squeeze of fingers. "We don't have a lot of time. I wanna do this before he gets back."

"Okay, sweetheart. What you need?"

"Look after him?"

Pete hid his affront. "A' course."

"No, Pete. *Look after him.*"

Big Petey continued to hide his affront. "Jackie, you don't gotta ask that. Me and all the boys got you covered."

"I mean Chaos."

"I know."

"I mean get him to earn his patch."

Pete gave her fingers a careful squeeze. "Jackie, baby, *I know.*"

She stared at him and whispered, "You know."

"You're ours, he's ours. Just gotta figure out a way around it to make him understand it."

"I'm yours, he's yours," she said so quiet, he almost didn't hear her.

But he saw the wet gather and fall out the side of her eye.

So he leaned close. "Hey, hey, hey, none of that. You got nothin' to worry about. We got him."

The tears still in her eyes, she looked at him hard, like she was trying to read any hint of lie on him.

There was none, so she couldn't find it.

"I should have gotten him to you earlier," she mumbled.

"He needed to be with you. You know that, Jackie. No way he'd commit to a club when his only commitment was you."

"I shouldn't have done that to him, made him feel like that."

"Darlin',"—Pete leaned even closer—"you didn't. You raised that boy right. Any good son will look after his momma."

She nodded vaguely, fatigue showing even starker on her face.

"Not gonna have the energy to eat that Blizzard when it gets here, you push yourself too hard," Big Petey warned.

"I'll just take a bite. All I need. I asked for Oreo, Harlan's favorite."

Of course she did.

"He'll eat the rest," she finished.

It'd taste like dust, but Harlan would eat the rest.

"Help him find a good woman, Pete," she begged. "A pretty one, with sass and class, with a brain in her head, like Tack found."

"You got it."

"Make sure she's sweet too."

"I will."

"Tell the boys—"

Another careful squeeze of her fingers. "Don't gotta tell 'em nothin'."

"Tell them anyway," she whispered.

"I will, sweetheart."

Suddenly, her face got fierce, and he saw a little of the old Jackie there.

Even now, wasted to nothing, she was beautiful.

Harlan got all his momma. That thick, leonine hair. That long, strong body. Like she willed it, and maybe she did, there was nothing of his father in him.

Harlan McCain was all Jackie.

"I don't regret it. Not a second of it," she declared.

"I know."

"Got him out of it, no regrets in that."

"I know, girl."

"No regrets," she whispered, her eyes fluttering.

"Nothing to regret, Jackie."

"He'll do you boys right," she promised.

"Not a doubt in my mind."

Her frail fingers curled a bit around his then went slack as her eyes closed.

Pete instantly felt panic, but when he raised his gaze to the heart monitor, he saw the slow but steady blip.

He took her in, seeing her there in that bed, but remembering how she used to be. Tall and golden, not beaten down by a life that would break most, standing strong because that was Jacqueline McCain, and because she had to for her boy.

Then Big Petey bent in, kissed her forehead and whispered, "Don't worry about a thing, Jackie, we'll take it from here."

He lifted her hand and kissed her fingers too.

And he got out of her room before Harlan returned.

He didn't leave the hospice though.

He found a shadow and became one with it, so he saw Harlan return with the Dairy Queen cup in his hand.

Pete gave it time before he moved stealthily down the hall, positioned himself outside her door and peered around the jamb.

Harlan's back was to him, but he saw him bent to his momma, giving her a taste of Blizzard.

She'd woken up for him, because they were eking out the last dregs, trying to make a miracle by making what was proved finite, last longer.

Then the tall, handsome man sat in a chair beside his mother's bed, and he ate the Blizzard, chatting with his mother until she fell asleep.

It didn't take long.

Big Petey watched as Harlan then got up, and he knew by the sound when that DQ cup hit the trash can, there was a lot of ice cream left.

He was right, it had tasted like dust.

Harlan went back to sit by his momma.

Big Petey moved away from the door, out to his trike, and he waited to call Rush until after he got home.

———————

Present day...

Big Petey stood by the graveside, looking down at the arched, ivory marble headstone with the pretty flowers etched in at the top, and underneath, it said:

Jacqueline Mary McCain
Loving Mother
Beloved Mother
*"Think of the days of me and you,
You and me against the world."*

There were flowers at the base, because of course there were. Hugger was in town, and Di had just left. He'd brought his woman to meet his momma, because that was Harlan McCain.

The flowers were creamy Calla lilies.

Jackie's favorite.

Big Petey set the frame by the blooms that were beginning to curl and brown.

In that frame was a photo of Diana holding Chief, Millie's grumpy-faced cat to her chest. Hug was close to them both, his fingers buried in the cat's ruff, but his eyes were on Diana.

His face was soft, so was hers.

They were smiling at each other, bright and blinding.

"She's got class and sass, she's a fighter, got a heart so big, you wouldn't believe, and as you can see, she's gorgeous," he told Jackie. "And, woman, she loves him somethin' fierce. *Somethin' fierce.* Her mother said something mean to your boy, and Di cut her right out. No hesitation. It was a sight to see, I promise you. She *cut her right out.*" He paused and added on a mumble, "Woman is a bitch, though."

There was nothing after his words died, just the chill late-October air.

"We had it, darlin', now Di's got it, make no mistake," Big Petey promised. "She's got him. He's all good now. He's got family, and only thing left for him to do is make more."

The marble had nothing to say.

Big Petey touched the top, feeling the cold like a burn on his fingers.

"You can rest now, gorgeous. It's all good," he murmured, patted the marble and took in a deep breath.

Then he left Jackie to rest, walked to his trike and rode, the cold air biting his face, the chill wind in his hair.

It might not do any good for his joints, but in that moment he didn't care.

Because like he said, finally, after years of struggle, war, pain and betrayal, it was all good.

And anyway, anytime he was riding, all his life, Big Petey felt nothing but free.

EPILOGUE
"ROLL ME AWAY"

Diana

About two weeks later...

HUGGER MOVING WOKE ME UP.

I was tucked tight to his back, and since it seemed he wasn't getting out of bed to go to the bathroom or something, I kept hold on him with my arm wrapped around his waist.

I realized he was answering his phone when he grunted, "Yeah?"

I opened my eyes to see it was still dark out, but it was early November. Days were shorter, and unlike most of the rest of the world, we Phoenicians didn't have a problem with the shorter days, because they brought the cooler temperatures, and the city woke up for what felt like an eight-month Mardi Gras.

This was my thought when I felt Hugger's body turn to stone.

Any sleep still lingering vanished at the vibe coming off him, and I pushed up to a hand in the bed to try to see his profile.

The light was dim.

I still saw his face looked carved from granite.

My stomach curled into itself.

"When?" he bit off like a quiet bark.

But I heard it.

I heard the pain.

Oh *no*.

What was happening?

I pressed closer.

"Okay, yeah," he said. "Yeah. We'll be up." A pause and a final, "Yeah. Soon's we can."

He took the phone from his ear.

"Honey?" I called when he just lay there, on his side, unmoving.

He continued to lay there, on his side, unmoving, his arm with his phone in hand resting on the bed like it had stopped working, his eyes aimed at nothing.

Now I was getting scared.

"Honey?" I asked more urgently, trying to push his big body to its back so I could get a look at his whole face.

Suddenly, he dropped his phone to the bed and reached out to turn on the light.

I blinked against it, and when my eyes became accustomed to it, I saw he'd fallen to his back and he was looking at me, but even so, his handsome face had a blankness to it that was terrifying.

He lifted both hands and rubbed them over his face, something he did a lot in the mornings when he was in the midst of a Morning Hugger Haze.

But this wasn't about that.

When his hands fell to his sides, I climbed onto him, chest to chest, and caught his jaw in both hands.

"Harlan, what's going on?" I demanded.

"That was Tyra," he said.

Oh God.

Why was Tyra calling so early in the morning?

Hugger told me.

"Pete died in his sleep last night."

I didn't know it until that moment, but the world had rushed out from under both of us.

Unable to hold it up, my head fell, my face landing in his chest.

Hugger sifted his fingers in my hair, cupping the back of it.

On a violent buck, my tears came, hot, hard, fast and furious.

Hugger rolled us to our sides and tucked my face into his throat, holding me close as I sobbed into his skin.

He let me, and after a very long time, when the tears were beginning to fade, he whispered, "We gotta go up to Denver."

I took my red, wet face out of his neck, looked into my man's beautiful, gaunt one and whispered back, "We gotta go up to Denver."

IN THE FUNERAL PROCESSION, Dad drove the rented SUV.

I sat in the passenger seat.

Nicole and Larry were in the back.

Hugger was on his bike, one of the ones at the front of the procession.

The roar ahead of us was deafening.

This was because it wasn't just Chaos up there on their bikes leading the hearse to the cemetery.

Every member of Resurrection. Every member of Aces High. And about two hundred other bikers from all over the country whose lives Peter Waite touched were riding too.

And this was led by a police escort and tailed by it.

I'd never seen an honor guard so impressive in my life.

I wasn't surprised in the slightest.

I'd watched them start to roll out, and noted there was a broken part of the procession up front, an open space, an empty space.

A space a Harley trike would be.

I'd had to look away, that empty space had so gutted me.

But I couldn't stop thinking about it.

As we went, people pulled over, stopped, gawked, and they had no clue at all they saw a man glide by on his final ride, a man they'd never know was good and true, down to the marrow of his bones. They'd never know who rolled past them. They'd never know they were privileged to be in the presence of a man who might not have done great things in his life, but he did a whole lot of good, and the world was a vastly poorer place without him.

We hit the cemetery, cars and bikes everywhere, and Larry, in the seat behind me, got out quickly so he could open my door and help me out.

It was cold. Before we came, I'd had to rush to the mall to buy an overcoat. And gloves.

I didn't feel anything.

Dad and Nicole joined Larry and me, Dad taking my hand, Nicole wrapping her arm through mine, but before we could move, Larry made a noise.

Like I was in a trance, I was watching them take the casket out of the back of the hearse.

Tack, Hop, High, Hound, Arlo and Boz were the pall bearers, but the rest of the Club were lined up to follow Big Petey's final journey.

The only non-bikers allowed to follow the Chaos pack did so. I'd met them the day before too. Their names were Hawk Delgado, Brock Lucas and Mitch Lawson.

I'd met all their women as well, they were somewhere around (I didn't have it in me right then to look for them), as was Mace (who apparently was married to Stella Freaking Gunn, the famous rock star!) and a bunch of other hot guys and their gorgeous wives who I would later learn were known as the "Nightingale Men" and the "Rock Chicks." And finally, there was a tragically handsome man introduced to me the day before as Knight Sebring, who was with his equally beautiful woman, whose name was Anya.

The casket was black, no flowers, but the Chaos insignia had been painted on the top.

"Buttercup, I think you're supposed to go with Rebel," Dad murmured in my ear.

I blinked and looked up at him, only to follow his gaze, seeing Rebel standing some way away, closer to the gravesite, her attention on me.

"Go on, hon," Nic encouraged, a hand in my back giving me a gentle push. "You need to be with Pete's family now. We'll be close, promise."

I nodded, Dad and Nic let me go, and I woodenly and awkwardly moved across the turf that wasn't yet frozen in my spike-heeled black pumps.

When I got to Rebel, she curved an arm around my waist and guided me to the chairs set out by the freshly dug grave. There were massive arrays of blood red roses all around the bottom of the casket, hiding the hole in the dirt.

"Hugger needs to be able to lay eyes on you," Rebel murmured as explanation.

Yes, of course.

And I needed for Hugger to be able to lay eyes on me.

I nodded again.

She took me to the second row of chairs, and Archie, already in the row, held her hand my way.

I shuffled in, Georgie shuffling in after me.

Tyra and Tabby sat in front of us, Lanie beside Tyra, Elvira beside Tabby.

Renae, Pete's woman (and Rosalie's mom) sat beside Lanie, Rosalie beside her mother, then Millie, Carrie sitting beside Elvira, with Keely at the other end.

Rebel, the queen bee of Chaos now that her husband Rush was president, sat in our row, along with a woman I'd met the day before, Bev, who used to be married to Boz, but now she was married to someone else whose name in all the introductions I'd had the last couple of days, I'd sadly forgotten.

Then again, I'd noticed that once you were Chaos, if you did them right, they didn't let you go.

Family was family.

Always.

Obviously, I wasn't miffed at my placement. I was the newbie. And I saw that was how Rebel had arranged this, because she was a (semi-kinda-not-really-but-in-this-sense) newbie too.

All the women in the front had the most time in with Big Petey.

And the women in our row had their backs.

It was the biker way.

Children were jostled around, pulled into laps, given seats, and I would have had an issue with none of the woman saying anything when all the boys—including Rider and Cutter (Tack and Tyra's sons), Cody and Nash (Hop's boy from a previous relationship, and Lanie and Hop's son—Molly, Hop's daughter, was sitting scrunched up to Archie), Playboy (Tabby and Shy's boy—Princess was sitting in Lanie's lap), Travis and Wyatt (Carrie and Joker's boys—Dakota was much younger and sitting in his mom's lap), Wilder (Keely and Hound's son), Atticus (Rosalie and Snapper's son—Emmeline, their daughter, was sitting on her Grandma Renae's lap) and Rhodes (Rebel and Rush's boy—Ember, their little girl, was with Rebel)—cut away to go stand with the men (that being only the boys had gone), if Raven didn't go too, along with her older sister Clementine.

Both of them headed right to Joker...and Hugger.

The minute Raven got to my guy, he picked her up and planted her on his hip. The minute she was put where she needed to be, she rested her little cheek on her Uncle Hugger's chest and wrapped her little hand at the side of his neck.

I felt my throat get scratchy.

And *damn*, but I loved my man.

Clementine wasn't a big girl, she wasn't such a little girl anymore either, but that didn't stop Joker from doing the same.

Rounding out this kid business, Cleo and Zadie, High's girls and

Millie's stepdaughters, had taken hold of Wren, Shy and Tabby's middle girl, and they were tucked in beside Georgie.

Last, I saw what appeared to be someone waving out of the side of my eye, so I focused beyond the chairs, and I felt my chest depress when I saw Maddy, wearing black, standing there, eyes red rimmed, between Elias and Emmylou (the latter whose eyes were red rimmed too).

She looked melancholy, of course, but unbroken (which was so Maddy), and best of all, like she'd gained some weight.

I blew her kiss, and she returned it, adding a sad little smile.

We settled in, a mass of people behind us, and I watched as the bikers in front of us fanned out in an arc around the other side of the casket.

They were all wearing their cuts.

For most of Chaos, their cuts were leather jackets with the Chaos patch on the back, only a few of them wore leather vests. Hugger had explained he didn't wear it in Phoenix not only because it was "hot as fuck," but because, when they were on missions, they didn't wear their patches.

He also explained Resurrection never paraded their club info in public.

But all of Resurrection were wearing their cuts that day.

The sky was gray and ugly, like my mood.

But it was a sight to behold, two hundred and fifty some bikers curving around the casket of just one. I'd never seen a turnout this impressive for anyone, except a head of state or a royal.

Chaos, obviously, was up front of that crowd.

A movement in front of us caught my eye, and I looked to see Carrie now had her head resting on Elvira's shoulder, Dakota had climbed into Elvira's lap and Vira had wound her arms around the little boy.

Only Vira's profile was visible to me, but from what I could see, silent tears were rolling down her cheeks as her back remained straight, and her gaze stayed locked to the casket.

I'd never seen anyone cry with such dignity before.

And I loved she gave that to Big Petey.

Tabby was a mess, and Tyra wasn't far behind her. They were curled into each other, holding on for support, but faced forward.

It didn't take long before everyone had arrived, took their positions, and Tack, center casket, standing between Rush and Hop, didn't delay in taking a step forward.

His gaze never left the casket.

Quiet greeted him, so when his gravelly voice sounded loud, it was like a thunderclap.

"Fuck you, old man, for being mortal."

I couldn't stop my mouth from forming a smile, because it was sad, but it was apropos.

Tabby let out a cry-laugh.

Tyra held her closer.

"Fuck you more for convincing us you weren't," Tack went on. "We all have our place in this brotherhood, but you held every place. Wherever we needed you. However we needed you. Whenever we needed you. You were there. Warrior. Wiseman. Healer. Priest. Hand-holder. Babysitter. Brother. Father. Granddad. Uncle. Husband. Partner. You went through the worst with us, and it was a rough ride, but you walked through fire with us, and finally, when we got smooth sailing, you fucked off. And gotta say, 'cause I know you like it honest, Pete, it pisses all of us off."

It was definitely going to be the weirdest eulogy I'd ever heard.

And I could tell, absolutely the most perfect.

Tack put his hand on the casket and bowed his head.

Tyra, Tabby and Elvira all let out audible sobs when he did.

I knew why.

I'd heard all about Kane "Tack" Allen, and I'd seen that movie, and from what I heard, saw and knew, nothing bowed that man. He'd been through hell, personally and with his Club, and he'd guided his brothers out of it, his family, their families, and he'd done it eyes forward, head high, back straight, shoulders squared, vision strong.

Now he was bowed...

By the loss of Big Petey.

"Only thing we got to hold on to is you lived a life where you owned the wind, and in your time, you were wild like it. Wild like fire. Wild like the wind. And now you're finally free."

Not taking my eyes off Tack, I dug in my purse for a Kleenex.

Tack kept going.

"You were loved, because you were loving," Tack told Big Petey direct. "Best father there was. Best brother there could be. Best man I've ever met. There were times when it felt like the angels deserted us, but they never did. There was an angel among us. And that angel was you."

More sobs, these now coming from all around, including me.

"Tell that girl of yours we miss her," Tack ordered. "And ride steady, my brother. We'll catch you on the flipside."

He took a moment, lifted his head and stepped back.

The second he rejoined the arc, Rush shouted, "On three!" and lifted his hand, three fingers extended.

One went down, the next, and the next.

And then the entire biker contingent shouted, "*Wind! Ride! Fire! Free!*"

Oh God.

I was sobbing openly now.

Rush stepped forward and yelled, "Four wheels move the body, two wheels move the soul."

All the bikers raised a shout.

Okay, dammit, I was close to bawling.

Fortunately, there was quiet for a moment so I could get it together before Rosie and Tabby got up and went to Renae. Rosie took her mother's hand and helped her out of her seat. She tried to take her daughter from her mom, but Emmeline held close to her grandma as she rose, and Rosalie gave up as they all walked to the casket.

Tabby, known to all as Pete's surrogate daughter who stepped in when his girl was lost, bent and kissed the casket first. Rosalie rubbed her mother's back as Renae did it last.

As they stood there, taking their own moment, Emmeline studied the casket and whispered, "'Bye-bye, Pawpaw."

Renae released a silent, but visible hiccoughing sob.

And me?

Yep.

I was bawling. It wasn't loud, but it was totally bawling and all around me I could hear sniffles, coughs, and quiet weeping.

Renae, Rosalie and Tabby returned to their seats, and the second their asses had found them, the bikers all began to move to their bikes.

I twisted to look for Dad, but Georgie caught my hand.

"Sit still, babe, not over yet," she whispered.

Honestly, I couldn't take much more.

But I would. I had to.

For Big Petey.

And for Hugger.

I sat and watched the wave of bikers make their way to their bikes.

Millie turned to our row and murmured, "Ringing out the dead."

I didn't know what that meant, but by the sound of it, I wasn't sure I was going to like it.

Hugger had been so quiet, so lost for the last three days, I didn't have the heart to push him on specifics. He told us where to be and when we had to be there. That morning, when they'd arrived, surprising us both, he'd let Dad, Nicole *and* Larry give him a hug, showing openly how shocked and touched he was they'd come.

But mostly he was stuck in his grief, and all I could do was stick close and make sure he knew I was there.

After a while, I heard all the bikes coming to life, and ran my gaze down that long, thick phalanx of Harleys.

Tack was at the front.

Rush was on his bike at the very back.

Suddenly, Tack revved his engine and then all of the bikers did it, one, two, three, four, five times.

The bikes went silent, and after a couple of beats, Rush revved his bike once.

"The Last Rev," Keely's trembling voice said. It broke when she finished, "It's done."

God, how beautiful.

"Now we can go," Archie whispered and stood.

I stood with her and searched, finding Hugger astride his bike close to the front of the pack.

He wasn't near.

But I knew his eyes were on me.

I touched my hand to my heart and my lips, then sent it fluttering in his direction.

Again, he wasn't near.

But I saw him jerk up his chin.

Archie and Georgie escorted me to Dad, Nic and Larry.

And we headed back to Chaos.

A PARTY RAGED outside the Compound, but inside, where only Chaos, Resurrection, Aces High (and Dad, Nic and Larry, and close friends to Chaos) were allowed, the mood was somber.

I had my eyes on my man sitting at the bar where all the brothers were hanging, drinking tequila and brooding, while the rest of us gave them a wide berth.

Dad, Nic and Larry had their eyes on me.

But it was Nicole who curled her fingers around my wrist.

I looked to her.

"Go to him," Nicole urged.

I wasn't sure.

I was the new girl. I didn't want to do something stupid and mess up.

"None of the other ladies are doing it," I replied.

"Then break the seal, sweetheart." Dad was now close. "Those men need their women."

"And these women need their men," Nicole added.

Shit.

Should I?

I watched Hugger throw back a shot of tequila.

He had a beer on more than the rare occasion, but he wasn't a big drinker.

He'd barely put the glass down before Shy filled it.

And Shy had barely filled it before Hugger threw it back again.

Shy didn't bother with a glass, he just took his slugs direct from the bottle.

Fuck.

I had to make a decision.

A decision for my man.

I made it.

I walked to my guy, my pumps sounding loud in the solemn quiet.

Some of the men watched me coming, but I couldn't tell if I was doing wrong or right by the expressions on their faces.

Even so, I kept going.

And when I got to him, I put my hand on Hugger's back.

He twisted to me.

"Hey, honey," I whispered.

I barely got the second word out before he turned fully to me, pulled me so forcefully between his spread knees and into his arms, my breath clean left me, and he buried his face in my neck.

I not only heard but felt the powerful hitch in his breath.

I fisted my hand in his hair, wrapped my other arm around him and shoved my face in his neck too.

I sensed all the other women finding their men as I held on to my own.

I didn't know how long I stood there with my guy, my sisters with theirs, before I heard Elvira say, "Fuck this. Enough. Petey would be so over this shit, he'd spit."

I peeked out from Hugger's neck and saw her man, another gorgeous one (which seemed all that Chaos attracted, even if Malik wasn't Chaos) was setting a Bluetooth speaker on the bar, and she was queuing something up on her phone.

Within moments, some piano notes and drumbeats filled the room.

By the time Bob Seger's voice could be heard, Hop was singing with him.

It barely got to the second line before Tack, Boz and Hound had joined in, and they were doing it loud.

It wasn't even the next verse before High, Snap and Shy joined in.

Everyone in the Compound gathered around the bar then, and we all sang it (though I didn't know all the words, I'd heard the song, so I did my best), and with each word, we were singing it louder, a Chaos and Friends chorus of Seger's "Roll Me Away."

Some arms were linked, some thrown over shoulders, some curved around waists, but all of us were in some way connected so there was a circle of love around that bar, shouting out rock poetry.

Singing Big Petey off on his last ride.

Halfway through the song, people were smiling, eyes were lighting, breath was being breathed back into a loving family who'd lost their cornerstone and hadn't known what to do.

Until then, when they realized the man who formed that cornerstone did it so strong, it'd never crumble.

And they realized the man who set it would always be part of the very foundation of the beauty that was built on top of it.

Because, when Chaos hit their next time, with Peter Waite's support, grit and guidance, they got it right.

IN HUGGER's room at the Compound, I left the bathroom after cleaning up.

Hugger and I had just made love.

It wasn't that we never did it that way, we did. Though it was rare. We preferred to get physical, raunchy, rough, intense.

But that night, he took his beautiful, sweet time with my body, I did the same with his, and in this moment, at the end of this dreadful day, it was perfect.

Hugger's room at the Compound, I'd noticed the time before, and again right then, was clean and tidy, like he always was everywhere.

He'd been so conditioned to take care of the little he had, even when he had more, he did the same.

The week before, I'd considered it a minor triumph when he left his clothes on the floor of our bedroom, rather than what he normally did, gathering them up and putting them in the laundry hamper, when he had an early meeting with Buck about the properties they were looking at.

I was maybe the only woman on the planet who wanted her man to loosen up when it came to keeping their place tight.

But in the end, if he didn't, he didn't.

I'd take him any way he came.

When I got close, Hugger lifted the bedclothes that were covering him from the waist down, so I could enter the bed, something I did, finding my place right on top of him.

When I settled in, he traced his big hands up my back and said softly, "Why am I the only guy existing who's considering going back to condoms, so my baby doesn't have to haul her ass to the bathroom after sex?"

Okay, okay, *okay*.

Oh-freaking-*ficial*.

I so totally *loved this man*.

"Deal, from here on, I clean you up," he continued.

"Deal," I agreed.

His eyes moved to the side and back to me. "Your phone's been goin', baby."

I'd heard it, vaguely, during sex, but obviously only very vaguely.

I sighed, reached out to nab it, thumbed it and showed it my face, then scanned the texts.

I put it back on his nightstand and turned to him.

"Texts from Bernie, Charlie and Mel. Also Gerard. And shocker, Annie remembered too. They want me to tell you different versions of you and your family are in their thoughts."

"Sweet. Tell 'em thanks," he muttered.

"Will do," I replied and stroked his beard. "How are you hanging in?"

"Feel absolute shit...and totally great."

I didn't get that, but I stayed silent and let him do what I knew he'd do.

Give it to me.

He did.

"When I lost Ma, I didn't know what I was heading into, and that was shit, but more, I did it alone, and that made it impossible to maneuver. That's why I got stuck in it. I didn't know how to pull myself out, and I didn't have anyone to show me the way."

My poor baby.

I continued to stroke his beard.

"Losing Pete isn't any less shit," he carried on. "Having lost someone before and knowing how bad it's going to be isn't any less shit either. The difference is havin' my brothers, my family." His hands stopped roaming my back. "And havin' you."

I melted into him.

Or, I was pretty melted into him, so I *oozed* into him.

"Babe, your dad, Nic and Larry showing was all kinds of cool," he whispered.

"They like you," I whispered back.

"Yeah," he grunted.

"No, they really, *really* do," I teased, but it was still the truth.

He slid his hands to the cheeks of my ass and gave them a squeeze.

I smiled at him. It wasn't beaming but it was genuine.

Then I took a breath and let it flow.

"And I love you," I said.

Hugger went solid under me.

Then he rolled us so he was on top.

"Say it again," he ordered.

I smoothed the hair away from his handsome face, gazing into those warm, intense, beautiful brown eyes, and I whispered, "I love you, Harlan McCain."

He slanted his head and kissed me, hard, wet, long and *deep*.

When he broke it, my lips were bruised but my eyes were stinging with tears because Hugger was a tremendous kisser, but that was the best yet by far.

And I knew why it was.

But he was my Hugger.

So he told me.

"Love you too, baby," he said.

A tear slid out of the corner of my eye.

Hugger caught it with his thumb, dipped to rub his nose against mine...

Then he kissed me again.

And we made love again, long, slow, sweet and beautiful.

We fell asleep in each other's arms in the Compound on Chaos.

Where I was meant to be.

And where my man was born to be.

BEFORE WE LEFT to go back to Phoenix, we were delivered one more brutal, and velvet, blow.

Renae gave us the Christmas presents Big Petey had ordered for us.

Renae, being that kind of woman (in other words, *awesome*), even wrapped them in Christmas paper, although it was still well before Thanksgiving.

We opened them in front of her, though I knew Hugger didn't want to, and I didn't either, because we knew they'd be blows.

We did it because she was hanging in there, but she was also broken. This was the second man she'd lost (Rosalie's father died before Renae met Big Petey), and if she wanted to see our reactions, we were going to let her.

The good news was, it didn't make me cry.

I loved my present, and Hugger's, with every fiber of my being.

They were black tees (mine a babydoll—man, did Big Petey pay attention or what?).

They had the Chaos logo on front, and on the back of mine it said, PROPERTY OF HUGGER.

And on the back of Hugger's it said, PROPERTY OF BLUE.

They were everything. They were life.

And after we got home, I called Rebel to find out where Pete got them.

I ordered three for Hugger and three for me, so there'd always be a clean one at hand.

The ones Big Petey got us, I had mounted in a shadowbox and hung on the wall behind the head of the table in my dining room, where Pete belonged.

And now he'd always be there with us.

Always.

Six months later...

HUGGER WALKED AHEAD of me down the path. Caught up in looking around, he didn't notice I'd stopped to take an up-close picture of a cherry blossom.

Once I got it, my gaze sought my man.

He'd stopped too and was breathing deep, taking in the delicate fragrance all around, the beauty of the place, the trees a dreamy, soft-pink landscape, a four-story, bright-red building with green roofs with the famous Japanese swoops at the edges decorating the distance.

I lifted my phone to snap a photo of him just as he turned to look for me, found me and smiled at me.

I returned that smile before I looked down at my phone to see the shot.

Damn, he was beautiful.

I heard a call I didn't know what it was because it was in Japanese, so I looked up and saw a woman rushing toward Hugger.

But her little boy was standing close to him, staring up at him like he was some fantastical being who had fallen to the earth.

I understood the sentiment.

The woman made it to Hugger, bowed repeatedly and spoke, trying to pull her boy away.

Hugger just smiled, reached out and mussed the boy's hair, and I wasn't really close, but I could swear I saw him wink at the kid.

The kid's giggle reached me, though, and I didn't miss his face mostly taken up with a big, bright smile.

My heart swelled.

"Thank you," I whispered to Jackie McCain.

Then I hurried toward my man, so busy pulling up the translation app on my phone, I didn't notice a gentle breeze blew through the cherry trees, setting petals to floating all around us.

And for a beautiful moment in time, our vacation became a downright dream.

Because we got a visit from Heaven.

Hugger

One and a half years later...

Every time he came, it was like this.

Candles, flowers, bottles of bourbon, whisky, tequila, and the odd beer. Patches, flags and a shit ton of pictures.

In the mess around Big Petey's headstone, Hugger tucked one more picture.

It was black and white, depicting a blurry blob.

But he tucked it anyway between a shot of Rider tickling Princess so hard, he had to hold her up so she wouldn't fall from laughing, and a pic of Joker and Travis, with Travis standing on a step stool, bent over the hood of one of Joke's builds.

Not far was a photo of Jag looming over Archie's shoulder as she lay in a hospital bed, Arch holding the newborn Graham in her arms. And another of a bunch of his brothers, their old ladies, Hugger and Di, all crunching into tacos at the Taco Festival in Phoenix last year.

Also not far was the faded picture of Diana wearing a strapless wedding gown with a lot of lace and a long slit up one side that had two skirts. One that was straight and had a little lace train at the back, and there was a big floof of another one over it, falling from her waist, which looked fantastic as she was walking down the aisle, but fortunately she got rid of it by the time it came to party.

You could just say, Nolan and Di putting their heads together with Nolan's money meant Hugger's wedding to his woman had been far from a chill affair.

It gave his brothers never-ending fodder to hand him shit about, even if at the time he didn't see any of them balk once at the open bar, shoving perfectly cooked prime rib in their faces, the extravagant dessert buffet, or busting a move on the dance floor.

But Hugger wouldn't have had it any other way.

Di had looked so fucking gorgeous, it was hard to lay eyes on her (but he put in the effort and managed it).

And she'd been so damned happy, he wouldn't change a thing.

Even the fact her mother didn't show, mostly because she wasn't invited.

But on Di's side of the pews, the front one was filled with

her dad, his now wife, then fiancée, Gisele (a woman who was age-appropriate, elegant as fuck (because she was French), gorgeous, sophisticated and hilarious—Hugger thought she was the shit, Di adored her—needless to say, with pool parties and dinners, and Di and Gisele cooking French food in his kitchen, and Gisele having two kids of her own, also (so far) one grand-child, Nolan hadn't sold his house), Di's gram, Nicole, Larry and Larry's kids.

With them and the rest of the church packed nearly to standing room only, on both sides, his woman had love to spare.

None of those pictures around Pete's stone were in frames, but they were weighed down, which was what Hugger made sure to do with the newest one.

Over time, the heat beat down on those photos, the wind frayed them, the rain and snow made the images run.

And all that meant what was in those the images sunk into the stone, the dirt, and the bones below, right where they were intended to reach.

When he straightened, he stared down at the stone and shared, "Her name's gonna be Jacqueline Waite McCain."

"I suggested Petra as a middle name," Di, standing at his side, chimed in.

He looked down at his wife.

"We're not namin' our girl Petra," Hugger said for the fiftieth time.

"Why not?"

"It sounds like a video game."

She scrunched her nose.

"Exactly," he decreed.

"Peta?" she tried.

"That's bread."

She screwed up her face.

Damn, she was cute.

"Petronella?" she tried again.

"Sounds like fuel you'd put in a lantern." He looked down at the stone. "Seems my woman doesn't like your last name, Big Petey."

"That's not true!" she cried, also to the stone. Then she turned to Hugger and got desperate. "Petunia!"

He caught her by the neck and yanked her to him before he bent his head and laid a heavy, wet one on her mouth.

When he lifted away, he stated, "It's gonna be Waite."

"'Kay," she breathed.

Oh yeah, she was cute.

"You cold?" he asked.

"Freezing," she whispered.

He rubbed his nose to hers and looked again at the stone.

"Gotta get my woman home, old man, and get her warm. We'll see you when we're back in town," he said.

"'Bye, Big Petey," Diana added. "Love you."

Yeah. Love you, Pete, bottom of my soul, Hugger thought.

Then he wrapped his arm around his woman's shoulders, feeling her arm circle his waist, and, holding her close, he took her to the bike he'd borrowed from the garage.

He got on first.

Di mounted up after him, curled her arms under his pits, her fingers on one hand into his shoulder, the other she flattened against his chest, and she put her chin to one shoulder.

With Di settled in where she belonged, Hugger started the bike up, revved their farewell-for-now to his brother, and he, his woman and their unborn baby girl rolled away.

The End

The Wild West MC Series will continue.

CAST OF CHARACTERS
WILD WEST MC SERIES

Chaos Motorcycle Club
(*with children*)

- Tack and Tyra
    - Rider
    - Cutter
    - (Rush and Tabby)

- Shy and Tabby
    - Kane (Playboy)
    - Wren
    - Caroline (Princess)

- Lanie and Hop
    - Molly
    - Cody
    - Nash

- Carissa and Joker
    - Travis
    - Clementine
    - Wyatt
    - Raven
    - Dakota

- High and Millie
    - Cleo
    - Zadie

- Hound and Keely
    - Wilder
    - (Dutch and Jagger)

- Rosalie and Snapper
    - Atticus
    - Emmeline

- Rebel and Rush
  - Rhodes
  - Ember

- Dutch and Georgie

- Jagger and Archie
  - Graham

- Hugger and Diana
  - Jackie (on the way)

- Big Petey and Renae
- Dog and Sheila
- Arlo
- Boz
- Brick
- Roscoe
- Tug
- Bat
- Speck
- Chill
- Saddle

Resurrection Motorcycle Club

- Beck (Wash)
- Eightball (Eight)
- Muzzle
- Hardcore (Core) and Hellen
- Linus
- Brain

Aces High Motorcycle Club

- Buck
- Cruise
- Ink
- Gash
- Driver

KristenAshley.net
NEW YORK TIMES BESTSELLING AUTHOR

Join the next Rock Chick Generation
on romantic adventures as they
expand the Nightingale Investigations team.

Avenging Angel
the story of Raye and Cap.

READ MORE FROM KRISTEN ASHLEY

Avenging Angel

Rachel Armstrong has a burning need to right the world's wrongs. Thus, she becomes the Avenging Angel.

And maybe she's a bit too cocky about it.

While riding a hunch about the identity of a kidnapper, she runs into Julien "Cap" Jackson, who was trained by the team at Nightingale Investigations in Denver. Now he's a full-fledged member at their newly opened Phoenix branch.

It takes Cap a beat to realize Raye's the woman for him. It takes Raye a little longer (but just a little) to figure out how she feels about Cap.

As Raye introduces Cap to her crazy posse of found family and his new home in the Valley of the Sun, Cap struggles with his protective streak. Because Raye has no intention to stop doing what she can to save the world.

But there's a mysterious entity out there who has discovered what Raye is up to, and they've become very interested.

Not to mention, women are going missing in Phoenix, and it seems like the police aren't taking it seriously.

Raye believes someone should.

So she recruits her best friend Luna, and between making coffees, mixing cocktails, planning parties and enduring family interventions (along with reunions), the Avenging Angels unite to ride to the rescue.

AVENGING ANGEL
AVENGING ANGELS BOOK ONE

To all the Rock Chicks out there.

They're all for you,
but this one in particular
is my love letter to our history...
and our future.

Chapter One
Natural Badassery

"I'm gonna go in."

"Are you *insane*? You can't go in!"

"I'm just gonna have a look around."

"What if you're right? What if this guy is the actual guy?"

"Then I'll call the police."

"What if he sees you?"

I sighed. "Luna, this isn't my first rodeo."

"Exactly!" she cried in a Eureka! tone. "So, yeah, let's talk about that, Raye."

Sitting in my car, talking to my bestie on the phone and casing the house in question, I cut her off quickly before she could start in—*again*—about how she felt about what I'd been up to lately.

"I'm just going to wander across the front of his house and look in the windows. No biggie."

Truthfully, I was hoping to do more than that, but my best friend of all time, Luna, didn't need to know that.

We'd had chats about what she called my unhinged shenanigans, or my lunatic tomfooleries. Then there were also my deranged mischiefs (Luna read a lot and her vocabulary showed it).

But I did what I did because, well...

I had to.

Luna spoke into my thoughts. "Okay, so if *I* kidnapped a little girl from my church, and *I* was holding her for things I won't even contemplate why someone would do that, and some woman I'd never seen in my neighborhood casually strolled in front of my house and looked in my windows, what do you think *I* would do?"

"Sic Jacques on them, whereupon he'd lick them and dance around them and race away, only to race back, bringing his toys so they'd play?"

Jacques was Luna's French bulldog. He was gray, had a little white patch on his chest, and I considered myself for sainthood that I hadn't dognapped him yet. I was pretty sure I loved him more than Luna did, and the Tiffany's dog collar I'd splurged and bought him (which she refused to let him wear because she said it was too bougie, like that was a bad thing) proved my case on that.

"This isn't funny, Raye," Luna said softly.

That got to me, her talking softly.

She was yin to my yang, Ethel to my Lucy, Shirley to my Laverne, Louise to my Thelma. Dorothy to my Rose/Sophia/Blanche (and yes, I could be all three, dingy, sarcastic and slutty, sometimes all at the same time, I considered it my superpower).

You get the picture.

We were opposites, but she loved me.

And I loved her.

"I promise to be careful. It's gone okay so far, hasn't it?" I asked.

"Luck has a way of running out."

Hmm.

I struggled for a moment with the use of the word "luck," considering I thought I was pretty kickass, but I let it go.

There was a little girl missing. And I had a feeling I knew where she was.

"I need to do this, Luna."

It was her turn to sigh, long and loud.

She knew I did.

"Call me the instant you get back to your car," she ordered.

"Roger wilco," I replied.

"You don't even know what that means," she muttered.

"It means I heard you."

"Yes, it also means *you will comply with my orders.* That's what wilco is short for."

See?

She totally read a lot.

"Okay, so, samesies, yeah? I heard you, and I'll call."

Another sigh before she said, "You won't call because either, a, you'll be tied up in some villain's basement, and I'll then be forced to put up fliers and hold candlelight vigils and harass the police to follow leads. This will end with me being interviewed, weeping copiously, naturally, saying you lit up a room in a Netflix docuseries about solved cold case files once some hikers find what's left of your body at the bottom of a ravine in fifteen years. Or, b, you won't get anything from the guy, so you'll start devising some other way of figuring out if it's him or not. You'll then immediately begin scheming to implement plans to do that, at the same time you'll remember you forgot to buy tampons for your upcoming cycle, and you need to pop into CVS, after which you'll realize you're hungry and you'll stop by Lenny's for a cowboy burger and a malt."

She was hitting close to home with that first bit, and she knew it.

Including when my period was coming, something she always reminded me to prepare for because I always forgot, and as such, was constantly bumming tampons from her. Though, her remembering this wasn't a feat, since we were together so often, including working together, we were moon sisters.

"I will totally call," I promised.

"If you don't, I'm uninviting you to my birthday party."

I gasped.

"You wouldn't," I whispered in horror.

Yes, you guessed it. Luna threw great parties, especially when she was celebrating herself.

"Try me."

"I'll call. I'll absolutely call. Long distance pinkie swear."

"Lord save me," she mumbled, then stated, "If you hit Lenny's, *definitely* call me. Since I brought Lenny's up, I now realize I need a malt."

After that, she hung up on me.

I leaned forward and put my phone in the back pocket of my pants, my eyes on the house that was just right of the T at the end of the street where I was parked.

There was a light on to the right side of the front door.

He was home.

He was home, and he might be the kind of guy who grabbed little girls to do things it wasn't mentally healthy to contemplate.

Maybe Luna was right. Maybe this was madness.

Though...

Her name was Elsie Fay. She was six years old. She had a cute-as-a-button face.

And she'd been missing for nine days.

What could happen, even if he saw me?

He wasn't going to storm out of his house and confront a stranger who was out for an evening stroll.

I was just getting the lay of the land.

I was correct in what I said to Luna.

No biggie.

That said, better safe than sorry.

I leaned across to the glove compartment, opened it and nabbed my stun gun. I then got out, locked the doors on my bright yellow, Nissan Juke (not exactly a covert car, I needed to consider that on upcoming operations) and shoved the stun gun in my free back pocket.

I'd dressed the part. Navy-blue chinos and a navy-blue polo shirt with a yellow badge insignia at my left breast.

Sure, under the yellow badge it said PUPPY PATROL, and this was my uniform when I did moonlighting gigs for an online dog walking/pet sitting service. But if you didn't look too closely, it appeared official. If someone asked, I could say I worked for code enforcement or animal control or...something.

I'd seen in an episode of *Burn Notice* that the best way to do something you weren't supposed to be doing, somewhere you weren't supposed to be doing it, was to look like you were supposed to be there doing what you were doing.

And if a burned TV spy couldn't guide me in a possibly, but not probably, dangerous mission, who could?

Okay, so I was seeing some of Luna's concern.

Nevertheless, I walked up the sidewalk toward the house in question like I'd personally designed the neighborhood. I hooked a right at the T, walked down the street a ways, crossed, then walked back up on the possible perp's side of the street.

And then across the front of his house.

Good news, his window shades were open.

More good news: I was right, he was there. And as I'd already ascertained, and this cemented it, he was sitting, watching TV, and he looked the nondescript everyman version of your not-so-friendly local kidnapper. The image of a man whose neighbors would appear on TV and say, "He gave us a bad vibe, but he was quiet and didn't cause any trouble, so..."

I kept walking, thinking she could be in there.

In that house.

Right now.

Scared and alone and so much more that, for my mental health, I refused to contemplate.

Not many homes in Phoenix had basements, and his place was a one-story ranch. I couldn't imagine he'd be stupid enough to keep the shades open in a room he was keeping a kidnapped little girl in, but who knew? Maybe he was.

I couldn't call the cops and say, "Hey, listen, hear me out about this guy."

I had to have something meaty.

At the end of the street, I turned right, then hooked another right to walk down the alley. It was dark, impossible to see the words PUPPY PATROL on my shirt. I was counting the houses in my head at the same time coming up with a plausible explanation of why I was wandering down the alley should someone stop and ask.

I hit his back gate without seeing anyone and tried the latch.

Of course, locked.

If I owned a home, I might lock my back gate to deter intruders. But it'd be a pain in the ass when I took out my garbage.

If I was holding a little girl I'd snatched, I'd definitely lock it.

Hmm.

The dumpsters and huge recycling bins were just outside his gate. Perfect.

This meant I could get into his yard to look in the back windows, though I might not be able to get out.

I'd figure that out later.

I climbed on top of the dumpster (not easy and all kinds of gross), stood and looked over the top of his fence.

Clean landing on turf.

He should xeriscape. We were in a water crisis. No one should have lawns anymore in arid climates.

Right, I totally needed to learn better focus.

I looked at the house.

Light on in the kitchen with no one in it (did this man *not* hear about climate change?). No lights on in the other side of the house. I couldn't tell from that far away, but it seemed like no blinds were closed over the back windows, because I could see the light shining in from opened doorways to a hall.

Except the last room, but it might just be the door was closed.

This could mean he had nothing to hide.

It could also mean he was an idiot.

Well, I was currently harboring fifty thousand forms of bacteria on my hands and clothing from my climb onto the dumpster. In for a penny, in for a pound.

I put one foot to the top of his fence then leaped over. I landed on soft knees and it still jarred me like a bitch.

Ouch.

Right away, I set the pain aside and returned my attention to the house.

No movement in the windows. I didn't think I was making that much noise, but, if he could hear it, I hoped my climb onto the dumpster sounded like someone taking out their trash like people often did at seven at night.

Though it appeared I was good.

Sticking to the fence, I moved left, forward, then crouching, I went in.

Coming up from the crouch just enough to see over the windowsill, I noted it was a window to the dining room, through which was a galley kitchen, through which was the living room and him sitting in a recliner watching the Diamondbacks on TV.

Okay, good. He hadn't heard me and come to investigate.

Onward.

Crouch-walking under the window, I hit a back patio. The first window there, from the dim light shining in from the rest of the house, I saw was a bathroom.

The next room, door open from the hallway, more light shining in, appeared to be an office.

The next room, there were blinds, they were down and closed.

"Shit," I whispered.

I went around the side of the house, which was rife with mature trees, not a lot of room to move. I shimmied my way in, but the blinds on the window on that side were also closed.

Open windows everywhere else, except this room.

That was fishy.

Right?

Still not enough to call the cops.

I couldn't now say, "I have a feeling about this guy, and the blinds on one of his rooms are closed, though I can't tell you how I know that. So obviously, that's cause to break down the door and search the house ASAFP."

They weren't going to rush an urgent call to assemble the SWAT team on that intel.

Time for tampons, Lenny's and scheming some plan to find a way to get into that house and check that room.

I was thinking a trip to a T-shirt printer and some time on my computer creating a bogus notice from the city for a mandatory visit from pest control.

Gophers.

I'd heard gophers were a sitch in the Valley.

Though, not so much inside houses.

Again, I'd figure it out.

I was about to move out of the trees, hoping the lock on the gate was easy to navigate from the inside, when I noticed movement at the window.

I froze.

I'd brushed against the trees, but I didn't think I'd made much noise. Surely not enough he'd hear me three rooms away over the TV.

That was when she appeared.

Just her head.

Dark hair: messy.

Cute-as-a-button face: terrified.

Lips: moving with words anyone could read, even in the dark.

Help me.

Adrenaline surged throughout my body, making it tingle top to toe.

Tears flooded my eyes, making them sting.

My heart clutched and memories battered my brain, trying to force their way in.

I couldn't give them free reign or they'd paralyze me.

It took mad effort, but I held them back using the aforementioned adrenaline and the sight of her face in that window.

I was right.

She was there.

I had to call the cops.

Now.

I put my hand to the window, nodded to her, tried to smile reassuringly, my mind cluttered.

Should I call from where I was? Would he hear me? If he did, what would he do with her? He had access to her. I did not. He had access to his garage. I did not. And I was at least a five-minute run away from my car, and in my current situation, couldn't even easily get around to the front of the house to see which direction he'd have gone. Had a neighbor heard me, one who would maybe warn him someone was lurking on his property, or they'd called the cops and their sirens would do it? Would me being in his backyard, trespassing, mess up the investigation?

I had to get to the alley and make the call.

Pronto.

It's going to be okay, I mouthed back to her. *Someone will be here soon.*

Panic filled her little face. Even if I suspected she couldn't read my lips, my guess was she knew I had to leave. She shook her head.

I pressed my hand into the window, not that she could notice the added pressure, so I got closer and mouthed, *Promise. Hang tight.*

She kept shaking her head, but I was on the move.

I didn't stick to the fence. I ran right to the back gate.

The latch locked from the inside, but with an easy twist and lift, the door opened.

On instinct, I looked back to the house and froze yet again.

I saw a shadow moving through the hall across the door of the bathroom, headed toward the back bedroom.

"*Shit!*" I hissed.

I sprinted back to the dining room window and didn't bother crouching.

I looked right in.

I was correct about that shadow.

He wasn't in his recliner anymore.

He was headed to her.

"No, no, no, no, no," I chanted, panic creeping in, attempting to take a firm grip.

To force it out (because that would paralyze me too, and no way could I let that happen), acting fast, even though I was not able to think as fast, I had to go with it.

I went to the patio door and knocked, loud.

And I kept doing it until he showed at the door.

Okay, good.

Or, also, bad.

What the heck did I do now?

The door was made of glass.

Through it, he looked at me.

He looked at the patio beyond me.

He looked at me again.

And I looked at him.

On the wrong side of middle age, my guess, closer to sixty than forty. His shoulders were broad. His hair was thin. He had a little gut. He needed a shave. And he had to be four or five inches taller than me.

I had a stun gun and thirty years less than him.

But he could probably take me.

Expressions chased themselves across his face. Shady. Incredulous. And regrettably, he ended on angry.

He opened the door and demanded, "Who are you and what are you doing on my back patio?"

"Hi!" I exclaimed. "I'm so sorry." I pointed to the badge on my chest. "I work for Puppy Patrol?" I told him in a question, like he could confirm I did. I didn't wait for his confirmation, I babbled on. "And I was walking one of your neighbor's dogs. He slipped the leash and ran off. I'm trying to find him. He's a little Chihuahua. I'm freaked! He'd be a snack for coyotes."

"We don't have coyotes in the city," he informed me.

"Yes, we do," I contradicted. And we did. I had a Puppy Patrol client (actually, it was a Kitty Krew client, same company, brown uniform, whole different ball of wax) who'd learned that the hard way. "They come down from the mountains and in from the desert, easy pickin's for people who let their cats go outside and stuff."

RIP Gaia.

"How did you get in my backyard?"

"Your gate was unlatched," I lied. "And I could swear I saw little Bruiser dash in here from the alley."

He leaned out to look toward his gate.

I leaned back, my hand moving toward my pocket and my stun gun.

When he looked back at me, I knew he saw through my story.

And it was on.

I didn't have time for the stun gun. Not now.

He lunged.

I tried to evade.

He caught me anyway and pulled me right inside.

Totally knew he could take me.

Damn it!

We grappled.

I went for the gonads with my knee and hit his inner thigh.

This caused him not to let me go, but instead grab my hair and pull, *hard*.

Jerk!

I went for the instep, slamming down on it with my foot, and that was better. He yelped, his hold loosened, I ripped myself away from him (pulling my own hair, because his grip hadn't loosened that much, *ouch!*), and I yanked out the stun gun.

He recovered too quickly, nabbed me, and even if I knew he could take me, I was still surprised at his strength when he wrenched me around at the same time throwing me down to the floor with such force, I hit the tile and skidded several feet. My head then struck a corner of his kitchen cabinet.

Worse than the hair pulling. Seriously.

While I blinked the stars out of my eyes, he came after me, reached down to grab me again, and I remembered I had my stun gun in my hand.

I turned it on, heard it crackling, his attention went to it, and ill-advisedly in our current positioning, I touched it to him.

He went inert, then dropped, all two hundred some-odd pounds of him landing square on top of me.

"*Oof*," I grunted.

Fuck! I thought.

I dropped the stun gun to try to shift him off, when my breath that had just come back stopped because he was suddenly flying through the air.

He landed on his back several feet away from me, his head cracking against the tile with a sickening sound.

But I didn't have any attention to give him.

I didn't because there were two men standing over me, and these two dudes could totally take me. I didn't know who they were. They might be associates of the bad guy. But they were so gorgeous, for a split second, all I could think was that I'd be okay with that (the them taking me part, that was).

One was tall, very tall, with black hair, green eyes and an age range of thirty-five to a very fit, healthy-living, great-genes forty-five. He also looked familiar, but I couldn't place it in my current predicament. And last, he'd had some goodness injected in him from, my guess, a Pacific Islander parent.

The other one was also tall, very tall, just not as tall as the other guy. I'd put him in the thirty to thirty-five age zone. He had dark-brown hair, full, short, but the top and sides were longish and slicked back in a stylish way. He had a thick brown beard that was trimmed gloriously and gray-blue eyes.

For a second, I thought he was Chris Evans.

Then he spoke.

Angrily.

"What the fuck are you doing?"

Wait.

What *was* I doing?

Oh yeah.

Suddenly confronting a Chris Evans doppelgänger, I'd forgotten about Elsie Fay (that sounded really bad, but trust me, with these guys, who wouldn't?).

I shot to my feet and dashed through the kitchen.

That was as far as I got before I was whipped around with a strong hand on my arm and Chris Evans was in my face.

"Again, what the fuck are you doing?" he asked.

"Who are you?" I asked back.

"I asked first," he returned.

"Do you know that guy?"

"What guy?"

"The one who owns this house."

"No."

Okay, I was going with he was a good guy. Maybe a cop. Maybe they were onto this guy like I was.

Yeah.

Anyway, if they were in cahoots with the bad guy, they wouldn't have cracked his head on the tile.

So I was going with that because there was no more time to waste.

"Elsie Fay," I said, tore my arm from his hold and raced through the house.

I made it to the door to the room at the end of the hall and was in such a rush, when I turned the knob, I slammed full-body into it because it was locked.

I then grabbed the knob and jostled it and the door violently, like that would magically open it.

I was pushed aside with an order of, "Stand back."

I did as told.

"Are you a good guy or a bad guy?" I belatedly asked in order to confirm.

"Even if I was a bad guy," he said while positioning in front of the door, his eyes aimed at it, "I'd tell you I was a good guy."

Excellent point.

He lifted a beefy (those thighs!), chocolate-brown-cargo-pants-clad leg and landed his boot solidly by the door handle.

The door popped open.

I slipped in front of him to enter the dark room.

I immediately tripped over something, but stopped, righted myself and called into the darkness, "Elsie Fay?"

No movement. No sound.

Chris Evans entered behind me, *close* behind me. So close, I could feel his heat and the natural badassery that wafted off him (this apparently happened with guys who knew how to bust open doors with their boot), and I felt him move.

On instinct again, I spun and whispered, "Don't turn on the light."

The other guy was standing in the doorway.

I turned back to the room, and gingerly, my eyes adjusting to the dark with weak light coming in from down the hall (trying to ignore the fact this room would be pitch black without the door open, and how that would affect the mind of a little girl), I called, "Elsie Fay? It's me. From outside? You know, the window? You're okay. We're gonna get you out and call the cops and your parents and—"

I didn't finish because a six-year-old hit me like a bullet. She slammed into my legs so hard, I nearly went down. And I would have if I didn't run into Chris Evans and his hands didn't span my hips to hold me steady (told you he was close).

I didn't have time to consider how those hands felt on my hips.

Elsie Fay was clawing up my chinos.

I bent and pulled her into my arms. She was heavy, as six-year-olds were wont to be, too big to be held, too young to realize it, though in this instance, she needed it, and I didn't have time to consider her weight as she clamped onto me with arms and legs. She, too, fisted her hand in my hair and she did it tighter than the bad guy. She also shoved her face in my neck.

"It's okay," I whispered to her. "You're okay. You're safe now. Okay?"

She said nothing.

I turned to Chris Evans and his hottie partner.

"Is he neutralized?" I asked.

"Yes," the hottie partner answered.

"Then let's get her out of here," I stated, and didn't wait for their response.

I pushed through them and got that little girl the hell out of there.

Avenging Angel is available to purchase in all formats

NEWSLETTER

Would you like advanced notification about Upcoming Releases? Access to exclusive content? Access to exclusive giveaways? The first to see a new cover reveal? Sign up for my newsletter to keep up-to-date with the latest from Kristen Ashley!

Sign up at kristenashley.net

ABOUT THE AUTHOR

Kristen Ashley is the *New York Times* bestselling author of over eighty romance novels including the *Rock Chick, Colorado Mountain, Dream Man, Chaos, Unfinished Heroes, The 'Burg, Magdalene, Fantasyland, The Three, Ghost and Reincarnation, The Rising, Dream Team, Moonlight and Motor Oil, River Rain, Wild West MC, Misted Pines* and *Honey* series along with several stand-alone novels. She's a hybrid author, publishing titles both independently and traditionally, her books have been translated in fourteen languages and she's sold over five million books.

Kristen's novel, *Law Man*, won the *RT Book Reviews* Reviewer's Choice Award for best Romantic Suspense, her independently published title *Hold On* was nominated for *RT Book Reviews* best Independent Contemporary Romance and her traditionally published title *Breathe* was nominated for best Contemporary Romance. Kristen's titles *Motorcycle Man, The Will*, and *Ride Steady* (which won the Reader's Choice award from *Romance Reviews*) all made the final rounds for Goodreads Choice Awards in the Romance category.

Kristen, born in Gary and raised in Brownsburg, Indiana, is a fourth-generation graduate of Purdue University. Since, she's lived in Denver, the West Country of England, and she now resides in Phoenix. She worked as a charity executive for eighteen years prior to beginning her independent publishing career. She now writes full-time.

Although romance is her genre, the prevailing themes running through all of Kristen's novels are friendship, family and a strong sisterhood. To this end, and as a way to thank her readers for their support, Kristen has created the Rock Chick Nation, a series of programs that are designed to give back to her readers and promote a strong female community.

The mission of the Rock Chick Nation is to live your best life, be true to your true self, recognize your beauty, and take your sister's back whether they're at your side as friends and family or if they're thousands of miles away and you don't know who they are.

The programs of the RC Nation include Rock Chick Rendezvous, weekends Kristen organizes full of parties and get-togethers to bring the sisterhood together, Rock Chick Recharges, evenings Kristen arranges for women who have been nominated to receive a special night, and Rock Chick Rewards, an ongoing program that raises funds for nonprofit women's organizations Kristen's readers nominate. Kristen's Rock Chick Rewards have donated hundreds of thousands of dollars to charity and this number continues to rise.

You can read more about Kristen, her titles and the Rock Chick Nation at KristenAshley.net.

facebook.com/kristenashleybooks

instagram.com/kristenashleybooks

pinterest.com/KristenAshleyBooks

goodreads.com/kristenashleybooks

bookbub.com/authors/kristen-ashley

tiktok.com/@kristenashleybooks

ALSO BY KRISTEN ASHLEY

The Colorado Mountain Series:
The Gamble
Sweet Dreams
Lady Luck
Breathe
Jagged
Kaleidoscope
Bounty

Dream Man Series:
Mystery Man
Wild Man
Law Man
Motorcycle Man
Quiet Man

Dream Team Series:
Dream Maker
Dream Chaser
Dream Bites Cookbook
Dream Spinner
Dream Keeper

The Fantasyland Series:
Wildest Dreams
The Golden Dynasty
Fantastical
Broken Dove
Midnight Soul
Gossamer in the Darkness

Ghosts and Reincarnation Series:
Sommersgate House
Lacybourne Manor
Penmort Castle
Fairytale Come Alive
Lucky Stars

The Honey Series:
The Deep End
The Farthest Edge
The Greatest Risk

The Magdalene Series:
The Will
Soaring
The Time in Between

Mathilda, SuperWitch:
Mathilda's Book of Shadows
Mathilda The Rise of the Dark Lord

Misted Pines Series
The Girl in the Mist
The Girl in the Woods
The Woman by the Lake

Moonlight and Motor Oil Series:
The Hookup
The Slow Burn

The Rising Series:
The Beginning of Everything
The Plan Commences
The Dawn of the End
The Rising

The River Rain Series:
After the Climb
After the Climb Special Edition
Chasing Serenity
Taking the Leap
Making the Match
Fighting the Pull
Sharing the Miracle
Embracing the Change

The Three Series:
Until the Sun Falls from the Sky
With Everything I Am
Wild and Free

The Unfinished Hero Series:
Knight
Creed
Raid
Deacon
Sebring

Wild West MC Series:
Still Standing
Smoke and Steel
Smooth Sailing

Other Titles by Kristen Ashley:
Heaven and Hell
Play It Safe
Three Wishes
Complicated
Loose Ends
Fast Lane
Perfect Together
Too Good To Be True